SOPHIE PARKES was
1985. Following degrees fi
and Manchester Metropoli
studying for a PhD in creati
Hallam University. She wc ⸻ Award in
2017 and has published a biography of musician, Eliza Carthy,
and co-wrote the autobiography of endurance athlete Dave
Heeley. *Out of Human Sight* is her first novel.

Follow Sophie on Twitter: @sophparkes

OUT OF HUMAN SIGHT

SOPHIE PARKES

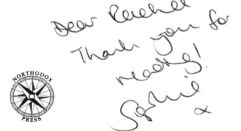

Dear Rachel
Thank you for
reading!
Sophie x

Northodox Press Ltd
Maiden Greve, Malton,
North Yorkshire, YO17 7BE

This edition 2023
1

First published in Great Britain by
Northodox Press Ltd 2023

Copyright © Sophie Parkes 2023

Sophie Parkes asserts the moral right to
be identified as the author of this work.

ISBN: 9781915179135

This book is set in Caslon Pro Std

This Novel is entirely a work of fiction. The names,
characters and incidents portrayed in it are the work of the
author's imagination. Any resemblance to actual persons,
living or dead, events or localities is entirely coincidental.

All rights reserved. No part of this publication may be
reproduced, stored in a retrieval system, or transmitted, in any
form or by any means, electronic, mechanical, photocopying,
recording, or otherwise, without the prior
permission of the publishers.

This book is sold subject to the condition that it shall not, by
way of trade or otherwise, be lent, re-sold, hired out or
otherwise circulated without the publisher's prior consent in
any form of binding or cover other than that in which it is
published and without a similar condition including this
condition being imposed on the subsequent purchaser.

For Eileen Crisp and Len Evans

1

Millie could see the open door to the inn as she turned on to the track. There was no sign of the dray; the barrels would have been unloaded earlier. She searched the green bowl of the valley for her uncle, cocking his gun at a rabbit or checking his traps.

She pushed the hair out of her eyes, but it flayed her cheeks again, pulling at the pins jammed into the back of her head. The wind was so fierce that she would have to pin it all back up when she got home. Another task for the list.

Why her mother had chosen this afternoon to run out of yeast, she didn't know. Why should it be her duly dispatched when Jane would've done just as well? The bakestone was Jane's domain, after all. However, she would've made a fuss, while Millie was soft, unable to say no to Mam's inconvenient requests. She, Tudor, and Mam, were all soft compared to her sister. *From your father*, Mam had said on more than one occasion, *her temper is from your father and his before him.*

She barely remembered her father, of course, but the comment about her Granda had surprised her. Granda seemed too quiet, too absorbed in his work, to have a temper. Or if he did, he swallowed it when Millie was around, when she was threading her fingers through the cob's forelock when the dray arrived, or collecting up the feathers from her uncle's recent shoot, or borrowing yeast.

She looked up to the heavens, the sky the colour of newly carded wool, and closed her eyes momentarily in apology. It wasn't Mam's fault; it wasn't anybody's fault. Yeast was yeast, and if some were to be had, it too would soon be used.

The inn door remained open. Her uncle was not amongst the tough hillocks of grass, harder still the closer it grew to the hillside. He wasn't fixing a fence post, one hand clamped to the hat on his head, nor was he taking apart his gun on his knee, raised on the stile. As she scanned from one hillside to the next, there was no man nor beast visible, only the grasses swaying. The weather was coming in; the clouds hulked in front of her eyes. She fixed her hair behind her ears and ran towards the inn.

'Tom?' She pushed the door back on its hinges. She had seen grown men swing on that door, kicking their feet up from the stones and hanging from whitening fingers, her Granda smiling from the bar, but threatening recompense for any damage. 'Granda?'

It was cool in the inn. Cold. She felt her knee twitch. A good inn should never be cold. There wasn't a light in the grate nor a candle on the bar. She wrapped her shawl about her. Millie was alone, she was certain of that. She would hear her Granda's boots on the flags otherwise, his constant cough hassling his whiskers or his perfunctory barks to his one remaining son.

She knocked a chair, heard it screech against the flagstones. The sound made her wince. Her eyes adjusted to the gloom. The tables and benches had been pushed together; overturned chairs, their limbs wrought together as though frozen mid tumble. Had there been a party, or a fight? And there was a smell, distinct. Tom had been hunting recently then, separating feather from sinew from bone. Her pattens ground glass into the stone. A pane was missing; she could hear fingers of wind sifting through the roof slates, the beating of the rain.

'Granda!' she shouted this time, her voice vanishing so quickly she wasn't sure she had said anything at all. The chimney cleared its throat, sent ash spiralling out of the grate. The blood at her wrists quickened. It was nothing to worry about, she told herself. Men living alone rarely kept house like the one she would, like Mam would. They didn't seem to notice the cold.

But then she heard a moan, low. She skittered over the glass, her hands reaching for the bar. Sacking lay in the doorway between the bar and the snug. She went to whip it away, bundle it under her arms to put away for washing, folding, or whatever her grandfather wanted. Which was when she noticed the boots. Boots and legs. The red of his kerchief. She bent over it. Him. Bent over him; her grandfather's body, his nose and brow beaten into his face, a soft, bloodied mess. She stepped back; saw her grandfather's shirt ripped open at the collarbone. She thought of the bright blood in the eggs she had cracked against the side of a bowl that morning and how she needed yeast. And teeth, teeth caught in the soup like tiny nuggets of stale bread. A faint whistle came from his mouth, the red stickiness bubbling. She crouched over him, grasped at his collar with shaking hands.

'Platts.' His lips puckered and his breastbone rose and sank.

'What? What?' She knelt to him this time, lowered her ear to the stinking soup. The inn smelt of blood, mineral, insides out. 'What, Granda?'

Her hair swung out of its pins, caught his blood. She roped it back, stared at the red on her hands.

'Pats,' he murmured. Though his eyelids were pasted shut, black, red, brown, she could see the eyeballs roll beneath their twin shrouds, see his beard pulse. His breath heaved, his chest breaching up through the ripped fabric, then sinking as quickly.

3

His head lurched to the side. Only his lobe remained attached to his head, a scarlet inkwell above it. His ear glittered on the flagstones. Her ears rang, her vision flickered and her fingers felt detached as she sank them into his flesh, hefted him to her, but he was gone.

'Tom!' she screamed. 'Tom!'

She must have let her grandfather go as his body lurched away from her, heard the dull sound as he dropped back to the stone. Her hands groped the walls, fingers pinched at the doorframes as she steadied herself. She was noisy now, like a bird trying to find an open window. Her pattens chattered on the stone, her hands thumped and slapped the wood, the plaster. There was a deep, guttural pant, rhythmic and regular that she realised was hers. It hurt her throat, but she seemed unable to stop it.

The snug was bare, unassuming. She retreated, backtracked, and pushed open the door behind the bar. Her legs and arms groping at the stairs, her hem hampered and heavy. Her hands felt the stairs in front of her as her eyes seemed incapable. She was a dog on the stairs, mouth open and dry tongued. 'Tom!'

Her uncle's body was prone on the bed linen, his feet bare, his arms splayed apart like one of the birds, which hung from the rafters. His hair was matted but shining, the shape of his body traced and silhouetted by blood-soaked linen.

Bloodied handprints marked the stone; there were smears along the stairs. She noticed the drag and weight of her skirts and saw that they were reddened and sorry.

She ran, hands out, hair streaming behind her, her mouth open and silent.

A light shone in the window of the first Binn Green cottage. It may have been a candle on the sill; it may have been several dotted about a room, a family enjoying a meal together. She thought of them briefly, as she ran towards it; the rain blinding her path, and thought of their forks held aloft as they heard her slamming her fists against their door, against the heavy hardwood.

Then she noticed the knocker and grasped at it, her fingers sliding against the wet metal. The door was opened a crack. Her hand reached for the latch and air rushed out of her mouth. The face of a small thin maid, eyebrows folded together, mouth a whiskery o, fell back into the darkness before the door was opened again, further; this time, a man, and another man behind him holding a leather bag, a doctor, and she wanted to laugh at the coincidence of it.

Somehow, she managed to say something, raise the alarm, for soon they were following her back along the lane, back towards Bill O'Jack's. The men holding their sodden hats to their sodden heads. And soon running faster than her, their shoes sidestepping the worst of the mud. Millie's skirts fell heavier and her breaths became shorter and that noise in her ears – the loudest of Sunday bells, the loudest of looms – scorched the inside of her head so that she could barely remember why they were running and why the door to her grandfather's inn was open.

The men stopped when they reached the door, one taking out a handkerchief from his breast pocket. She couldn't decipher the look they exchanged. Though she could see things – the low wall in front of the open door, the darkness beyond the door itself – the sight wouldn't give her the meaning it used to.

'Stay here,' the man with the handkerchief said, and he blotted it against his nose and mouth, held it there as she had seen a mill inspector do. She sank to the wall then leant her back up against the stone and closed her eyes, the rain washing her face, seeping into her clothes.

A cold hand touched her elbow. It was the man with the handkerchief, crouched low so his small, brown eyes were level with hers. He no longer held the handkerchief.

'Are they dead?' Millie asked, her throat squeezing out the words through a gap just small enough for the breaths she had been holding back. The same pulse at her wrists throbbed in her head.

The man nodded, as the other, standing behind in the doorway, set his leather bag to the floor.

'This man 'ere's a doctor,' the crouching man said, though Millie knew there was no need for a doctor in what she had seen. 'He'll send for help. But we best get you home. Where do you live, Miss? In Greenfield?'

She must've nodded, for the men supported her and lifted her to her feet. They looped an arm each through hers and shuffled away from Bill O'Jack's and past Binn Green. She listened to the scrape of her pattens against the track, the rain against the men's hats. She usually covered the short distance in half an hour or so, but like this – the track liquid beneath her feet, her ribcage as heavy as the copper her Granda used to wash the linen – it felt like hours. As the track began to harden and grasses on the verge to thin, she could smell the smoke of the cottage fires as families sought out their evening meals.

2

Her face was fiery as she prised her eyelids apart, noticing a cobweb in the corner of the ceiling. Blinking, tears gathering, misting her vision. Blinking again, she submerged, feeling a presence, coaxed her eyeballs right and saw Jane reading, a small book open flat in her hands.

'Oh!' Jane said, shifting, 'You're awake! How do you feel?' She closed the book and draped her cool fingers over Millie's forehead. Millie shuffled upwards under the coarse sheet, noted the burning in her eyes, the back of her throat, her stomach. She closed her eyes, swallowed, felt the flat of her stomach with a shaking hand.

'How long?' Millie asked, her question snatched away by a cough. The air rasped her tonsils.

Jane leant forward, peered into Millie's eyes.

'What?' Millie asked. Jane didn't answer, dropped her gaze.

'We put you to bed about five yesterday evening.' Jane picked at her nails.

'And now?'

'It's afternoon, coming up for three.'

'Where's Mam?' Millie shifted herself upwards, heard the straw in the mattress crackle.

'She's laying the fire, though I told her not to, that I would do it. She insisted I sit up here with you.'

'Have they found them?' Millie spoke again. 'Have they found who did it?' Jane raised her head, her mouth twitching as though to answer. The motion set off a succession of tiny movements in her face: her eyes blinking, her eyebrows leaning in together, then lifting high as though attached to marionette strings.

Millie felt sweat gather at her hairline, stream along her spine. She moved the thin blanket to swing out her hot feet onto the floorboards. Her stomach bubbled.

'Wait! Wait!' Jane took Millie's arm as she stood, her knees weak. 'Slowly. Take your time.'

Millie coughed a little, her breath rattling around her chest. A death rattle. Had she heard her grandfather's death rattle there in the narrow hallway between bar and snug? There had been a groan, a moan, as she had knelt over his bloodied face, his features pulpy, like the molasses she had seen him feed the cob. Had that been his death rattle?

Suddenly, thin liquid shot from her mouth to the floor. Her throat burned and Jane's feet darted away.

'Sit down, Millie.'

She did as she was told, held her temples. Her mother opened the door, called her name gently. Feet thumped at the floorboards in the bedroom, then the stairs, voices low and urgent.

'I'm sorry,' Millie repeated as she heard Mam and Jane wringing out the rags. The sound of water slopped against the floorboards.

'There's naught to be sorry for, my lass,' Mam said, but her voice broke and the endearment fell away. Millie opened her eyes and Mam reached for her hand, eyelashes blinking furiously, her mouth twisting into a caterpillar. 'You should never've seen what you did. Nobody should.'

Mam pulled Millie into her, their tears soaking the sleeves

of her nightgown. Jane looked away; a wet rag suffocated in her hand.

Mam's shoulders slowed, her breaths lengthening, evening. She set down her hands on her apron. 'We must be brave. You, Amelia, the bravest of all.' She hooked a finger under her daughter's wet chin.

Millie nodded and swallowed. 'Mam, have they caught them? The people that did it?'

Mam paused. She gave her head the briefest of shakes. 'Now, that poor brother of yours is downstairs and as white as a sheet. Let's get him some bread, shall we? And I'm sure you'll be positively *aching* for some, Millie, my girl? Why, you've missed three meals!' She counted them on her fingers to be sure. 'One of each. You'll waste away!'

'But, Mam, is there any bread? I didn't get the yeast!' Millie stood, blinking.

She wasn't even sure where her grandfather kept it. Had the door to the scullery been closed? She'd seen the lye in there. But the yeast?

'Don't you worry yourself about that.' Mam patted her arm. 'That's the last thing to be worrying about.'

Bread lay untouched on the table. Tudor poked at the fire and immediately the room was too hot, too insufferably hot. Millie plucked at the collar of her shift and took a mug of recently boiled water. Jane and Mam sat at their wheels and span. They didn't sing the songs or make up the nonsense verse they usually did. Instead, the family listened to the creak of their feet against the wooden wheels and the pop of the kindling. It was unusual to be silent in this home, to listen. Were Mam, Jane, and Tudor listening for something else, Millie wondered, listening for footsteps and news to be brought to the door?

'Mam, I can't just sit here; I can't watch you and Jane work. Give Tudor and me something to do. Please?' Millie said, her voice louder than she intended. She looked about her for piles of raw wool. 'Carding, teasing, anything.'

Tudor agreed with a bob of his head, which made it look as though his skull could topple from his neck at any time. He couldn't take his eyes from the flames. He needed to occupy his hands.

'Here, then,' Mam said, nudging out a bucket of unturned wool from behind her stool. 'Tudor can tease, you can card, and then you can put the finished lot in here.' She gestured to the large basket between the wheels.

It was children's work, picking the dust and dirt from the grease, brushing it from one hand card to the next. She had spent more evenings in this way than she cared to remember, but it was comforting to have them tell her what to do, to feel the warm wool between her fingers. The sound of it, too, like a horse scratching against a fencepost or a brush against the sole of a boot. Rhythmic and substantial. The sound of a job being done, of progress being made.

But it wasn't enough. This silence, this avoidance of the truth, of the left-unsaids. Millie couldn't bear it. 'Tell me, Mam, has there been any news?'

Mam shook her head, concentrated on the fine skein before her.

'They know nowt, Millie,' Tudor answered, his eyes wide. 'The yeoman are out, the constables are stopping everyone between here and Holmfirth, but there h'aint no clues. No evidence. Nothing.'

'They might come back.'

Mam's knee rose and fell beneath her apron. 'They shall be found. God will see to that.'

'Did I tell you what Granda said?'

Mam nodded slightly, but Millie continued regardless. 'Was he trying to tell me something?' She found two heavy tears on her cheeks and her throat swelled with mucus. 'It's that word he said. "Pats", or "Platts". What do you think he meant? What do you think he was trying to tell me? You don't just say a word like that now, do you?'

'Hush now,' Mam said quietly.

'But Mam,' Millie said, and Mam set her hands down in her lap wearily to listen. 'It wasn't a sound that slipped out; but a signal, a sign. It takes effort to make that sound. Don't you think?'

'We've got theories,' Tudor said, though his hands shook as he spoke.

Millie sat up straighter, galvanised. 'And why would someone do this? What had they done to deserve this?'

'Nothing,' Mam said, quickly. 'And don't for a minute believe this to be the fault of our kin.'

'I don't, I don't-' Millie said just as quickly.

Mam looked upwards, a fat bead of a tear sitting at the corner of her eye. 'You concentrate on being fit and well for the day we set our relatives to the earth; let other people do the wondering.'

'When? When is the burial?' Millie asked, turning to Jane.

'Friday,' her sister replied. She moved her head to the window. 'There's somebody at the door,' she said, rising, untying her apron. Three firm raps sounded. As Millie flinched, she noticed Mam, Jane, and Tudor do the same. Jane's eyes widened; Mam chewed at her lips. 'Go upstairs, Millie, you're in your shift.'

Millie mustered energy and made her way upstairs, but it was her name that Jane called. She wondered who it would be, and why they would call so soon, when she had but a shift on. She pulled on her stuff dress over the top.

'Millie! There's a gentleman here to see you.'

A yeoman, perhaps even a dragoon, stood at the doorway, his hat under his arm. The bright blue of his jacket looked absurd; it seemed to reek of colour in an otherwise colourless home.

'Miss Bradbury?' he asked through his moustache. Raindrops hung on to the ends of his whiskers, but he didn't wipe them away.

'Please sit down,' Jane said, bundling away the wool, the needles, and pincushions from the kitchen table. He obliged and sat on the edge of a seat, as though he wasn't accustomed to it.

Millie stood, watched his eyes trace her hair, then the shape of her head, then further down, his eyes travelling across her stuff dress.

'I believe you've witnessed a tragedy, Miss. I am here to take down your evidence so we can find the culprit.' He spoke to her stockinged toes, hastily stuffed into her pattens.

'Are you a dragoon?' Tudor asked, and Millie heard Jane tut.

'Yeomanry,' he answered without looking up. 'What did you see when you entered The Moorcock Inn, Bill O'Jack's, yesterday, Miss?'

Millie sat down, and, despite the heat, began to tremble, wondering where to start. She looked between Jane and Mam, heard Tudor shuffling in front of the grate. She began with her walk to the inn. The silence of it, the door ajar. Then she described the image that remained with her: the unruliness of the furniture, her grandfather in the short hallway, her uncle upstairs and lifeless. She told him about the blood, though her vision swam at the mention of it, and the red of Granda's kerchief. Her raising of the alarm. He listened, making notes, until she came to the end of her speech and faltered, searching for a suitable ending.

'And you didn't notice any people, anyone on your way to and from the inn? Any men lurking about outside?'

She shivered. 'No.' She imagined men crouching at the low wall, watching her entry; men with bloodied clubs in their hands, broken bottles ready to thrust her way. She hadn't thought of that.

'Thank you,' he said and folded his notes into his breast pocket.

'Have you any information? Is there anything you can tell us?' Jane said as he rose.

'Not yes, Miss, but we will endeavour to keep you informed.' He nodded at each of them in turn, then span on his heel to the door. 'I shan't keep you further. I'll be on my way.' He left as quickly as he had entered it.

'Well,' Mam said.

'Do you think he has a horse outside?' Tudor asked. He ran to the window, squinted through the poor light and the heavy rain. Granda loved horses. His father had kept one for his rounds when he was younger, and Granda had treated it like a sibling, a pet. He showed Millie how to wisp the dray's cob until its flanks shone.

Millie sat where the yeoman had sat. His buttocks hadn't warmed the seat. She trembled.

'Get your sister a brandy, Jane,' Mam said suddenly. 'She looks as though she needs it. And me, one for me, too, please.'

Jane took the brandy down from the highest shelf and sloshed it into three mugs. They watched in surprise as Mam downed hers as though it were water.

'Purely medicinal,' she smiled weakly, 'nothing the preacher wouldn't do himself.'

Millie and Jane each took a sip. Millie felt the warmth of the liquid loop the twists and turns of her insides. It didn't make her better exactly, but anchored, grounded.

'Oh Mam, I didn't mention what Granda said to me. Do you

think I ought've?' Millie stood facing the window, squeezing her hands into fists, then releasing them.

Mam sat back at her wheel. She blinked hard, dazed, like the rabbits when Tom took them from his snares.

'Yes, perhaps you should've. Shall I go to see if he's left the lane?' Jane paced on the rug, thinking.

'Someone else is here!' Tudor trilled from the window. 'It's Johnny Barkwell!'

'Johnny?' Millie looked at Mam and Jane in surprise, pushed her empty mug away from her. Having vomited only two hours earlier, she was sure that he'd be able to smell its legacy. Which was worse: vomit or brandy? She straightened her dress, though it was futile as it hung in great, haphazard creases, and hastily twisted locks of her hair.

Tudor held open the door like a magician. Johnny crowded the front door, taller than the hatstand. His necktie was loose, and she wished to reach up, set it right. He clamped his hat to his breast; his other hand held five bright daffodils. The corners of his red mouth brightened into a smile but then fell again, as though he'd remembered better of it.

'Tudor,' he said, breathlessly, 'Mrs Bradbury.' He stepped into the room, turned about as though he was seeing it for the first time. 'I came as soon as I could.' He grasped Mrs Bradbury's hand and held it like a secret. 'I cannot believe…'

Mam turned her head, flapped her spare hand as though he was flattering her. He wasn't this time. 'Johnny, dear boy,' she murmured.

'And Millie.'

His cool grey eyes settled on her.

Johnny Barkwell had come to visit her at her home. He had even brought her a gift.

'Look who's here,' Jane said, looking pointedly at Millie, her eyes narrowing, as if trying to convey some urgent message that Millie couldn't follow. Millie stood, hovered over her seat, and as Johnny took the chair opposite, she settled back into hers, her wet palms grasping at the daffodils he held out to her. She laid them on the tabletop, moving aside the mugs. She saw his nostrils pulse as they detected the brandy. Mam melted away into the house, but Jane stood behind him, her hands on her hips.

'How are you?' he said, leaning forward in his seat. His eyes, seal coloured, dominated his face, and she felt the ferocity of his concern. She had kissed those eyelids once.

'Thank you for asking; for coming to visit.' She turned in her seat to face him better and banged her elbow on the pocked wood. He took it, rubbed it gently through the coarse cotton. She wondered if Jane could see, but noticed she, too, had left the room. They were alone. Her stomach began to flutter.

'I heard the news this morning. Mr Dunne was standing on the doorstep of his shop, telling every one of us as we passed by, as he's wont to do. I came here as soon as the bell rang. I couldn't believe it; not a word. But I know when Dunne's genuine. You could've sent a message to me; you could've let me know right away. I would have been here.'

Millie blinked slowly, felt her brow crease. 'You, Johnny? Why would've we..?'

'I could've helped, Millie, I *will* help.' He placed his large hand over hers, smothered it. It was surprisingly soft, given the large furrows writ across his skin. She looked down at it. His nails had been picked clean with a knife, squared off. Few men of the valley would go to such lengths, she thought, and here he was.

A fly landed on his ear. His eyes didn't leave hers, even as he shook his head, raised his fist to it.

'That's very kind. I've been asleep most of the day. In fact, since I've been home, I've been a-bed. I think; it's what I've been told, at least. Mam and Jane have been watching over me and Tudor-'

'Hush,' he said, 'you don't need to tell me everything.'

He draped his arms across the table. He was tired. His work was heavy, his day was long. And he had chosen to come here.

'I couldn't believe it when I heard,' he said again, 'and for you to find them, Millie…' He looked for Jane, Mam, or Tudor, but the family had vanished, upstairs, or out into the yard. 'I curse the bastards.'

She pictured him with the men at the market, laughing and joking, quite unaware he was steadily charming them out of the promises they had made to their wives for certain prices. She had heard about how Johnny held the men, even the older ones with a lifetime of experience, like the game in his traps: about the neck, without mercy, but with smiles on their faces as though Johnny had done them a favour. And still they came back for more, buying him ales in The King Bill, offering to cover his shifts if ever he needed. His name hung in the tobacco smoke in The King Bill and The Clarence and The Wellington; his name was passed between and snagged on the wire fences that separated one farmer's lot from another's.

His name was often mentioned in the women's weaving sheds, too, from behind cupped hands and through smiling lips, though they all conceded that it was on Millie Bradbury his eyes lingered most. It made her want to reach out and grab his hands, draw him to her. Of course, she had done, once.

But then she thought of Granda, of Tom.

'Thank you for the daffs,' she said, stroking their closed petals.

Johnny watched her. Millie could feel his eyes, his irises the colour of local houses, searching her forehead, her cheekbones, her chin. She couldn't look up. She felt her knees begin to tremble again. It sent up a chatter in her teeth, and she clamped shut her jaws as though swallowing a yawn.

'I'll be back at the mill tomorrow,' she blurted, head spinning as fast as Mam and Jane's wheels. Her hands felt light and heavy at the same time. She didn't know what to do with them.

'You should take another day.' He stood and ducked his head under a beam.

She shrugged and stood, too, but had trouble disguising her frailty. He shot out a hand as though to steady her. She longed for it on her hip, that large hand to hold her firm. 'I must go back sooner or later, and I'd rather it was sooner. And to see Alice and the other girls, and besides, there's the money to be got.' He knew it as well as she: if she took another day, Shipton would have her replaced.

'Why don't I speak to him?'

She could feel his eyes trying to find hers. She tilted her chin and looked at him, wished she had brushed her hair, washed her face, anything. 'That Shipton, he's only used to keeping the women in line. I bet a word or two from me would shock him.'

'No, Johnny, please don't do that,' though she was careful to shake her head so gently he would see that she wasn't defying him or thinking that she knew better. A simple preference, that was all. She needed to go back.

'Very well,' he said, exhaling through his nostrils like the cob that pulled the dray to Granda's. 'If you're sure.'

He straightened his collar and swiped at the invisible dust on his hat before placing it back on his head. He had his traps to check, he told her, but if she needed anything else, or changed her mind about Shipton, she was to send Tudor to his parents' house. She nodded meekly and hoped he would settle that red mouth on hers again. Instead, though, he took her hand and shook it like a baby's rattle, called his goodbyes to Mam and Jane up the stairs, and closed the door neatly behind him.

Millie realised she hadn't said goodbye, hadn't thanked him, and faced the closed door, wondering whether to run after him, but feared her feet wouldn't carry her.

At the sound of the door closing, Mam and Jane reappeared. Mam cleared her throat. 'That's kind of Johnny, h'aint it?' Mam said, eyebrows raised. 'He's always been a good boy.'

'Always sniffing around, you mean?' Jane said. 'And telling her to take another day!'

'What do you mean, "sniffing around"?' Tudor asked, appearing at the back door and knocking at the doorframe with the toe of his hobnail boots.

'Stop that,' Mam and Jane said in unison.

'I mean, he's interested in Millie,' Jane said, frowning.

'Well, of course!' Mam said. 'I've always said they'd be a good match; your father thought so, too.'

Millie's cheeks burned. She turned to watch her family.

'If he has intentions, he should make them plain,' Jane said. 'It's not right. Just look at her!'

'It's nothing to do with you,' Millie said, her cheeks hot, her lips dry. She had kissed him once, at the steps by the mill. If Jane had known-

'Can I have a brandy?' Tudor asked, his eyes wide. Jane poured him a smaller measure in one of the mugs. He sipped at it, winced.

Mam took up at the wheel again. The putter-out would come to collect their wool tomorrow.

'Well, I like Johnny,' Tudor said, rubbing his breastbone. Millie smiled gently at her brother and started to card the wool again, as Jane and Mam set their wheels to spin.

3

Millie knocked at Alice's door to walk to work as they did each morning. Alice's father greeted her as though she was a spectre, last night's drink flushing his face.

'Our Alice is gone, dear, gone already. I don't suppose she thought you'd be a-coming this morning, what with...' and he tailed off, deferring the door to Alice's mother. Her hands were covered in flour and she raised them apologetically, as if to insinuate that if she wasn't so inconvenienced, she'd take Millie to her bosom and crush away the sadness.

'I'm so sorry, dear; I couldn't believe it when I heard. Alice was beside herself; we all were.'

Millie wondered what Alice's parents might say when the door closed. But for the black ribbon in her hair, would it be difficult to detect she had so recently witnessed a tragedy?

At the mill gates, she could already hear the clatter and rush of the looms. Perhaps the noise would still the workers' lips, snatch away their questions and give up their condolences. Men stood and smoked hurriedly while weary women ushered in children. Millie kept her head down. She felt their eyes on her, the hush catching and spreading like contagion.

Inside, though the air was cold, she took off her shawl and hung it on her peg, setting beneath the waxed paper containing her bread and butter. The heavy doors that separated it from the corridor somewhat muted the noise from the weaving shed, though usually she would still hear the women singing, their refrains barked loudly above the din. However, this time, she supposed it was Bill O'Jack's that kept back the songs far better than any overlooker.

Millie's eyes adjusted to the darkness. Her loom was empty, waiting. Alice looked up, flinched at the sight of her, checking over her shoulder that Shipton was nowhere nearby, ran towards her and grabbed her hands.

'Millie! I didn't think you were a-coming today; I would've waited if I thought you were. Oh Millie, what news!' Alice chewed at her bottom lip.

The other women raised their heads at them, then lowered them as quickly. They had never seemed so industrious. The overlooker would be overjoyed.

'I couldn't stay away. Not when–' but Millie no longer knew how to finish her sentence. The Dingle girl, barefoot, a new scratch along the length of her nose, crawled out from beneath the machines to look at her. Millie gave her a half-hearted smile, but Alice told her to get back to work.

The overlooker approached, and the Dingle girl scuttled beneath the threads. Alice gave Millie a look – *we'll talk more* – and retreated to her own loom.

'Nowt to worry on, girls,' Shipton barked, though no one but Millie looked up. 'I've come to fetch Millie 'ere, not tell you off.' He moved closer to her so he could push the words directly into her ears. Hot breath and spittle. 'These are speshal circumstances, aren't they? Dark days.' He shook his greying curls. He normally took great delight in threatening Alice with fines for singing, and any of the women that should join her choruses. He liked to wind back the clock before the bell.

'Oh?'

'Yes, I've a gentleman here from the new constabulary. Wants to exchange words with you.' He thumbed towards the main door and she followed him. She realised she ached; her body, braced and tight, throbbed. Her head ached, her brain ached, and even her teeth ached.

The constable leant against the stone wall near the pegs where the women stored their things. Shining buttons ran up his middle and a large stiff hat sat on his head. He looked relieved when Shipton closed the door behind him and clutched his hat to his breast.

'My, that's loud. And you work all day in that?'

Millie nodded.

'I won't be two minutes with Miss Bradbury here,' the constable said and Shipton sloped off, disappointed.

'I'm sorry to disturb you, Miss.' The constable took out a piece of paper, looked at the information at the top and folded it away again. 'There will be an inquest into the deaths of, I believe, your grandfather and uncle on 11 April, which is, uh, next Wednesday. It will be at the public house, King William the Fourth, the King Bill. Do you know it?'

Millie nodded. She wasn't sure her voice could work.

'Good. Then I'm afraid I'm going to have to ask you to attend and give your account.'

Her thighs began to tremble violently.

'How will I do it?'

'Ah yes, well, there will be a coroner. A man who will oversee proceedings. He will be most pleasant and courteous to you, as you will be doing your family, your community, boundless service, as, uh, difficult and as painful as it may be. It is his job to hear all sorts of accounts, like yours – well, none as important or as painful as yours, I'm sure – but hear all the evidence and determine the cause of death.'

Determine the cause of death. There was no need for that; Millie could announce it to the weaving shed that very moment: by battery, by fist, by weapon.

'But what of a perpetrator?' Millie's stomach roiled. She put out a hand to the cool of the wall.

'That will take time, Miss, but rest assured: we have other constables like myself out across Saddleworth and beyond, as we speak now. But this is the first step, and your account will, uh, be very helpful. You will help us?'

She would have to stand and speak, hold her head aloft and relay the moment she entered her grandfather's inn, describe what she had seen there, in public, to a room full of strangers. Would she be able to summon her eyes and ears again, invite them to conjure up their memories? Would she then be able to speak those memories clearly, plaintively, knowing she would become a spectacle?

'Is there no one else?'

'No one has seen what you have; it would be most useful to all concerned if you were to tell it.'

Slowly, she nodded.

'Good. The inquest will be in the afternoon, so you'll be able to work your morning, and then come along to the King Bill for midday. We shall arrange some kind of compensation for your loss of your afternoon shift.'

He touched the brim of his hat and made to leave.

'Will there be many others present?'

The constable looked grave. 'This event has caught the attention of many. I suspect the room will be full.'

He thanked her again, before striding away through the gates.

Shipton appeared from the shift manager's office and escorted her back to the looms as though she were a patient at Bedlam.

Theresa and Alice had been talking together at Alice's loom, but at the sight of Shipton and Millie, Theresa took her place at her own, head bent.

'Oh Millie, we don't know what to say,' Alice said, once Shipton had disappeared. 'Everyone's been coming to me to ask what to say to you, if I know how you are. And here you are and there isn't a word in my head!' Her eyes welled with tears.

'I'm not sure there is anything to be said,' Millie replied, starting up her loom. The wool was a neater quality than the fibres she had been working on last Saturday, softer. 'Is this the London Pride?' She had to raise her voice for Alice to hear it, and the effort made her ears buzz.

Alice looked puzzled for a moment and glanced down at her hands. 'Yes, it was changed over yesterday. We've got to mind it; he's threatened fines if we damage it, or leave it lying about. It's been imported, see.'

Soon Millie's shoulders felt their familiar burn, and she longed for butter to rub into the hard skin of her fingers to stop the wool from catching and raising it. She and the women stayed silent for the rest of their shift, their hands darting back and forth, their mouths buttoned shut. At dinner, the women took it in hasty turns to eat their bread and butter beneath their pegs, their looms watched by those who had already eaten. When the bell finally rang, the women filed out in tired silence. Even the children kept close to their mothers, grasping at their hands and picking up the pace as they took their short walks home. The older children disappeared into the alleys, their voices low in their collars, their eyes shaded by their hats and shawls.

Alice took up Millie's hand. 'I can't walk home. I promised Mam I'd help her with the babby up at Little Haigh. It's got an awful cough.'

'Of course,' Millie replied, 'you go.'

'We'll talk properly tomorrow, though?'

Alice ran as soon as Millie nodded her head, and Millie watched her dodge the knots of subdued workers.

Johnny, though, was smoking at the low wall in front of the mill. She watched as the workers, slower to get away, exchanged quiet words with him as they passed. He winked and took off his hat at the women, telling them how lucky Mr Bartriss that evening would be, to have his fill of Betsy's pie, and Betsy had flushed as red as a pig left out in the sun. He made arrangements with Frank to have a look at his traps and see why he hadn't caught a single rabbit since Epiphany; he told old Mr Jarvis that he knew of a buyer for the sow, if he was still looking?

But when he saw Millie, she saw him bring his features into line, lose the sparkle from his eyes. It was as quick as a player taking a mask down from the shelf, though she knew it was his concern, his desire to please people that made him tailor his emotions so. He was like one of those painted creatures she had seen in the Sunday School encyclopaedia, those lizardy things that changed their colour to their surroundings. And she admired him for that; too many of the mill folk were caught up in their own worldly woes to be so attentive to others, despite what they would attest in church on a Sunday morning.

Her heart took up its thump again. If it were Johnny's grandfather and uncle slain, he would be mad with fury, sweeping aside the jackdaws from the chimney pots and railing to the sky. He would not stop until he had found the perpetrator, and would set everyone quivering in their boots, innocent or guilty. It would not do for her to be morose, muddled.

He sat up as she approached, ignored the one or two that were coming in for the night shift that moved their heads to him in greeting. For her; he was waiting for her.

'Amelia,' he said, standing.

She crossed her hands beneath her shawl and pulled it closer.

'How do you feel? How was Shipton? Do you wish you had taken another day?' His voice was gruff from tobacco and tiredness, but he coughed it into something softer, sweeter.

She sighed and stumbled on the uneven path. Her feet in their pattens felt like the weights Mr Dunne used in his shop. 'Shipton said he couldn't give me any special considerations, and I don't want any, but anybody would think it was I that was the villain,' she said. 'Nobody knew what to say; only dear Alice stayed close by and even her tongue seemed stuck to the roof of her mouth. They all know it; they didn't need the detail from me. So they avoided me like I had a disease.'

He shook his head, his hair dancing about his ears. 'I'm not at all surprised. These people will have spoken about nothing else the moment they heard about it from Dunne, yet they can't even bring themselves to offer you comfort. You! Who has been by their side, operating these looms with your blood and your sweat since you were tall enough...'

'Oh, Johnny, I can't blame them. What would I say if the boot were on the other foot?'

She thought of the whiskery old maid that had closed the Binn Green door at her hammerings, returned for her master. She had probably gone right back to her silver polishing or her stew stirring, her arm shaking a little from the news. What choice had they but to continue? Nobody would be bringing them the smelling salts.

'You're too good for them, Millie; *we're* too good for them.'

She had no answer. Perhaps she could have tried Shipton to stay at home another day; she was a good enough worker, never known to cause trouble afore. And Johnny would surely have brought him round. But it was done now, of course.

They turned out onto the road. The other workers had fled, like rabbits to their warrens. Normally, the older women stood in clusters for a time, dissecting the gossip of the day, while the men went to the fields, the farms, and the inns, the children playing in the streets until they were dragged away. She'd never known them to scatter so quickly.

'See, me and my men know the score; if this had happened to one of them, there would be no uncomfortable silences, of that, I'm sure.'

Johnny had a little piecer, an eight-year-old boy with terrible eyesight and a father that threatened it further by blackening his eyes most evenings, and a big piecer that was much older than Johnny but saw in him a leader, a light. Together, his lads worked hard to win his praise and respect.

Johnny nodded at an old man Millie didn't recognise, passing in the opposite direction. He had a sack draped over his shoulder.

'Rabbit. He traps behind Dunne's shop. Anyway, it doesn't matter how hard we work; it could be harder, or faster, or more careful. And there will still be the same load to get through tomorrow, some shipment going somewhere, and we'll never see the finished thing, never lay claim to it.'

She enjoyed listening to him speak, how he was so certain with the words he chose and their meanings. How he paused to suck at his pipe, and how he expected the listener to respect those pauses, too, to take the time to consider his words and the emphasis of them, how his intonation dipped at the closing of each clause. His speech commanded attention; he wasn't letting words fly for something to do, or to fill the dead, dull air.

She wanted to lean in to him, for him to put his arm around her shoulders as though to curtain her off from the world. She wanted to feel his stubbled jaw against her face, her neck.

They turned right again; Chew Valley Road was up ahead. The lanes grew shorter, the houses smaller. Millie felt crowded in, watched.

'A constable came to see me today.'

'A constable?' He stopped suddenly, then moved on again. His eyebrows drew together.

'Yes, I'm to testify at the inquest, being held next week.'

'No,' he said, taking her hand. He didn't look about him to see who might be watching. He was too concerned for her. 'No, you mustn't do that. Think of all you've been through. Why should you go through all that again? Send someone else in your place; that doctor up at Bin Green. When is it?'

Millie was taken aback at Johnny's insistence. She had found Granda and Thomas; it was only right that she tell the authorities how and when.

'It's at the King Bill on Wednesday. But I've already told them I would: I'm to work in the morning and arrive at midday. There will be a coroner.'

'A coroner? Oh Millie, you don't want any of that grief, you have enough of your own. All those pairs of eyes on you; all those gossips twisting your words.'

Millie felt a wave of panic. Would the coroner be alone? Or would there be constables, the Peelers that kept order in Manchester, and yeomen? She trembled. She'd had to speak in Sunday School, and that was bad enough. But they would need the truth, wouldn't they? And she had some of that truth, at least. She thought of Granda in the corridor to the snug, the last sounds he made, and Tom, upstairs, lying alone. The darkness of the inn. The broken windowpane.

Something gripped her inside, told her she needed to do it. The constable already had her word.

They stopped to face each other. The householders of five terraced houses could look out now and see Johnny Barkwell holding the hand of Millie Bradbury, see Johnny's face creased in worry.

'I need to help them catch whoever did this,' she said slowly.

'Your testimony won't do that, Millie.'

'Why not?' The wind was getting up, and she felt rain mar her cheeks.

'You found them and raised the alarm. What more could be gleaned from that?' He turned to walk towards her house, pulled at his collar and her hand. The rain grew more determined. 'And you bury them on Friday. What more is there to add?'

Perhaps he was right. But she had told the constable. What would Mam say?

They rounded into her street and stopped. Tudor, Ed, and two other boys were kicking a large stone between them. She thought she heard their front door open a creak; she would know that sound blindfolded, tested against the others in the terrace.

'Look,' he said. 'I've got an offer for you. Because life is precious, we can't delay our decisions.'

'Yes?' Her tongue stuck to the roof of her mouth and she remembered the tongue of her grandfather, lost in a wet, muddled mire. Guilt pulled at her stomach like a needle and twine. An offer?

He studied her nails. She looked away; she wished she had used Mam's nailbrush. She had a thin crescent of grime in each one.

'It has only been you, Amelia Bradbury, only ever been you. You have more sense than the rest of them put together.'

She snorted in denial, regretted it.

'And you are the most beautiful,' he said, tipping up her chin with his finger. Those eyes, those iron-grey eyes. 'Aren't you?' She squirmed like a fish on a hook. 'I have an offer for you that's been a long time in the making. Will you be my wife?'

She stepped back from him, looked up at his face. He smiled, his red mouth widening. His eyebrows leapt and the lines at his eyes appeared.

'What? Now?' she said, and heard a laugh – her own, from her own lips. She could laugh. She smiled again. The needle and twine in her stomach took another two stitches and her eyes smarted. She thought of Granda, how he should be there and wouldn't be.

Johnny laughed, too. 'Not this very second, Amelia no; but soon.'

Something tickled inside her throat and she coughed gently to dislodge it, coughed again. Her stomach lurched. It was happening. It was truly happening.

'When?'

'Millie! I didn't expect you to ask me "when". More that you'd answer yes or no!' His laugh grew louder then, and Millie spotted Tudor break off from his game to watch them. Next door's baby mewled. She glanced at the doorway for a sight of Mam or Jane.

'Of course, it's a yes, Johnny! It's always been yes!' She smiled wide and lifted her fingers first to his collar, then to his cheeks, and pulled his face to hers. A soft kiss, sweet. She felt her face redden in the rain, the droplets like sleet on her hot skin.

'Well, thank the Lord Almighty for that, because you did have me worried a fraction,' he said, a laugh still weaving through his words. His hands moved from her wrists to her waist. She sank back to the street. His height; his breadth of shoulder.

'Gentlemen,' Johnny said, tipping an invisible cap to the four boys. Ed elbowed Tudor in the ribs, and her face burned again. 'See you tomorrow, Amelia. But think on what I've said: just because you've given your word to a constable, doesn't mean you need to do it.'

She nodded and watched him walk to the end of the street, swinging his arms like he had never seen a day of hard work.

Mam opened the door as Millie approached. She had on her apron, the little wire spectacles that cut into the bridge of her nose.

'Well?' Mam said, with bright eyes.

'Hello, Mam,' she replied, taking down her shawl and shaking it. She was hot. Her heart was beating fully in her chest. She saw Tom lying as still as stone, and the needle and twine started up again. How was it to feel happiness at a time like this? Was it truly happiness?

'Did Johnny Barkwell just ask you to marry him?' Mam stood with her hands on her hips, two great whalebones protruding from thin cloth.

Jane was already seated at one of the wheels, her jaw set as the yarn made its way round the frame. Mam had on the water to boil. Two pies sat on the table. Millie eyed them, looked up at Mam.

'From Mr Dunne. Isn't he kind? I have a handful of early beans to go with them. But you haven't answered my question. Did Johnny Barkwell just ask you to marry him?'

Millie sank into a seat at the table, unlaced her boots. Her skirts were wet, and her hair was thin to her scalp. She smiled and enjoyed the stretch and crease of the skin around her lips.

'Well, yes, as a matter of fact, he did,' she replied, taking the pins out of her hair one by one and setting them on the table.

'He asked you to marry him just after your own kin has been brutally murdered?' Jane said. Her brow had gathered into a thick black line across her forehead, like the brim of an unflattering felt hat. 'Unbelievable! I hope you told him no?'

Mam laughed, darted forwards, threw her arms about Millie's shoulders. 'Oh daughter, such wonderful news! Light in't darkness! My daughter – married. And to such a fine young man as Johnny? We always knew it was to be, and now it is! Oh, I must go and see George and Esme.' She shook her daughter gently, soft tears seeping into her collar.

'I'm so glad you're happy, Mam, you looked so stern, I-'

'Stern?' Mam's laugh grew louder.

'Are you both out of your minds? Have you lost your wits?' Jane threw up her hands. 'Have you quite forgotten our father's relatives who aren't yet lying cold in their graves because their corpses haven't been pieced together? This is not the time for jollity, or marriage, or any other whims and fancies!' She faced Mam and Millie as their embrace fell apart.

'This is exactly the time,' Mam turned to her and pointed a finger. 'This is precisely the time when your sister – this family – needs happiness and the chance to move on from such wicked circumstances-'

'But what man, what monster, proposes *marriage* to a woman just days later?'

'A man that has your sister's best interests at heart, that's who. A man who understands that his love and protection can soothe and mend!' She jabbed in Jane's direction with an arthritic finger. 'I will not see my eldest daughter jealous of my younger daughter's proposal-'

'Jealous? Of Millie? And Johnny Barkwell?' She wrinkled her mouth as though the mutton had turned green.

'I think you should shut your mouth, Jane,' Millie said.

'I think you-'

'I think you've said quite enough,' Millie said, holding her head high. She moved towards the stairs, folded her shawl under her arm. 'I've accepted Johnny's proposal and I expect I will be married before the summer is out. Now, if you don't mind, I'm going to get out of these wet things and then help Mam with whatever she needs help with.'

As she climbed the stairs, she dug her hands into her hair and eased it away from her scalp. She allowed herself a grin, despite the feeling in her stomach, the images that flashed each time she blinked. She was to be a wife; Johnny Barkwell's wife.

4

The marriage proposal had travelled across the factory floor as quick as the children that scuttled between their skirts. It was a relief; a well-worn topic of conversation, easy in their mouths. The women took it in turns to appear next to Millie at her loom and put forward their questions, the same few that she recognised she had asked others in the past. From Betsy and Dora: where would they be wed, and when? Who would be present? From Bridie: Had the banns gone out? From Lizzie, who would surely later put forward her sister for the job: Who would make her dress? And Theresa, elbowed forward, so it seemed that she had agreed to ask it on behalf of others: Would there be ale afterwards?

She answered each slowly, picking at thoughts that seemed about right, and made mental notes to discuss them with Johnny later. Each woman went back to her station with Millie's latest answer and distributed it to the others, so that by the end of the day, a full picture of a wedding emerged. She wondered what Johnny would make of it. She hoped that he was the kind of man that would see a wedding for what it was: the binding together of two people, rather than the superstitions and fripperies that often accompanied it, though she knew he was unlikely to be seen at the altar in patched trousers. He would be sure of a bright handkerchief, too, or a splash of borrowed cologne at his jaw. She should start thinking about her dress right away; she needed to please him, ensure he was proud of the new wife that hung off his arm. But at Theresa's question, she stalled. *Would* there be ale afterwards? Johnny would have it, undoubtedly, but would Mam think differently of it, especially after Bill O'Jack's?

After Bill O'Jack's. She scoffed at herself. Even she was veiling the truth. *After the murder of her grandfather and uncle.* And who would supply the ale, if not Granda and Tom? She had always imagined their presence at her wedding, Granda's eyes shining, Tom spinning a woman beneath his arm, both congratulating Johnny. *Aye,* Granda'd say, *he were always the husband for you.* Of course, he'd never had said as much while he was alive, but he'd once mentioned what a hard worker Johnny Barkwell was and Millie had felt a blush race upwards from her toes on the spot, for that was the utmost compliment in Granda's book. He'd seen her face pinken, and she thought she'd recognised a smile beneath his whiskers. Her eyes smarted, and she looked away so she wouldn't spoil the London Pride.

Her news seemed a welcome substitution for the silence that had followed her reappearance at her loom, and the women whiled away the subsequent two days at the looms with talk of other weddings: of Saddleworth weddings gone wrong, where crooked seams fell apart or drunken fathers couldn't be roused, of delayed vicars, errant employers and unreasonable landlords.

'But your wedding will be different,' Alice had announced to the others at dinnertime. Betsy had offered to mind the looms while the others ate their bread together beneath their pegs. 'Yours, Millie, your wedding with Johnny has been written in the stars since we were childer.' A few of the women had laughed at that and clanged their flasks together.

'Ark at the poetess in the corner!' Lizzie shouted, her belly shaking with her laughter.

'Written in't smog, more like!' Theresa said.

The honey from Millie's bread dripped onto her smock when she raised it to her lips, so she had bent her head to it, dabbing at the stickiness so she didn't have to look at their faces.

'It has!' Alice had insisted. 'We all knew that Millie Bradbury would have a good and happy marriage. She's always worked so hard and been so kind.'

And the women had piped down, muttered their agreement.

Millie instead tried to strike up a discussion about who would be next, but Theresa chattered on.

'And Johnny Barkwell, Millie,' she said, raising her eyebrows. 'He's only ever had eyes for you.'

The women agreed again.

'And you for him, h'aint it the truth! A match in proper heaven, if ever I saw it!'

'And there's some that would switch for your place, Millie, I tells you. Oh, for a tall, broad-shouldered man-'

'With sense in his head-'

'-I'd prefer teeth in his head-'

'Neither! It's what in his trousers that counts!'

At that, there had been unanimous laughter, enough to prompt Shipton to his feet to quieten them and warn of a delayed end to the day. Millie's cheeks burnt and though she smiled, her stomach ached, her chest tightened.

Back at the loom, her fingers faltered on the warp. She had trouble filtering the chatter like she usually did, and instead let the noise accumulate in her ears. The sound grew, evolving new threads, weaving themselves together, distorting fuzzily, and the mass pressed against her ears, her mind. She thought again of Granda and the whimper he had given when she had leant over him.

It could be easy to slip back in to what she knew, to pick up where she left off, and never have to talk with the others about what she had seen. The other women craved ignorance, and she could honour it. The silly stories of life could distract; perhaps could even heal, over time.

But by Thursday night, she had no choice but to face it. William and Thomas would be buried in the morning. She had heard the rooting around in her mother's bedroom, Mam pulling out her widow's weeds from the box she kept underneath her bed. Jane had held up her Sunday dress to the light, grumbled at its frailty.

'I should be honouring my kin with something better than this sack,' she said. Millie silently agreed; her own stuff dress was permanently stained at the ankles and needed taking in again at the waist. Tudor told Ed he wouldn't see him that evening and paced in front of the hearth until, finally, he asked what happened at a church, and how different it'd be to chapel.

Jane smiled gently. 'Burials are quick and quiet, brother,' she said, using her handkerchief to dab the dirt from his cheek. 'We can't afford anything else.'

It was a response that seemed to please Tudor, for he sank into the kitchen chair and listened to Mam's stockinged feet in the bedroom above.

The walk to St Chad's soaked them to the skin and drowned any words that dared to float between them. Millie and Jane linked arms with Mam, Tudor kicking stones beside them. They each looked down, the water running along their eyelashes and noses. If they shed a tear, Millie realised, it could be disguised quite easily.

Through the sound of the rain against the track, she strained for footsteps, for Johnny's footsteps, fast, his feet thudding in his broken boots.

But he wouldn't come, he couldn't. His little piecer had been ill, passing out, and Johnny had been doing the work for two. He wouldn't be able to leave his work.

But soon they would be kin, and Johnny would have to be present at all occasions like this: for he would be the head of a family, a household. She imagined her arm through his, their forearms pasted wet together. Looking up at him graveside, watching as he blew plumes of smoke into the rain and stood tall, commanding more eyes on him than the vicar.

The track to the church wound further round the valley than she had remembered, and she was glad they had set off when they did. The mist hung in clouds so low it was though they could be reached out to, grabbed and pocketed, while the trees stood with shoulders hunched, heads bent. It was a dowly of a day.

Mr Dunne greeted them at the stone steps like they were about to enter his shop rather than the church, and, encasing their hands with his meatier ones, introduced the vicar to each of them in turn. He had taken care of it all, Mam had said. She had been so grateful; she wouldn't have known where to turn. At bed the night before, Jane had shaken off her mother's comments with a haughty toss of her head. Hadn't Mam buried Father, after all? Isiah Dunne seemed to be increasingly involved in their mother's affairs. Mam knew as much as other Saddleworth women about births and burials; Mr Dunne should stick to keeping shop and collecting rent. Millie knew Jane was right, but felt too numb for anger and had closed her eyes in response.

The men were to be buried together, in a clearing at the bottom of the new graveyard. 'They will find peace there,' the vicar had said, but Millie was surprised at how isolated their grave was to be. No others came close, as though theirs were bodies infected with disease.

As they gathered at the graveside, with a few of Bill O'Jack's' old regulars, faces Millie recognised but whose names she had never known, their numbers swelled in the mist. Millie looked over her shoulder. There was a man with parchment, looking furtively about him as he scribbled onto pages, curling with the drizzle. She spotted the constable who had spoken to her at the mill, in deep discussion with two other men that had taken off their hats in respect. His had remained on his head, though through forgetfulness or officialdom, Millie couldn't be sure.

But beyond them were a crowd of other people: stick thin old men and bowed women, younger women with babes in their arms, men with pipes that somehow remained lit in the weather. There were a few children, too, standing stock still as though struck with passion or grief. These faces were unfamiliar, but she presumed they were local, their presence to spread support and solidarity, rather than gossip. When the vicar spoke, whispers skittered out between them, to ensure each had heard what was said. But there were pointed fingers, too, and they didn't look away when her gaze met theirs.

'Don't mind them,' Mr Dunne said beneath his moustache. 'Spectators, hangers-on.' Millie's head snapped back. The sextons had begun to lift the heavy earth back into the grave. Her body heaved. The wet air settled on her face, coated it, mixed with her saltiness. Her eyes stung. She felt Mam shudder next to her.

There wouldn't be a headstone. It was costly anyhow, but one of the constables had warned Mr Dunne at the possibility of visitors, people paying an unhealthy homage to the final resting place for Granda and Thomas. It was to be a plain mound where they lay for eternity. For a fleeting moment, she wondered how her grandfather and uncle would look side-by-side, like two twigs, broken and blown down; Granda short, Tom almost a foot taller with a breadth of shoulder that rivalled Johnny's. But it wouldn't do to think like that; what were bodies without minds, without breath?

'There now,' Mam said, as though she had finished a day's work at her wheel. The vicar closed his hands and his Bible and under the patchy canopy of a large tree, the inn's regulars came to Mam and she shook their hands in turn, thanking them for their attendance, before they moved off into the wet.

It's a long road without a turn, Granda had been fond of saying. His and Tom's road had come to an abrupt end. Millie thought she preferred a long road than none at all.

'T'was wise, not having anyone back to Bill O'Jack's, Mrs Bradbury,' Mr Dunne said once they were gone. 'There would've been all sorts there to gawp through the windows. And once they'd got the ale inside them, they'd be no shifting 'em.'

'Is it over?' Tudor drew closer, and his sisters smiled sadly and told him yes.

'Come,' Mr Dunne said, throwing open his hands, 'the Reverend has kindly invited us into the church for tea.'

'Oh, when will it end?' Jane spoke into Millie's ear. 'Can't we just go home?' Millie opened her mouth but closed it again when she found she had nothing to say.

Despite the darkness of the graveyard, where the tall trees and mist had closed in on them, the church itself sat high on a knoll so that there was light enough to refrain from using candles. Millie looked up from the pew. There was a second floor where bellringers or a choir could sit. Perhaps they would on her wedding day, if it could be afforded.

A small woman with a worried expression appeared from the vestry and rattled teacups and saucers as she brought through teapots and fruit cake on a low trolley. Millie watched it arrive and felt her stomach twinge.

'We're being treated like royalty,' she heard Jane mutter.

The vicar spoke to Mam and Mr Dunne as the worried looking woman began to pour tea into cups. She handed a plate of cake to Tudor.

'Funerals are so we feel that things are done and dusted,' Tudor said, crumbs of fruitcake falling from his mouth and into his lap. 'That the whole chapter's finished.'

'Who told you that?' Jane asked. 'Ed again?' Tudor nodded and swilled the tea around in his teacup. 'And he's the fountain of all knowledge, of course.' Jane squeezed water from the ends of her hair. It rained onto the pew.

'Well, he's probably right,' Millie said. 'But this feels a bit different somehow.'

'The tea and cake, for starters,' Jane said.

If Johnny were here, he would be listening to the vicar, holding Mam's elbow to steady her. She pictured him at the altar waiting for her, but quashed the thought. Not today.

'Why *is* Dunne here, anyway?' Jane said, sitting up again, her voice a little louder. Millie hushed her.

'But what has this got to do with him?'

'Mam finds it a comfort, so let him be.'

Tudor drained his teacup and set it down alongside the hymn books. He picked one up and idly flicked through it.

Jane twisted the ends of her hair and pinned them back to her head.

'Can I have more cake?' Tudor asked, setting the book down.

They looked between them, wondering who would play the authority. Granda had once told Millie that he feared Tudor would be soft without a father, that he'd become a Mary Ann. Millie shrugged.

'Yes,' Jane said, finally. 'Though it's a shame, we are best fed on the day we bury our relatives.'

Mam, Mr Dunne and the vicar briefly looked over at them, as Tudor reached for the trolley. The worried looking woman had vanished. Sitting back against the pew, as straight as he had been instructed in Sunday School, he pushed the remaining pieces of fruitcake into his mouth one after the other.

'Tudor!' Jane laughed.

Mam strode over. 'Do you mind? It's not right, you three sitting here and laughing.'

Jane and Tudor pulled their mouths into line.

'Try not to be hard on them, Mrs Bradbury,' the vicar laid his hand on her shoulder. 'Many feel a mix of emotions on days like these, especially the young.'

'Yes,' Tudor piped up, 'Ed told me about a woman who buried her sister and laughed so hard the vicar had to tell her to stand away from the mourners.'

The vicar looked taken aback but gave Tudor a deft nod of his head before leading them out of the church.

'Honestly, you three,' Mam said, once they were outside. 'What were you thinking?'

'It was nerves, Mother,' Tudor said, casting a look over his shoulder. Mr Dunne was shaking the vicar's hand. Mam made one of her little grunting sounds that Millie could never quite decipher.

The path led them past The Church Inn where a man stood outside, leaning against the wall. As they approached, he took his pipe from his mouth but didn't remove his hat. Millie recognised him as the man who had been pawing at the parchment, graveside.

'Excuse me there,' he said, falling in step with them. Mam slowed her pace in surprise. 'Mrs Bradbury?'

'Yes, as you find me,' she replied curtly.

'*The Manchester Guardian*. I wondered if you'd answer a few questions?'

'Ah, no, if you don't mind,' Mam said, flustered, flapping her hand and looking away. The man continued to walk alongside them.

'It's nothing scurrilous, mistress. It's purely to set records straight. And you want people to know the truth, don't you?'

'What truth?' Jane intervened, and the man looked over at her. His eyebrows twitched together. 'What truth is there? That we've just buried our grandfather and uncle, and we're a grieving family? Is that the truth you seek?'

'Jane,' Millie and Mam warned.

'Do you stop every family that walks between the church and this fine establishment after they have buried their kin?'

'Well, no…' the man began, but Jane continued.

'There is no other truth, then, and you should be satisfied to leave us well alone. You can put that in your paper.' Jane took her mother by the arm and led her quickly away. The man smiled and shrugged at Millie, Tudor and Mr Dunne, who had just caught them up.

'Everything alright?' Mr Dunne asked, looking between them.

'Absolutely fine,' the man replied, lifting his hat from his head and retreating back to the doorway of the inn.

'What did he want?'

'Nothing,' Millie and Tudor answered simultaneously. They hurried to catch up with Mam and Jane.

5

His cough was enough. The King Bill fell silent. Millie had never seen it so full, had never seen any building so full; no church, no mill, no factory. She felt the thrum of expectant bodies, torsos tall with withheld breath, soaped armpits sweating. Heads bobbed over shoulders and ears for a better look, peering, she knew, at her and her eyes flickering between the coroner and the floor.

She looked for Johnny, but knew it was futile. Even if he hadn't his loom to operate or his traps to set, he'd find some other task to occupy him. He didn't think she should be here; his presence would be endorsement. It'd be the only time she went against his wishes.

The coroner's second cough was shorter. He read from his papers; his half-moon spectacles poised on his nose.

'This inquest seeks to reveal the truth behind a terrible crime that has taken place in our community, one of such grave, tragic circumstances unlike any we have witnessed previously. On the afternoon of Sunday 1st April 1832, two men – William Bradbury, publican and gamekeeper, and his son, Thomas Bradbury, gamekeeper – were discovered brutally murdered in their own home, the well-known but secluded public house, The Moorcock Inn, or Bill O'Jack's in local parlance. Bill O'Jack's is situated along the Holmfirth Road, a long, tiresome road that links this village with Holmfirth, and it is such that the inn is frequented by thirsty travellers, by merchants and navvies, those that use the road for their trade and employment.

'It is my duty, as representative of the law and the Crown, to establish the cause of death. There will be pictures painted today, ladies and gentlemen, that are most unpleasant. I urge anyone of a weak disposition or a faint heart to leave, and I especially entreat the paper-writers present, the journalists, to restrain their ramblings in respect of those that may come across their reports in the public.'

Millie heard shuffling, of whispers being passed back and forth, but nobody rose to leave.

'Well then,' the coroner continued, 'I would like to invite Miss Amelia Bradbury to tell us what she witnessed that terrible day.'

Millie rose. She tried to clear her throat as the coroner did before each address, but she felt the breath lodge as though she had dry bread there. Her ears popped and crackled as she swallowed.

'Now, in your own time, please tell us your reason for visiting Bill O'Jack's that Sunday afternoon.'

Her voice sounded small in the contained air, thin. But he didn't ask her to speak up or to repeat her answer, only to explain her family's relations to the deceased.

'My father was the brother of Thomas; the son of William Bradbury. He died almost ten years ago.'

The coroner nodded swiftly. 'And at what hour might this visit of yours been, for the purpose of securing yeast?'

'No earlier than two in the afternoon, sir.'

He asked her then to describe the route she would take to the inn, and any landmarks or people she may have passed. Her voice grew in strength as she described the singular route to her grandfather's public house: the lane that gave way to that long, lonely road which continued to rise up and away from Greenfield. She described the moment the road paused as if wondering how to continue, and it would be there that travellers would see the well-lit windows or smell the smoke from the chimney of Bill O'Jack's.

'But there were no lights that day, Amelia?'

'No, sir, it was still light, though the clouds were gathering. I was surprised as the door was open but it was not yet drinking time.'

'And this would be unusual?' The coroner asked over his glasses.

'Oh yes, Granda – William – opened around six on a Sunday. The door would only be ajar if the inn was to be open or when he was taking on supplies. But there was no sign of the dray. And the wind was picking up. The door should've been closed.'

She shook, her cheeks burning with the attention of so many faces, her body sweating though she felt chilled. She set one hand on her hip to steady it.

'Please, Amelia, do take your time, but can you tell us what you saw when you arrived through that open door?'

She nodded, focused her attention on the coroner's brow, on the hair she could see protruding from his ears.

Millie recalled the darkness of the inn, how the cloud cover made the bar very gloomy and she would've expected candles or a fire in the hearth. She mentioned that the tables were overturned, the glass from the window smashed and scattered across the floor. She watched his quick hand make deft movements across the paper in front of him.

She paused, waiting for another question. He nodded for her to go on, so she breathed deeply and told of the moment she had discovered Granda; the muffled sound he had made, how she had mistaken his poor, pummelled body for laundry to be done.

She wouldn't cry, she wouldn't cry in front of these people. Instead, she clenched her fists at her skirts, breathed evenly through her nose.

'I appreciate that this is difficult for you. Can you tell all assembled here today whether your grandfather was alive then, and whether you managed a discourse?'

Millie tested her vocal cords. 'I knelt over him. I can't remember if I spoke his name, but he seemed to be trying to say something.'

'And what was that something?'

'It sounded like "Platts", or "Pats".'

'And what did you make of that?'

Millie's set her shaking hands to her hips, then folded them in front of her. 'I don't know, sir.'

'Well, do you think your grandfather was trying to say something in particular?' The coroner's half-moon glasses had slid to the tip of his nose.

She nodded. 'I've been thinking on it since. A word beginning with "p" takes effort.'

'You mean,' the coroner said, 'you don't believe a man would say a word beginning with "p" involuntarily? That he purposefully meant the word to be got across?'

Millie nodded. She felt her pins loosen, sweat tickling the backs of her thighs.

'And what do you think your grandfather meant to tell you?'

'We thought he could be trying to alert us to the person, or people, who – beat him. But we thought it could have been simply what was on his mind at the time, things concerning him; you know, if he's in a daze.'

'And what conclusions did you draw?'

Millie had feared this. She glanced over at Mam, but she was looking straight ahead, at the chipped paint of the windowsill, or the crooked window itself. Mr Dunne, seated beside Mam, returned her glance instead, pressed his moustache into a smile. Millie turned back to the coroner.

'It's all just theories, sir, speculation; I wouldn't want to draw anyone else into this.'

'That's quite all right. Amelia, I am asking you for your thoughts alone; nobody will be implicated until a firm line of inquiry is established.'

She wrung her hands, felt the sweat of each palm, and slid a hand down each thigh to dry them. 'Well, if it was "Platts" he was saying, then there's Reuben Platt, one of his regular customers; a friend, you might say.'

Millie heard the shuffling of the congregation. They had all turned to look at Reuben Platt. She knew it.

...Until a firm line of inquiry was established.

She grabbed at her skirts, felt her hands twist the material.

The coroner nodded and made a tiny note. 'We shall be hearing from him shortly. What else?'

She cleared her throat. 'Then there's the platters, renting some of Granda's fields at the moment.'

'Platters?'

'The Travellers, sir, Gypsies.'

'Why do these platters rent your grandfather's fields?'

Millie pictured the small caravans – vardos, Granda had called them – and the hairy horses they grazed there. They liked piebald horses best and allowed their manes and fetlocks to grow unfettered. She had seen Granda patting them, watched as they nosed his empty pockets, their long ropes tethered to stakes in the ground.

'They come for the reeds that grow up there so the women

can make baskets to sell. The men work on the farms.'

The coroner continued to write as he spoke. 'And did any platters work for your grandfather or your uncle? Was there any hostility you knew of?'

'I don't know my grandfather's business, sir; I am just his granddaughter. He would never tell me of his work, who supplied his beer.'

'But you would know if these platters caused your grandfather's problems, would you not? I expect the entire village would know.'

The vardos nestled close together at the edge of the plantation. She had seen the dark flashes of children playing close by.

'Perhaps; yes, probably. And I've not heard anything like that.'

'I see.'

'My brother, Tudor, suggested the final thought.'

'Tudor Bradbury? Is he here?' The coroner took off his glasses to scan the room.

'No, he is at work, along with my sister.'

'So, what did Tudor come up with?' The coroner tapped a temple.

'At the mill, there's been a great deal of talk about the Pats arriving here to work on the canal.'

'Ah, you mean the Irish labourers?'

Millie nodded. 'I'd heard of them, though I've not seen them in the flesh.'

'And would your grandfather have any connection to these men?'

'I couldn't tell you, sir. Whether they drink his ale, I couldn't say.'

The coroner made more notes, quickly and firmly. He looked up again at Millie, swept his glasses off, and let them swing from his hand.

'Thank you, Amelia. We all appreciate your time in recounting your hardships. You may take your seat and we will now hear from-' he checked a second sheet of paper, '-a Mr Reuben Platt. Mr Platt, please rise.'

Millie dropped to her seat, her legs like full lant jars, heavy and uncompromising. It was done. It was the right thing to do, she was sure of it, though her body shook and her collar was wet with sweat.

She saw Reuben Platt stand, recite his name and occupation – 'fuller' – but then her ears began to buzz and her vision flicker. She closed her eyes, concentrated on her lungs, imagined the sacks within her ribcage expanding and contracting. She felt her mother take her hand.

Reuben Platt had little to say. He answered the coroner's questions sparsely, without detail. His right leg juddered.

'And where were you on Sunday evening, if Bill O'Jack's didn't have your custom?' the coroner asked.

'Ah, but I don't frequent old Bill on a Sunday,' he said quickly, his red whiskers trembling. 'Never have. He don't open 'til the evening, but I spend my Sundays with my mother. I was there then, too, sweeping out her grate.'

Finally, he asked the doctor to speak.

Mr Higginbottom told of the alarm being raised by a young woman hammering at the door of one of his patients. She had evidently witnessed an ordeal, he said, as her eyes were wide, and she had trouble getting the words out of her head.

'I knew of Bill O'Jack's; it's a name well known around here, and I have seen it from the road when I travel to Holmfirth, which is a semi-regular occasion: I have a clergyman friend there who I visit every month or so. It's also the nearest public house to the cottage of one of my regular patients. But I've never been to the inn.'

'Why have you never visited?' The coroner asked, taking off

his glasses again. He began to clean them with a small cloth. 'Does it have a poor reputation?'

'Oh no,' the doctor shook his jowls vehemently, 'no, if it has a reputation – and it may or may not do – I shouldn't know it. I rarely drink and I do not enjoy public houses; they are not establishments I frequent.'

'And why were you close by on this occasion?'

The doctor looked over at Mr Whitehead, coughing neatly into a handkerchief. 'Mrs Whitehead is a patient of mine, has been for some time. I see her regularly.'

The coroner asked the doctor to describe the inn as he found it. He detailed William's injuries, referring to his notes, and their possible cause: fractured skull from repeated blows to the head, most probably with a large but blunt instrument; fractured jaw and broken and missing teeth as a result of further blows to the face; a grave loss of blood; a severed ear from a grappling or bite from the perpetrator. He confirmed that he hadn't searched for a weapon, that there hadn't been anything obvious.

Millie felt Mam's fingers close about her own and hold them tight. It was not a grip of love, like she might experience in front of the hearth of an evening, but of desperation that Millie was present and made of the same stuff, of true flesh and blood. They would endure this together.

The coroner wrote as the doctor spoke. When the doctor stopped, so, too, did the coroner.

'Could you please describe how you found the son, Thomas Bradbury?'

And on it went again: the doctor's analysis of a very simple death – 'a hard, quick blow to the head from behind, a rough fall and a broken neck' – and Millie's churning, undulating stomach like a year's worth of women's pains had arrived at once.

Eventually, the doctor reached the end of his speech, mopped his brow with a new handkerchief and retook his seat. A wave of shuffling rose and fell.

'Well, ladies and gentlemen,' the coroner said to his papers, 'we have heard a great amount this afternoon, but there is little evidence on which to draw, few clues to probe. At present, I can only record that this is wilful murder by person or persons at present unknown. As a result, the session will resume when the constables have further lines of inquiry. I will also take the advice of the constables as to whether a financial reward for further information is appropriate.

'But before I do, I would like to thank all those present for your quiet and your patience, and to reassure you that we will find the culprit, or culprits, and we *will* bring them to justice. It is my duty to God and the King to oversee that procedure and ensure that justice is done.'

The coroner set down his empty glass, slid his papers into his bag and took leave of the makeshift courtroom.

It was as though the play had been performed and the audience didn't know what to make of it. They stood in clumps, speaking hurriedly, glancing at those who had spoken. Women fanned themselves with the ends of their shawls while the landlady went from room to room, opening windows to let out the hot air and intrigue.

'You're a good girl,' Mam said, smoothing down the collar on Millie's Sunday dress.

Millie's eyes filled with tears before she could will them not to, but she would not allow them to spill.

'You spoke well, Amelia, especially given that you had been so heartily dissuaded.' Johnny, with his father, George, at his side. He gave her a wink, then allowed his face to fall with sombreness.

'You were here? You heard?'

'Of course,' he said, nodding sadly. She felt her face pinken, watched his eyes fill. He was sore that she had endured such suffering. For her to suffer would be to cause him sufferance.

'There were people outside, you know, trying to get in. They couldn't hear, of course, so the people at the front passed messages back. *The Manchester Guardian* was here, too,' George said, as though she should be impressed. Millie watched his son, the jaw that clenched and rested, then clenched again.

'You mustn't stay any longer,' Johnny said.

'Thank you for coming, dear; George,' Mam said in a small voice, 'it is nice to see such friendly faces amongst all this-'

He pressed his hand to the small of Millie's back and ushered her towards the door. 'There will be happier times here,' he said in her ear and Millie nodded, childlike, and grasped at Mam's cuffs.

Mam nodded deftly at each as they parted.

'Goodbye,' Millie said over her shoulder as the men fixed their hats on their heads.

Her temples throbbed so hard she could imagine each pulse rippling the air, sending out signals to the night. She rolled her head back, let a staccato sigh float up to the ceiling.

'Millie,' Jane said. Her voice sounded far away. 'Go to sleep.'

'I can't,' Millie said.

'Well, try.' Jane sounded more like Mam than Mam did.

Millie sighed again, but quieter this time. Imagined the sigh as a little cloud, rising to the rafters with all the other clouds, from Jane, from Mam, from Tudor. She thought of Johnny and the first time they would share a bed, their two clouds mingling, joining together beneath their own ceiling. She inched a leg across, imagined it touching the flesh of another human being; it being normal that their legs should touch. Then wondered what would happen next, as that flesh connected. It would be the time for it; it was bed where it happened, she knew that much. And she knew about the hardness, about the firmness in his groin. She had seen one hand move to his lap when she had kissed him at the mill that time. Alice had told her that her mother had said, in a moment of jovial transparency, that men became uncomfortable if it stayed that way for too long *without release.*

And she wondered at that phrase, because although she knew that bit involved a wife, she couldn't quite fathom her part in it. She knew she was to lie still and obliging, and that he would take his pleasure from her in the dark, and if she were a good wife, then there was no harm in her seeking happiness in it, too, especially when the children arrived. She and Jane had often speculated about it when they were much younger, about the seed they knew the man possessed and that it somehow had to find its way to the flowers they cultivated themselves.

But as they had grown older, as their mam had asked them to raise their necklines, lower their hems and bow their heads, as men made comments under their breath or clucked their tongues as they passed them to the mill gates, Millie and Jane had dropped their conversation on the matter altogether. It seemed too looming and too real to put into words.

And now she would be a wife in just a few months. She pictured herself at the bakestone, pulling feathers from a bird, sifting the coins through her fingers at Dunne's shop. How different would it be to now? She did all of those things for Mam, and Tudor was often treated like the man of the household: his dinner made for him, his boots repaired. But perhaps Johnny would be the kind that split their duties; she knew he was a decent fellow, good to the men below him. He understood that many hands made light work. They could be a true partnership, a team perhaps, like the two lead horses at the head of the coach. No cuss words, no bowed heads and fearful children.

It had been inevitable, their pairing. Millie and Johnny had known each other since birth, it seemed. Their fathers had been in the same business of wool and game – but whose father hadn't round here? – and his mother went to Chapel, too, so that eased things on a little. And he had a sister the same age as Jane and yes, his sister was proud and too fond of fine clothes despite not having any and yes, Jane positively despised her, but they could bring her round. She smiled again, picturing Jane arm in arm with Gertie Barkwell, gathering flowers in their aprons or knitting with Mam beside the grate. She snorted.

'Millie! It's been a long day; tomorrow will seem longer still if you don't go to sleep.'

'My mind's too busy,' Millie whispered.

'Of course it is. But calm it. Count sheep; it's not long before we have their wool in our hands.'

It was alright for Jane; she didn't see the bloody faces of her grandfather and her uncle each time she allowed her mind to rest. She had to occupy it, busy it, else the scene reappeared. His body in the doorway, smaller than she would have anticipated, his clothing assaulting him with its errant flaps and tears. Her uncle, like a little girl's doll left on a bedspread, limbs splayed as though dropped from above, abandoned.

And, she allowed herself the thought, Jane hadn't been as close to Granda; she hadn't known him like Millie had. Nobody had, she was sure of that.

It would do no good, she told herself. Her grandfather and uncle had suffered enough. It would not help to pace up and down that afternoon in this way, wearing down the soles of her boots, wearying her feet like this. She was not the constable or the coroner, it was not her duty.

But her Granda's face. It was there as soon as she closed her eyes, like it had been branded onto the inside of her eyelids. At the mill that afternoon, a skein she had drawn apart curled into a replica of his beard. How it had smeared itself across body and flagstone.

Tudor had said the inn had been left open. Ed had told him more people were arriving to look at the scene for themselves. She saw them gingerly pushing open the door as she had done but stepping into the gloom fully expectant of what lay ahead, wanting to witness it, see the truth first-hand, to satiate their own curiosity and retell it to their neighbours. They would ape at the blood on the walls, sidestep the biggest puddles and nod knowingly. They would toe the shattered glass, their soles on the stone the only sound for miles, save for the pulse of their own blood in their ears, a welcome reminder of their own fortitude and safety. And life.

She needed to go back. She needed to find where Granda kept the yeast.

She sat up. Jane had slipped into sleep. Millie held her breath as the straw in the mattress hissed when she planted her feet to the floor. She took her shawl from the door.

Her mother's breathing was as regular as a saw against timber. Millie timed each exhale with a step on the stairs.

'Where are you going?'

She wheeled round. Tudor's eyes shone bright with excitement. She pressed a finger to her lips, shushed him.

He sank his arms into his jerkin and pulled the collar close.

'I'm coming too,' he whispered.

'No, you're not.' Millie ushered him back to the threshold.

'You're going to Granda's, aren't you?'

'How do you..?' Millie began to shake her head, but changed her mind. She nodded once, quickly, sharp. 'Yes, but please, you can't tell a soul, lest of all Mam or Jane. Nor Johnny, neither. I need to see it again.'

She squeezed her hands together, bit her lip. She could trust Tudor.

He hastily tied his laces. 'Well, let's get there quickly then, before it's noticed we're gone.' He closed the door with a click.

Clouds sagged over the road out of Greenfield, illuminated by a toenail moon. Breath tumbled out of their mouths, but deadened instantly, dissipated. The silent road that rose in front of them was just as it was during the day: deserted, barren. Soon they would take the hidden dirt track that sulked down into the valley. Only locals and people that took the Holmfirth Road regularly – the wool sellers, the cotton merchants, nomadic preachers, navvies – knew of the existence of Bill O'Jack's. Its name was passed between experts like a fine cloth or horse: only visible to those that needed and appreciated it.

'What will happen to the inn now?' Tudor asked, kicking at the dirt.

Millie shrugged. 'I honestly don't know.'

The track was beset with puddles cut through with gorges from cartwheels. The moon peered into the snatches of water as though it was searching for something. Millie hitched up her skirts. She pictured herself running the opposite way, grabbing at the air, her skirts forgotten and beaten by the mud, pummelled by her incessant feet. Her breath shortened.

'Why did you want to come here tonight, Mills? Why not tomorrow after work, Sunday after chapel, why now?'

The inn lay coal black on the next brow, hunkering down, bracing itself against the hillside.

She couldn't tell him about the yeast. It was the mutterings of a madwoman. 'I couldn't sleep.'

'Many people can't sleep but they aren't out here, getting stuck in the mud.'

'You sound like Jane,' Millie said, picking up the pace. She wondered what Johnny would say if he knew she was out here. She wouldn't tell him; he wouldn't need to know. When they were married, that's when she would tell him everything; there would be no secrets.

The trees breathed and sighed. Millie fixed her eyes to the front door, closed this time. As they reached the cobbled courtyard, they noticed a scrap of paper pasted to the door, almost blue in its whiteness. Millie squinted.

'What's that?'

Tudor read aloud. '"The murders at Bill O'Jack's. See for yourself the scene of the most talked about crime in the country, with your knowledgeable guide and host, Isiah Dunne, a personal friend of the Bradburys. Call at the Greenfield Village Stores for more information." Personal friend?' Tudor spat. Below it, an excerpt from *The Manchester Guardian*.

Millie read, read again, the words joining hands and dancing. She ripped down the paper and squashed it between her hot hands before pushing open the door. The moon poked a silvery tongue through a window, throwing light across the flags. The bottom pane had been blocked with a wedge of rough wood, but still the tables and chairs were scattered, glass winking beneath.

'What a ruckus!' Tudor said. He lifted up his boot to inspect the glass he had squeaked against the stone.

'Left as it was; better for Mr Dunne's visits, I suppose.'

It was colder here, much colder. But still, Millie's face burned.

Tudor took out a candle from his jacket and lit it. 'It looks the same, then?'

She nodded, imagined Mr Dunne's exaggerated goosesteps over the fallen furniture, his call for quiet as his bloodthirsty punters witnessed the rattle of the windowpanes, the howl of the chimney. She gripped at the bar to steady her feet. To steady her feet where her grandfather's feet had once stood.

'And Granda was found in here?' Tudor asked, his eyes searching the shadows. She pointed towards the snug, the dark stone before it. Closed her eyes.

His voice had sunken small against the stone. She pictured Granda's face, mauled and bloody, his mouth desperately trying to form sounds she could recognise. It had glistened, sparkled, his blood and flesh and bone and muscle, all stirred up and laid out. She had internalised that smell. She could conjure it up at any time she chose. Farms, of new lambs and dung, of birth and life, death and decay, mould. Of sour and freshness, hide and hair.

'Yes,' she said through her hand, though she didn't look to confirm.

'There's still blood,' she heard him say quietly to himself. 'Anyone could step in it.'

He appeared at her side, took her hand. His skin was rough like her own. He held the candle up to the bar. The mirror that leant up against the wall was mottled, in need of polish, while the shelves were furred with dust. Had it always been unkempt, or did it seem so in Granda's absence? She recalled him rubbing beeswax into the counter as carefully as a groom to the flank of his mount.

The handbell Granda used to call time was leaning up against a stopped clock. The dirty ribbon tied to the handle harboured a small key.

'Of course,' she said aloud, stepping over the glass to reach it. 'He kept it in the cabinet.'

'Kept what in the cabinet?' she heard Tudor ask, but she ignored him, instead reaching for the small wooden cabinet lodged in the rack that held the glasses. She brought it down, set it on the bar and fitted the key to it. The lid opened easily. Inside, yeast, and three other small jars. She held them up to Tudor's candle. 'Sugar, salt. Coffee. Granda's important stuff.'

'He locked it away?'

'Away from prying eyes and drunken fingers,' she replied. He disdained any extravagance – *why put butter on the bacon?* he'd say – and locked away the only luxuries he had. 'Come; we've seen enough.' She steadied herself against the bar, untied the ribbon from the bell's handle and set the small key in her waistband. She didn't look for Tudor's expression.

'Can't we lock the door?' Tudor asked, as she closed it behind them.

She shrugged. 'Mr Dunne probably has the keys; he has his fingers in all sorts of pies,' and she shuddered, thinking of the pies he had left Mam.

She wedged her hands into her armpits to warm them. He kicked stones, stiff hillocks of grass, the bare earth.

'Stop that. You'll ruin those boots.'

'They didn't deserve this, Millie, did they?'

Millie wondered how long it would be before the knocker-up was out in the streets, until the crying of next door's colicky baby would commence, until Mam threatened Tudor with no breakfast if he didn't come down the stairs that instant. She didn't even have energy to yawn.

'Nobody deserves such savagery,' she said.

Millie didn't linger with Alice and Johnny after the bell. Mam and Jane visited Father's old aunt in Quick every Thursday night, and Millie aimed to steal a few moments to herself to begin her dressmaking in earnest.

She found Tudor slouched low in a kitchen chair, though, pulled close to the grate.

'Tudor! You still have on your jerkin!' Millie said. He flinched, but his eyes didn't leave the flames. 'It's a bit warm for a fire and your jerkin. Aren't you well?' Millie reached out to touch his forehead, but he ducked his head away. He usually met with his friends after the bell, slunk around with them in the ginnels until bed. 'What's the matter?'

He turned, shouldered off his jerkin. 'Ed Munton told me that Mr Dunne is selling everything from Granda's place. All the tables, chairs, glasses, everything. Tomorrow, Friday, there's an auction. I had to pretend to Ed that I knew all about it. The whole lot, Millie!'

'What?' Millie held on to the back of Tudor's chair.

'Bill O'Jack's is going to be sold, and everything in it.'

'But what's Mr Dunne got to do with it?'

Tudor shrugged and began to unlace his boots.

'Well, who'd Ed heard it from?'

'I don't know.'

'Perhaps he has it wrong; it could be hearsay, someone with the wrong idea.'

But Millie doubted her words. She could hear Mr Dunne making Mam the offer – *Best to be shot of it all. You have suffered enough. I shall take full control; you shan't have to lift a finger* – and creaming off a share of the profits.

After all, you've a wedding to pay for now.

It was too soon. What if there was a clue lying there, awaiting discovery? She thought of the cabinet with Granda's salt and sugar, coffee and yeast. He had worked so hard to look after Bill O'Jack's, to make it the inn it was. She was sure she could feel the key in her waistband glow with heat.

Mam and Jane appeared at the back door. A curtain of rain fell from Mam's felt hat as she removed it from her head.

'I could wring this out,' Jane said, hanging up her shawl in disgust. Their boots squeaked against the flags as they prised out their damp feet.

'You're back soon,' Millie said dully, knowing her sewing plan was destroyed. Jane told her that they had made their excuses when they saw that their relative already had a visitor, a neighbour infamous for her loquaciousness.

'Oh Millie, have you not even made a start on the potatoes?' Mam cast her eye across the kitchen. Millie took up a knife quickly, but set it down again. 'Tudor?' She looked to Millie. 'What's happened? Something's afoot.'

Millie took a breath in. 'Ed Munton told Tudor that there's to be an auction at the inn tomorrow.'

'Ah.' Mam pulled a chair close and sat back in it with relish. She circled her ankles in turn. 'Yes, though I did intend to tell you this evening, it seems that Greenfield's done my work for me. I should've known; nothing stays quiet for long in this place.'

'But Mam, Mr Dunne? What's he got to do with all this?'

Mam held up her hand. It looked small, wrinkled, like it had wilted in the rain.

'Mr Dunne suggested it, and a very good, kind suggestion it was, too. I hadn't given the contents of that poor place a thought, all that furniture your grandfather collected over the years, and Mr Dunne brought it to my attention, sayed that we shouldn't leave it a-festering. Why, in that secluded spot, it could all disappear to tinkers and other ne'er-do-wells. No, he is right; it must go, and it must go immediately.'

'But really, Mother, so soon?' Jane said, folding her arms.

'Yes. There's already some *unusual* people paying the inn visits. Apparently, keen to - well, I don't know what, frankly.'

'Didn't Dunne tell you that he's the cause of most of that?' Tudor asked, still facing the fire.

'Oh, you mean his opening up for people? Keeping an eye on it? That I don't mind at all; I'm grateful for his thoughtfulness.'

'You don't mind him taking the coin for it, neither?'

'He's a businessman, and he's doing us a service. I mind not a jot.'

'But what if there are clues to be found?' Millie asked, 'If it all goes at auction, we might never find the perpetrators!'

'A few broken glasses are not going to help us bring our kin justice, Amelia, else it would have occurred already. I'm quite confident of that. Isiah – Mr Dunne – has been granted permission to go ahead.'

Jane shook her head slowly. 'And are we not granted permission to give our thoughts and feelings on the matter?'

Mam rolled her eyes. 'There are no thoughts or feelings to be had on matters such as these; only common sense and common decency should prevail, which you three seem to lack in abundance.'

Mam stood, shook off her gloves and submerged the potatoes in a basin of water.

'But Mam, does this mean the inn will be sold, too?'

'No, it doesn't,' she said. She employed a weary tone as though she'd answered the question before. 'I'm not sure what we'll do with it; we can decide later in the year. Now, if you've quite finished picking apart your deceased relatives' doings, then can one of you set a pot going and another of you take over these potatoes while Jane and I get out of our wet things? We'll catch our death and we've had enough of that in this family.'

6

Millie could see Johnny across the road from the mill, his stance unmistakeable: hips jutted forwards, one long leg bent, his hulk held languidly, threatening to topple over. One hand rooted in his pocket, the other raised his pipe to his lips at regular intervals. She watched him as he nodded at his companion, a greying man whose name she couldn't place, listening and pausing the conversation every time someone passed and bade him good evening. Millie felt the base of her stomach shift, as though it, too, was listening, perched on the drystone wall next to Johnny.

Through the steady line of workers, each in their uniform greys and browns, the faded shirts and off-white aprons, Johnny spotted her and Alice and dipped his forehead.

'Amelia, Alice,' Johnny said solemnly, blowing out a sluice of smoke. The other man touched the peak of his cap, his skin the same grey, and took his leave. The three of them watched him walk quickly along Manchester Road.

'Was that John Bates?' Alice asked.

'Aye, the bore,' Johnny said through a half-smile.

'I thought he was having a hard time of it?' Alice said again.

John Bates? Millie thought. *Why are we talking of him?* Then something made her watch his back. He walked quickly, nodding at the other men he passed. *Bates? Pates? Patts?* He had left the minute she had arrived. Was he hiding something?

'Yep, a man who's only recently left the mill to inherit his uncle's farm, but he's already in the mire with it,' Johnny said.

'Poor man,' Alice mused. They set off along Manchester Road in the same direction. 'Are you helping him out?'

There, Millie thought to herself, *he's just a poor man in hard times. I can't go around suspecting any poor soul.*

'I'll see what I can do, but there's nowt more tiresome than debt and woe,' Johnny said. Millie watched as the wind ruffled the hair about his ears. 'Anyway, I thought you might be in need of another body. Make sure old Dunne doesn't get too involved in proceedings.'

She was lucky, she knew that. Someone was smiling on her. To have witnessed such a tragedy but to have since been afforded such kindnesses. Combined, she thought, Alice and Johnny knew all there was to know about Millie Bradbury. If she were to collapse now, they would know to whom to raise the alarm, where to take her. In the event of her sudden, unexpected death, they could spin an elegant, accurate eulogy.

'That's very kind of you,' Millie said, and wanted to laugh at her formality. That wasn't how real wives and husbands conversed. She knew that as much. But neither Johnny nor Alice seemed to notice.

'Tell Johnny about the burial,' Alice said. She didn't need Alice's prompts, either, but nevertheless recounted the drizzle of the day, the tea and cake in front of the vestry, the man taking notes.

'Imagine, Millie,' Alice said, without thinking, 'your name could be as famous as Joan of Arc's! Or Mary Queen of Scots!'

The clouds busied themselves over the hills. Their shapes cast over the moors so that the slopes flashed bright green and grey, alternating. As workers dispersed, closing their cottage doors behind them, the road grew quieter, the wind gaining confidence in its voice. Nicks between homes grew bigger and ginnels gave way to open ground; coarse thickets of mountain grass cropped cleanly by rabbits.

'Why did they live out here, Millie? It's a shame; if they'd lived amongst the rest of us...' Johnny tailed off.

She felt her face frown, but straightened it out again.

'But Bill O'Jack's was well known,' Alice began, plugging the silence that Millie had left. 'People knew to rest there.'

'Yes,' Millie added, but stopped. It had been their home; it was how her Granda and Tom had made their living. It was hardly their fault. People should be able to live anywhere, grind out a living from anything they could turn their hand to.

But, as she scanned the bald plains, her face flushed with the shame of it. They could've chosen something a little more sociable. Is that what Johnny believed, too?

'*Thomas* and *William Bradbury* were well known, you mean,' he said.

Millie wondered at his words. They were well known, in the same way that any publican was known in the area. As hospitable men whose attitudes would change as fast as the clouds if men were to mistake them for fools. And what Saddleworth man worth his salt would prefer to take up the mantle of the fool?

The Holmfirth Road stretched out before them, its summit invisible beneath a plucky wisp of cloud that sank lower than the others. The road was lined by drystone walls to keep farmers content and wallers in work. But then there was that section that broke off, like it was pausing for breath or clearing its throat, just enough time to allow a lane to break away and hunker down. It ran parallel for a short while to the Binn Green cottages before making its own path to the front door of Bill O'Jack's.

She hadn't returned since her night visit with Tudor. She presumed Mr Dunne had replaced the sign they had torn down, perhaps even substituted it with something more permanent and statelier, in wood or etched slate. And how many of his grisly gore seekers had passed through its open door today, taken a memento? She imagined men and women, their eyes bright with imagination, turning over the walking sticks Granda had made himself; picking through her uncle's calfskin gloves; admiring the knocks and scratches in the dark furniture, hoping for a blot of blood or some other mark of misfortune.

Just think, that poor old fella would've drank from this.

He may have slept in this on his last night on this fair earth!

Millie stopped. Retched.

'Love! Aren't you well?' Alice bent over her, stroked the knobs of her spine. Millie's words were lost in a burning that seared her throat. She felt Johnny's hand on her sleeve.

'I knew this was too much for her,' she heard Johnny say to Alice. 'She needs to rest; what she has witnessed...'

Fine, she mouthed. *Fine. It's nothing.*

She let them steady her upright, converse silently over her head as though she were a child.

A phaeton approached at Binn Green, the driver tipping his hat. Two ladies, one older, one younger, paused in their conversation behind gloved hands to stare.

'Imagine being so rich that you can summon your driver and go wherever you please,' Alice said.

'Those, if my eyes don't deceive me, were the Mellwoods from Brighouse. Their old man's a mill owner,' Johnny said. 'So, imagine having the mettle to come all the way from Brighouse to root through some poor old bugger's belongings.'

It wouldn't be the words she'd choose, though Granda was – had been – undeniably poor and old. But the essence of it was true enough. It made her heartsore, that her grandfather and uncle, who had spent their lives working, shoring up their inn and trapping their game, were reduced to a sack full of blood-spattered clothing, mooned over by strangers.

'From Brighouse? They've come all the way from Brighouse for the auction?'

'They won't be the furthest neither, I'll bet. Trust me, if I had that sort of money, I would not be using it on a phaeton to the

Holmfirth Road.'

The lane to Bill O'Jack's was like a plough had run furrows through it, so deep were the banks of earth gouged out by multiple cartwheels. But no carts were standing beside the front door, no horses or ostlers were hastily stomping life into their feet.

'It must be over,' Millie said with relief. She could help sweep the flags, draw the curtains upstairs, close up the scullery, like she would in any household, then accompany Mam home.

The rain hit them without any warning, great sheets of water slashing at their sides. They ran, Millie and Alice scooping up their skirts, their boots sinking even in the coarse grass that bordered the sticky lane.

Millie hammered at the door. Mam ushered them in, shivering at the remnants of the downpour they brought in with them.

The bar was bare, the mirror gone, the shelves empty and free of dust. She couldn't see the corner of the cabinet in the glass rack, nor the handbell with dirty ribbon on its handle. The flags were swept, the tables and chairs had vanished. The horseshoes her grandfather had hung from the rafters, the brasses and dimpled copper kettles; all were gone. Even the poorly inked sketches of local scenes had been taken. The candles were almost out. The rain swiped at the windows, hammered on the roof.

'It's all gone!' Millie exclaimed.

Mr Dunne clapped his great hands together, his moustache leeching across his face in triumph. 'Yes, isn't it marvellous?'

'We've been overwhelmed with custom,' Mam explained carefully. 'We've had people as far as York! Leeds!'

'I suppose they would've taken the bricks and mortar if we'd let them,' Millie said, pacing the room where, only recently, she had picked her way over a tangle of wood, metal and glass. It looked bigger, more like a chapel in its nudity. She ran a hand over the sill that cut the wall in two, its wood stained with rings from pint-pots. 'And everything upstairs?'

'Gone; the lot,' Mr Dunne replied. He rocked on his heels. He would no doubt afford new shoes with his portion of the profits, Millie thought; perhaps even a new tailored waistcoat to flatter his paunch. 'One man, I think he gave his name as Smith, took off with poor Thomas' bed on the back of his cart!'

'And nothing left to remember them by?' Alice asked quietly, taking Mam's hand.

'All the memories are up here,' she replied, tapping her temple.

Johnny coughed suddenly, coughed again, his breath catching. He huffed in, his coughs throwing him off, and he didn't know whether to breathe in or out. His torso shook, and they all silenced to watch him. He waved them on, as if to ignore him, but Millie stepped forward.

'Johnny? Are you alright?' She bent over to look at his face, felt the key against her flesh, but he turned away. There wasn't a stool or chair to pull under him, so she planted a hand on his shoulder, steadied him to the floor. He nodded, coughed again, nodded.

'I'd get you a glass of water, but there's neither glasses nor water,' Mr Dunne smiled, his lips like newly sheathed sausages, glistening.

'S'nothing,' Johnny whispered into his clenched fist. He buffeted his chest. 'I'm fine.'

She kept her hands fixed to Johnny's shoulders.

'I'm fine.' Johnny cleared his throat, his voice returning. 'Fine.' He scraped Millie's hands away and stood, mopped his face with a no longer white handkerchief he produced from his breast pocket. 'Well, it seems there's nothing more to see. Shall we escort you home, Mrs Bradbury?'

Millie could see that Johnny was right. Barren rooms swept and polished, windowpanes fixed and locks firm. What more could Millie add? Even if she were to summon the inn's regulars, the crotchety old fullers, the tanners and slaughterers, the masons, the sextons and the spinners, the weavers and the labourers, even their tobacco-crackle laughter couldn't return this place to what it had been: the home of her Granda and her uncle. The place where she'd learnt about life, death, and the confusing, contradictory and joyous parts in-between.

Mam nodded. 'Aye, there's no point staring at the old place, is there?' She trooped to the door. Mr Dunne extended a hand behind her as if he were a gentleman shepherding her to his carriage.

'How are you, love? How are you feeling?' Alice whispered to Millie as they followed.

In truth, her body was hot and sweating; her ears hummed in that familiar way they seemed to do these days; her knees seemed light and bendy, as though they could fold in on themselves.

'I'm well, Alice, and all the better for you being here.' They squeezed each other's hands lightly and joined Johnny, Mam and Mr Dunne pooled in front of the door.

'Well,' Mr Dunne announced, as he jangled the keys like a gaoler. 'Well,' he said again as the key's click in the lock satisfied him. Millie watched as he opened his coat and placed the keys in his breast pocket. At least Mr Dunne hadn't got the key she held. The cabinet might've gone to a thief from Thirsk, but she had the key Granda had tied to ribbon, the key to the things he worked hard for and held dear.

Mr Dunne looked out from the door. The rain had stopped, the wind had retreated back behind the hills. They walked the darkening road in silence.

7

The pieces had been cut slowly and carefully, stored away in the trunk under her bed. She decided to work on the jacket first as that needed the most concentration; clean lines, as the men at the markets would say. She settled in to the chair next to Mam who was already darning, an ever-growing pile of greys and browns and tans, socks, stockings, vests.

'Set yourself your own candle ready. You'll need it with those tiny stitches of yours,' Mam said, pushing the flint and touch-paper towards her. 'Nice and slow and steady.' Mam knocked her arthritic ankle against the table's foreleg, the sound of bone against wood already irritating. Millie tried to focus instead on the silvery thread.

'Are you not going out with Jane?' Mam asked. 'I think she'll be disappointed.'

'I couldn't wait to get started, Mam. Now that the pieces are cut, I couldn't wait.'

Millie listened as Mam told her story about the sewing of her own wedding dress, done in secret as her father didn't approve of the match.

'But your Granda, he was as pleased as punch.'

It was something she'd heard often enough, but with her own wedding dress in her hands, it seemed different somehow. Real.

'Thank the Lord you won't have to go through that.'

'I'm not sure Jane's as pleased as punch,' Millie ventured, more despondently than she'd intended.

Mam shook her head and laughed. 'She's only put out you're first; she'll come round.'

There was more to it than that – the look she had given her when Johnny had turned up, the veritable lack of enthusiasm on the proposal since – but she couldn't quite place what it could be.

Millie looked up as Jane breezed in, securing her bonnet at her chin. She saw her sister's face fall when she recognised Millie's hands engaged so delicately.

'Come on, Mills, it's Whitsun! You've got weeks to do that! What's a little evening at the fair? Especially since you made me do the Walk this morning!'

'I wanted to get started. I was so excited. And the fair's always the same, the same old shies, the man with one arm challenging boys to box him. It bores me to tears.'

'Oh, you bore me to tears sometimes, Millie, honestly. The only time when there's entertainment on our doorstep and you'd rather sit at the fireside and sew like we do every other night of the year.'

'Don't be so dramatic, Jane,' Mam said, the jigging of her ankle growing in volume and regularity.

'Please stop that, Mother,' Millie wheedled.

'See! You should come out with me, take the air–'

'I've had quite enough air already today, thank you, and I've had quite enough of being stared at by our neighbours. I want to sew my own wedding dress for my wedding, which, in case you'd forgotten, is now only eight weeks away. There's naught wrong with that, is there?'

Jane huffed. 'Well, who shall I go with? And don't say Tudor,'

Jane wagged a finger at her mother.

'Alice will go with you,' Millie replied curtly. And Alice would, even though Millie knew how quietly afraid she was of her elder sister.

'Fine. Though it seems I shan't have a say in the matter once again,' Jane replied.

She let the back-door ring with her departure.

The ticking of the clock and the rhythmic judder of Mam's ankle was punctuated occasionally by the mewing of the baby next door.

'I don't know what she does to them babes,' Mam wondered aloud, 'for they're always vocal. I swear you three were positively mice in comparison.'

Millie carefully considered each penetration of the cloth, making sure her fingers were tucked well away, one bethimbled so as not to draw blood. She made each stitch small and straight, and after every two or three, paused to roll her shoulders or move her head from side to side.

'I must say, my lass,' Mam began suddenly, the gaps between words diminishing as though she had tried them out in her head first. 'I always knew you were a strong, unflappable girl. There wouldn't be many in your situation as bold as this, preparing to be wed after all you've so recently encountered.'

'Why, thank you, Mother,' Millie replied, rethreading her needle. The light, as Mam had predicted, was proving elusive.

'You've shown yourself to be resilient. You'll make a wonderful wife; of that, I am sure.'

'And Johnny a wonderful husband,' Millie added.

'Oh, I don't have any doubts about that. He's a clever one, a determined thing. Think of what your two bright minds together will bring.' Mam's ankle finally ceased. She had said her piece, and Millie's heart stilled and her stomach settled. She felt at ease for the first time in many weeks.

As Tudor brought in a rush of cool air, Millie realised how stuffy the room had become.

'Did you see Jane?' Mam set down her darning and blinked. He reached for the bread knife, but she shook her head. 'No, save that 'til the morning. Have a cup of tea if you're hungry. But I think first you should go and find her. It's later than I expected; I thought she'd be home by now.'

Tudor sighed and put back the knife. Millie could see him eyeing the bread beneath the brown paper.

'I've only just got back. And now I've got to go there again?'

'I'll come with you, Tudor. I'm all stiff and hunched over from sewing.' Millie stowed away the jacket in her trunk.

Tudor shrugged at his sister and slunk out of the door. Millie hurried to follow him, grabbing her mother's shawl by mistake.

'How was the fair?' Millie could hear it still, the shouts and cheers and laughter that sounded, in the absence of anything else, as though the fair was much larger and fuller of people than she supposed it truly was. She heard an organ play a tune she dimly recognised but couldn't put a name or words to. She wondered if Johnny was there.

'Quite good,' Tudor said. 'There was a man with a monkey in a cage.'

'A real one? A real monkey?'

'Yes, it was quite still. It just looked at us from behind the bars.'

'Where did the man get it from?'

'Africa. That's what someone said, anyway.'

Millie and Tudor seemed to be the only ones walking back towards the fair; most were coming away, carrying home sleeping babes or draping tired arms around the shoulders of their wives.

The pasture was still well populated, though. A number of the stalls had fires burning in front, and pockets of people gathered at them, talking and laughing. Millie could feel the cool wet from the grass seeping into her boots, smell the frying meat.

'Have you got a ha'penny, Millie? Ed had gingerbread; I want some.'

'Where do you think she'll be?'

'Talking somewhere, probably. Have you got ha'penny?'

'No, Tudor, shhh. We'll have to walk up and down until we find her.'

The fires illuminated the faces that they took shy, discreet looks at. Sometimes they weren't quick enough, and the faces jerked upwards, away from the flames, to exchange glances. Millie pressed her lips into a practised smile. They smiled back, the mouths shortening, their eyes shrinking, when they realised who it was: Millie Bradbury, the woman who had discovered the blood-spattered bodies of her own grandfather and uncle, who had to stand and testify, who was set to marry before the summer was out.

Past a coconut shy, a ballad singer had a small crowd gathered. Millie could tell the singer was at the culmination of her song: she had her eyes closed, her head tilted back, the words slowing. She wasn't a musical singer; the notes she returned to were too similar, bunched together, but she had character. Her small audience was rapt. As the applause rippled around the group, the singer opened her eyes and held out small sheets of paper for her congregation to buy. One woman turned around. It was Jane.

'Looking for me?' Her dark curls raged about her head and her jaw was set. She had stuffed her bonnet into her pocket. Alice appeared at her shoulder.

'Yes,' Tudor said, 'Mam wants you home.'

'Come on, then, childer, if Mam wants me home, we shall all go home.' Her voice implied it was the last thing she wanted to do. Jane picked up her skirts and brushed past them. Millie rolled her eyes at Alice.

'She's been quite entertaining, actually,' Alice whispered. 'She's been getting us to talk with the fair people, with the stallholders. It's true, you know; they don't have proper homes. Imagine that! Always travelling from one place to the next.'

'I should go mad,' Millie said, winding Mam's shawl tightly about her.

'And that singer, she learns different songs every week. There's hundreds of singers in Manchester apparently, some in Oldham, too.'

'She didn't sing as well as you,' Millie said, linking arms with her.

'But she had something about her. There was something about the way she sang it. Something I couldn't do. It was like she had a secret, and she'd only show bits of it to us.'

'That all sounds rather romantic,' Millie said. 'Wasn't she just an old, toothless beggar?'

'Probably,' Alice agreed, 'but the pennies were mounting up. Your sister even bought one.'

Jane strode ahead and Millie, Alice and Tudor had to pick up their feet to stay with her.

'Has she been like this all night?' Millie whispered to Alice. 'What's going on?'

Alice shrugged. 'I think she would've stayed all night if we'd let her.'

'We're in for it when we get home,' Tudor said.

'She really thought she could stay all night?' Millie shook her head. Jane was delirious. She had to be.

Many had prolonged their short journey home by a stint at the King Bill. They could hear singing inside, but, melded together with heat and ale, the words were incomprehensible. Dark hulks of men clustered together outside, cloistered in inward facing circles to protect their beers.

In the lane opposite, two men supported another sunken man between them. They held his arms about their necks, strained under his uncompromising weight and daft feet.

'Come on, laddie, left, right, left,' one encouraged. The man in the centre appeared not to be listening, his head lolled forward in sleep or lethargy.

'Blimey, what a sight,' Tudor muttered, as Jane hushed him, mouthed that they should pass by quickly and quietly.

'It's Jane Bradbury! It's Millie, my Millie!'

They looked back. It was Johnny Barkwell, slung between them like sodden wool.

His feet slapped against the dirt, found purchase. They watched his ankles steady, his hips. He stood. He swayed. The two men held out their hands like parents to a toddling child.

Millie felt the cold suddenly, a sharp metallic twang in the back of her throat, Alice's eyes on her cheeks.

'Johnny Barkwell,' Millie said plainly. 'You've had a good evening, then?'

'That's my Millie,' he said, looking to his two pillars so that they understood. They did; they knew it, they said.

'Shall I take him home?' Millie asked the men. One was Jerred Buckley, the smaller man who seemed embarrassed at her presence, his eyes fastened to her damp feet. The other man, taller, broader, shook his head, fixed her with a grey stare. He had remarkably blue lips, like a child caught amongst the sloes.

'We wouldn't want that, Miss, nor would he. 'Tis not far, we'll take him,' he said. His voice was low, rumbling.

'Make sure you see him in, won't you?'

The taller man nodded as if it was obvious that he would, that he already planned the same.

Alice threaded her arm through Millie's again.

'Quite the Methodist there, Mills,' Jane smirked. 'Taking full advantage of that Beerhouse Act-'

'Oh, shut up, Jane,' Millie retorted. 'He's allowed a drink, for god's sake.'

'I think he's had more than one,' Tudor added.

Millie quickened her pace.

'Where's she going?' she heard Johnny ask, bewildered. 'That's my Millie. She'll be my wife.'

She blinked heavily, rounded her shoulders. 'Did you know that other man, Alice? Not Jerred; the other?'

Alice pursed her lips, thinking. 'Yes, isn't he a Broadbent?'

'Isn't everyone a Broadbent?' Tudor said, and he and Jane laughed.

But Alice and Millie ignored them. 'Yes, a Broadbent. Paddy, I think.'

They exchanged goodnights and Alice turned onto her own street. The three siblings walked on, Tudor gently humming the tune that the organ had played to soften the silence.

As Jane opened the door, they saw Mam wake with a start, blink heavily. Automatically, she picked up her sewing. 'They found you then?' she called brightly. 'How was it?'

'I thought it was good. There was a man with a monkey,' Tudor said, setting his boots down by the table leg. Mam ushered him to move them.

'Never mind the monkey. It appears we were the stars of the show.' Jane reached into her pocket and unfolded a piece of paper, handed it to Mam. Millie leant over. Squat inky letters staggered across the page.

'What's this?' Mam whispered, frowning. She squinted, held the paper away from her, squinted again.

Tudor peered over his mother's other shoulder.

'Oh, only our own bloody broadside.'

'What do you mean?'

Tears pooled in Jane's eyes, but her thick eyelashes swatted them.

'The printers of Manchester, or London, or wherever our fame has spread, has found money to be made in our story, in "The Great Crime of the Century". The singer had it for sale. Of course, we're old news now, so she didn't choose to sing it and so I don't know the tune. Perhaps we should set it to "Barbary Allen", then everyone can join in!'

Jane's jaw was hard, her words fighting to slip out between her teeth.

'We shall ignore it. Nothing but gossip, pure gossip.' Mam folded the sheet and held it out to Millie. She set the kettle on the stove, lit it. Millie could see her hands shaking. She opened up the paper and read.

THE GREAT CRIME OF THE CENTURY
Did you hear the sad old tale
Of the Bradburys slain in their house of ale?
It happened on the Saddleworth Moor,
Beyond their threshold, their own front door.

Why, pray sit back and this song I'll sing
Of the coldest, bloodiest crime this spring.

It was on an evening cold and dark
When the moon shone bright and the curs did bark
A young lady sought her kin to meet
Across the moors of bog and peat.

Why, pray sit back and this song I'll sing
Of the coldest, bloodiest crime this spring.

She tripped along the road well known
To her grandfather's inn and home
But when she arrived there, quick and neat
She found warm blood a-clotting at her feet.

'This is vile,' Millie muttered. She couldn't finish reading. The illustrator had obviously never seen Bill O'Jack's nor the Holmfirth Road; it looked nothing like it. She folded it and tucked it into her waistband next to Granda's key.

So, it was true: their story had outgrown them. Her family had become known beyond the boundary stone. It would follow them now; it would be a legend that would dog their family for years, for generations. Whatever she did – the children she raised, the neighbours she served, the duties she performed – would be outweighed, overshadowed, by that afternoon in April, *the warm blood a-clotting at her feet.*

The song had that right at least: the blood did pool; it would have clotted there, if she'd stayed long enough to let it. Granda rasping and moaning as it leaked out of him. What had he done to deserve it? He'd had a life much like anyone else in these parts: hard winters, backbreaking summers of slog, barely a penny to his name. He'd suffered the death of his first wife, his second, some children in infancy. It was true his fortune had changed once he had Bill O'Jack's, but he wasn't Lord of the Manor: he still rolled in the barrels from the dray, washed every last glass in the house, swept the boards, set the traps, blew the bellows into the grate for any warmth that cruel, unforgiving landscape would afford. What had he done to deserve such notoriety? Truth, his son had a reputation for grudges and cuss words, and Millie herself had seen Granda turn men from the door, their fists pummelling. They didn't go to church, they liked beer. But how did that set them apart from the other men of Saddleworth? And what would they have made of their newfound fame? Granda would have loathed it, would've taken all the glasses down from the rack and begun cleaning them one by one, whether they needed it or not. She'd seen him do the same after a quarrel with Tom, though it had soon blown over.

She thought of Johnny. They were well known, he had said, Granda and Tom. It was them that were well known, not Bill O'Jack's.

Millie screeched, her hands grabbing at the air. She shook her head from side to side, felt her shawl fly to the floor. Her boots knocked something. There was a clutter, a clash of metal or fired clay with the flagstone. She howled, wailed, felt something surge through her, something bigger, more powerful. God, perhaps; God making her kick and writhe, testing her resolve. Her throat scorched from the noise she could hear, a banshee trapped in the walls, until Millie realised it was she who proffered the sound.

She felt other hands at her then, cradling her torso as they lowered her backwards, downwards. The surge abated. Her body wilted against the flagstones and she cried, every muscle weakened and waned.

'To bed, take her to bed,' she heard someone say, a woman's

voice. Mam, it was Mam. And the hands carried her, heaved her up the stairs and pulled a thin sheet up to her chin as though it were her shroud.

8

The summer was unusually fine. The sun rose punctually to light their way to work, and shone so intensely, so relentlessly, that the women dripped sweat into their wool. The men were rumoured to strip down to their waists at their stations, and the women whiled away the hours by picturing and comparing each man in turn: who would have the softest hair, the broadest chest, the darkest nipples, the biggest belly.

The Platters took to watering their horses in the Tame, while the Irish navvies ceased work on the canal under the midday sun and instead worked into the night, their eyes and teeth glinting in the twilight. Mr Dunne brought Mam some ice he had made in the icehouse at the back of his shop and they had laughed as it melted before their eyes, drinking it down and exclaiming they could feel its passage through their insides. Jane, Millie and Tudor had rolled their eyes at each other.

Johnny cursed the lack of activity at his traps. 'All the blighters are hiding in the shade,' he said, with a laugh, and Millie had smiled at the thought of small, noble rabbits, hares and pheasants outwitting him.

Still there was no news from the constables, and even the newspapers had begun to tire of Bill O'Jack's.

Though the mill was hardest in the heat, Millie made sure she retained just enough energy to continue with her dressmaking into the night. Mam looked over her stitches in approval, asking her where the pieces would fit, but Jane ignored it as though it were an invisible cloak Millie sewed. Jane didn't ask how it would look when it was finished, how her sister had decided on the style. Instead, she looked over Millie's head and scanned the room and, when her motive was questioned, stated she was seeking a particular book or her knitting needles or anything else so unrelated to dressmaking that Millie could scream.

One evening, when Jane sought the letter from a cousin that she was suddenly moved to answer, Millie set down the underskirt she was close to finishing and beckoned Jane to sit.

'What shall you wear to my wedding, Jane?'

She watched her sister scan the shelves in the kitchen, the cracked crockery that lined the cupboard.

'Oh, I don't know, I haven't given it much thought.'

'No, that's quite right, Jane; you haven't given my wedding much thought at all, have you?'

Mam raised her head from the back of the easy chair.

'Why don't you wish me well, like everyone else seems to want to do?'

'Oh, go away, Millie, get back to your dressmaking.'

'I thought you'd be pleased for me, at least. Or do you not care for me?'

Jane's eyes settled on her then. She frowned slightly, a twitch at her eyebrows. 'You know how much I care for you.'

'Do I?'

Jane looked as though she had walked into a room she didn't recognise. 'Of course.'

'But you don't want me wed?'

Jane sighed. It sounded to Millie as tired and weary as an old maid.

'It's not that I don't want *you* wed, I – well. I know I don't want marriage for myself, but I-' and Jane struggled for the words.

'You don't want it for yourself, so you don't want it for me?'

'Millie,' Mam intercepted, 'you're talking in riddles.'

'Well, to be quite honest,' Jane said slowly. Millie knew that Jane was going to tell the truth and that the truth would hurt, and Millie would disagree. That's how it would be. A chasm between them which could never be stitched together again. Millie braced herself.

'To be quite honest, I don't know how you can consider marriage now, at this time. Granda and Tom; we still don't know what happened to them. I fear everyone's getting back to normal. It's not even mentioned at Chapel. So, if everyone gets back to normal, will we forget them, too? Is this what it's about? Forgetting?'

Jane's lip quivered. Millie watched it move. The skin cracked into tiny grooves. She listened to Mam breathe in and out through her open mouth. There was truth in it, truth in what she said. The humming in her ears intensified again. How could she forget Granda and Tom like that, and pick up with Johnny as though nothing had ever happened? But Johnny, the presence of Johnny, the added weight of his family – didn't that make her feel safe? Didn't that make them all feel safer? And she wouldn't forget them, not ever; she would never forget that day.

Mam cleared her throat. 'Millie's getting married, whether you like it or nay. I suggest you enjoy this time together; you shan't have it like this again.'

The sisters looked at each other. Jane's eyes softened.

'Show me, then,' she said quietly, pointing a jagged fingernail at the fabric in Millie's hands. 'Show me how it fits.'

Millie stood and lay the dress against her, holding her arms out so the sleeves draped over them. She pinned the neckline to her chest with her chin. The stitches were invisible to the naked eye, she was sure of it, though she couldn't help but focus on the little section at the back where her hem hadn't been straight and she'd had to shake it out and pin it again. But the tiny buttons down the middle were straight. It was not beautiful fabric. Gertie would laugh at its lack of sheen, its practicality, but it was new. If she looked after it, it would keep forever. She watched Jane take in her labour, survey the nips and tucks.

'Your waist will look tiny, Millie,' she said, looking up at her. 'Look how it comes in!'

'That's how they do it in society, you know.'

'It will look lovely, of that, I'm sure. But there's something missing.' Jane ran upstairs, her skirts swishing against the floorboards. When she came back downstairs, she held out a small paper parcel.

Millie set down the dress on the back of the chair and took the parcel from Jane. She peered in. Her Sunday School prize.

'Oh, Jane, I can't take these!' She drew the gloves out of the paper and turned them over. 'You've never let me *look* at them before, let alone touch them!'

And Jane shrugged. 'You've got occasion for them. I h'aint.'

Millie saw Mam smile as Jane took back her seat with the letter from their cousin.

Tudor licked his fingers and pasted his hair behind his ears. He hadn't soaped it, as it still hung in dirty hanks. She saw his realisation that this wouldn't do, saw her own gentle disappointment reflected in his expression. He took down his cap from the door handle, settled it into position, and blinked hopefully.

'Oh, Tudor,' she said, snatching it off his head. 'You can't wear your everyday cap to my wedding, to your sister's wedding. Haven't you got anything else?' Knowing full well that he hadn't. He should have had his hair cut, too. But still, what did he know? 'Couldn't you comb it, at least?'

He took the comb she had left on the mantelpiece and chased it through his hair. She watched him part it on the side, flatten it against his skull and frown at the uneasy face in the glass.

'Better?' he asked, turning to her. It looked exactly the same; worse, if it dried in saliva-stiffened peaks.

'Yes, much,' she replied, poking her toes into the shoes she had borrowed from Mam. An image came into her mind, of Johnny slipping off her shoes, holding her stockinged foot in his hand like it was a baby bird. Something, somewhere at the base of her stomach, fizzed.

'Your sixpence, ma'am.' Tudor held out the coin on the flat of his palm.

She looked at him.

'Have you *saved* this, Tudor?'

He shuffled. She could see him consider the reactions to the two tales he could tell.

'Nah, Mam did. I intended to, but it didn't really happen.'

Millie smiled. 'Fair enough. It's good of Mam. I'll have to save it, pass it to Jane afterwards.'

'You're supposed to keep it, I think, for luck.'

'Do you think I put my foot in first, then the coin?'

'Nah.' He peered down at her foot. 'Sixpence first. Definitely. And Jane said it's got to be your left one.'

'Jane said what?' Jane pushed open the door.

'You told me the sixpence has to go in Millie's left shoe.'

'Ah yes, that's right,' she said, leaning against the doorframe

89

and folding her arms. 'That's what Theresa said, anyway.'

Millie dropped the coin into her left shoe, let it settle in the centre, and placed her foot on top.

'It feels really strange, like I'll forget and think I've a stone in there.' She stood, tightened the strap around her heel. The buckle took a little persuasion to push on past the groove in the punctured leather where it usually lay. 'It doesn't help that these are too big, of course.'

Millie looked at the clock. It was past ten. In an hour, she'd be married: she'd be a woman with a new title, a new surname. Amelia Barkwell, Mrs Millie Barkwell. It was nicer than Bradbury, sweeter. It made her think of shaded forest paths. Bradbury was cartwheels in compacted earth.

'We wait until quarter to eleven?' Tudor meant it as a statement, she saw, but as his eldest sister closed the door, his uncertainty curled it into a question. She told him yes, and they listened to the tick of the clock on the mantelpiece and his boots on the floorboards.

At the door to St Chad's, Tudor stiffened and shot his arm through Millie's.

'How do they know we're here? And when to go in?'

Millie's stomach swilled. She thought of melted lard, of a flannel wrung in a bucket.

'Oh Tudor, I don't know, I-'

A man's bald head appeared at the door. He lurched his face upwards, peered along his nose.

'We're ready for you,' and he smiled a real smile, so that lines appeared at his eyes. He wedged open the door, ducked into the church.

Tudor puffed out his chest. The organ made them both start,

Tudor turning it into a rock onto the balls of his feet.

Millie was no longer in charge of her face. Her eyes welled immediately, her mouth twitched upwards, her lower lip trembled, sweat gathered at her brow. She focused on the short journey towards the vicar, the same man that she'd last seen at the burial. She squinted. He seemed to be looking in their direction. One foot scuffing in front of the other, she felt faces turning towards her. Tudor strode stiffly beside her as though he had on a back straightener at the half-timing school. She felt as faint as she had the last time she was here, as otherworldly, as though she was watching her life from above.

Then Johnny. He was tall, broad; taller and broader than she'd realised. He coughed into a clenched fist, did it again, then his mouth widened into a grin. George grinned too, and she thought she saw him elbow his son. She had been right: there was no patched jacket for Johnny, but something dark, closely fitted. A nick or two on his throat where he'd caught himself with his blade. A red kerchief at his pocket. Red! She wanted to laugh. Only her almost-husband would choose something as brazen as a red kerchief! And then she thought of Granda's red kerchief, swaddling his blood-soaked collar, and her breath caught in her throat. Was it coincidence or a tribute?

'Well look at you,' he whispered when their elbows brushed. She smiled, her lips sticking to her teeth as her muscles finally took charge and rose, bloomed, but looked ahead at the vicar who wore the same expression as the day they set her relatives to earth. He was her reminder that these were unusual times. That the feeling of guilt in her stomach, like silt or sediment, hadn't fully evaporated.

And then the vicar began to speak, and Millie could hear her heart in her ears, the booming of her own blood. Her buttocks trembled, she was certain her hem was tickling the stone floor, and she wondered if the congregation had noticed, whether they could see the skirt of her dress shaking. It could be round the mill by Tuesday, that Millie Bradbury was so terrified to be married that her dress shook with tremors.

Then she heard Johnny recite his name, and she looked up again. He was watching her firmly, fondly. Each time he took his lead from the vicar, he spoke evenly. Then she heard her own dry mouth crack open, the spittle snapping her lips shut at the completion of each word. And then Johnny smiled, dipped his forehead as though doffing his cap, and drew her close. He smelt of soap and something earthier: wood or wool. *Soon*, she thought, as she squeezed the brittle stems of heather between her palms, *I won't notice his scent at all; it'll become part of me, mine.*

Mam patted Johnny's arm. 'Oh, I'm so pleased, so pleased,' she said, while Jane smiled satisfactorily, as though she had overseen the whole thing and it had gone to plan. Tudor stood between Mam and Mr Dunne, dazed.

Esme Barkwell moved in to the circle standing on the church steps and joined with the stroking of Johnny's forearms, up and down, as though breathing life into them.

'Come on, George, dear!' she called, turning to pull her husband by the hem of his waistcoat and knocking him off balance so that he wavered like a top. Millie saw Mr Dunne snicker, attempt to catch Tudor's eye to share the joke, but Tudor was watching Gertie plump the curls on top of her head. Millie wondered if she should have put her own hair in rags; hers felt too thin and close to her skull.

'To the King Bill!' Johnny announced, his fist raised. With his other arm, he hefted Millie to his side.

'Of course, it's a shame,' she heard her mother say in a small voice behind her, 'we'd always hoped that special occasions would be held at Bill O'Jack's.'

'And it won't be the same,' Johnny wheeled round to face Mam and his own mother. 'Of course it won't. I always dreamed of our wedding party in that place, Millie's grandfather presiding over the bar. The King Bill is a consolation. But we'll make it jolly, won't we?' His fist pumped the air again so that Mam and Esme laughed together, took each other's arms. Being on the arm of such a live wire left her breathless, and she watched as his actions, his enquiries to other members of the party – 'Alright there, old boy?' to Tudor, when he lagged behind; 'Finally, the chance to buy my old man a drink as a proper man!' to his father – brought out smiles in return.

'I do admire your dress, Jane,' Millie heard Gertie say, and she silently hoped that Jane's reply would be polite, especially as all three women knew it was the same dress Jane wore for Chapel every Sunday – the addition of the lace at the cuffs hadn't had quite the transformative effect Jane had wished for. But Jane thanked her quietly and listened to Johnny's sister witter on about the plans she had for her own wedding, despite the absence of a bridegroom.

Millie smiled and nodded at the faces that ballooned at the cottage windows they passed, or the women that looked up from their front steps or abandoned their neighbourly conversations over their broom handles. They paused, smiled politely, knowingly; Millie could see their eyes soften, briefly consider their own wedding days and the long walk from church to hostelry, their toes pinching in their borrowed shoes and their hands sweating in the palms of a man they barely knew. Millie was lucky; Johnny she knew inside and out.

9

Millie saw Alice spot the wedding party, waved, and ducked behind the heavy red door of the inn. As she and Johnny approached, the door swung open and Alice, Alice's mother, the other girls from the mill, their mothers and brothers and fathers, so many faces turned towards them, mouths red and open, eyes bright. So much genuine happiness that Millie laughed, shook her hands from Johnny, and clapped them together. He dropped a kiss on her brow, then moved to the bar, his back echoing with the generous thumps of men's hands.

It could have been a completely different place to where the inquest was held. Pockets of people laughed, chatted animatedly together, leant against tables or sat together. Chairs and tables were set about in clusters, rather than the austere straight lines of April, where the people had been stiffened into rows. It was a happier time, Millie thought. And Granda would wish that for her, too. She thought of his happiness: the satisfaction he took in his own bar, when he stood back to admire the gleam of the glasses, the shine of the wood. He would take the damp pot towel from her hands and sling it over his shoulder to announce the completion of a job well done, and magic barley sugars from his pocket as her reward.

George Barkwell knocked on the door with the flat of his hand, cleared his throat and announced the new Mr and Mrs

Barkwell. Millie looked for Johnny but he was hunched over the bar, deaf to the well wishes, so she rolled on to the balls of her feet, lost in her too-big shoes and mouthed 'thank you', catching the eyes of as many as she could. She saw Johnny slide a beer towards Tudor.

'A little surprise for you has just walked in,' Alice said quietly at her shoulder. Millie looked about her as a man entered and removed his hat. In his other hand, he held a fiddle case.

It was the Saddleworth fiddler, Joe Kershaw, from Slackcote. 'A nice surprise, h'aint it?'

'Mrs Barkwell?' Joe asked, tucking the hat under the arm that held the fiddle case so that he could offer his hand. She took it gently and enjoyed her first address. His eyes were small, his tie was neat and his congratulations were said in such a sombre manner that Millie thanked him as though he had offered his condolences. He knew, then. 'Where would you like me to play?'

Millie scanned the inn, flustered. She looked for a space where he could play uninhibited, but left plenty of room to dance. It was Joseph Kershaw! He couldn't be hidden in a dark corner!

Tudor came forward with a heavy stool. Joe took his seat, lay his case across his lap and began to rosin his bow. Millie stared after him.

'We thought you'd be pleased,' her mother said at her ear. 'It was Jane's idea-'

'-and he agreed, right away,' Jane cut in.

'But he must've cost a fortune!' Millie watched him tease the pegs at the fiddle's scroll, listen as he plucked each string in turn.

'No, that's the very best bit; he-' but Mam silenced Jane with her hand.

'He's a good Christian man,' Mam concluded.

'Thank you, thank you,' Millie said, wheeling round for

Johnny. He was still at the bar, with George and that tall man with the blue lips she had seen somewhere before. Mr Dunne stood to Johnny's left, laughing when the other men did, but it was as if Johnny hadn't noticed he was there. He leant away from Mr Dunne, his shoulders square towards his father.

Millie heard the slap of her borrowed shoes on the flags as she walked to Johnny's side to tap his shoulder. The laughing ceased, and the men turned. Johnny's eyebrows raised. The taller man with the blue lips hissed as if she had come to chastise Johnny. She straightened out her brow, cheered her lips into the happiest smile she could summon.

'Yes, my love?' Johnny asked, giving the man with blue lips a wink. It was the man from the night of the fair, the one Alice had called Paddy Broadbent. He was either deathly cold or he stained his lips with blueberries, but neither seemed likely.

'Look what Mam and Jane have arranged! Joseph Kershaw's come to play for us!'

Johnny looked over at the thin man, still tuning his violin.

'That's very kind of them,' he said. 'We should give him something to play for, shouldn't we?'

He led her to the stone flags. Joe Kershaw took his cue and struck up a lively jig, the melody peeling and tumbling, his toes and heels the percussion. Johnny spread his fingers across the small of Millie's back and jolted her into a spin. They bounded around the square Tudor had carefully demarcated, Johnny's boots grazing her ankle bones or scuffing the very tip of her shoes. Sometimes she felt her toes land on his, but Joe's bow bounced so quickly that her feet were soon in the air and she hadn't time to mutter her apologies.

Her temple pressed into the coarse hair of his jaw. They settled into a rhythm that depended as much on each other as it did their individual co-ordination, and their bodies knew when to turn to avoid the couples that joined them. Mam and Jane, Gertie and George, Alice and Theresa. Tudor stood at the side, clapping in time, hesitating whenever the fiddler wheeled into the next tune.

'Know this then?' Johnny asked, and she realised she had been pressing his hand each time his bow vaulted down the scale, reminding her of the way Tudor heavy-booted his way down the staircase. She wouldn't hear her brother's morning footsteps again.

'Yes,' she replied, 'but I can't remember what he calls it. He played it at the Temperance Picnic.' Johnny snorted in her ear. She felt warm spittle land on her neck.

'What's funny?'

'Temperance Picnic!'

'What's so funny about that?'

'Mean old pussywillows, scared of the ale, the only pleasure left for the working man. Of course they can take that away from us, too! What pleasure will there be left?' He extended his arm, span her quickly beneath.

'I don't know about that; I wanted to go because it was a nice day, and Jane-'

'It's enough to make anyone thirsty. Temperance! Here,' he said, passing her hand to Jane, who dropped Mam's. The three women looked at him as he moved back to the bar.

'Oh, he is handsome, h'aint he?' Mam said, her cheeks pink with exertion. 'A fine, fine fellow. Look at how he fills his fustian!'

'Mother!' Millie and Jane cried, and she laughed, fanned her face.

'Jane, you take her now. I'm done in.' Mam threw an arm about Tudor and they moved to the sidelines, out of the way of the circling couples.

'Your new husband likes his ale, for a Methodist,' Jane said through gritted teeth.

Millie rolled her eyes. 'Keep your opinions to yourself,' Millie hissed, clipping her sister's shin with her toe.

Johnny tapped a knife against his beer. The fiddler stopped with his bow suspended above the strings. He took down his fiddle and tucked it into the crook of his arm. The women stopped, too, looked over at Johnny, waited.

'Thank you, Joe, lad. What wonderful music, eh? A favourite of my wife's, my *new* wife's, and a favourite son of Saddleworth. A show of hands for the fiddler!' Joe allowed himself a smile as the room erupted into applause, the thumping of fists against wood. 'But now I think it's about time I made meself a speech.'

'Go on, lad!'

She saw the crowd hold their breath and their drinks.

'It's been a dark few months for Saddleworth, especially for my new family-'

'Hear, hear,' Mr Dunne roared, his flat palm striking the bar. Johnny gave him a half nod and continued.

'-but it's family, good friends and neighbours that help us carry on, recover.'

He paused for a swig of beer and wiped his mouth with the back of his hand.

'And in joining my family with the family of my new wife, we're strengthening a bond that already existed. Me and Millie, we'll just pull those knots ever closer. Won't we, Amelia?'

She nodded, exchanged meek smiles with Alice, then Jane, Mam and Gertie.

'Hear, hear,' Mr Dunne said again, his fist thumping the bar like it was dough.

'And she's a fine one, ain't she? Just look at her!'

And they did all turn to look at her at his command, whispered 'ah' as though she were a child in ribbons and petticoats. Millie felt her cheeks burn and looked past them, through the hallway, into the light of the lane.

'So, I ask you to join me in a toast to my new wife, Millie Barkwell. A fine lass!'

'A fine lass!' they echoed, holding their glasses aloft.

Joe Kershaw began again as the men crowded the bar. Millie watched as Tudor elbowed his brother-in-law to let him in. To lean on the bar as Johnny did, he had to raise himself up on his tiptoes and thrust his weight forward.

'Your Johnny's quite the orator!' Alice said with her hands. 'I could see him on a Sunday morning, preaching in a square in Ashton, the people hanging on his every word.'

'Preaching?' Millie laughed. 'You've got to be joking! I'm astonished we managed to get him to church today!'

'No, not preaching then,' Alice conceded. 'Perhaps our next representative in Parliament?'

'He'd need an estate for that, and an estate—' Millie cast her hands about her, '—we don't quite have.'

'Agitator then? Trade unionist?'

'Probably more like it,' she agreed.

'So then, you're a wife, a wife to Johnny Barkwell!' Alice said, her grip tightening with excitement. 'And how does it feel? Or should I ask you that in the morning?' She gave her a wink that Millie pretended not to see. 'You can't be a prude *and* a wife, my love; never the twain shall meet. And I want to know absolutely everything! It's your duty to dispense all your newfound knowledge to us lowly, innocent valley maids.'

'And what're you two talking about so furtively?' Alice's

mother appeared with Mam behind her.

'Millie is promising me housekeeping tips,' she replied instantly, drawing her friend close and kissing her cheek.

Mam's eyebrows arched as Alice's mother's laugh leapt from her mouth like a racehorse on Whitsun.

'Well, good, patient Lord, you need it, Alice Ann. Do you know,' she said, turning to Mam, 'that she managed to burn *porridge* last week? Porridge!'

Her mother kissed her on the cheek, but when she stood back, Mam wouldn't meet her eye.

'Come on, Jane; Tudor, where are you?' Mam asked, though he was right behind and held out his arm for her. Mr Dunne doffed his cap and smiled twice as hard, as though compensating for Mam. Millie thought she saw him wink at Johnny, but it went unreciprocated. Instead, Johnny kissed the hands of Jane and Mam.

'Thank you,' he said between kisses, 'thank you for raising such a daughter.'

'Oh, be off with you!' Mam said, blushing and fanning her face with her fingers.

Jane looked past Johnny's sleeve to roll her eyes at Millie. 'And what a daughter!' she said with a groan. Millie narrowed her eyes, twisting her lips into something she then decided not to say. Not on her wedding day.

'A wonderful wedding, you lovely pair,' Mam said to the dusk. 'Your father would have been proud. That Joe Kershaw makes a pretty tune, don't he? Right then, Jane, Tudor, let's leave 'em, the new couple.'

The foursome clattered up the lane. Mr Dunne turned to wink again.

'Has that man an eye problem, Millie?' Johnny smiled.

'He has a problem of the heart, I know that much,' she answered drily.

'How so?'

'It hankers after my mother, that I'm sure of. And Bill O'Jack's, I should imagine, if I know anything about Isiah Dunne.'

'Oh dear, oh dear. Poor Millie Bradbury.' Johnny clucked his tongue. She raised her eyebrows. 'Or should that be poor Mistress Barkwell?'

'That's more like it,' she answered, rubbing flat the goose pimples that rose on her forearms.

He missed the door handle the first time he reached for it, but the second time, he opened the door and ushered her inside. The landlady was drawing dust into a corner with a besom.

'You'll be wanting upstairs, then,' she said, eyeing the dirt.

'Yes, please, ma'am,' Johnny replied quickly, but with eagerness or impatience, Millie couldn't deduce. Her heart began to throb. She was sure he'd be able to see it beating, the cotton pulsing at her breast. Her feet and knees ached from the constant tensing and balancing required to keep Mam's shoes on her feet.

'Right, then,' the landlady said, resting the besom against the doorframe. She held out a key to Johnny. 'Up the stairs, to your right. There's only one room up there; you can't go wrong. Privy out the back. I'm next door in the clogger's cottage if you need me. But I daresay you won't.' She swept again, though the dirt was already neatly formed in a triangle.

'Come then, wife.' Johnny took her hand and led her upstairs.

He unlaced his boots and kicked them beneath the bedstead. She stood by the closed door, watching his long white toes emerge from his stockings. He dropped them onto the floor.

'Are you going to stand and watch?' he asked, his face upturned and serious, like a Bible on the lectern, but his voice soft. She smiled for him.

'No, I-' but he patted the sheets next to him.

Her shoes came off easily. She hitched up the skirt of her dress to her knee, just enough so she could wriggle her stockings down into two fistfuls. She looked at them, pale, and balled into her hand. Alice had told her that a person's clenched fist was the size and shape of their brain. It wasn't big. She wedged them into the toes of Mam's shoes.

'My, is this how long you take in't morn? It's fair wonder you ever see a full wage!'

Johnny's clothes heaped at his feet. She looked across quickly and noticed the fine tufts of hair across his chest, like cobwebs against a whitewashed wall. She thought that there was hair further down, too, but that was only out of the very corner of her eye. She turned her back so he could see the buttons along her spine and willed him to be gentle. She had sewn on each and every one.

She felt his fingers move quickly, the cotton loosening at her shoulders. Anyone would have thought he'd done this before, but she pushed it from her mind, instead thinking back to the time behind the mill, his wet mouth. She had always hoped it would come to this.

'Let me look at you, then,' he said, turning her shoulders squarely as her wedding gown fell to the floor. She smelt the warm sourness of the beer towels at Bill O'Jack's, heightened when Granda boiled them in the copper.

She felt his eyes creep across her shift. The walls were in need of a new coat of paint; small flakes were dotted around the skirting boards. And there seemed to be a patch of damp in the top corner; it had discoloured, and the plaster bulged precariously. The landlady hadn't noticed; perhaps she didn't care.

'I have been thinking about this day, this moment, Millie,' he said softly. She flinched as his fingers traced the edge of her shift. 'My fingers aren't cold,' he said, almost hurt.

'No, no,' she replied.

She noticed dust gathered yellow at the doorframe. Perhaps she should offer to clean the room before they left in the morning. *The morning.*

Gently, he lifted the shift over her head and she heard him breathe in. Or perhaps it was an exhalation. She couldn't be sure.

His thumb found the cleft in her chin, brought it to his.

'Look at me, Millie, your husband.' His voice was low, and she did as she was told, blinked furiously as her eyes met his, the proximity of it. He scooped a hand around her back, like he was swaddling a newborn, and pressed his chest against hers. They dominoed down against the coarse sheets. His left hand was elsewhere: first it brushed her thigh, then it tapped a knee, then she felt its movement in his own lap. She closed her eyes. She was askew on the bed, the bedframe digging in to her pelvis. She always imagined she'd be beneath sheets, straight and comfortable. Here, she could fall, could catch her head on the bedframe. Her knees were bent now, her soles flush to the linen. He guided one of her knees left, the other right, and she thought of the new lock at Uppermill, how it was surprisingly easy to guide the timber to the bank and let the boats pass through. She was exposed now, and she clamped her eyes shut, pictured the two seams beneath her eyelashes. Is this what giving birth would be like? Your whole, your being, your self, left open to cold prying eyes and fingers? She waited, she waited for the pain she knew would well up, that she'd heard mentioned with laughter between Mam and her friends, between the mill girls.

She continued to wait, told herself to stay calm, to breathe. What use was rushing these things?

She felt his body cover hers like a shadow, hands on either side of her. She'd seen a gypsy girl at a fair like this, her long sleeves pinned to a plank of wood with cudgels thrown by a dark smiling man. The girl had winced each time a cudgel left his hand but had smiled broadly once the applause rang out.

There was something smooth against her, something cool. Skin, smooth skin.

'Come on, come on,' she heard him growl and she opened her eyes. His brow was taut where his eyebrows knotted together. He looked south.

'Here,' he said, grasping her hands and rolling on to his back. 'You try.' He pushed her hands to his lap. She felt his penis nestle there, amongst his hair, rough as old wool. 'Like this.' He shook her hands violently, it squirming between her hands and she thought of vegetable gardens and clawing roots from the earth. She closed her eyes again and he let her hands go. Without his guiding them, hers felt weak and foolish.

'Try a little harder.'

She shook her hands again. 'How about this?' Her arms ached, her wrists tense.

'No,' he said suddenly, turning away from her. She watched his elbows juddering, his shoulders hunched. His back was white and mottled with moles, like he'd been flecked with ink. She could make her own constellations. She traced a line from the largest in the centre outwards to a cluster where she visited each in turn, imagining the route of the dray, picking up the empties.

'It's no use.' He swatted her hands away from his back and

stood, rousing his trousers from his ankles and fastening them at his waist. He slotted one arm into his shirt.

'Where are you going?' she asked. Though she folded an arm across her breasts, he didn't look back at her.

'For a drink, a smoke, the privy,' and the door wheezed shut.

That was not how it was supposed to be. She knew that much. She drew her legs under the sheets, looked down at her naked body, the notches and the knolls, the sheer blue-whiteness of it all. Was it her fault? Had she done something wrong, or not done something at all? She wouldn't cry, she would not. She would ask him, sit him down and ask him honestly how it all worked, how it should be, and how she could contribute. That would be the right thing to do: she knew strong marriages were built on honesty and transparency, on duty and willing. She had heard the minister say so. She drew the sheets around her and waited for him to come back, refreshed and ready to try again to claim what was rightfully theirs.

But when he pushed open the door with his free hand, she saw a face closed to honesty and transparency, unaware of duty and willing. His eyes were hard, downcast. His hair hung over his ears, his mouth sour, not even mollified by the ale he clutched.

'There's naught to worry at, my love-' She offered him a hand which lay untouched.

'I'm not worried.' He spoke evenly, crisply. Each letter sounded and sharp. 'It's been a long day.'

'Aye, a long day and a beautiful one, at that.' She placed her hands on his waist, but looked into his eyes. If he agreed, he didn't show it. He moved his glass in a circle so that the ale rocked into a foam.

'Millie, I have news.' He set the glass down on the Bible lying on the table beside the bed. She hoped it wouldn't leave a ring.

'Oh? News?' She clasped his hands between hers. His news

would be hers now: the traps fat with pheasant each evening, the prices they fetched at market. His work would be her work: the washing of his clothes as well as her own, the plucking and dressing, the fetching and carrying.

'Yes,' he said, the last of the ale disappearing down his throat. 'We're going to the Canadas.'

A cold washed through her, like the time Tudor had tipped the sluice bucket onto her head. How old had she been?

'What?'

She pictured Tudor's face, surprised at his own audacity, fearful of her reaction.

'A boat leaves Liverpool next Tuesday and Mr and Mrs Barkwell are booked. Our tickets reserved.'

He continued to look at the yellowing wall. She waited for him to crack a smile – had you there! – but he blinked slowly, calmly, his long lashes fluttering up, fluttering down. Fans made of peacock feathers used to cool emperors and sultans. She had seen drawings in the Sunday School encyclopaedia.

'What?' she asked again. She needed repetition, clarification. Concentration this time. The Canadas? She hadn't heard him right. The encyclopaedia, the Canadas. Where men in furs made shelters of ice? And great stags roamed? 'For how long?'

'My wedding gift to you, Millie, is a new life, one of opportunity and prosperity.'

When she didn't speak, he continued, his voice gathering pace, volume.

'I don't want some horse-shit hovel for you, wetter and woollier as the years drag on; our children doing the same work as our ancestors: cleaning the wool, carding the wool, drying it out on fucking great sticks in fields owned by men living in London. Our children, hungry, working their arses off in mills only for their children to die with lungs full of cotton. And what for? What fucking for? For wages that barely fund the bread on our tables? For men to be replaced by machine? For God and the fucking Temperance Movement?'

The glass shattered as he struck it against the Bible. The smithereens slid, hid.

Millie sat still. She thought that if she sat as still and as motionless as she had seen the rabbits do when they smelt the scent of the fox or heard the cock of Tom's gun, that his voice would return to its low whisper, that the glass would breathe in, pick itself up and hoist its parts back together.

'Well?' He looked at her this time, his lips a thin grey line. He rubbed at his cheeks and the stubble rasped at his skin.

'Greenfield is my home.'

'The Canadas will be your home,' he said firmly, looking away again.

'I don't want to leave my family.'

'*I* am your family. And what when Tudor takes a wife? Someone might even have Jane, and good luck to them. And old Isiah Dunne is desperate to get his fingers onto your Mam – what then? You think they will stay around these damp, festering hills? They'll see a chance like this and they'll leap at it; they'd say goodbye in a finger snap!'

'They wouldn't; Greenfield's our home.'

'Ah, and such a fine home! Where your kin are murdered in their beds!'

The cold made Millie shiver, the cold of the ice of the Canadas got into her bones, set her teeth rattling like the snakes that lived on that huge great continent; the shudder of cold, wet seal skin draped across her shoulders.

'I can't leave. I'm not leaving.'

'You are; we are. Mr and Mrs Barkwell, on The Great Countess that sails from Albert Dock this Tuesday hence.'

'I shan't be there.'

He gripped her wrist, sank in his square nails.

'You shall; you will. We're making a better life for ourselves; you'll thank me.' She shook off his grip and turned to face the wall, buried herself beneath the sheets and blew on her fingertips to warm them.

In the morning, the pain arrived as she thought it would: short but searing, like a hot knife, but there wasn't as much blood as she feared, just a few spots to show she was alive.

Afterwards, he lay back in a sheen of his own making, pleased with himself. He tapped her thighs.

'Oh, you're a good girl, Millie Barkwell, I always knew you would be.' And she wondered what the compliment was for, as the string of stickiness she understood to be the important stuff leaked out of her.

He threw her wedding gown to her and fastened up the shirt he hadn't bothered to take off.

'Come on, let's get out of this hellhole; we've got people to tell. We'll be the talk of

Saddleworth; we'll be the envy of all.'

Millie couldn't think of a word to say, not a syllable or sentence entered her head. Silently, she put on her underwear and presented her back for her husband to button up.

'That's my girl.'

10

The floorboards had been freshly scrubbed by Esme; she couldn't imagine Gertie on her hands and knees, her skirt shifting in the squally dirt and dust, in preparation for her brother and his new bride.

There was a small rag rug beneath the window and a chipped vase next to the washstand in which some hasty stems of heather stood in shock, recently purpled. Esme wouldn't have the opportunity to play the role of mother-in-law, of a matriarch in a growing household; those roles would have to be performed by letter. And could letters even be sent as far as the Canadas? If she were to write – and Johnny couldn't, so it would fall to her – she would hardly be able to describe the truth of what they saw and experienced: the colour of the sky, the shape of the land, their lodgings. How to put those new things into words? It would all be interpretation, her poorly worded descriptions, and the reader's own interpretation of that. And then what would be left? An impression, a falsehood?

'It's only for a few days now,' Johnny whispered, placing his boots at the foot of the bed. 'Imagine the fools that do this for life!'

She would never have thought she would wish for half a room in the Barkwell household, a two-up-two-down in the street that petered out at the foot of Cadishead Mill. But now she did. She could stay here forever, swapping pleasantries with Gertie and helping Esme to scrub floorboards and pick heather if it meant she could stay in Greenfield, remain married, remain a daughter and a sibling.

'Only a few days and then we'll be shot of it.'

'Johnny.' She perched primly on the edge of his bed, close enough to him that she could feel his warmth. She lowered her voice. 'Look at the effort your mam has gone to; she wants us here. You're a Saddleworth lad, Johnny.' She heard him sigh. 'We don't need to go anywhere; we've got it all here.'

'It's not enough. Being from a place is not enough; I need something else. I can't spend my life facing the same old – the same old disputes, the same old farmers and traps and mill owners – seeing the likes of Mr Dunne grow fat because he has no decency to wait until corpses grow cold.' He sat up and gripped her forearms, pulling her towards him. 'Millie, I'm serious now. This isn't a joke, or some kind of trick. You are my wife, and I am offering you the chance to go somewhere where there aren't any mills or murder or rain, where kids might actually grow up straight-backed. I'm – we're – better than this.'

'But how do you know that this new place doesn't have all that?' she retorted, her jaw tightening so that she had to force the words through her teeth. 'How do you know that the Canadas aren't full of those things too?'

Johnny shook his head, eyed the whorls in the thick woollen blanket his Mam had knitted.

'It'll be just the same, Johnny, just the same. The land might be bigger, there might be different game on it and the people might speak differently, but we're under the same sky.'

'Exactly. The same sky. I'm not asking you to commit a sin, Millie; I'm not asking you to stop going to Chapel. It'll still be you and me, Millie. We'll still be living and breathing. We'll be living better, breathing clean air.'

'But this makes no sense!' she said. She was louder now. She ignored his signals to quiet. 'I love my family; why should I leave them?'

'Because you're not a child, Millie. You're a woman. You're my woman.' He shook her. 'Look, I have always wanted you. I have always wanted you to be my wife. You have miles more sense than the rest, and I thought you'd leap at this chance. And besides, when we get there, we could send for your Mam and Tudor; Jane, too, if she wanted. Then they'd have the chance to make a new life, too.'

'They won't want to; I don't want to,' she said, shaking her head, shaking her body in his hands. He tried to steady her.

'You will, you'll see. Now compose yourself and we'll go to help Gertie with breakfast. Then I presume you'll want to go to Chapel and I am quite sure your Lord would not want to see you in this state.' He smiled then and raised her chin to look at him. She thought back to the men at market, how Johnny was known to be firm but fair. This wasn't fair.

He closed the door behind him. She could hear him in his stockings on the stairs, the rumble of his Adam's apple as he addressed his sister.

She screwed up her face, threw herself onto the thin sheets and cried. The sheets grew hot and wet and the fibres scratched at her skin, wounding her for her ungrateful misery. She beat the sheets wearily with tiny, futile fists. He couldn't frogmarch her to the port; he couldn't take her there on a scaffold. But he could take another, or he could go by himself. If she refused, then what?

Johnny was picking at a trap with a knife, tightening a hinge, while George watched. Neither looked up as she entered, but

Esme set down her sewing.

'Good morning, Mrs Barkwell! Oh, how funny that sounds! 'Ere, you sit where I was, and–'

'No, no,' Millie protested, 'I'll help Gertie.'

'We've actually got enough eggs this morning,' Gertie answered. 'There's normally one hen that doesn't lay for some reason or other. Not the same one, neither, it changes from day to day, else we'd have her in the pot. They take turns to deceive us.' She spoke to her own reflection in the kitchen window as she wound strands of hair around her fingers.

Millie smiled weakly and took up the bread knife.

'Oh yes, if you wouldn't mind.'

'What will the new couple be doing after Chapel?'

The trap snapped shut when Johnny let it go. It was like a skull, the jaw of a skull. Funny it should trap smaller skulls within it.

'I've got the traps at Bill O'Jack's to check,' Johnny said. Millie looked over, but his eyes didn't leave the metal skull. She didn't know he set his traps at her Granda's place, her Uncle Tom's land.

'And Millie?' Esme said, sinking back into her seat.

'I suppose I'll go and see Mam and Jane, see if they need any help.'

'Quite right, quite right,' George said, watching Johnny again.

'Though you're welcome to stay here, Millie dear, remember this is your home now. You must do as you please,' Esme said, first to Millie, then to Gertie. Both women nodded, and Gertie brought the eggs to the table.

'Which reminds me,' Johnny said suddenly, standing. His chair screeched on the flags behind him. 'We have some news to give you.'

'Oh?' Esme glanced at Millie's stomach, then up at her face questioningly.

Millie swallowed, followed Gertie with the bread and butter. The butter dish was rough with chips.

'Yes,' he said, pasting the butter to his bread in one hand. He harpooned a peeled egg. 'Millie and I are leaving for the Canadas.'

'What?'

'Come again?'

Gertie let out a laugh.

'We'll be leaving from Liverpool on Tuesday; our passage takes around ten weeks.'

'A fine joke, my lad! He always was a joker,' Esme began to explain over the table to Millie, but Millie concentrated on salting and slicing her egg.

'What do you mean, Johnny, my boy?' George spoke softly. Millie heard him turn in his chair to face Johnny.

'I mean exactly as I say. I've been saving for months, perhaps even a year now, for me and her to emigrate. The time is come; we leave on Tuesday. Gertie can have my room; you'll have fewer mouths to worry on. And we'll have a new life.'

At that moment, Millie wondered if she had ever truly heard silence. The road to Bill O'Jack's was quiet, but it was often interrupted by the caw of jackdaws or a sigh of wind; her family home, even in the dead of night, had its silence interrupted by the mantelpiece clock, Mam's snores. Here, there was no clock, no breath escaping from nostrils, no neighbours choosing that moment to shout at a child.

Eventually, George dropped his knife. The ring, as it chimed to the flagstones, startled the family into questions and retorts and exclamations. Millie chewed her bread slowly, felt it clag in her throat.

'And when did you think you were going to tell us?'

'As I planned; today, once we were married.'

'Did you not think to tell us before?'

'And what difference do you think it would have made, except for giving longer to dissuade us? It has long been our plan-'

'And so Millie has been involved?'

'No, it is my wedding present to her, the chance of a new life.'

'In the Canadas? So far? Lord, you've never even seen the sea!'

'Precisely. There is more to life than Greenfield, Mother.'

'Don't speak so condescendingly, John.'

Millie watched the conversation flicker between them. She couldn't add to it; she had nothing to say. She let the noise of their voices accumulate as she did in the mill. Once it reached a particular volume, it became part of her, as natural and as integral as her heartbeat. She saw Esme cry, raising an old handkerchief to her face as George consoled her, pointing at their son. Their voices grew louder still. George reddened. Hands beckoned back to her, eyes flitting between herself and Johnny.

Mam cried wordlessly when Millie told her. Jane got up and walked out. Tudor put his hands on his hips, paced like an overlooker. She could see him wondering what to do, what to say. He was the man of the house, she'd heard Mr Dunne tell him, but he didn't know how to wear his position.

Millie picked at the hem of her cuff, knowing she would have to mend it.

'But so soon?' her mother asked, snorting suddenly. She could hear the snot bubble and crack in her nostrils. 'But at all? Oh, Millie, I didn't expect this. Did you? Did you expect this?'

And Millie shook her head gently. No, she hadn't expected this. She had expected to move in with the Barkwells, for a year, two, however long it took them to find independent rent for their own place and endure another family's finicks and foibles.

But this development, this was something else. When Janey Nield married Eli, they walked to their new cottage in Dobcross. And though the walk couldn't have taken them longer than two hours, Janey spoke of it as though she was walking to the moon: who would care for her mother as old age approached? What if Dobcross women had a different washing day?

But men went away all the time: to sea, to the farms, to the great houses outside the boundaries, to seek their fortunes, make their mothers proud. Mostly they came back, sometimes with a wife and children in tow; sometimes they made a new life for themselves elsewhere, their mothers regaling neighbours with the latest letter at church. But the women seldom moved further than Oldham, Manchester at most. Why would they, when they had their home, their work, their family? And she and Mam and Jane had the added complication of Bill O'Jack's, of course. *Complication*, she thought; the deaths of her kin had become an inconvenience to her.

'Johnny says we can send for you all when we're set up; you can meet us there. We can get a house, and find jobs for us all, then write to let you know, and-'

Mam looked at her. 'At my time of life, Millie?'

'What will Johnny do?' Tudor perched on the corner of the table. For once, Mam didn't warn him about ruining the seat of his trousers.

'Johnny says there'll be so much work to try his hand at that he'll have a choice. He wants to get into the sawmills, there's plenty enough of them. He can keep on with traps, though the game is different there,' Millie paused as Mam's eyes widened, 'and there's so many houses going up that they'll need hands to build them. He'll even be able to build our own.'

'Johnny can't build a house! What will he build it from?' Tudor scoffed, but Millie's narrow, stony eyes saw off his smile.

'He says he'll have so much work that even I need not work.'

'Not work?' Mam asked, lifting up her face. 'But what would you do?'

Millie shrugged. How was she to know? She had no idea where she was meant to be going, what kind of amenities there would be, the people she would meet. All she could think of was the dog-eared encyclopaedia in the Chapel's library and its picture of the men in their dome shelters made of snow and the round incisions they made in the ice to fish.

'I could tend a garden.'

'And from whom would you learn to do that?' It was Mam's turn to scoff. She shifted her weight to her feet, her thinning ankles still managing to support her, and began to sort through the wool. Millie could see that she wasn't doing it properly, that she'd have to do it all again later before it could be left for the putter-out.

'And what of your grandfather and your Uncle Thomas?' Mam said quietly.

Millie felt Tudor's eyes on her. 'What of them?'

'You will leave us when your relatives have so recently been set to the earth?'

'I don't want to go! Can't you see that?' Millie shouted, her hands flailing high above her. She saw Granda's face, his lips meeting desperately to tell her something. *Platts, Pats.* 'Why on earth would I want to go to the Canadas? Where I don't know a soul and a soul doesn't know me! When I am perfectly happy here! But what choice do I have?'

'Then we'll petition him,' Mam said, examining each clump of wool more closely, quicker now. 'We'll show him it's a poor idea. Surely his family don't want him to go?'

'I'm sure they'd sooner have a room free and one less mouth to feed; two without me,' Millie said dully, toeing the ash fallen from the grate.

'Clean that; you'll make a mess.'

Millie did, kneeling down and sweeping and scrubbing until her kneecaps burst into song.

Mam rapped on the door and Jane drew in her breath. Millie could see her growing taller, holding her head high. They had been taught that once, at the village school, when they were half-timers. Good carriage could keep a book aloft on their heads and would help them later in life when the mill's machinery pulled on their muscles and bones and bent them out of shape.

'I don't think this... I really don't think...' Millie began, but Jane wafted her away. It was Esme that opened the door, though they could see George sitting behind at the table, picking at his pipe with a penknife.

'Our new kin!' Esme beamed apologetically. 'To what do we owe this -?' and she broke off, hoping they would supplement her words.

Jane did as Millie knew she would, as she was puffed up to do.

'We want to talk to you. To talk to you all, but especially to Johnny. Is he here?'

Esme drew back and Johnny appeared. Millie watched as he raised his hands in greeting, his lips pulling into a grin as though his fingers controlled them with strings.

'My new family!' His hands swept the air to guide them into the house.

'I'm sorry,' Millie mouthed from behind, wringing her hands, but he pretended not to see her.

Mam loosened her shawl and declined the chair Johnny offered her. She folded her hands, shook them out, and refolded them the other way.

'The message we've come to bring is, well, it's more of a discussion than a message, I suppose. We've left Tudor at home and he'll be wanting his tea afore long, so we'll keep it sweet-'

Gertie appeared at the back door and shook off her shawl. Millie could feel Jane bristle.

'Oh hello, everybody!' she exclaimed in her little girl's voice. 'How terribly nice to see my new family! To what do we owe this pleasure?' Gertie bobbed a curtsey. 'Jane, Mrs Bradbury, Sister Millie,' she smiled.

'Well, then.' Johnny rocked in his boots, the soles squeaking gently.

'We want to know why you're going to the Canadas,' Jane said, placing her hands on her hips. 'We want to know where this plan came from, and what kind of man you think you are, taking Millie with you, when she's perfectly happy here; she's said so herself.'

'Jane!' Mam and Millie exclaimed, Millie's hands shaking as she went to grab her sister's elbow.

'It's true, h'aint it?' Jane flashed her eyes around the room.

'Well, then,' Johnny said again, drawing out the chair next to his father. He sat down and took the pipe from his father's hands and tapped it. The dottle and ash fell out onto the table. 'It is true. Me and Millie plan a new life there. And would her family really stand in her way, after all's she suffered?'

'No, but-' Mam began.

'Yes. All she knows is here.'

'She will get to know somewhere else, abroad; she will prosper. We both will. Which is why we're doing it.'

George stroked his whiskers, sighed.

'We've spoken to him, Mrs Bradbury. Lord knows we haven't tried,' Esme said, 'but he's set on it. He's always been an obstinate wee thing. Look at him! Once his mind is made, there's no swaying him.'

'But he didn't consult her!'

Millie looked at her feet, twisted the ends of her shawl in her hands.

'And I'm not sure where it says that husbands have to consult their wives, especially on matters such as prosperity and occupation-'

'Easy, John,' George said, resting a hand on his knee.

'-but you'll have to see that I'm making the right decision, one you'll only grow to envy-'

Jane laughed, but it sounded higher in pitch than usual. She tossed her head.

'-when the prices drop further, the mills close down, the strikes rise up again.'

'Nonsense,' Jane said.

'We leave on Tuesday.'

'So I hear,' Jane said, 'but what time does that give Millie? She doesn't even know where the Canadas are – do you?'

'Jane, I…'

'What will you do there, Johnny? What plans have you made?' Mam said, laying a hand next to George's pipe on the table to steady herself. George sprang up and offered her his seat. She took it, drew Johnny's hand into her lap. 'I want to know my daughter will be cared for, given the opportunities you tell us are so frequent there.'

'I will take up in a sawmill; I'll run it, eventually.'

Jane guffawed, but Johnny didn't seem to notice. Millie saw

that his words only strengthened his composure, his conviction. He draped an arm over the back of the chair and leant against it, easy. He didn't look at her. He was enjoying the attention.

Maybe he was right, she thought for a second. Maybe they would be better off. She could try a garden. But then her mind clouded with ice and snow and she shivered.

'That I don't doubt,' Mam said, reaching forward for his chin. She pulled it upwards, close to hers. 'But Millie?'

'She will be by my side. She will share in whatever I bring home.'

'And how will you guarantee her happiness?'

'She will be happy; she will not be wanting for owt. And we shall send for you once we're settled, if that pleases you.'

Mam stared, blinked slowly. 'Well then,' she said, dropping her hands in to her lap. Johnny sat back against the chair. 'I am deeply saddened to see you go, both of you, especially my daughter. But I see that this is made final and our attempts to make you rethink will be thwarted.'

'I told you,' Esme added.

Millie saw Jane grab fistfuls of her dress in rage. 'So that's it then? We let them get on with it. Board a boat to the arse end of nowhere?'

'Jane!' Mam cried, patting at her waist. Johnny sniggered.

'He assures me 'e's got everything arranged,' George said. 'Mail coach to Liverpool on the Sunday night, a boarding house at the dock where all passengers lodge before they go.'

'Liverpool!' Gertie clapped her hands together. 'How I'd love to see it! It just sounds so...'

'Dangerous? Full of thieves and whores?'

'Jane!' Mam said again, snatching at her hand. 'We're going, come on. Goodbye, Millie, make sure you call this week after work.'

Mam made for the door and Millie hovered behind them, bobbed her head so that she might catch their eyes, but they turned their heads and lurched out of the door.

'Your sister has quite the mouth on her!' George said, his eyes wide. Esme shook her head sadly.

'She's just upset,' Millie answered, and stood there, watching the backs of her mother and sister recede. Straight-whiskered, Granda called Jane a 'church bell'; he didn't like women to get above their station.

'Understandable,' Gertie smiled as though she didn't understand at all, her eyes glassy, her cheeks rosy.

Millie looked to the door, back at Johnny and his family.

'I'm just going to talk to them; I'll be back shortly.' She slipped through the door before they could pull her back.

She called their names. Jane stopped first, turned. She whispered hurriedly to Mam, who then continued on her way, her forehead facing her feet.

'Where's Mam going?' Millie asked, when she'd caught up.

'I've told her to go on; she's too upset, Millie, especially with *my* conduct, apparently.'

Millie rubbed her forearms for something to do.

'I've got to ask, though: why *are* you doing this?' Jane's eyes had narrowed, the skin around her eyelids dry and creased into papery grooves.

'Doing what?' Millie frowned, her mind buzzing. Did Jane think she had consented to this? That she was part of the plan?

'Going along with things. You can say no, you know. You can refuse to go. Why would you want to go? With everything that's happened! Can't you see that Mam needs you here?'

'Do you think I want to do this?' Her mouth was dry, her

tongue stuck to her lips, the insides of her teeth, the roof of her mouth. She tried to free her words. 'Do you think I want to go?'

Why didn't Jane understand, why couldn't she see what little choice she had?

'You could say no, Millie, you could tell him no.'

'How could I? How can I? You've seen him! He's my *husband*, Jane.'

'And you've been married all of five minutes! I knew you shouldn't have said yes; I knew there was something about all of this.' Millie saw Jane's hands shake as she threw them about her, saw her try to bring them under control, down by her sides.

'You wanted me to turn him down? Why would I? We've always meant to be married-'

Jane snorted. 'I don't know where you've got this from.'

'Mam! Mam has always said that we would be a good match, that Father said it when I was young. And George and Esme, too, they always said it!'

'So that's it, then? People say things and then it happens?'

'When people you love say it, when family say it, then yes. They've got our best interests at heart-'

'But Johnny hasn't, has he? He isn't thinking about you at all. Why did you marry him? What was it he offered? That you couldn't have from anyone ese, another man, your family?'

Millie blinked, swallowed. There was that rush in her ears again, like water falling from the hills, incessant, cold.

'I- he, well-'

'Oh, of course, he's charming, he fills his fustian, he's handy with money. Everybody knows him, everybody likes him, reputedly. All of those things. But what does he offer *you*, Millie?'

'You haven't seen how he is with me, Jane; he's soft, he's kind. He truly loves me. He says he always has.'

'So much he'll take you from your family?'

'But it's not all about me, though, is it? In a marriage, you put others before yourself, and-'

'You're one half of this marriage, aren't you?'

Millie lowered her voice, looked about her. 'Jane, I'm not going to stand here and argue with you. We've been gossip enough for this village, and-'

'Fine.' Jane grabbed at Millie's forearm and led her to the cobbled ginnel beside Cadishead Mill. Millie shook her off. She could already feel a bruise.

The ginnel stank of urine and stale pipe smoke.

'I want to know why you married Johnny Barkwell,' Jane said, more gently this time. Millie looked up at Jane's eyes, softened into sorrow, and felt a sharp tang of irritation. What kind of question was that?

'I don't know what you want me to say,' Millie said. She noticed two abandoned glass bottles and kicked them. They skittered against each other, ricocheted against the wall, in a confusion of noise.

'Did you think he was your only option? That you would grow to be an old maid if you turned him down?'

'No!' Millie snapped. 'No! Do you think me to be so shallow?'

Jane shrugged her shoulders.

'No!' Millie said again, exasperated. Why did she think she could interrogate her so? What did Jane know of love? 'No, Jane, I married Johnny because I love him, because I've always loved him. I feel it here; I can't explain it. I shouldn't have to explain it. The fact that I declared it in front of my family, in front of God, should be enough.' She rubbed at her chest, her belly. Her insides ached. 'I didn't think this would happen, though. Who could've predicted this?'

Jane shook her head, kept shaking her head.

'What, Jane? What do you know that's different?'

'I think you can get him to change his mind; you can refuse to go.'

Jane didn't understand. She didn't know Johnny like Millie did. Esme, his very mother, had said he was stubborn, determined.

'I just want to be good, Jane. I've always wanted to be good. Some people say that because they have to; because their mamas tell them to and the preacher tells them to and the Bible tells them to. But I truly want to be good, do the right thing. I don't understand why that causes you such problems.'

If faces could cloud over like the sky – the eyes dulling, the skin losing its lustre – then Jane's was close. Millie watched her disappointment consume her, realise that she wouldn't convince Millie to feel differently. What could she do? Why didn't Jane understand she had no choice? She could hardly desert her husband.

'I best go and find Mam,' Jane said, moving into the weak sunlight.

Johnny was waiting at the end of his street, sucking on his pipe and looking out onto the hills. The sound of their pattens roused him.

He lifted his hat to Jane as she strode past him, but she didn't acknowledge it.

'What's the matter with her? Come on,' Johnny said, taking her wrist. 'We need some air; I've got traps to check.'

They walked along Chew Valley Road; his hand wrapped around her wrist. With his other hand, he took his pipe from his mouth and exhaled.

'Your sister. My,' he breathed, 'your mam needs to get a hold on her before she really goes too far.'

'She's just hot-headed, it's no bother,' Millie quickly replied. 'She's always been the same. Mam can't do owt about it.'

'Those Bradbury lines,' he muttered, laughing softly to himself.

'Where are your traps?' she asked, changing the subject. His grip was tight.

He nodded his head forwards. 'Not far.'

As they passed the terraces, she saw women scrubbing the doorsteps or bringing in washing, dried starchy in the sunshine. They rounded up children that hopscotched in the dirt. A parson closed the door behind him on one house, a man in sooty work clothes entered another. It was this part of the day she usually loved best, most of all, on a Sunday. It was like the moment before silence, the getting ready and anticipation of the early night, of tired little bodies scrubbed in baths before the fire.

Would it be the same elsewhere? Surely not. She she tried to push the thought from her mind.

'I won't have your family interfere like that, Millie, thinking they can dictate to me,' he said. He turned the bowl of his pipe upside down. The ash fluttered to the ground.

'I, no, I-'

'Don't make excuses for them. They'll see, you wait. This is the best thing we can do.' He stopped her, as though it was a lead rein she had about her wrist. He stood in front of her then, crouched slightly so their faces were level. 'You've got to trust me.'

'I'll miss them,' she said simply. 'They're my family.'

'And you'll make new friends and new family,' he said, patting her stomach gently.

He started again, leading her like the fat little ponies she saw the children of the manor houses ride.

He turned on to the road to Holmfirth.

'Whereabouts are your traps?' Millie asked again. She could already see the break in the wall that led to Bill O'Jacks.

'Down yonder,' he nodded forward again. 'I have some at the back of your old Granda's place.'

He thrust his hands in his pockets as the breeze rolled off the moors, tickling their necks and their ankles, thrusting a tremble through them. The Gypsy vardos lined the fencing that split the valley into pastures. It was the fencing that Thomas fixed after storms, the sound of hammering nails reverberating across the valley. At its lowest point, the stiles bridged a tiny sike that collected when the rains had been plentiful. Where Thomas had once told her he had found fish, which, as a seven-year-old girl, she had believed; now, she thought it must have been his idea of a joke.

'I'll stay here,' Millie said at the top of the track. The inn seemed dusty and cold, even from here, without lights in the window or people congregating around the front door, ales in hand.

'Don't be foolish,' Johnny said, pinching her wrist again. It astonished her his hand could encircle her entire wrist in one go. 'You can't stay here. Plus, I need your help. Come on.'

As they neared the inn, Millie's heart began to beat, and sweat collected at her neck. She shook off his hand.

'I shan't go in.'

'We won't go in, I told you; I promise.'

The grass lay a path down to the fencing. They heard a shout from the inn. It was Mr Dunne. He waved and jogged down the incline towards them. His stomach jiggled with the movement.

'Mrs Barkwell, Johnny,' he said, clutching at his chest to regain his breath.

'Can we help you, our noble friend, Mr Dunne?' Johnny

asked with a wide grin.

Mr Dunne raised his eyebrows, his gaze nipping between their faces. He settled on Johnny.

'Er... no, no, not really. Thought I'd say my greetings, that's all.'

'What were you doing at my grandfather's place?' Millie asked, her voice small in the slack.

'I keep an eye on it for your mother, Amelia; it's all arranged, you know that.' He reached into his breast pocket and took out a handkerchief, dabbed at his shining head.

'But now, what were you doing just now?'

'A small group of people called at my shop and wanted to see the inn for themselves,' he replied.

'Where were they from?'

Mr Dunne frowned at the question, shook his head slightly as if to avoid a fly. 'I don't know, Yorkshire, perhaps. Near the coast. Does it matter?'

Millie didn't reply.

'And you? What are you fine young couple doing here?'

'Checking my traps,' Johnny said, resettling his hat on his head and striding towards the fence.

'Good day, Mr Dunne,' Millie said, and followed her husband. She heard the shopkeeper echo his response.

'I don't understand him. Can't he leave us in peace? Doesn't he realise that perpetuating these tours of the inn, taking money from these bloodthirsty *savages*, is to prolong our suffering?'

'Savages, eh?'

A rabbit lay in his first trap, one leg snapped and bloody, its eyes vacant. Johnny lifted up the latch and grabbed the rabbit by its ears. Its leg remained in the trap and he kicked it away with his boot. Millie held open the sack and Johnny dropped the rabbit in. Though he was careful not to show it, Granda had been impressed when she'd shown him her first skinned rabbit. *Look 'ere*, he'd said, flicking torn skin with a nail. *You've got to be careful not to tear it.* She'd never torn it again afterwards, even though it was the job she liked least, and hurried through it.

'Do you think we'll ever find out what happened to them?'

Johnny crouched, examined the stitching in the edging of the sack. His hair was so full, so lush, she took out a hand to touch it, but thought better of it.

'There's nothing to go on, is there? They'll give up, I know it.'

Johnny didn't answer. He turned the sack over in his hands as if it was the first time he'd seen it, then stood and turned to face the Gypsies' vardos. A woman was sitting on the brightly coloured steps of one, rummaging in a reed basket. She looked up, caught sight of Millie and Johnny, and climbed into the vardo, letting the curtain fall behind her. The basket lay abandoned on the steps.

'Don't they ever talk to you?' Millie lowered her voice.

'The men-folk do, on occasion; their women, never.'

'And the childer?'

'Rare.'

Five moles were strung by their noses on the highest wire. Their hands had fallen open as if in surrender.

'Will you take those to skin them?' she asked.

'Questions, Millie! Never known so many questions!' But he turned his face and offered her the smallest of smiles. She blushed and vowed to ration them. Johnny walked to the next trap where another rabbit, larger, bulkier, lay.

'Make sure you say your goodbyes,' Johnny said, as the rabbit sank to the bottom of the sack. He levered open the next snare. 'This is your last week here. Don't forget that; remember to tell Shipton tomorrow.'

Millie's heart pounded. He was sincere. A week. One more Sunday afternoon and they would be gone. She had never ridden the mail coach. She had never even made it to Manchester. And now she never would.

'How do you say goodbye when you don't want to leave somebody, Johnny?'

She regretted her question.

The third rabbit was sticky with blood. It had been caught in the abdomen, worsened its wound in the struggle, and grass and seeds had stuck to it. Millie closed her eyes as it dripped into the sack, which Johnny tied and threw over his shoulder. His other traps lay deeper in the plantation.

'Johnny?' She strode after him, slowed him by the elbow.

'You'll find a way,' he said, and wrenched his arm free from her grip.

11

Mam and Esme Barkwell had arranged a picnic for them, at the ing where the Tame swelled at the Wellihole. The two mothers set down their baskets in the long grass while Tudor and Gertie smoothed out old blankets for them to sit on. Alice unwrapped the bread, still warm from the bakestone, and removed the dishcloths from the basket of ales that Tudor left to rest in the grass. He kicked off his boots, pointing his toes into the grass so his mother wouldn't spy the holes in his stockings. Ed, behind him, threw pebbles into the water that clunked like the gulps of a drunk man. Jane drew Millie down to a blanket and kept her hands on her wrist.

'Can you believe it's come to this?' Jane asked, looking about. 'Can you believe my little sister is getting on a boat and sailing off to a new life?'

Alice peeled the shell from a boiled egg, agonised over the tiny pieces and collected them into the lid of the butter dish.

'What do you think, Alice?'

Alice shrugged and began another egg. 'I wish her good luck, of course.'

Mam and Esme ceased their conversation to listen.

'I don't know where he got the idea from,' Jane said, fanning her face with her hand. Millie began to butter the bread, passed a stack of slices to Jane.

'Well, you can stop wondering,' Millie said flatly, 'and butter these.'

'What if you're called upon for evidence, or another inquest?'

'She won't be,' Mam cut in.

'That's right, because they've forgotten us already. Forgotten my poor Granda and my uncle Thomas-'

'Forgotten? Hardly likely; I'm still stared at wherever I go. The factory floor falls silent the minute I walk in-'

'Let's not talk of this,' Mam said firmly, raising her hands up. 'Millie and Johnny leave Greenfield tomorrow. Let's talk of happier times, please. The happier times they're likely to encounter.'

But as the bread and boiled eggs were passed around, conversation ceased entirely. They listened instead to the water curdling at the bank, a pair of mallards hooting as they crashed into it, webbed feet first. They listened as Mam and Esme shifted every few minutes, their joints unused to sitting flush against the flat of the unforgiving earth. And Millie watched the hills above them, traced their silhouette against the moving clouds with her eyes, and vowed to memorise the shape.

Millie saw her friend shake the crumbs from her fingers and clear her throat with a mouthful of water from the old milk bottle she had carried there. She knew she was about to sing from the way she began to deepen her breath.

It was 'Nancy of Yarmouth'. Alice addressed her in song, her mouth smiling at the words, and Millie smiled back, though felt tears lodge in the corners of her eyes.

'Here's a health to sweet *Millie*,' Alice emphasised, 'as we sail on the main, and I hope to old England we shall come again.' She lifted one of the bottles from the basket to toast. Millie nodded; the action spilling tears onto one of her cheeks. She threaded her fingers through the coarse grass and snatched roughly at their roots, tearing them from the heavy clods of earth.

'My! This looks like a good spread!' Johnny arrived, standing over them and rubbing his hands together. George sat where his wife patted the grass beside her. 'Though we've brought salt as I couldn't have boiled eggs without it,' and he held out a dirty handkerchief, folded tightly.

Alice's mother and Theresa arrived behind them, Theresa shaking out her shawl to sit on it. Alice's mother joined Mam and Esme, groaning softly as she tucked her legs close to her body.

George passed Tudor and Ed an ale each, and Mam looked hard at Alice's mother as she spoke, instead of watching Tudor drink from the bottle.

'Nice afternoon for it,' George said, sinking into the grass between Tudor and Ed. 'You'll miss your sister, I expect?'

Millie didn't wait for his answer, but addressed Johnny instead. He crouched next to her.

'I didn't see you after work?'

'No,' he said, loosening his collar, 'I stayed longer, made sure I said goodbye to the lads proper.'

'Are they sorry to see you go?'

He shrugged; a smile ghosted his lips. 'Ah, they say so, but there's plenty more where I came from. I'll be a distant memory in no time.'

He unwrapped his handkerchief and dunked a boiled egg in the salt.

'Here he is!' Johnny said, suddenly looking up. Mr Dunne strode over the grass, flattening it with his boots. He had on a felt hat pulled down to his ears. 'And where's he dug out that hat? The Civil War?'

'Hello!' Mr Dunne called, 'Hello! I've left the shop with

Little William, so I can join you for an hour!'

The women shuffled along the blanket to make room for him. He unlaced his boots and set them aside, where they glowed with a warm scent. George settled an ale into his hand.

'Good of you to come, Isiah,' Mam said, handing him an egg. Johnny offered up his handkerchief of salt and Mr Dunne twisted his egg in it before popping it whole in his mouth. Millie could see his tongue push the egg from one side of his mouth to the other before his great teeth bore down on it, puncturing it.

'Well, I had to see the new couple off on their adventure, didn't I?' he said, bits of yellow and white mush visible. 'You're off tomorrow then, your mother tells me?' Millie nodded. 'Liverpool and then on your way. Fancy! Now, Liverpool, what can I tell you about that?'

Millie heard Johnny mumble, but she couldn't make out the words.

'Well, you must keep your items close about you as the place is run riot with pickpockets. Pickpockets and Irish,' he said, wagging a sausagey finger. 'Don't let anybody give you directions in the street. If you get lost, ask in a reputable looking shop; a bookseller or a tobacconist. Otherwise, you'll be led astray. Speak clearly and slowly; they won't understand you, nor you them. Don't make eye contact with the women at the dockside.'

Millie swallowed. Mr Dunne was renowned for his tall tales and bluster, especially when he was in his cups, but if this was true of Liverpool, what would the Canadas bring?

'When have you been to Liverpool?' Tudor asked, leaning back against his elbows.

'Oh, many a-time, m'lad, for supplies,' he said, his mouth

bending into a smile. 'You get it cheaper the moment it gets off the ship, before they've decided what price to give it. Catch 'em unawares, make 'em fluster.'

'Like what?' Tudor asked again.

'You know… sugar,' Mr Dunne replied, his eyes darting from face to face as he thought. 'Well, sugar, mainly.'

Millie saw Tudor and Ed exchange glances, their eyebrows shuttling up their foreheads and back down again. They didn't believe a word.

Johnny hissed Tudor's name.

'I meant to sort this before, but with everything that's going on,' Johnny said, his palms open to the air, 'I hadn't got round to it. See,' and Johnny cleared his throat, leant back against Millie. Mr Dunne's words died in his mouth and everyone listened to Johnny. 'See, with me going, I won't be able to trap on the land around the back of your Granda's place anymore. How about you take it on?'

Tudor blinked slowly, glanced at his mother, who frowned.

'I don't know, Johnny,' she said, 'with the mill and-'

'No, no, it's logical. Ideal piece of land to learn on.'

It could provide them with a useful income now she would be gone, but he would need someone to guide him. She saw Mam sit up straight, consider it.

'What do you think? Good?'

Tudor nodded once, stuttered.

'Now, Johnny, I'm not sure it's wise. Might the sensible thing be to sell it? Wouldn't you say, Mrs Bradbury?' Mr Dunne said, puffing out his chest.

Mam's lips wrinkled, puckered at one side of her mouth, then the other.

'Nay, we'll be making it easier; keeping it in the family,'

Johnny answered.

Mr Dunne wobbled his head on his neck, took off his hat and fanned it in front of his face. Sweat glistened from the creases in his face.

'I shall advise him, then, I shall be his advocate,' Mr Dunne said, and Johnny smiled.

'Of course you will. Of course.'

Tudor knotted tall blades of grass in his fingers. He seemed bewildered. He didn't know the right way to answer, whether he should be happy at the prospect, or concerned about his new privileges. He wanted to please Mam, his departing sister, Johnny.

'Good, that,' Ed said, plopping another pebble into the water. 'Your own traps.' Millie saw a small brown fish dart away into the reeds.

George shifted to his knees and raised his bottle of ale, tapping his finger dully against the neck. 'It seems we had only speeches about these two just yesterday, but it's time for another one.'

But no one rose their faces expectantly as they had done at The King Bill. No one smiled or corroborated with a 'hear, hear!' Instead, Esme stroked Mam's wrist gently, Alice and Jane looked into their crusts, Millie into the thick hair of her husband.

'For my son has always been an ambitious one, even when he was in his britches. He didn't listen to his mam; he certainly wouldn't listen to me. And still, he ploughs his own furrow. I'm convinced we'll be toasting his success in the Canadas; he and his pretty wife, Millie.'

Millie glowed, watched Johnny's face, the muscles under his beard pulsing. She wasn't pretty, that she knew, not in a Gertie sense of the word. So, if she wasn't pretty, what was she? And if ambitious meant willing to leave her family, willing to leave this, then she certainly held no ambition.

It came down on her then, like a cloud. It choked her throat. She coughed into her hand, knocked on her chest, struggled for air. Jane thumped her back as if she would spit out a seed, but Millie continued to gasp, her throat closing. She fought back the smarting at her eyes.

Tomorrow, she would be gone. This time tomorrow. Gone.

12

From the dock, the ship blocked out any view of the sea, so Millie couldn't inspect it to determine its colour, gauge its temperature and volatility. She hadn't anticipated the sheer glacial size of The Great Countess. The ship was white, a bright white like goat's froth in the sun. She gazed up at the three masts, thin reeds that looked as though they would snap at the stiff breeze that Johnny had said was always to be found at the shore. Clumps of beige sacking bandaged the masts, bound in place by ropes. Sails, she realised, that would unfurl at command and somehow propel them across the ocean. She squinted under the rays, sharper here than those tempered by the hills of home, and noticed a man halfway up the central mast, his hands animated in work. He shouted down to the deck, and she noticed other men, too, shifting ropes and buckets. And there were passengers milling about, confident and merry, pointing back at Liverpool, up at its many spires. She saw gentlemen chatting together in groups, poring over newspapers, their bellies laughing. She wondered what Granda would've made of the scene. *Pompous so-and-sos,* she could imagine him saying, *what are they so afraid of that they're climbing aboard a ship that size? What are they running away from?*

Johnny gave her a nudge. She let the hand shielding her eyes fall to her side.

'Ain't she a beauty?' he said, as though he had taken a pheasant from his trap. 'But there's no use looking up there; that's for the moneyed and connected, your mill owners and your merchants and your politicians and their fancy ladies. Probably the clergy, too, knowing them.'

He pointed lower down the boat, beneath the smart navy ribbon that ran around the perimeter of the deck.

'No, that down there is for us.'

But she couldn't see what he was pointing at. There were no windows, no places where she could go to gulp in the great lungfuls of sea air that Mam had ordered her to do.

'Exactly,' Johnny said, rubbing his hands together. 'Below deck is where the fun is to be had!'

Millie couldn't imagine what fun could be gleaned from almost three months' passage on a ship with no windows. She followed Johnny through the throng of people that had gathered, her heart still pounding in her chest, as he patted the working men on the back and dipped his forehead at their women. But there were men of all kinds: old with great whiskers and tall hats, carrying remarkably similar briefcases, and canes, umbrellas and newspapers, as though they had all been purchased from the same shopkeeper.

There were younger men in their Sunday best with small knapsacks, some quietly smoking in the shade of the carriages recently parked up, others talking loudly in accents she didn't recognise. There were serving men carrying boxes, taking them from one cart and adding them to another. Ladies held parasols or children's hands, and talked to worried looking maids. There were fewer women like her, with shawls wrapped tightly despite the late summer heat and small cases containing their few meagre possessions: a second dress, another set of undergarments, a brooch or looking glass, a Bible, a needle and thread. She wondered whether they should have brought more food with them; even the poorest looking people were checking on their waxed paper packages, counting them out and repacking them into baskets.

'It'll go mouldy in moments,' Johnny said too loudly, so that she wheeled on her heel and pretended she was looking elsewhere. 'We'll share with others; buy from the cook. We'll be alright with our biscuits and oatmeal.' He patted his pack with the flat of his hand. He knew what he was doing.

Millie spotted one woman, probably a few years older than her, but not yet twenty-five, who was regaling her husband with a tale that made him laugh outright, kept laughing and wiping his eyes as Johnny and Millie neared. She was short and her shapeless clothing gave the impression that she would be in proportion if put through a mangle. As they passed, the woman paused to wink at Millie. Her husband's eyes creased shut with laughter. Millie nodded shyly back and wondered what story she had told. Once they were settled, and they had work and lodgings to call their own, she hoped she would be able to make Johnny laugh like that.

There were more people now, and Johnny couldn't push forward any further.

'They're lining up,' he said, peering over the hats in front. 'Best join 'em.'

She wondered if this was what the march to the gallows felt like, an involuntary shuffle forward, limbs leaden and brain furred, the inability to turn and flee despite the overwhelming desire to. She preoccupied herself by watching the surrounding feet, how they inched forward, nipped at the heels of the feet in front. Mostly, the shoes were new, as though they had been purchased especially for the journey. They were covered in a fine dust that would need to be wiped away with a handkerchief. She could see no clogs, no pattens, no boots like Johnny's with their cracked leather scowls. She hoped Johnny knew what he was doing.

'Ah, we're in the wrong place. We need to be in line for the steerage, over there,' Johnny pointed, and grabbed her wrist. She fell in behind his broad shoulders, watching the shoes grow dustier, dirtier, the soles thinner. 'Excuse me,' he said buoyantly, ignoring those that turned to face him quizzically, cross at their jostling. His body, animated with excitement, further exacerbated her feelings of dismay. How could he be so happy to leave his family behind, to leave everything he knew behind?

'Is this for the steerage?' Johnny asked a man squinting in the sun. The man took out his pipe and pushed out his words through the gap previously plugged by it.

'Aye, can't you tell? We're the ones that have known a day's work,' he said, smiling and hooking a thumb in the direction of the other queues. 'And they're loading them up first, of course, packing them away into their fine kitchens and their fancy feather beds before we sully the scene.' The two men began to speak amicably.

Steerage. It was a peculiar word. She wondered if it was from below deck that the ship's course was determined. She pictured huge great wheels, men shining with sweat, beholden to thick, winding ropes, and shuddered.

The man looked down at her as though she was a child, offering a paper bag of boiled sweets. 'And we're excited, are we?'

'No, dreading it,' Millie replied, plainly, and bent to rest her case on the dust. She used the movement to collect herself. She was not sure she had ever been so curt.

'She's afraid of the seasickness,' Johnny answered quickly,

tapping his stomach, and the man nodded, told him to acquire the menthol eucalyptus liquid that sailors swore by. Millie could tell Johnny had never heard of such a thing. She rolled her eyes to herself and counted the pebbles that dotted about her case.

She thought of the other couple she had seen and how the man had enjoyed his wife's company, that no one else on the earth could have tickled him in that way, at that time, as she had. Millie wanted that, too. She wanted to be Johnny's confidant, to feel as though whatever he faced in the mills or the fields, that he could come back to her and there would be safety and security and comfort. Even fun and liveliness! She could provide that, she was sure; she just needed to be granted the opportunity to advise, to provide.

But where they were going, there were no mills as she knew them; she couldn't imagine the fields, as vast and open as she was led to believe, without a hedgerow or a drystone wall. How could she provide that safety and security and comfort when she didn't know a bear from a mountain lion, a gorge from a canyon, a lake from an ocean?

She felt Johnny turn from her as he and the man chattered on, but his excitement had stiffened into fury. She had behaved inappropriately. What would the man think? She had embarrassed Johnny, embarrassed the man. She willed the trembles in her knees to subside. But he had to know she was here against her will; that when she gave her assent at the altar, she was exhilarated for their future, but ignorant for the actual future her husband had in store.

A steady wave of sound grew from the front and drew nearer, a cacophony of shuffling feet; straightening of collars, ties and hats; of women checking their bags and children's faces; of men repeatedly patting pockets for the tickets they had only recently located. Men turned to women to exclaim 'here we go!' and women nodded their replies, gathering up their children and bags, checking the horizon nervously, looking to God for His mercy.

Feet began to move again, toes crashing in to the heels in front, hems catching under soles. Slowly they crept forward, Johnny toeing up dust and small stones as the man fell into conversation with another. Millie slid in small, uncertain steps.

'Why did you have to be so rude, Millie?' he hissed. 'It's so unlike you.'

'Sorry,' she said, automatically. 'I-' but she couldn't continue. She wasn't truly sorry.

A man with round spectacles and a peaked hat snatched their tickets from Johnny's fist, held them up to the sky and screwed up his eyes at the text before ripping them roughly and handing half back. She would not be wished a fine journey, let alone a happy new life.

It thickened then, bodies lining up the steel ramp to the boat, which clanged with the squall of quickening boots, like hooves at a sheep fair. As Millie slipped behind him, Johnny reached to grip her wrist again. She felt as though the bones in her forearm would break.

'Stay close,' he said, as a surge of people gathered behind. Men held on to their hats as the breeze - fishier now, saltier - threatened to lift them from their heads.

The ship felt solid underfoot. She wondered if it was wedged into the seabed, because she didn't experience the bobbing she anticipated. It didn't dip with the jostling bodies, the men racing past them to claim their berths. It couldn't be floating yet.

She was surprised to see how much the ship's interior resembled a mill, with a network of pipes spidering across off-white walls, high ceilings crowded with large wooden boxes and crates. Around the perimeter, men sank into hammocks and swung from them ceremoniously, calling to their friends or leaning back and laughing, their elbows triangling out from their heads. Millie froze, felt others push past her. How would she and Johnny live like man and wife like that, in a hammock, in full view of everyone? There wasn't even a curtain by which they could conceal themselves.

She felt her arm tug. Johnny was looking at her, his eyes small. 'What?' he said with a spasm of his shoulders. He followed her gaze. 'No, those are for the sailors, the single men; we're through here,' and he pulled her wrist in the direction of a dark corridor, choked with people checking papers and conferring with strangers.

Bodies rolled into the slatted bunks, more pew than bed, like mice scurrying into nooks beneath the hearth. She saw adults push children out of the way to claim beds for themselves. Those with straw mattresses were seized first and curtains were quickly drawn to demonstrate possession, some fashioned from blankets magicked from knapsacks.

'Here,' he said, throwing glances over his shoulders. He tossed his knapsack into a dark corner. Millie couldn't tell whether it was a person or belongings that lay claim to the bottom bunk, but Johnny leapt up the ladder and held out his hand. 'You come up here; shan't have no wife of mine lying low with the dust and the dirt.'

Millie climbed up and set her case at the last slat. She lay back, pulled Mam's blanket from her case up to her chin and hoped no other bodies would join them. It was quieter here, darker. As her eyes adjusted to the gloom, she heard the steady drip of water. She noticed that the bunk was framed by a thick brown curtain, one corner missing, torn or chewed. She shuddered. It was a good job that she and Johnny were slender; Mr Dunne would have had to dangle out a leg, half his torso. If she shared that observation with Johnny, would that amuse him?

Johnny loosened his boots and leant back against his hands.

Still, she thought, *this* for ten weeks?

Johnny pulled the curtain across, the metal rings skittering across the crooked pole. The curtain didn't quite fit and left a narrow belt of light at her feet where she could view the corridor perfectly. A man was pulling another man out of a bunk by his lapels and demanding to see his ticket. She wondered if they were to stop and look back at her whether they would be able to see her eyes bright in the darkness. She watched, making a triangle with her arms behind her head like she had seen the men in the hammocks do.

She smelt bacon.

'Are you hungry?'

He pulled back the curtain and offered his hand.

'She speaks! I thought you'd taken a vow of silence!'

How else can I show my displeasure? she thought. She considered telling him those exact words, but she hadn't the energy. That instant, she wanted dripping on warmed bread and to fall asleep on Johnny's shoulder.

'Come on, my wife shall have the fattest bacon on this ship!' he said, drawing her away. He nipped her buttock with the nails of his thumb and first finger before pushing his hand through her arm as though she were a lady.

13

Johnny insisted she took the heel of the loaf from the seller. She looked at it doubtfully: her stomach felt too small for such a hunk of solid food. But once she began eating, she realised how hungry she was. The bread was slick with fat and slid down her throat with ease.

'We'll be eating better than this, don't you worry,' he said, crumbs falling from his lips. The lines that she always wanted to kiss appeared at his eyes. Her stomach, reinvigorated, gave a little leap.

'But what will we eat? And where?'

'I h'aint a clue. Come on, let's have a look round.'

Now that the other passengers were employed in finding their berths and their bearings, their number seemed fewer. The corridors and passageways were quieter, darker. A newspaper seller unpacked his boxes. Alongside his newspapers, he set out small books. Millie walked closer and saw he had collections of short stories, anthologies and miscellanies. A cobbler sat smugly beneath his sign that advertised soling and heeling, awaiting his first customer. A tobacconist beckoned to Johnny, waved him over with brown fingers, but Johnny shook his head.

'His tobacco will be wet, mark my words,' he muttered. 'I don't trust his face.' Millie studied the tobacconist; there was nothing wrong with his face. A lazy eye, perhaps, but who could help that?

A man wearing the same peaked hat as the ticket tearer was besieged with queries. No sooner had he satiated one then another was upon him. This time, a young couple, their toddling daughter barefoot, pointed plaintively at a piece of paper they held up before him. The man shook his head. The husband pointed again, but the official refused to follow his finger, looked over his shoulder and spoke to the next passenger, a man that held his pipe in the air. The husband turned away, exasperated. His wife pulled on his arm, then gave the daughter a deft slap for pulling at hers.

'Ah,' Johnny said, snorting his relief, 'the bar.'

It was makeshift, a counter made from packaging boxes sanded smooth and propped up by beer crates, presided over by a short man in spectacles and a woman drying and stacking pint glasses.

Johnny nodded to the bartender and ordered two beers, sliding one to Millie. Two men in sooty work clothes supped their ales in silence. Their features were as lost to the soot as their clothes, but their eyes, wet and white, caught her like torches.

'You got the right ticket then?' the bartender said, smiling.

Johnny raised his eyebrows.

'Some of these ships are dry, you know, the captains too fearful of their passengers falling overboard. Or so they say. And some won't let you smoke, neither, get you chewing tobacky instead.' The bartender leant heavily on his wrists.

'Ten weeks without beer?'

The bartender nodded, solemn. 'But not this one. He couldn't care how many of us wash up on the other side. Aye, there's always a few lost along the way.'

The bartender fixed his eyes on Millie. She felt her lips rise to a smile, instinctively, though she felt sick. He smiled back.

'But he'll take care of you, love, won't he?'

Millie gave the slightest of nods.

The ale was warmer than Granda would have liked, and the froth clung to the edges of the glass as though it had been piped in as a decorative afterthought. She wished Johnny had saved their money.

'And now she inspects the ale to see if it's to her liking!' Johnny whispered. 'As though she's the very connoisseur!' She wasn't sure if he was teasing or cross. The softer lines at his eyes disappeared, but the lines in his forehead deepened, solidified.

She rose the glass to her lips and downed the lot, wiping her mouth with the back of her hand. She could feel the ale's journey downwards, its melding and curdling with the bread and bacon fat. She imagined the liquid and the solid combining. She heard the two sooty men clapping.

'Well, well,' Johnny said, 'I trust it's to your taste?'

'Granda wouldn't have stood to stock it, but I suppose we're a captive audience here.'

'Hark at 'er!' Johnny pinched the bridge of his nose, closed his eyes. 'And to think I've known you since we were childer; I would've never had you down as a doughty one!'

'Got a light, pal?' A man leant in to Johnny, holding a beer in one hand, his pipe in the other. Millie recognised him as the laughing man, his wife who had engendered his mirth at his elbow. The men juggled flints and touch-paper and pint glasses, spoke hurriedly between sipping and drawing on their pipes. The woman held her shawl in her hand and used it to wipe the sweat from her face. She was shorter than a child, shorter than a grandmother, but her quick, flitting eyes, and her red mouth that seemed to dart from one side of her face to the other, had gravitas, knowing.

'I had to send you a wink,' she said, 'when I saw you afore because I hadn't seen a mite so miserable!' Her voice was soft, her words curling at the edges like parchment at a flame. Millie wanted to laugh; no wonder her husband had roared so. It was a voice that commanded humour, whether she meant the effect or not. 'And you couldn't even afford me one in return!'

'I'm sorry,' Millie reddened, 'I wasn't sure-'

But the woman cut her off, pulled forward her long plait, and set it over her other shoulder.

'Only playing with you, petal, trying to poke a smile into that wan face of yourn. Now yours is a face that's accustomed to smiling. So why the change of affairs?'

Millie was struck by her forthrightness. Though Alice could ask her anything, and very often did, there was a dance they performed as she led up to the question she desired to ask, encircling associated issues until she arrived at the nub. Here, with this doughy woman with her curranty eyes, Millie felt ambushed.

'Oh nothing, nothing at all. I was worrying that - Our tickets... I wasn't sure,' she stuttered. 'The usual; terribly dull stuff and nonsense,' she finished quickly. She wished to use her shawl as the woman was using hers, stippling the ends across her pink cheeks to remove her sheen, but she daren't. Mam wouldn't have stood for it; she hated girls fiddling with their hair, their cuffs, their hems. And grown women that did it? The devil would find work for idle hands to do, she'd quote, and Millie, when she was older, realised her mam didn't use the phrase in the same way as others did.

The woman blinked and nodded, but Millie could see that she didn't believe her answer. 'Where are you going?' the woman asked instead, and Millie frowned.

'To the Canadas?' Millie hesitated. Weren't they all?

The woman nearly spat out her ale.

'Well, of course, petal, we all know that, we're all a-going there.'

Millie looked about her, considering it properly for the first time: all these people, to the Canadas, for good. What made this new place's reputation that all these people were leaving their homes on such a scale?

'But where in the Canadas?' the woman pressed.

Millie looked at her blankly. Her mind felt like wool in warmed water. She watched Johnny's hand flutter in the air as he spoke. He had only said the Canadas; there was no talk of names of villages or towns. But it was plural: the Canadas. There must be more than one place to choose from.

'Why, he ain't even told you?' The woman scowled at Johnny. 'I bet he's telling my Adam right now, but he doesn't even think to tell his own wife!'

'It's not like-, no, it's not. I, to be honest, it's my fault. I hadn't even thought that far ahead.'

'That far ahead? It's your life, petal,' she said, leaning forward, leaving a clammy hand on Millie's forearm. 'No talk of Toronto, or Halifax, or…?'

'Halifax?'

'Nova Scotia, my new friend, Halifax in Nova Scotia, a town full of shipyards and our Scottish brethren. The natives are sick of them already, I've no doubt. You know Halifax in England then?'

Millie nodded, felt her hair sag in its pins. 'Yes, it's not all that far from where I – we – live. Lived. Not that we'd ever been.'

'Not far?'

'Do you know Saddleworth? Near Oldham as the crow flies, but it takes some effort by foot or horse.'

'Hilly, then? Yes, the name rings clear, if only – Saddleworth. Say, isn't that the place of those godawful murders? Those poor fellas left for dead in their own home? An inn, weren't it?'

And Millie froze, felt the warm water of her mind harden

to ice, the creak of it along her spine as that stiffened, too. Her ears pulsed, blood thickening, great shards damming the flow to her heart, her lungs, her throat closing in.

'Oh dear, oh dearie me. You knew them, petal?'

Millie nodded, tried to nod, summoned her head to rock on the great cold stump of her neck.

'Now I'm sorry for that. I'm sorry for your loss. Let's have a wee sip of this,' and Millie bent her head to the stranger's glass as her warm, bready hands stroked warmth into Millie's arms and shoulders. 'Now I shouldn't have brought that up, should've realised what a small world we live in! Aye, small enough to board a ship and sail to a whole, new one! Tell me instead: when were you married?'

It was true, then: the deaths of Granda and Tom had made famous the name of her home, ringing like a bell from pump and well, to public house, to church gathering. She pictured Mr Dunne pushing open the door to the bar. *This is where the intruder would've arrived; the upturned tables and chairs were flung over in a fit of passion!* Granda wasn't a gossip, a show-off. He'd have hated being known.

'Last week,' Millie croaked.

'Last week! Why, you'll be with child by the time we dock, then!' And the woman winked again.

'Haven't you any childer?' Millie asked because she felt she ought to, though didn't really care to hear the answer.

What did Dunne do, now that Bill O'Jack's was emptied of its belongings? Were people still arriving by the cartload, to spot Granda's blood on the cold stone flags?

'Oh no, not us,' the woman said. 'They flow out of me like water, the poor things.'

It took a moment for Millie to realise what the woman

meant, and she came to.

'That's dreadful; I'm so sorry to hear that.'

'Don't be; it's how it's to be. And there's naught we can do about it, so there's no point fretting. Now, say we have another ale, and you can tell me your name?'

Annie and Adam Henderson had lived in Annie's father's cottage in Oswaldtwistle with her father and two brothers. Millie liked the way in which she said the name of her hometown through her teeth. There was too many of them, she had said, especially once her father remarried and the new wife brought forth her children, too. When Adam had heard about the ships leaving from Liverpool, Annie was quick to encourage him.

The woman played with the end of her plait as she spoke. 'Oh yes. There wasn't anything to stay around for.'

Millie marvelled at her ease. Did she not care for her family? When she seemed so warm!

'Oh!' Annie said suddenly, throwing her arms wide. 'We're off! Come on fellas, we mustn't miss this!' She grabbed Adam by his hand and, Millie and Johnny following, wound their way through the dark corridors to the small pools of light that indicated the opening to the deck. They could hear the cheers of the passengers above them, the stamping of boots and the clapping of hands. The cold metal rungs of the steps upwards clanged with hurried feet. It was a cacophony, a chorus of impatience, apprehension.

As they broke free of the gloom, they shielded their eyes. Men threw up their hats, their children. Women smiled, but wrung their hands, their foreheads creased with worry. Tobacco smoke lifted from them like steam and the clouds mimicked the phenomenon, high above, fleeting.

'We're off! We're off!' Annie shrieked, her hands high above her head. Her little mouth widened, and Adam threw his arms about her as the noise of the other passengers grew. Millie's ears rang with it.

The ship was moving, but Millie couldn't feel the sensation beneath. It was like standing still, but with the dockside receding and the waving hands on the shore growing smaller. It wasn't an unpleasant sensation. Not yet, at least.

'Goodbye, goodbye!' Annie called, and Adam joined her enthusiastic waving.

The city, from the boat, seemed larger than Millie had realised when she had been there, on foot. It was tall, built up. There were many windows, opened at odd angles; spires peppered the skyline. She heard a bell toll morosely. Birds soared past on high, wheeled and cawed, looping in the air, while at the dockside, carriages rolled away. The people looked like insects, toiling back and forth. It seemed so pointless from her viewpoint, so futile. One journey this way, another that, and so little to show for it.

The cheers fell, replaced by an animated chatter, children's outbursts hushed by their parents who proceeded to talk over them. The gulls coiled back to shore, and the wind whipped at the flags, high on the cables and ropes above, as loud as the looms.

'Well, that's that then,' Johnny said, finishing his pint. 'Another?'

'Aye,' Adam replied, and Annie threaded her arm through Millie's as they moved back to the bar.

You don't mind?' she nudged Millie in the ribs. 'Adam says I move awful quick, but I tell 'im that for all we know, I might be dead tomorrow. And you don't mind, do you?'

Millie wasn't sure if she meant her arm or the ale. She wasn't sure she wanted either, but allowed herself to be swept along.

Adam and Annie had left the bar citing tiredness, but Johnny hadn't yielded. His hand was on the second glass even before he had finished the first. Millie took him by the arm.

'Slow down,' she hissed, but Johnny refused eye contact, instead looking after the path Adam and Annie had made through the crowd. She knew they should have followed them, taken their leave past the swaying hammocks to their own dark alcoves. He shook off her hand. 'Take less drink, Johnny. There's no need for this. You'll feel so unwell tomorrow. And there's the seasickness to think of.'

His words were drowned in the beer he swilled down. A sweat appeared at his brow. She saw droplets run into his eyebrows.

What was she supposed to do? Stand here like his keeper, accompanying him as he drank himself into a stupor so she, aid, carer, helper, fool, could help him back, undress him, see to his head in the morn? She looked about her. Only one woman remained, a sharp featured woman with her petticoat showing. She laughed raucously at the bar. A man cupped her breast and her group laughed again. Millie looked away.

A fiddler started up in the opposite corner. He was an old man, older than Joseph Kershaw, and poorer, too. His beard made a cushion for his chin against the wood and his boots rose away from their soles, open mouths accompanying him in song. He had thrown down his hat for coins, but the men had turned their backs to him, talked loudly. He played faster than Joseph, scratchier, his right hand barely gripping the bow so it looked as though it could fall at any moment. It wasn't as beautiful a sound, it didn't have the depth to it that Joseph had, but still Millie listened.

'You'll have a dance then,' Johnny said, finishing his glass. He grasped her by the waist, but she pushed him away.

'No, Johnny, not now. Not here.' The men they knocked into scowled, frowned, turned back to their laughter and vowels.

'Come on, I know you like to dance, and there's a fiddler a-playing,' Johnny said, but Millie's hand slipped out of his like a fish. Still his eyes roamed about the walls, anywhere but her face.

'No,' she said, low and quiet. His feet crashed into hers and the momentum sent her into the back of a young lad.

'Watch it!' she heard him yell, but she didn't make for an apology.

'I'm going to bed,' she said.

Johnny stumbled, righted himself, looked about for his glass. 'You won't go alone. Stay here until I'm ready.'

'No,' Millie said again, and swallowed hard. The rims of his eyes had reddened.

He encircled her wrist with his fingers, but his grip was weak, clumsy. She turned on her heel and began to weave through the crowd, ducking under arms, shouldering past men that sweated and gestured. Their tongues were ale-slowed; once they understood that she was a young woman alone, she had passed before they had chance to comment.

The corridors were quieter, the shadowy forms of sleeping bodies at their edges. Millie didn't care to look too closely. She focused on the route ahead. Left, right at the pipe as tall and as wide as a tree, rumbling. Their berth was then fourth on the left, the shabby curtain no shabbier than any of the others, but she feared the fleas it harboured and pinched it away with the very tips of her fingers. She wouldn't change into her shift; not now, not without Johnny. She would instead draw the sheet to her chin, clamp her eyes and jaws shut as though she were already dead. Sleep, sleep, sleep, she chanted to herself, don't think of anything else, not Johnny, not this ship, not the Canadas. Sleep brings strength, and she needed an arsenal of it.

14

She woke surprised to find she had slept, and undisturbed. Johnny faced away from her, his bulk flattened by the coarse blanket; his hair tossed this way and that. She leant in to him and smelt the farmyard smell of beer, of Bill O'Jack's. Though Millie had seen him take a drink often enough, Granda rarely smelt the same. Tobacco and pipesmoke were stitched into his fustian and fingernails. Despite scrubbing his fingers, Granda's had remained the same brown-yellow as sickly babies, of the tobacconist who had beckoned to Johnny. She thought of the gentlemen she had seen leaving their carriages in Liverpool, unsheathing their hands from gloves, and passing them to their men. Did their footmen, butlers, and serving men hold their pipes to their lips for them, too? She couldn't imagine a mill owner with stained fingers. How would he hold the cloth?

Johnny rolled towards her, opened an eye.

'Morning, sailor,' he whispered, smoke grating at his words. 'A smile!' He touched her bottom lip with his forefinger and traced the line of it. Would he like it if she stained her mouth red for him? He scooped her closer; wound his arms about her, so she understood her thinness. If she could have more meat in the Canadas, then she may have the chance of looking less like a child. 'And you're in your clothes? What, did you fall asleep the moment you climbed aboard without me to supervise?'

Johnny whispered again, his voice cracking. He smiled this time, and she thought fleetingly of the women in the mill, how they had spent afternoons describing his smile, how he closed his eyes when he laughed, the bright red of his mouth. How they hoped to make him laugh. Their husbands, brothers, and fathers, too. But they had all decided, conceded, that it would only be Millie who had the chance. A wife to make him truly, wholly happy. And here she was.

'Well, we'll have to change that,' he said, picking at her stays, and she hoped the man who lodged beneath them had gone to seek his breakfast.

The number of bodies in the corridor had grown, most huddled under blankets, but many stretched out in their clothes, their eyes gently shut. There were more tickets than beds, it seemed. Two young children, barefooted, chased each other.

'Sea air will keep us well,' Johnny said, leading her up the steps to the deck. She shaded her eyes at the brittle sun's glare, the cloudless sky that only amplified it. Still, large birds circled them. They looked back to shore. Whether the land they saw was Liverpool, it was hard to say; it had melted into an indistinguishable mass, like wet wool drawn out across flagstones. How sea captains knew that to be England, she could not understand.

'Millie! Johnny!'

Annie had a darning needle in her hand. 'Well, this is already my last thing to mend. I'll be ripping holes in our clothes to mend them soon enough; we'll go stark raving mad on here, I tell you.'

Adam took out a grimy deck of cards and gestured to Johnny.

'Say we leave the boys to it and have a little parade about this deck of ours, Millie?'

They walked to the perimeter of the deck, where the sea could be seen through the uneven gaps between the planks. It was green, then blue, then grey, then green again. White suds cropping and peaking, dying away, then rising, unprovoked. When Millie had pictured the crossing, she had imagined seasickness, crouching over pails and tiny children clutching their stomachs and wailing for their mamas. She had imagined sideways waves and huge seabirds, big enough to carry her away. But this sea was calm, and the sun tried its best. She hoped it would stay that way.

'What brought you aboard this great adventure then, Millie-May?' Annie asked. She couldn't leave her plait be, it seemed; if she wasn't picking at the ends and retying it, she was tossing it over one shoulder then the other. Millie wondered whether to grab hold of it and lead her about the ship like an animal. It would give Annie's hands some rest, if nothing else.

'It was a wedding gift,' Millie answered, and immediately felt the fool. A wedding gift? Who was she, Queen Adelaide?

'Oh hark-a-monkey! A wedding gift? And what a gift! From whom?'

'From Johnny,' Millie said quickly, reddening. 'It was his surprise for us. A new life.' And when she put it like that, she wondered at her ingratitude. It *was* a gift; it was an opportunity. 'Mam, and Jane and Tudor, my siblings, they'll join us later.' Her face felt hot; surely Annie could tell a falsehood when she heard one. But saying it aloud at least made her feel better; it made it feel a possibility. That she would see her family again.

'My, as sweet in the heart as in the face!'

They leant against the rail that separated boat and life from sea and death. Tudor had revelled in telling Millie that the cold of the deep sea would shock a man's body into death far sooner than drowning would. The breeze was more playful here, teasing their hair and skirts, cartwheeling across their forearms and raising their skin into goose pimples.

'I wonder what's down there?' Annie said, leaning further. Her shape made a silhouette across the water.

'Whales, sharks, certainly a mermaid or two,' Millie said.

'Those poor mer-people! Imagine being caught up as a fish! You should never get the stink out!'

'I shouldn't think they notice.'

'Like the Oswaldtwistle fishmongers, the poor sods. The only women that marry into those families have come from fishmonger families themselves.'

Two ladies paraded in front of them holding parasols over their heads as they leant together, talking gently. Their full skirts swept the dirt, hushed against the wooden boards. Their skirts were too heavy, too stiff about their crinolines, Millie supposed, to hold them up, away from the spray splattered decking, too much effort for the creamy white wrists she could glimpse poking out from the sleeves that ballooned from the shoulder. The two ladies walked slowly, assuredly, and were not roused from their conversation by the bonnet ribbons whipping about their faces. One gown was a light brown, a pattern across it that Millie couldn't quite decipher. Ferns, maybe, or grasses. The wearer seemed older than the other perhaps, fuller at the waist, but their faces could not be seen for confirmation. The second gown was an impractical dove grey, soft and sure to stain.

'Now look at them!' Annie whispered. 'Flashy and thin, set to break. They shan't last ten weeks here.'

'But a man told Johnny that they have fine feather beds and kitchens aboard. I think I should manage if it were me.'

'Ah, but what when they get to the Canadas? Those harsh

Sophie Parkes

winters?'

Millie was certain that there would be more of the same, with the finest wool and fur. The rich only went where they knew they could expect the same luxuries as home, and she thought of the Mellwoods in their phaeton, the younger staring down at them from her seat before her mother told her to stop.

Despite the wind, the ladies' necks were exposed, their shoulder blades visible at the tops of their gowns.

'Why, they must be clumst! They don't know what they're missing; they could have shawls like ours!' Millie exclaimed, holding out hers, the wind whistling through the holes and teasing its tired ends. 'We're quite warm beneath them.' She fastened hers around her, squirreled into it. 'I wonder why they're here, on this deck? I'm sure that man told Johnny that the rich folk kept to their quarters. If I had plucked ducks for dinner, I shouldn't come about here.'

'And that's why they do it, my Millie love,' Annie answered. 'They can leave their sumptuosity, all the food of the high seas, and take a look at us like we're animals in cages, dirty and wanting. Then they can retreat, telling tales of ghastly men begging for bread and dirty, barefooted children, and shudder, being thankful for their lot.'

'I hope they truly are thankful for their lot,' Millie said.

'Well, I wouldn't change places. Look how slowly you have to promenade about! I think a bairn could crawl faster, a tortoise.'

Millie smiled and watched the two women reach the railings and look overboard to the sea. She wondered what they were talking about so softly, out of the way of their own class. Perhaps they, too, were talking of their menfolk and what the Canadas would bring. Perhaps they, too, had to leave parents behind, siblings; perhaps their husbands had purchased their travel without their knowing. The only thing that kept them sane was their friendship. Those low, snatched conversations which reminded them they were not alone.

Annie beckoned for them to pass the ladies quickly. Millie fought the urge to look over her shoulder at their faces, to determine their ages, whether they were troubled about leaving England and everything they knew.

'I must ask, Millie-May, but those crimes in Saddleworth: did you know owt of them?'

She had never been asked outright, for the women at the mill had already known. Mr Dunne had done that job for her.

'Oh Lord above,' Annie continued, her voice lower, the sing-song removed. 'I knew I shouldn't ask such things. You have turned as white as that surf down there. You knew 'em, didn't you?'

Millie nodded, trying out the words she could use to answer. None seemed to fit and her mind slowed, her hands began to shake. She was unfit even to describe her poor grandfather and uncle's fate! She should not introduce herself a relative, she could not honour their legacies. She saw Granda reduced to a simpering bundle of clothes in the corridor, easily mistaken for sacking; her uncle as though he had been struck by a bolt of lightning. Could she even remember what they looked like before that day? She saw her Granda's coarse white whiskers, his red kerchief. And Tom had been reduced to a broad-shouldered silhouette, more Johnny's shape than her uncle's. Would she forget them entirely?

Millie could hear Annie's talking, could feel her grasp at her hands and lead her away from the railing. There were footsteps near the ladies, perhaps? She and Annie sank to the deck.

'I shouldn't have asked. I shouldn't have. I've been warned my mouth will lead me into all manner of mischief, and now it has.

And quite innocently, too-'

Millie held up her hand to silence her. She needed to listen to the sounds of the boat first, the background sounds of the childer playing and the women talking, the wind snapping the sails. Then she could let in Annie's talk, listen and respond.

'I'm sorry, Millie, and we have known each other for such a short time. I didn't mean to cause you such suffering.' Annie's plait hung limp along her back. Tears welled.

'It was my Granda, Annie, my poor Granda and his son, my uncle, Thomas. They were at home, alone. And we have no reason for it, why anyone should want to... do *that*. At all, but to my poor Granda.' Millie breathed deeply through her nose. Her trembles began to cease. She felt the heat of the small key in her waistband. She was sure that it glowed red when she was reminded of Granda and Tom, as red as the blacksmith's wares when set to heat. It didn't, of course, she knew that, but she also knew that God would remind her of her burden for the rest of her life. She would repent, that she knew.

'I'm so sorry,' Annie repeated.

'Aye, but it is done now. And we are here.'

They listened to the seabirds chatter to each other overhead.

Johnny and Adam were silent, brooding over their cards, when Millie and Annie returned. The news about Bill O'Jack's had sent Annie quiet, but Millie could see that Adam's silence made her uneasy. She set about filling the space with words.

'I must occupy these hands, Millie, else I'll find them – well, He knows where. Have you any darning? Perhaps we can do it together?'

Millie replied that she would bring some with her the next time she went back to the berth; for now, she was content at sitting quietly and in the sun. Annie's eyebrows pumped at that and promptly she began to interview Johnny as she drew out a stocking for darning. Her stitches were spidery, inelegant.

'And what kind of work will you be after, Johnny?'

'A sawmill,' he replied. 'Timber. There'll be plenty of it. Clean work; heavy, but clean.'

'We've been talking about that already, Annie love,' Adam interjected. 'He sounds like quite the merchant back home in those damp hills; quite the squire. We'll have high hopes of you in the new land, Johnny Barkwell. It won't be long before he'll be owning some kind of enterprise-'

Millie thought at first that Adam was teasing him, mocking Johnny for his ambitions, but he neither winked nor laughed. Adam was already lining himself up to be first in Johnny's shadow.

Annie agreed, as though she was regularly consulted on such matters as timber and forestry and sawmills. 'A sawmill for Millie. Ah yes, now Johnny Barkwell will see to that. He'll be running the place, all these men doffing their caps to him, and you two will be living like royalty, all the riches you could wish for.'

'No riches, thank you,' Johnny said, shuffling his deck. 'I'll be happy as long as we're fed.'

Millie couldn't identify the game they were embroiled in.

'What, you mean you wouldn't enjoy those fine clothes and those carriages, all the meat you could wish for, and men to bow low every time you but laid an eyeball on 'em?'

'I couldn't imagine owt worse,' he replied. He stopped and looked up, first at Annie, then at Adam. 'For to be rich is the cause of woe.'

'The *cause*?' Annie set aside her stocking.

'To be rich,' Johnny said, placing two cards down confidently and watching Adam's face, 'is for others to be poor.'

'But all men would trade places in an instant,' Adam said, placing his cards down in retaliation. 'Everyone knows that. It's just luck, or bad luck, depending on which side of the river you're born.'

'And that luck, or lack of it, should govern you for the rest of your life? No matter how hard you work, how hard you pray, how little you drink or beat your wife?'

Millie felt her cheeks flush red, but nobody watched her; the cards, and the hard, grooved hands that held them, retained their attention.

'Aye, it's not right, Johnny m'lad, but it's the way of the world.'

'Well, it shouldn't be. And it might have been the way of the world in Yorkshire, in Lancashire, in the whole of King Bill's England, but it shan't be in our new world. I shall see to that.'

"ark at him!' Annie laughed, nudging Adam gently. 'We've a martyr in our midst.'

'Oh, I don't intend to martyr mesself,' Johnny said, revealing his cards.

Millie could see Adam was now tasked with beating Johnny's hand with whatever lay in his. Secretly, she hoped Adam would; Johnny seemed so quietly sure of himself.

But Adam flinched, chuckled, and threw down his cards. Johnny didn't even crack a smile at his own victory, as though it was guaranteed. Instead, he dealt the cards again.

'Well, what about you, Millie? Have you got such lofty ideas as your fella here?' Annie asked. She still seemed to be darning, but Millie couldn't see where she needed the extra stitches. Perhaps she was going over the same stitch for something to do. It was an awful waste of thread.

'Oh, I don't know,' Millie shrugged. 'I haven't given it much thought.'

'You haven't given it much thought? It's your new life!' Adam said, taking up his pack.

'Shhh, leave her be,' Annie said in one breath, swatting her husband's arm. 'She's only young. Young people don't give much thought to the future.'

Millie winced. She wasn't that much younger than Annie, and she cared deeply about the future, about her future. Marrying Johnny had been the first steppingstone in the life she had imagined would stretch out before them. Then one of those cottages set back from the lane, Chew Valley Road, with a flowerbed out in front. She could have trained roses around the door, like a real country wife. Children at her heels. They'd have taken a lodger if they'd needed to; they'd have kept a wheel in the cellar or the garret to turn once she was in from the mill. He'd have kept on with the traps. It would have been a simple life, but she had imagined laughter, love.

And what now?

'I could grow things,' Millie thought aloud.

'Yes, yes, you could, my petal,' Annie replied, tapping Millie's knee. 'I'm sure you could, though it won't be the easiest way to make your fortune.'

Millie and Johnny soon settled into the routine of the steerage: rising as late as their bellies would allow, finding food and water, and eking out the day with Annie and Adam. The evenings would lapse into the bar and Millie quickly began to loathe that sweaty little box, where laughter grew louder and in frequency, and Johnny seemed to forget they had a small, finite amount of money they could depend on until they were able to find work on land. He chased one ale down with another; spilled those belonging to others when his gestures grew unwieldy and had to repay them; and joined single men in their games, quite content to leave Millie in the company of Annie and Adam, who didn't remark on it. She grew weary of going to bed alone, picking her way over the bodies clustered in the hall and slapping back the hands that rose up to worry her skirts, and waking before Johnny and his scent of sodden straw and cereals.

It was the dawning of their third week that Millie lay awake, listening to the sounds of the women calling their children for breakfast. The meagre pebbles of bread counted out into their dirty hands. Johnny's mouth was open, his eyes shut though twitching, his dark hair pasted black to his wet forehead. Sleep sounded in the rasps and heaves that alternated between his mouth and nose. She shook him awake.

'Johnny, I can't move while you're here, snoring. And it's late, anyway. Let's go and find bread.'

He blinked slowly, revealing bright white eyeballs shot through with red. The watery rims where lashes met skin were angry, and she angrier still.

'Come now, Johnny.'

He slid himself upwards, plucked at the collar of his fustian. He looked about him, dazed.

'What's the matter with yerself?'

'*You* are what's the matter. All this ale.'

'Ah, the Temperance has come to find me after all.' Johnny lowered himself back down to the bunk, closed his eyes.

'Johnny!' Millie hissed. 'Is this what I'm to contend with? A drunken husband every night of the week?'

'Yes, and why not? How often does a working man get to enjoy himself..?'

'Well, I shall have to amuse myself then, shan't I?' Millie reached over his body for the ladder. His fingers closed around her wrist.

His eyes still closed, his breathing even, he lowered his voice. 'Not without me, you shan't.'

She moved one bare foot over his, but his eyes snapped open and he pinioned it with his boot. She suppressed the cry of pain and focused on the tread of his boot, its pressure on her skin. It was nothing. She thought of Granda and his lips opening and closing, despite the blood, his blackened skin.

'So, I am to be a prisoner in my own bed?'

'Foolish girl,' he said, closing his eyes again and releasing her hand and foot. She fumbled with her hands and went down the ladder, ignoring the splinters that needled her.

15

Leaving Johnny asleep, Millie began to spend her days with Annie. They would meet soon after they rose, pooling their bread supplies and dreaming of the meat they would have in the Canadas. 'Extra fatty, it'd be, with all that blubber to protect them from the cold,' Annie told her.

Annie no longer asked where Johnny was, but Millie guessed she had asked Adam to rouse him, or at least entertain him before the evening's drinking began, because they were always together in the afternoons, when Millie and Annie would find them playing cards or smoking in a shady corner of the deck.

'The calm before the storm,' Annie had said once, watching Johnny, whose head still throbbed, for he occasionally reached up through his thicket of hair to press a temple. Millie hated Annie for that second: hated that she recognised Johnny's flaws, hated her for her husband's apparent lack of flaws, for their own loving relationship. And then she hated herself for feeling such spite and jealousy.

And Johnny had begun to look away when Millie appeared, to look out to sea when she spoke, allowing the conversation to die. Even when he came back to the bunk from the bar and clawed at her stays, he closed his eyes or, worse, turned her over so that her head beat the wall repeatedly and the water that trickled from its secret leak fell instead into her hair. Once, when she refused to turn and lay flat beneath him, she held up her hands to his face, took his jaw between her fingers. His eyes danced somewhere about her hairline.

'Look at me!' she said with urgency.

He smiled then and looked her directly in the eyes. It was a smile made stupid with ale. 'Oh, she's liking it, is she?'

'Johnny! I'm your wife! Please look at me!'

'Aye, and a pretty one at that. And ripe for the taking.'

She closed her eyes then, for he wouldn't take long and sleep would soon follow.

Once they had run out of clothing to mend, Millie and Annie taught each other rhymes they knew, games and chants they had learned as children, or looked out at sea, daring to imagine the beasts that moved in the waters below them. When the waves became fierce and the bile rose up in their throats, they steadied each other, wiping away the vomit that clung to their hair. When the ship's captain claimed it to be a fine enough day to allow passengers to dry their clothes on the deck, they washed their scanty pile together, tying their sleeves together to prevent them from flying away.

It was a Saturday morning – the tallies on the inside cover of Millie's Bible told them so – when, sitting on deck, they pretended they could see the first strip of land, the first rocky outcrop signalling the Canadas. Annie imagined a throng of small, curiously dressed people awaiting their arrival, waving and shouting with smiles on their faces. But Millie had smiled at that and told her it'd more likely be boulders of ice, cliffs of granite and no people whatsoever. It would be a cold, fractious welcome, like an old aunt who lived a day's walk away and reluctantly let relatives in her house.

'Your fella's an impressive one, Millie-May,' Annie suddenly said.

'What do you mean?' Millie frowned.

'It's *his* knowledge, *his* way,' she continued. 'People sit up and listen when he talks. Even I do, and I know a good talker when I hear one.'

Millie lifted her eyebrows. Annie obviously hadn't seen him drunk as much as she.

'He has his own flock, doesn't he? Wherever he turns! Adam's simply enamoured with him; I've teased him more than once.'

'Yes, I suppose so.'

'People take him seriously, see him as a man of his word.'

'Yes.'

Millie didn't know what Annie wanted her to say. Yes, she was right, it was one of the reasons Millie had always admired him, that her Mam did. She had heard Tudor showing off about his connections to Johnny Barkwell, to Ed and their other friends. At the time, she had felt pride, confidence. She could walk with her head high. He had chosen her, after all.

'But, if you don't mind my saying, my flower, that is, until he takes a drink.'

Millie shrugged. 'He's a man; he takes a drink.' She tried to sound as nonchalant as she could, but Annie narrowed her eyes.

'Now, there's no pretending with me, petal. We both know this is trouble. Has he always liked a drink?'

She was going to be lectured; lectured by a woman that only just made five feet in height and had a voice like a circus act. Millie wanted her to stop, to shut up, to mind her own business. What business was it of hers, anyway? Johnny was hardly leading Adam into trouble. No, that gangly man, with his soft brain and his soft heart, had his formidable wife to answer to, Millie thought, crossly, and gritted her teeth.

But she thought of the night of the fair, when Jane had found the broadside, and Johnny had hung between two men like damp linen on washing day. *Quite the Methodist there*, Jane had said, *taking full advantage of that Beerhouse Act.*

Perhaps Annie only wanted to help.

'Aye,' Millie said. 'He does, and he always will.'

'You've never thought of the Temperance?'

Millie snorted gently. 'He wouldn't entertain the thought. He's certain it's just another ploy to curtail the working man.'

Annie's eyebrows bobbed. 'Well, it is, really. Still, it's a shame, for it's not much fun for you.'

'I'm not sure anyone joined this ship for *fun*, Annie.' Millie didn't want to be rude, but Annie didn't know Johnny. She couldn't get the measure of him from six, seven, weeks at sea. Millie didn't fully know Johnny, it seemed, and she had known him all her life.

Annie ignored the comment. 'But you do seem somewhat – now, how can I say this? Annie, dear, do pay mind to your words – a little *afraid* of your husband. Perhaps afraid is too strong a word. *Wary* might be better; yes, *wary*.' Annie began to inspect her fingernails, pushing one nail under another to dislodge the dirt. She wiped each in turn across her apron.

Millie could hear her heart beat, feel it. It was as though she had summoned the ship's drummer boy to beat beneath her, the vibrations of the goatskin tickling her ears. She liked Annie, but she wasn't sure she could love her – not as she did Alice; Annie seemed so much older, wiser than Alice, and without the mischievousness. But she wouldn't see Alice again, not now. And Annie, well, they were destined for the same place, the same country. They could work together, they could share their difficulties.

Clouds had gathered thickly, resolutely, overhead.

'Well, aren't you wary of Adam?' Millie asked, her voice thin.

Annie burst out laughing and wiped her eyes with the corners of her apron. 'Of Adam? No, of course not! Why would you be wary of him? He's as soft as a damson in the down. I should think there were times when he's wary of my tongue, but that's about it. No, no, my, what a thought.'

Millie frowned.

'Oh, my love, I wish I had said naught at all. Your face is the very picture of the clouds up above, and I didn't wish to upset or confuse you. It was a mere observation, a watching of a man and his new wife, and I meant nowt by it.' Annie lay a hand on Millie's forearm and they looked down at it.

'I don't feel wary, Annie, not at all; I have known Johnny and his family all my life. I have always known I would marry him; I may as well have been betrothed at birth, like a lady,' Millie said, standing. Annie looked up at her, surprised. She shielded her eyes.

'Like a lady?'

'I am a new bride, Annie; I have no conduct book, just a few hasty whispers into my ear from a mother I shall never see again. I didn't choose to leave my home, my country. I didn't wish to make this journey. But I am, as my husband wills it so.'

She spoke faster now, her words gathering momentum, her hands drawn into fists.

'I'm so sorry, my petal, I don't mean for to cause you-'

'And here I am, nineteen years of age, having never left my village and now I stand aboard a large ship in the – largest – sea and I don't know where I am going. I don't know where I shall live, I don't know how we shall earn our money, I don't even have any money, for the coins I know are in my husband's pocket and he seems to drink them so merrily, and-'

'Millie, love-'

'Let me finish. And I have never met anyone who calls me love or petal or flower and who seems so earthly wise and earthly knowledgeable, and I have never felt such a fool.'

She pushed her hands to eye sockets, forbade the tears from falling. At her shoulders, she felt Annie's hands, hot even below the rolling sky and above the roiling waters.

'Shush now.'

'And my poor kin, my own dear father's kin. My Granda.'

She heard Annie inhale deeply.

She said no more.

Children nearby started to play a noisy game, clashing their hands together. Annie ushered them away.

'I am so sorry, my petal. What an unforgiving, cruel thing. I haven't been able to forget what you told me. I cannot-'

'And I have left them so quickly, so suddenly, left my poor mother to contend with dragoons and yeoman and coroners and auctions and other such things. And, and-' she cleared her throat, '-and I know not whether we shall ever find the truth.'

Millie saw Annie rub away a tear with a knuckle. The words died in their throats as they looked out to sea, the blues and greys competing so that sometimes it was difficult to discern air from water. Annie patted Millie's forearm, each pat growing longer, reaching her wrist, until she took her hand.

'Oh Millie,' she said, her voice small, 'what you have suffered, I could only imagine.'

'I wouldn't imagine, if I were you,' Millie replied, 'it's too vivid an image. It's only been five months, yet it feels like five years, fifty. I shall be awaking to that image for the rest of my days. I'd do anything to cast it from my mind, cast it out to the sea, for it to sink to the depths. For fish and worms and whatever else slithers down there to pick it apart, to eat it. My, I sound like a madwoman!'

She managed a smile, though Annie didn't reciprocate, and took out the key from her waistband.

'It's enough to make anyone take a trip to Bedlam,' Annie nodded. 'What's that?'

'Oh, it's just a key of Granda's. I needed some kind of keepsake to remind me. Else I think I really would go mad.' Millie stroked it, knotted and unknotted the dirty ribbon, then pushed it back into her waistband. She couldn't lose it; she didn't want anyone to take it. She had heard how hastily her Granda's stuff had been fought over at the auction.

'You're made of strong stuff.'

'What kind of stuff?' Millie asked.

Annie thought for a moment. 'Not wool, and not cotton; you've seen too much of that. Something friendly, though, so you won't be stone, nor iron.'

'Glass?' Millie proffered.

'Oh no, no,' Annie shook her head, 'too showy, not enough to it. You're practical. You're woody, yes, definitely. You can support a household; you can light fires.'

'Wood?' Millie laughed, throwing up her hands. Annie caught them again and drew them into her lap.

'Yes! Now there's nothing wrong with that. Natural, made by God Himself. Standing there, high on the hillside, observing everything that a-goes on, biding your time.'

'Ah, but what of those splinters?'

Annie pretended to examine the pads of her fingers. 'Nothing to worry about, just a sharp little reminder that you're there. Tells people – like that Johnny of yours – to treat you well, look after you.'

Millie drew still again, buried her hands in her armpits for warmth.

'And he is, isn't he? It sounds like he has your best interests at heart. Taking you far from turmoil so that you might start again, afresh, anew.'

Millie nodded once, quickly.

'Now if we can just find him something better to do of an evening. Why, there's a preacher tomorrow night.'

Millie couldn't help but laugh. 'Oh, Annie, a preacher? I was lucky to get him in front of one on our wedding day. He won't listen to a preacher when there's ale to be had.'

'I'll ask him then, and Adam, too. He can't say no to us.'

Millie shook her head. She wouldn't be one of those women, nagging and wheedling at her husband. He could do as he pleased, as far as she was concerned. He could have his fun, as long as he pulled himself together by the time they reached the Canadas. There – she felt liberated at that. She had made a decision.

'Thank you, Annie,' Millie said, turning to her. 'Thank you for spending time with me, asking after me, concerning yourself with my-' she searched for the word '-circumstances.'

Annie patted her hand, threw her plait over her shoulder.

'Now, now, Mistress Millie, you can't go all soft on me.'

But she grinned, showing a row of squat yellow teeth that reminded Millie of Saddleworth cottages in the morning sun.

Annie surprised Millie: she had been successful in encouraging Johnny along to see the preacher. He stood on a makeshift stage of boxes in one of the quieter ends of the steerage, and his wife or daughter – Millie couldn't tell which, as she seemed decades his junior, but had no likeness in the face – held a candle sombrely as he spoke, and stared straight ahead as though she had heard it all before.

He was the kind of preacher that spoke in waves, the sentences gathering pace so that the climaxes were lost in a rush of speed and spittle. His arms flailed as though waves crashed about him; his white hair stood up on end as his body shook at the command of the gnarled, hooked finger he used to point at the thirty or so people that had gathered to listen. She had heard better.

Johnny looked at the floor, while Millie looked between Johnny and the end of the preacher's finger, its blackened nail. She feared meeting the eyes of the preacher in case he recognised her, though she wanted to laugh at her self-importance: how would he recognise her? He spoke with an accent she didn't know; no-one but Annie had asked her about Bill O'Jack's. There was no connection to be made. The key dug into her flesh, caught the edge of her ribcage, and she imagined a bruise blooming. Good, she thought, she deserved it.

Annie and Adam leant together, the very picture of goodness; like a pastoral painting of a shepherd and his mate, and Millie curled her lips at the bitterness she felt at her throat. She realised she wasn't listening. Perhaps it was he who had mentioned shepherds. She watched him rage on, his words rolling in his mouth before he unleashed them, his finger steadfast and threatening; his wife or daughter beside him, stony-faced. If *she* wasn't listening, then how could she expect Millie and Johnny to?

The preacher came to an abrupt end. His mouth fastened shut, but he left his finger in the air as if it was its own being, no longer attached to him. Annie burst into rapturous applause, like a clattering of hooves over cobbles, and the rest of the party followed. Millie joined in but noticed that Johnny folded his in his lap. He raised his head and fixed his eyes on the preacher, as if noticing his presence for the first time.

The preacher nodded his head and summoned to his woman to light his path away from the dank corner of the steerage.

'Well, I haven't heard the likes of that for years,' Annie breathed, looking between them all. 'He was something special, now, weren't he?'

'What was he?' Millie asked, and she heard Johnny grunt, mutter something under his breath.

'Couldn't tell you. He weren't like the Presbyterian folk we get,' Adam said, 'but it didn't matter, love, did it? He was one of the best I've seen.'

Millie wondered at the quality of preachers in Oswaldtwistle. His performance had only inspired her for sleep, rather than the passionate, dutiful serving of the Lord. Was she turning into Jane, she wondered, suddenly? She had never found herself so critical as she had in the past seven weeks.

'See you i'n't morn,' Annie said, taking Adam's arm.

'See you i'n't morn,' Johnny repeated in a thin, weedy voice as soon as the couple were out of earshot.

'Grow up, Johnny,' Millie said, and set off back to the bunk.

16

'We've only another fortnight, petal,' Annie had cooed when she had seen Millie rub her stomach carelessly, and Millie felt embarrassment at having been caught. It was their job to be brave, to cajole the men when they were feeling low and hungry. Of course, Johnny had remained silent on the subject, had offered up his crusts to Millie, who had passed them on to Adam, an already gaunt man who didn't suit further fasting. He had taken to planning his first meal in the Canadas at regular intervals, exchanging the potatoes for more meat, swapping the cabbage for potatoes, then back again.

But today, this morning, Millie was hungry, hungrier than she could ever remember. She watched Johnny in his sleep, saw him open and close his mouth, and wanted the same for herself: to open and close her mouth, for her saliva to meet something else, something substantial, that she could swallow down and numb the hollow.

He licked his lips regularly to moisten them; she could see his eyeballs twitch. It couldn't be a restful sleep. She had known that face for as long as she could remember; there wasn't a time she could think of when Johnny Barkwell wasn't there. He had barely half-timed, working at the mill as soon as they would have him, but still, she would see him in the streets, at Chapel. As a boy, he would help his uncle shoe horses, and trapped with his father as soon as he was old enough to hold open a sack. She would see him then, a sack that almost grazed the ground when it was slung over his shoulder. He would always nod to her, but he only spoke her name when they were older, when he tried to catch her eye on her way out of the mill.

But now this face seemed different. There was a constant frown settled heavily on his brow, even in sleep, and the blood in his eyelids – red threads like glowing webs of tiny spiders – were visible. The jaw harder set, the lips chapped. Then there was that scent that made her think of the dray's cob. It stirred something within her: to kiss him, even to hit him. She wasn't sure. Occasionally he opened his mouth to chew the air, dreaming of the bread they had hidden in his pockets and her apron. They couldn't leave any in their berth; it would soon be stolen.

She was rarely truly hungry. She wasn't accustomed to eating regularly and fully, anyway; a lifetime at the mercy of the fields, of mill wages, of luck and fortune had seen to that. But there was something about being at sea: the salt in the air reminded her of the thick cut chips they ate at Wakes Week. That, and the rumours that the ship's stocks were running low, that containers of bread and biscuits had been allowed to grow green.

She worried the corner of her apron. She had mended it twice before, but each time the thread had come loose, slipping through tired, gaping holes. The fabric had also thinned; she could see the shape of its weft, the delicate threads that sat alongside each other, at right angles. This one – and she pulled the fibres away from each other, prised them apart – could have been made near to home. It was cotton; not the fine stuff to sell, but the odds and ends, the scraps that made the lower grade. It could have been made in Ashton, Mossley, or Oldham. Greenfield was mainly wool; though she had done some cotton in her time, she wouldn't be contracting cotton lung any time soon.

A small rectangle of her apron, tapered at one end, came away. Johnny slept still. She pushed the fabric onto her tongue, lapped it round and round her mouth. She could feel it soak in her saliva. It tasted of nothing. She had imagined an earthy taste, something of dust or mildew or mould, something to detect it had once been a living thing, a fibre. She summoned more saliva and swallowed it down, feeling it inch along her gullet. Her stomach quelled its noise, expectant.

Johnny didn't wake, but his face threatened it, an eyebrow lifting, the corner of his mouth tugging at the surrounding muscles. Was it hunger that did this? The drink?

'Millie! Millie!' She heard Adam, his feet clattering to a halt. 'Johnny! It's Annie!'

'What?' Millie threw open the curtain. Johnny was already behind her. 'What is it?'

'She has a rash. Oh, I'm so afeard – will you come?'

Millie felt a tug on her wrist. Johnny. 'You go, I'll stay here.'

She nodded and followed Adam, avoiding the limbs that sprawled out of bunks. Adam's strides were long where the decking afforded him, and Millie struggled to keep up.

'Wait!' she said between breaths. 'What rash?'

'All over,' he said quietly, snapping back his head. 'I've heard of this, a rash that covers the body, the belly, then they're gone. I heard that there were people on this boat with it, wrapped and thrown overboard overnight.'

Millie shook her head. 'No, Adam, no, that's just silly rumours. Can you imagine-'

'It's the truth of it. A fella told me last night, he'd been one to wrap 'em. Saw 'em plosh with his own eyes, right in, sunk beneath the waves.'

'Well, what was it? What caused it?'

He stopped before their berth. Millie could see the shape of Annie's foot pressed into the curtain.

'Typhus, they say.'

He threw it open and Annie's eyelids flickered. 'Now, what you been causing a fuss for, Ad? Millie and Johnny don't want to be bothered with this, some nastiness on my body. Who wants to see that?'

But for all Annie's protestations, Millie could see she was uneasy in her skin. Gingerly, she drew herself upwards and pulled down her neckline. Millie leant forward. Tiny red welts peppered her skin, like a map-maker's work in progress.

'Unpleasant, h'aint it?' Annie looked down at her feet, kicked them gently. 'For a few days. I just thought it were lice or fleas or something, something to be got rid of. Simple, like. But then we heard – Adam heard – about this typhoid thingummy, bodies being launched into the sea, and-'

'Now, now,' Millie cut in, 'let's not worry about that. But sea air, that's the thing, isn't it? Before we came away, everyone told us to get great lungfuls of the stuff. Let's get you out there, up on deck. That'll be the thing to do.'

Adam danced between them, guiding his wife's feet to the floor, clearing a path before them.

'I can walk. I feel fine, really,' Annie whispered, as Millie craned in to listen. She was reminded of the two rich women and how closely they had murmured. 'It's these spots. They make me itch, then scratch, then I feel hot, then I feel cold. I imagine mice scuttling across me, insects.'

Millie hushed her. 'We don't want to alarm anyone.'

'Yes, or I'll be in the brine before we know it!'

Millie saw Adam's ears colour. 'Don't be daft!' Millie laughed softly.

The deck was where most people spent their days now. With little of the journey left, passengers stood at the railings, scanning the horizon. Annie and Millie had done it themselves and knew that after time, with little food and water, the mind could conjure up the biggest and most welcoming of shorelines, even imagined people to welcome them. A blink and it was gone.

Adam led them past the throngs standing at the railings. Children, tired of their parents' pointed fingers, had begun to weave around the collected skirts and aprons. Men smoked and looked up at them as they passed. Adam found them a quieter corner, a metal column poking up through the timber against which Annie leant her back.

'Well, I suppose this will be me for the next week or so, 'til we dock,' Annie said quietly, fingering the ends of her plait. 'Doesn't hurt, of course, this sea air of yours, Millie.'

'And the sun,' Millie said, although the sun wasn't visible behind the thick cloud which had accumulated above them. 'It's always good to feel sun on your face.'

Adam didn't offer any words. He looked as though he couldn't remember how to form them, his eyes darting between them, his throat bobbing but silent.

'You can go, you two. You can't spend your days here with me and my spots,' Annie said, looking out to sea. 'They'll keep me company.'

'We can't leave you here, Annie, don't be foolish. And this sea air and sun will be good for us, too. Won't it, Adam?'

He nodded too quickly.

'Besides, it's much fresher out here. That stench down there – you get used to it after a while, but when you forget, or take stock and sniff, my!'

Annie nodded, too. Slowly this time, sagely. Millie wanted to shake her, shake her hard so the spots would fall off. She shouldn't be afraid; they were so close to their destination. Land would be visible soon. One of the official men in their official caps had told her, though he hadn't specified when and where, what she could expect. She had come so far.

'Have you had chickenpox, Annie?'

'This ain't no chickenpox, my petal. This is something different, something deeper. I feel funny with it.'

'And you feel funny with the chickenpox, too. I remember Tudor laid out before the fire, telling us nonsensical stories and wondering why we were all howling with laughter.'

But Annie didn't smile in response.

'It will be fine, Annie, honest.' Millie went to clasp Annie's hand, but she drew it away.

'You mustn't risk it.'

Millie sent Adam away and sat down next to Annie.

They watched Adam leave, his steps short and light.

'He couldn't get away quick enough, poor love! Never been good with illness, always fears the worst. Can you guess what 'e said when I pulled up my shift to show 'im? "What'll I do without you?" Lorks! Thank you, my love, for rallying round. It's to our menfolk we look to for strength, don't we?' Her laugh sounded different, lighter, as though she had forgotten to breathe.

Millie wondered what Johnny would say in the same scenario. Little, probably, and take a deep draught of beer. She took Annie's hand and held it gently between them. 'This isn't anything to worry of, I can feel it,' she said. 'Look how far we've come! The only way you'll be leaving is the way you intended: through the dock to a new life. But you'll need some blankets if you're to stay out here. I'll be back.'

Adam and Johnny were sitting in the corridor when she returned, two ales and a pack of cards between them, and it wasn't even midday.

'How is she?' Adam turned up his face. Grey skin didn't contrast well with his red hair. He looked deathly himself.

Millie allowed a shrug. 'I'm no doctor. I'm a poor nurse. But she has her wits, her breath, colour. She's strong.'

'That's my girl,' Johnny grabbed at her thigh with a smile, though his eyes remained steadfast on his cards. She prised his fingers from her skirts.

Adam looked into her eyes, searching. 'I think keeping her on deck is sensible. We should keep an eye on her in shifts.' His head wobbled on his neck.

'There's nothing to be afraid of, Adam. She'll need you at her side.'

'Like I need my wife at mine!' Johnny said, outstretching his legs and leaning back on his hands. His cards lay face down in a fan. Millie bundled up her blanket in her hands. 'And she is leaving so soon! Where are you taking your only blanket, sweet wife?'

She hadn't a witty answer, so she decided not to respond at all.

Annie was sitting as she had left her, back to the metal column facing the sea. The wind had teased her hair from her plait into a fuzzy halo. She had never seen Annie so calm, so still. If she wasn't talking, then she was fondling her plait, nodding her head, picking her nails, tapping her toes, gesturing with her hands. But now, her hands were heavy in her lap, her head resting. It should have been peaceful, serene, a moment of quietude, contemplation. But knowing Annie's usual demeanour, it was unsettling.

Millie draped the blanket around Annie's shoulders and she felt her shift, as though waking from a dream.

'You read my mind, love. I was just beginning to feel a little cool,' she murmured.

'That's a good thing,' Millie said. 'We want to do all we can to avoid a fever.'

Though she hadn't a clue, not really. There hadn't been an outbreak of typhus in Greenfield for years. Perhaps it was the weather. The villagers joked that even the rats weren't hardy enough to withstand the year-round mist that left a wet rattle in most lungs.

They sat there in silence. There was enough noise on deck without them adding to it. Two girls, no older than seven or eight, played an elaborate clapping game, which involved chanting and spinning until they were dizzy. Millie and Annie listened to them, watched as one of the mothers came over to clip the shorter one about the ears, bidding her to make less noise. The girl waited for her mother to take a couple of a steps back towards the other women before taking up the game again, as determined as before.

'Tell me, Millie, if you don't mind my asking, what did you do when you found your kin there, in the inn?'

Millie inhaled deeply and told her about thumping on the door of the cottage at Binn Green. 'To be honest, when I think back to it, it's not as though I'm really seeing it; it's more like a dream. I see myself running away, see myself coming back with the doctor.'

'And how did you feel afterwards, there in your heart?' Annie rubbed at her chest. 'How about now?'

'I don't know,' she replied, looking out again at the sea, the brazen monotony of it. She would happily never have this view again, she thought. She had seen enough water for a lifetime. 'I don't know what I think. I worry I'll forget them.'

'Did you cry?'

'I railed, Annie, I screamed and shouted, but that was only afterwards. I fainted, clean out on the floor; I slept afterwards for a time. Perhaps I needed to rest after seeing what I saw. I can't explain it. I couldn't go to work, and I would normally come in dreadful trouble for that, but for some reason, everyone was kindly to me. I think I might've even got my full coin.'

'I'd bloody well hope so! You are but flesh and blood!'

'And then one of these new constables visits me at work and that causes all manner of whispering but everyone's too afraid to say anything, and then before I know it, I'm married and, on a ship, leaving everyone behind.'

Millie watched her new friend think for a moment, bite her lip. Release it.

'Millie, why is life so cruel? Why did that happen to your poor menfolk?' Annie wrinkled up her mouth like overworked pastry. 'Oh, hark at me,' Annie said, 'you mustn't listen. How can you answer such questions? 'Ere, I've two biscuits; one each.'

Millie tried to chew slowly, but the biscuit was gone by her third bite.

Each day, Millie sat with Annie on deck until she could bear the evening's frigidity no longer. Then, when Millie's shivers grew to tremors, Annie would send her away and Millie would walk quickly past the makeshift bar, vowing not to look for Johnny, before climbing into her bunk. Once, the man who took the bunk below had grabbed at her ankle, but she had managed to kick him away. Another time he had a woman in there with him, so ale-addled was she that she laughed loudly and shouted words in the wrong order until Millie hissed at her to keep quiet and remember that there were children sleeping nearby. 'Aye, and there'll be more a-coming, if they keep at it,' another woman's voice added in the gloom and Millie flounced back against the bed, cursing silently at this vile environment and why the hell she was there at all.

Otherwise, her body had become accustomed to the nights in the steerage: the damp air that roused a chorus of coughs, the vomiting and sex. She had even come to think of it as fucking, such was the routine robustness of what she had heard and witnessed.

One night, though, she woke prematurely, as hot breath smothered her eyelids. She could smell the hops, the sugar, how his body craved water.

'Millie, my Millie,' Johnny breathed, his hands reaching for her arms, the edge of her coarse blanket.

'Please, Johnny, sleep now,' she replied, rolling her head away for air cooler and fresher than his.

'No, Millie, no,' and his face reached for hers, ballooned over her. There was moisture then, and she put out a hand. He was crying. There were tears falling from his eyes, dotting her cheeks.

'What's the matter?' She put her hands to his cheeks.

His chin slotted into the hollow of her neck. With a lurch, his boots groped their way across her legs. She pressed herself up against the wall, felt the chill spread across her back. He rolled a heavy arm across her middle like a buckle to fasten her in.

He was drunk, a leaden weight. He was hot and smelled of hops and barley and sweat. He was fierce and noble and drunk. He was young yet wise, strong and tall, a man that delivered more with his words than his fists. Yet he came to his wife for comfort and snaked his body close to her slightness when he needed it. She tried out a smile in the darkness, stroked his cheeks. This was what it was to be a wife.

'Millie,' he whispered, his words collecting wetly in her ear.

'Mmm,' she muttered with her eyes closed, stroking, stroking. If she made soothing noises, if she stroked him, he would sleep. That's how it worked with animals and babies.

'Millie,' he whispered again.

'Yes,' she replied, her eyes still closed.

'I did it,' he said plainly to her ear.

The amount of drink: she was pleased he recognised it was an uneven path to ruin. He had memorised the lessons as well as she. She could forgive one or two. Men needed to loosen, to relax. This was his explanation, his apology. All would be well tomorrow. They could be true man and wife then, happy and laughing, a shared private language, like Adam and Annie. Finishing each other's sentences, knowing what the other would say. She wiped away his tears.

'You'll be joining the Temperance next,' she whispered back. She listened for his smile.

'No.' He reached for her wrist and clasped it. 'I did it. William and Thomas are dead because of me.'

She felt as wide awake as dawn. Her ear burnt as though he had taken a taper to her lobe, and it had caught her hair, the flames eating, consuming her scalp. The smoke to her throat. She coughed, she heaved. She asked him *what, what, what did you say*, and attempted to sit up, but his arm pinned her back, dropped anchor. His fingers tightened at her wrist.

'They owed me, Millie. Your kin thought they could play me, but they couldn't.'

His whispers were as loud and as clear as the preacher's. Could everyone on board hear? 'They were bad men, William and Thomas Bradbury, as bad as old Nick himself. We all knew it; even your mam knows it. They got what they deserved; it was God's will. So now we can start afresh and anew, as we planned.'

She thought she could hear the sea roar now, wailing and howling. Though it may have been her own throat, it might have been God Himself. She couldn't see Johnny's eyes, couldn't see whether they were open or closed, whether they still swam in his tears, but still he gripped her closely, his game in a snare.

'You're free of them now. This Earth is free of them. A good woman, a good wife, like you, shouldn't have been tainted. I've rescued you, and we'll start again. Now let's sleep. Things will be better now.'

It was the ale talking; she'd never heard so many words from him. Yes, it was the ale; he was mistaken. Or, more likely, he was trying her for a laugh, a wifely test. It was the drink; yes, this jest, this caper, fell on deaf, naïve ears. Perhaps she should have laughed! Then they both could have lain there and snorted, like she reckoned Adam and Annie did, to keep their spirits up. This was a game! This was marriage! She would have to think of her own trick next!

But there had been no punchline.

Her mouth opened, but she couldn't engage her voice. She felt the pulse in her ears, the throb in her chest. She held her breath, and he pulled her closer still. She felt his muscles soften. His breathing quickened, gained its own voice, again in her ear. He was asleep.

Her eyes blinked of their own accord; she couldn't see for the twitching. *Stop it!* she commanded silently, but her eyelids refused to obey. She tried to raise an arm, but he had pinioned both prostrate against her. The key stuck to her like a scab.

Johnny had done it. Johnny. How had she not known? The inquest; he hadn't wanted her to go. Did others suspect? Mr Dunne at Bill O'Jack's, asking what they were doing there. *Checking my traps.* How hadn't she known Johnny trapped there, when others seemed to?

But this was no lark. She could see the truth now. God could see that heart of hers engorged with the truth of it, that what he had said so quietly, so simply, was true. It was the drink that brought truth, too; that spilled secrets or proffered gossip from the slackest of lips, when hands were too slow to stifle it. And she thought to the mill and to the shop and to the fields of home and wondered what words had escaped there, what eyes were watching him and her and wondering. That stupid Millie, ignorant of her Granda's fate, too careless, so eager to be married and be gone, to desert her family still in their widows' weeds, when little did she know, it was to the murderer – the bludgeoner, the marauder – she would be bound. And it was her comeuppance, her trifle fairly dealt.

He had said that Granda and Thomas were *bad men*, that Mam knew it. What did he mean? The inn was a remote one, frequented by the knowledgeable few; it was not a den of vice, but a modest place of comfort. It was more than drink they served; it was laughter, laughter so rarely heard elsewhere in the valley. The men that congregated there were too weak to fight and connive and plot; they weighed the same as they had as children, as their own children whom they laboured to feed. Her Granda had taken time to show her things: to skin a rabbit, to trim the hooves of a horse. Her uncle made his own tools and was known to sing when he thought others weren't nearby. How could they be bad men?

And what made someone a 'bad man'? One who kills another? One who drinks and eats to excess? One who takes his hand to his wife? One who doesn't take up his prayer book, but takes out his cards or his dice instead? She had heard Tudor and Ed laugh about an old shepherd in Springhead who was rumoured to lie with his ewes. Was he a bad man? And could women be bad, too? What about the women at the mill that exchanged the words in songs for rude ones and sang them loudly in the red faces of men? She had heard about the women that let men into their houses after dark for coin. They frequented the inns, too, but she had never heard anything like that going on at Bill O'Jack's. Would she know if it did? Would that make Granda and Thomas bad men by association?

She jabbed him with her shoulder.

'Wake up and tell me,' she growled, freeing an arm. She found his chin, shook it sharply. 'Tell me why they were bad men, why you did this to them.'

'And why, dear Millie?' he whispered. 'So, you can tell the authorities on board this ship? So, our story will be known to all? So, you can see me marched off the plank?'

'Just tell me,' she hissed, rubbing the tears away with both trembling hands. She shook hard now, as hard as she had when she had seen her grandfather's face, when she had witnessed her uncle's body lying there, his own blood pooling around him. When she had been alone and hadn't known what to do but run and cry and scream.

'I had a parcel of land from them. It was mine to trap and snare. They continued to use it; I caught them, the Platters caught them and reported it to me. I warned them, your grandfather promised, but they were laughing at me; they thought they could have my money and my game.'

'But that could have been resolved, that could have-'

'And it has.'

'With death?'

His hand seized her throat, pushed her to the wall. She didn't know whether the wall was wet or cold, but a chill seeped into her bones. She felt it in her clenched teeth.

'I didn't intend for them to be killed. It wasn't even my hand that did it. I asked another to go to the inn, to rough them up a bit, frighten 'em. Only it went too far. I should have known. Now, no more, be quiet. Do you want others to hear you?'

She inhaled as if to speak, but his hand closed tighter on her throat.

'You mustn't want others to know. You'll be alone in a foreign country, a widow. Go to sleep.'

He gave up her throat and settled a sticky kiss on her lips.

She breathed, wriggled her toes. She heard that people thrown from their horses moved their toes: if they could do it, they knew their body was still in working order. Though she shook and her teeth gnashed involuntarily and her fists clutched at her linen, her body was still in working order. Deep, even breaths helped her refill, inflate every pocket in her body. She counted her breaths, in and out, counted them like she sometimes did the rhythms of work. It numbed the mind, numbed the soul, but kept the body awake, alive.

17

But she did sleep. She must have, for she awoke. She had lain straight all night, as straight as death entombed. Her back ached from holding it stiffened.

She didn't need to remember what he had said; it hadn't left her.

Johnny was still sleeping, his face turned to the wall. She slid over him and to the floor and walked quickly away, wrapping her shawl tightly around her. She jabbed her pins back into her scalp.

An official touched the peak of his cap at her as she passed through the door to the open deck. He didn't betray any expression of disgust or concern. Though she was sure her face was blotchy where it wasn't wan, though her hair was hastily affixed, though her eyes stung small, he had perhaps seen worse during his time officiating the lower decks. She sidestepped to avoid two rats, racing and merry, their tails streaming out behind them.

It was bright, the smarting yellow light of a ship in the middle of the ocean, and though she felt it warm her arms, it was temporary. The sea air snatched the rays away, scooping up her skirts. It slammed into her then, forcing the breath from her lungs. She let it buffet her, wound her. She wouldn't try to stop it or fight back.

She leant over the rail and watched the ship – such a large thing – cut through the water elegantly. She was reminded of skates Tudor had borrowed from the preacher's son and fixed to his hobnail boots when the mill pond at Uppermill had frozen over. He had managed two or three steps before he had fallen to his knees, but those steps, short lived, had been as graceful as the ship shearing through the surf.

The smell of the salt in the seawater was strong. It surprised her, but it was unmistakeable. It tingled on her tongue. If she were to cry now, the salt from her tears would mingle with the salt in the sea. It wouldn't take much for her to push her body through the railing and let go. The captain, the officials, the other passengers. They wouldn't even hear her splash. Nobody would follow her, anyway. If Tudor had been correct, her death would be instant. It would be better than living with this knowledge.

She heard a sigh and turned. A few feet ahead, tucked behind some crate or freight or other, a woman was kneeling, her eyes downcast. She was either in prayer or washing clothing or some other small things. Millie took a couple of steps, leant forward. She could see a man in front of the woman, leaning back against the boxes. His eyes were closed, but his mouth hung open. His shirt was untucked, his trousers unbuttoned. The woman was kneading and scooping at the dark hair of his groin in a steady rhythm, her eyes also closed, her mouth hovering over him. Millie moved away, turned hot in the face, let the wind cool it.

This was not where she should be.

Not on this ship, not on the sea. She moved back to the door to the deck. The same official stood on the other side, watching the people as they rose begin to seek bread and tobacco and fresh water. She slumped down to the door, tucked herself behind a large coil of rope, and pulled the shawl over her head. She counted her breaths. The same air that Mam would be breathing, the same sunshine that Jane and Tudor would be feeling.

'Alright, miss?' She pulled her shawl from her head. A man in the same uniform as the previous official, but with a different whiskered face bent over her. She nodded quickly, opened her mouth and closed it again. 'Are you not very well? Alone?'

She shook her head this time and thumbed towards the door. 'Husband,' she replied. It was his turn to nod, and his gestures were large, overstated, as though he was talking to a simpleton. She feared he was. Her mind had clouded over, closed up, like she had seen the wildflowers do in the verges of the Holmfirth Road.

'You get back inside there, missy. He'll be wondering where you'll have got to,' he said, delivering his lines over his shoulder as he moved on in his rounds. She was relieved to receive an instruction. Her body obeyed. She scrambled upwards; her torso so light it could be sloughed off by the briny air.

She managed to command her feet to walk, but she was wondering where to go when she heard her name. She turned her head. Annie was standing in her corner of the deck, a broad smile across her face. She had Millie's blanket folded in her hands. Adam sat at her feet.

'I swear it be a miracle, Millie-May. Look!' She pulled at the neckline of her shift. The spots had crusted over, each with a fine crown of yellow. There were fewer of them. 'They're like this all over! I can't quite believe it. It was your salty sea air that did it!'

Millie pulled her mouth into a smile. 'I had no doubt.'

'But I did. I wasn't so very brave, my petal. I heard about those bodies being flung overboard and I thought I'd be next. I think you were brave for me.' She handed the blanket over. 'I am going to wedge myself in with my old mate, Adam, here, tonight for the first time in days. And I will look forward to that rank odour of feet and unwashed bodies and dirty clothing, and savour it!'

Millie watched as Annie and Adam smiled into each other's faces, took each other's hands. Adam had softened into his height again, lost his stoop. Millie felt faint and held out her hand to steady herself.

'You look terrible, my petal,' Annie said, pressing her tiny hand to Millie's forehead. 'Seasick?'

Millie shook her head, nodded. 'And poor sleep,' she said.

There was a shout, several shouts, and the people on the deck were pointing upwards. White birds flew overheard, circling, some swooping low as if to take a better look at the deck. Some were smaller, with black head and beaks.

'They look just like the ones we saw in Liverpool,' Annie mused.

'They will do; they're seagulls, too. It means land is close now,' Adam answered, holding his hat to his head.

More shouts, more pointing over the ship's railings. Annie and Adam craned to see, while Millie pretended, pushing her body to face the way they were facing, moving her head upwards when others did the same. It was like the Whit Walks; doing as others were doing.

The passengers were hugging now, kissing each other. Men began to throw their hats up in the air and children went about retrieving them, passing them back to their fathers in amazement. They had never seen them act so recklessly. Millie felt as though she was in a dream. She touched the key in her waistband.

'Look!' Annie said, grabbing her arm and pointing. Millie rose up on trembling tiptoes. There was something in the water, lurking up into the sky on the horizon. Even though she squinted, and it seemed tiny, she knew it to be something substantial. More pellets appeared on the horizon, grey like the whales she had been told about, but had never seen.

It was land.

Annie and Adam grabbed each other by the waist. Annie leant into his armpit, her plait falling down her back and swinging. People gathered on the deck, oozing out of the doors and coagulating under the shrieking birds.

'We've arrived!' Adam shouted back at her. Millie vomited onto the deck.

Their predictions about their arrival had been simpler than reality. Once the ship neared the land, it took days still for the ship to navigate the course of the St Lawrence River; days where Millie pretended, for Annie and Adam's sakes, to emerge from and return to her bunk. Instead, she made herself a tight nest of coiled ropes and old sails on the deck and folded herself in to sleep there each evening, hidden from view. And when the last of the passengers left the deck each evening, she listened to the wind whip the sails and catch in the thick sheath of coniferous trees that grew either side of the river.

Johnny had arranged for the deaths of Granda and Thomas. She pictured him meeting a man, men, in a quiet corner of Greenfield and instructing them to his plan. They would jeer, she thought, salivate at the thought of ensnaring two defenceless men with punches; the opportunity for real action, perhaps, when they were usually hired for a curse word to a wayward wife. They would have the chance to use weapons this time, to beat 'em good so there would be no prospect for reprisal, retaliation. Possibly, if they were bad men, as Johnny had said, then these hired heavies wouldn't have been hard to recruit. Perhaps they had already volunteered, well ahead of any wrongdoing. *When you need us, Johnny, you'll know where to find us.*

She saw men lying in wait, Tom singing to himself as he closed up the windows at the first howl of wind and cursing the missed opportunity for shooting. Granda filling up the jars of yeast and sugar and coffee in the cabinet.

She sat up. The deck was dark, deserted, though she could hear the noise of the steerage, the feet, the laughter, the beer. She would have to ask Johnny. She needed to know more.

She hurried back to the bunk.

He wasn't asleep in the bunk. His blanket lay in a heap at the foot of the bed. Briefly, her heart pounded. He could have found another woman, rolled into her berth like the man beneath them.

She lay down, closed her eyes. She would wait.

'What have we here?' he whispered, and she woke to his hot, sour breath, his stubble tickling her lobes. He still cared for his complexion, then, even when he had borne a confession such as his. 'It's the errant wife, returned.'

He drew himself closer, stroked her hair.

'You know, if all the women on this boat were lined up and I could have my pick of the lot, I'd still pick you,' he said, bending a hair about her ear.

She was still a wife, that she could not escape, even if the marriage into which she had entered had been built on an absence of truth. Nor could she escape the boat and its bunks. They were on course to dock within four days, so strangers had begun to explain to her excitedly. She could endure four more days. Then would come fresh air, new surroundings, decisions. She could take stock on solid ground.

His fingers slid along her jawbone. When they reached her chin, he stroked her earlobe. Something in her twitched, a feathersome flutter at the tops of her thighs.

'Stop,' she said, catching his rough fingers in hers. 'Tell me two things.'

'Why,' he said, propping himself up on his elbow, 'that's the most you've said to your husband for weeks! I'd begun to think-'

She put her hand between them and lowered her voice.

'Stop. Two things. Firstly, who is the man that killed my grandfather? I need his name. Second: where are we going once we dock? I want the name of the town, the house. I want to know what will be provided.'

'There's no need to tell you the name of the man. You don't know him.'

'Try me.' Millie drew his blanket from him, gathered it over her breasts. He wrestled part of it back. 'Tell me who did it.'

'Fine. It was Patrick Broadbent.'

Pats. Platts. Patrick Broadbent. She thought back to the fair, the man with Jerred Buckley that had held Johnny upright, the man with the blue lips. Yes, Alice had confirmed it. *A Broadbent, Paddy, I think.* Had he spoken to her? Jerred had seemed ashamed, but the taller man… She tried to remember. The taller one had looked her in the eye, she was sure of it. But his face swam in her mind, blurred. Could she be sure? And had he been there at the bar at their wedding? She thought back to Johnny at the bar, clearing his throat ceremoniously. Her ears roared, and she wished to be rid of it.

'Yes. I said you wouldn't know him.'

'Is he a local man? Where do you know him from?'

'The markets, the fairs.'

'So, he's a tough man for hire? He frightens people.'

'That's right.'

'Because you wouldn't do it yourself?'

'No, I told you: I tried to reason with your relatives, but the Platters caught them, time after time after time. I'm not violent-'

Millie huffed.

'I am *not* violent. I'd not have chosen for this to happen. But that it has? As I have said, we can start anew. People will not be plagued by *your family*'s immorality.'

'My family's immorality?' Millie coughed.

'You have been blind to it! Didn't you know? It was the reason your own mam's father didn't want her marrying into the family! Your dear Granda's beer was water more than anything else; your dear uncle's wenching was known the length and breadth of Saddleworth-'

Millie had heard nothing of it. 'Wenching?'

'You've never been told of Uncle Tom's larks? Now I'm surprised! If there were ever a woman not come home when expected, it was presumed old Tom Bradbury had her and the message would go out. "Try Bill O'Jack's," and there'd be smirks, of course, for he was no looker, was he? I don't think he'd bathed in his life, and those lugs? Torn and bitten from fights in the Bill. And your poor Granda? Well, he'd turn a blind eye to it-'

Millie's chest tightened. Her breath caught in her collarbones, couldn't make it to her throat. She gulped for air.

'He probably joined in. It was a pretty location for all that caper-'

'Enough!' she said, hoarse.

It was lies.

Her breaths came short and shallow.

'You asked a second question.'

Tom prone on the bed. The bed carted away by a man. What was his name? Smith, Dunne had said. Did he choose the bed for its reputation? The bed on which-

'You asked where we would go in the Canadas, what town? I'm astounded that you've finally asked. Well, at first we will lodge, and then-'

'Where?' She heaved the word out of her mouth like a fisherman's catch onto the deck.

He thought for a moment. 'Well, it depends on when we dock and how rough the weather will be. It's October, so it's not cold yet, but it will be.'

'You don't know?'

'Millie, we don't know what we will find, what lodgings, what work. Adam and I have said we can live together, us four-'

'Annie and Adam?'

'Yes, you'd like that, shouldn't you?' There was laughter in his voice, mocking.

Johnny had no plan. It would be left to chance, opportunity, luck.

'And I mean it about the sawmill. There'll be so much work that me and Adam, we'll be rich men afore too long.'

'And me and Annie?'

'Oh, there'll be plenty for you, too. With all those people, there'll be babes to mind, and clothes to wash, stoves to watch.'

'So, we'll be domestics? But I've never done that!'

'Of course you have,' he said. He shot a hand underneath her shift and squeezed her nipple. 'What do you think you do at home? And all those years with your mam and Jane; all that work you did for naught; you'll earn a bright penny in the new land.'

But Millie wasn't sure. She wouldn't know anything until she saw it with her own eyes. She brushed off his prying fingers and rolled over, though he soon pawed at her again. She relented and closed her eyes.

18

A collective lull had befallen the deck. Passengers stood at the railing and pointed at the squat wooden structures huddled onto an island in the middle of the St Lawrence River.

'That'll be the quarantine station then,' Johnny had said, his arms folded against his chest. Annie and Adam had moved closer to the railings as the wind picked up and threatened to lift Adam's hat from his head.

'Quarantine?' Adam asked.

Millie could see ant-like people milling between the buildings. 'When they see how healthy we are, we'll be waved on, no doubt.'

She wondered where Johnny had retrieved his information and watched as eavesdroppers passed on his news. He performed perfect nonchalance when they were asked to walk down the ramp and onto the island, preferring to thumb tobacco into his pipe than touch the soil in astonishment or throw his arms around his wife as other men were doing.

Millie's legs trembled so much she had to reach out for Annie's hand. Her body felt the ten weeks of momentum even when she stood still. It was as if the island itself had no anchor and floated freely in the river. But the grass looked no different to the grass she knew from Greenfield; the soil, too, which gave her comfort. It was only the island's staff, people browned in the unobstructed sun, that seemed different, speaking to each other quickly, in a gruff tongue she couldn't comprehend. She stuck closely to Annie as the ship's officials ordered them to take their clothes to the wash houses lined up along the shore, to enable the ship to be scrubbed down and disinfected by local prisoners, so the rumours abounded.

When Millie and Annie were reunited with the men, smoking in the shade of a tree grown crooked from the wind, Johnny told them that a small number of passengers had been prevented from boarding the ship. Typhus, he had said, looking at Annie, and there were nurses that would be treating them for it, and not wanting a penny for it, neither.

The ladies and gentlemen Millie had glimpsed at Liverpool, and seen on deck from time to time, had evaporated. She wondered if she could similarly disappear. But Annie kept her close, kept her mouth engaged so Millie's mind couldn't wander, and, in time, the officials rounded them up and set them back on board.

The steerage still dripped, and moisture hung in the air like it did on the moorland roads. Millie felt it in her throat and her chest and she shivered beneath her shawl. They were caught in the crowd that streamed towards the deck.

'No blue flag,' Johnny nodded towards the prow. 'They'd fly one if we weren't healthy. But they're letting us through now.'

The wind grew stronger as the shoreline of the new town became bigger, real. It seemed unthinkable: that, for the price of a ticket, a whole new place could be presented, opened up, offered; a whole new place with a multitude of languages, of different food and industry and customs. A whole new set of people with their own mills and homes and children, where other husbands drank in inns and other women made friends over sewing at hearths. And now she was here with Johnny.

She turned her face so she could watch him take in the new horizon. The city didn't look dissimilar from the city they had left, though the light, inky and dusky, felt unfamiliar. There was the same jumbled skyline, the same tall structures leaning together, but the buildings were sculpted from a sandier stone that Millie hadn't seen before, and the roofs more colourful, oranges and reds that seemed too bold to be natural.

She'd always thought that you could tell a bad man by his features: a hooked nose, too-close twitching eyes, mouths that down-turned in sour, spiteful smiles. Johnny's jaw was square but softened by his hair which curled at his ears; his grey eyes were equine, watching and waiting; his lips smooth. He was strong, capable, but in a way that told of protection rather than savagery. How was he able to have done what he did, and to her family, of all men?

He spotted her watching him and without turning his head, placed his fingers and thumb around her wrist and pulled her towards him.

She thought back to Jane in the ginnel at Cadishead Mill. It was Johnny, only Johnny Barkwell. She had done as her mam had wanted, as her father had always wanted. And now she was here, in the Canadas.

The Great Countess inched towards the shore. As they neared closer still, she could see that some of the buildings closer to the harbour – boarding houses, she presumed, and inns – had shuttered windows and had once been painted white, though they were in need of a fresh coat.

The people Annie had imagined were waving frantically, hats scrunched into their waving hands. Millie squinted. They didn't seem curiously dressed from here; there were the same dismal greys and browns of shawls over heads and shoulders, the same full skirts. Children wore full pocketed aprons and held on to each other, eyeing the ship. Carriages waited behind dozing, blinkered ponies, as footmen polished metal and closed newspapers as they awaited their cabin passengers. It was the same scene as Liverpool: men running between vehicles carrying packages and parcels; women rounding up children and holding them close.

The deck woke from its silent curiosity and passengers darted back to berths and through corridors to retrieve belongings and to gather family members. Johnny held his knapsack with one hand and her wrist with the other, and watched, as quiet as he would watch his traps. Her own case sat at her feet as her heart thumped and her legs felt weak beneath her.

Annie and Adam joined them, their faces damp.

'We couldn't miss this!' Adam said, his arms about Annie's shoulders. 'We'll remember this for the rest of our lives!'

'Aye, and look at that for a city! My, it rises up with *opportunity!*'

'And meat!' Adam laughed. 'Think of all the meat!'

They listened to whistles blowing. The gaps about them closed as the whistles grew nearer.

'Set to dock! No pushing, no running!' one of the officials barked. In the same tone, he switched to another language, spittle clinging to his whiskers.

The faces stared as they had in Greenfield, eyes wide, a judging kind of fearful. They formed lines either side of the steel ramps and watched as Millie, Johnny, Annie, Adam and the other passengers, stunned into silence, processed through.

'Lodgings and inns! Rooms and beds!' A woman sitting on

an upturned bucket paused from the fish she was gutting to shout. 'Lodgings and inns! Rooms and beds!' Millie saw Annie nudge Adam, and he slowed in his step.

'No,' Johnny said, ushering him on. 'A fishwife h'aint finding our place.'

As the lanes narrowed, the shouts grew louder and more frequent, caged by the height of the buildings. Passengers from the ship peeled away, conferring with the voices that shouted the loudest or with most confidence. One man with a gummy smile and shoulders that could barely be contained by his fustian held a small audience of animated people, none of whom Millie recognised from The Great Countess. His hands cut the air, but the words, the speed of them, sounded like music, and the men in front of him deliberated and their womenfolk stood back, looking concerned and hopeful.

A lean man, younger than Millie, stood back from the scrum, his back against a low doorframe. 'Come rest your head, I'll find you a bed!' he chanted through cupped hands.

'This one'll do,' Johnny said, nodding towards him. 'He's got all his teeth, for one.'

'We'll let the men do the talking, eh?' Annie said, holding on to Millie's hands. Millie watched as the man straightened up and jingled the coins in his pocket. The three of them spoke quietly, bringing their heads together. They smiled in turn, flashing their teeth.

'Leave 'em to it, Millie-May,' Annie said, pulling her close and spinning her round so that she faced the street. 'My, look at those littlies.' Three dirty children, easily under five and barefoot, held hands as they trailed behind their mother or elder sister, a girl herself, who turned periodically to shout an instruction which they seemed to ignore, staring instead at the others around them. 'Out at this time.' She whistled through her teeth and Millie wondered at it, for children were out at all times at home, clean and with clogs or dirty and without, and it could only be early evening.

'And look at these fellas!' she breathed, as bandy-legged men filed past with heavy ropes wound about their necks. Millie peered into their pails, but they were empty. 'Going for their catch, no doubt.'

'But it's getting on. Don't fishermen work in't morn?'

Annie shrugged, scratched at the crusts peppered across her wrists. 'Who knows what they catch in these waters? It might all be back to front. Their fish might be like our badgers. And how funny these buildings are! Why, they reach right up to the sky! So narra, I'm sure I could touch a cloud if it I were to get on top. Those tiny little windows...'

They craned their necks upward.

'Why go to so much effort to make a window if you're only going to make one the size of your fist? No wonder they seem to be able to dry only a pillowcase beneath 'em!'

A threadbare mule clopped past, its driver flicking a switch across its pointed rump as its hooves slipped between the cobbles. The driver leant against a stack of boxes and parcels, behind which two boys alternated jumping on and off the cart.

'How are they doing?' Millie asked.

Annie glanced over her shoulder. 'Still talking. Well, that fella is. Our two are listening. He best be honest, they best make a sound judgement. You hear of these things...' she trailed off, and Millie shuddered. If Annie was anxious, then what hope-

'You shall be recently arrived, then?' A woman of similar height to Annie. Her face open and lined from the sun, her blue eyes glazed marble blind, plugged the gap between them.

212

Her accent was English, but Millie couldn't locate her. It was a simpler voice than Annie's, plainer, crisper at the ends.

'Aye,' Annie replied curtly.

'And you'll be wanting a bed, your bearings?'

'Aye, and it's being sorted,' Annie said.

'Good,' the woman said, moving her face closer to theirs. She reached out with leathery hands and found theirs. 'You shan't be needing me then. From the North? Am I right?'

'Yorkshire and Lancashire,' Millie answered.

'I thought as much. There's a moisture to your words. I can almost hear the cotton stringing your letters together. Very nice.'

Annie rolled her eyes. 'Yes, yes,' she said, and plucked the woman's hand from hers. 'We're just waiting to hear about our lodgings, so if you'd excuse us…'

'Of course, of course,' the woman began to shuffle away. 'But if you need an eye for detail, you'll find me around.' She laughed through her nose and left.

'Oh, I wasn't rude, was I, Millie-May?' Annie asked, turning towards Millie. 'I just – you know me by now, I'd love to chat and talk and confer, but not now, not when the men –how're they getting on?'

They whipped round to see the man pocketing paper and pointing to the narrow lanes that spidered out from the junction before them. Adam winked.

'Dear sweet Lord, they must've done it. Oh, thank heavens for that. We shall have somewhere to lay our weary bones, Millie, we shall and we have. Say we have – Adam?'

He beckoned them both over.

'This kind gentleman,' Adam said as the man touched the peak of his cap again, 'has a place where we can stay. All four of us, for as long as we like. He says it's spartan–'

'Modest, but dry,' he interrupted.

'Yep, but habitable. He'll take us there now.'

Millie watched Annie take Adam's hand and squeeze it. 'A bed,' she heard her whisper, 'our own bed on dry land!'

'Does he own it?' Millie asked Johnny, looking up at him as they followed.

'No, it belongs to the gentry a-course, a man who owes rows of the things, but has never set foot in 'em. And this fella works for a fella who works for him. But he seems genuine enough.' Johnny coughed and wound his arm around her waist. 'Come on.'

The lanes grew narrower, the buildings shorter and hollower, and the cobbles gave way to a sticky sort of sediment that made Millie think of the banks of the Tame, littered with the same kinds of rubbish: scattered bottles, tightly curled turds, fragments of metal and glass. At first, she held up her skirt, but when she noticed the other women in the lanes staring at her, she let it drop and held her arms stiffly at her sides. Still her ears roared with the absent sound of the sea. She blinked slowly, heavily.

People sat on the front steps of their homes, buildings primarily made of wood, of differing colours and lengths and weights, and patched with other materials, all scavenged, it seemed, for none matched, and each house was different to the next. Planed wood or sheets of metal served as rooftops or doors; an assortment of spouts, hollowed cans, and tubes for chimneys. Children dug holes or banged pots or lay quietly in the shade, while women kneaded wet clothes, hacked at vegetables or sat wistfully offering up indiscernible items for their inspection as they walked past. There were fewer men, but there were some standing in clusters smoking, one or two cleaning tools or mending ropes.

Millie watched Annie's head snap from left to right, nodding at the women whose eyes she caught. She was silent, taking it in. Millie wondered if Annie's stomach, too, growled with growing intensity; whether her heart felt leaden and lower in her breast; whether her eyelids pulled each time she commanded them to open. And this was their new chapter, their new world? This slum they could have found in Ashton-under-Lyne, but six miles from Greenfield? Where was this unbridled opportunity that Johnny dreamt of? She let her hand graze the key in her waistband.

'For a short while,' Johnny whispered into her hair.

And Millie wanted to shake her head, wanted to laugh. What fools they had been to believe, what fools they had been to pay for this. And they *had* paid for it, they *would* pay for it. Mam wouldn't come here; Millie couldn't allow it. She couldn't allow Mam's skirts to trail in pig shit, for the boots she stitched, and restitched and polished to become clogged with mud, for her to travel ten weeks, longer if the wind willed it – and longer still if the ship was to be quarantined – to find people in circumstances worse than home.

'S'it,' the man said, jerking his head towards a hut of grey clapboard sandwiched between two taller ones. It had three steps up to a platform the width of the house, open but with a flimsy roof above it, like many of the houses had. A space for leaving dirty things, she supposed, boots and pots, though she had seen a goat tethered in one. The front door looked as though it could be opened with a fingernail and there wasn't a window at the front. The man handed a key to Adam.

The clapboard shook as Annie took the steps in front of her. They were forced to hop over the missing planks in the platform in front of the door which opened as easily as predicted. It was one room, wide, with straw mattresses piled against a wall and a large trunk against another. A case or crate of some kind lay spread-eagled beneath a window in which Millie could see a stack of small plates and cups, a saucepan. As her eyes became accustomed to the dark, she could make out a copper in the back corner, against which pails and a rug beater leant. There was no rug, as far as Millie could see.

'We're lucky,' Adam said, pacing the floor. He raised his voice above the noise of his boots. 'This chap said that the last people did a flit and couldn't carry all their stuff; it normally comes as bare as a birthday.'

'Well,' Annie said, turning. She fixed her eyes on Millie. 'Well.'

Johnny blotted the light from the doorway. Annie's eyes glowed like twin stars.

'We can make it a home, can't we, Millie, love?' She began to laugh then. 'My god, a home. I've seen some in my time. And this will take some beating.'

Millie heard Johnny speaking to the man at the front of the house.

'Bit of sweeping and it'll be alright. Don't you think, Millie?' Adam turned to her. She could see that he was as hopeful as Annie, as keen to start their new chapter in the best light. Even when there was no light.

Though Millie was stationary, her body and ears lilted as though she was still on the sea. She closed her eyes briefly. She had aged then, she knew, her body felt different: thin and flat, but with a heaviness she hadn't detected before. She was nineteen, but she could add on a decade, she thought, two.

'Yes,' she replied, and staggered towards the mattresses.

19

Annie had found a broom propped up against the back door.

'You can be my eyes,' she told Millie. 'You can guide me to the biggest piles of dust.' And though Millie's knees trembled with the sea, she moved about the floor of the hut, her eyes adjusting to its dirtiness, and pointed.

'There, Annie, oh and there.'

Annie was brisk, her broom knocking dirt and dust into the chasms between the floorboards. A spider, its limbs as thin as cotton, groped at the splintered wood.

'Down you go!' Annie said, scooping it up and stuffing it back into the gap. 'And if those are as big as they get, I will be quite happy with that!'

But the dust continued to reappear. The windows, bunged with odd ends of glass and brick and board, shed crumbs of dirt each time a stiff breeze rattled. When Adam brought in a loaf and a curious squat vessel that turned out to be full of warm ale, loose earth fell from the treads in his boots and Annie hissed through her teeth and swept furiously at the wood that thinned beneath the front door.

Annie darted the broom carefully around the crates that Johnny and Adam had found in the lane and dragged in to use as tables and chairs. And as Millie began to chop the basin of potatoes that Johnny had bartered for tobacco, the brisk sound of the besom landed in between the smart chops of Millie's knife.

'We could earn a coin or two from this rendition. "The Two Housewives,"' Annie announced through her fist as though it were a bugle. 'We could be the newest performers in the new world!'

'Oh, aye, and what would people want to listen to this for?' Millie said from the potatoes, their skins coming away in hefts. She wrinkled her nose. Rotten.

'But they won't be as *together* as us now, will they? You have to be *together* to be a band; in tune, like. And we know each other now inside out, don't we? A ship to the other side of the world, locked up together in this hut. You've even seen me in my death throes!'

'Death throes? You had a few spots, your wits. I reckon it were chickenpox that had you a-scratching, not typhus.'

'I wonder what Adam would've done if I had been ploshed over the side. I wonder whether he would've had to be the one to do it, being next of kin.'

The two women fell silent at that, but for the sound of their sweeping and cutting. Annie was right, of course, nobody knew how they would cope with something until it happened. And how was she, herself, coping, Millie wondered? Was the lack of eye contact with Johnny common between newly married couples? She doubted it, but then there were surely few marriages founded in such circumstances.

Millie had become a prolific letter writer, writing almost daily to Mam, Jane, Tudor, Alice. When poignant conversations or peculiar sights occurred, she rolled them about in her memory afterwards so that she might better commit them to letter. But none of the letters had made it on to parchment as yet. She hadn't seen anyone with any; not on the ship, not in the short row of shops and hawkers they had passed. She doubted

Johnny would give up the coin for it, either.

But she had answered theirs, too, imagined great essays arriving daily, telling stories of mundanity that, in these unfamiliar surroundings, felt poignant, even sacred. Jane's fury at the lack of progress in finding the perpetrators, no new evidence, no further inquests set; Mam's gentle hand, little said in ink but great sentiment felt in her descriptions of spinning, minding next door's baby, her otherwise silence on the matter which Millie now knew more than she wished.

Could she tell them? Could she send a letter that told them of the truth she had learned? Perhaps she could find the address of Patrick Broadbent; ask Jane to get it for her.

But what then? Could she sit down, gather her skirts and her thoughts, to write a letter to a man she couldn't picture, a man whose name she didn't otherwise know, but a man who would risk the gallows at her husband's begging? What could she say to such a man?

Patrick Broadbent.

Alice had called him Paddy. There were plenty of Broadbents. It was a common enough Saddleworth name. But she couldn't think to which branch he was related. Those lips; so blue. As though his heart had forgotten to pump blood to them. And Granda's blood? Well, he'd have seen enough of that by the time he'd finished with him.

Patts. Pats.

'I don't think he would've have been able to do it. He'd have been blinded by his tears, poor lad.'

'What?' Millie asked.

'Adam. He wouldn't have been able to tip me over the side; he'd be shaking too much, shivering. Saying my name over and over. He'd be delirious, the poor thing, and they'd have to go and get some other poor sod, too familiar with doing away with relatives in the drink, and make him do it instead.'

'Oh,' Millie replied, 'yes.'

'I often wonder what's going on in there, Millie-May,' she said suddenly, pointing the broom handle at Millie's forehead. 'For a new bride, for a woman without any ties or responsibilities, other than for a husband that's more than a-capable of looking afore himself, you live in that head o'yourn. I know you've had an awful shock, but that ain't sadness I'm seeing, that's thinking. And thinking gets us all in trouble, there's no doubt about it. Talking, too, talking causes a trouble, but it's the thinking that's worse.'

'Oh, Annie, if my sister, Jane, could hear you!'

'Why?' Annie threw her plait nonchalantly over her shoulder. 'There's nowt good come of thinking. Thoughts don't change things; words do, and work does more.'

Millie thought for a moment. 'But how do your words or work mean anything if you don't think?'

'Because, my petal, they come from the gut, from your instink; they're God himself moving through you. Now, I ain't no God-afearing preacher, but I do know that if you surrender yourself, then all will be made well.' Annie turned to her then, laid a hand on her forearm. 'Surrender yourself, Millie. Let yourself go and stop thinking. I see these grey smudges under your eyes, like your brother has got you with a lump of coal. You look as tired as a new mother, yet your body's the size of a child's. Now, forgive my frank talking, but it comes from my heart. Give yourself to your husband, give yourself to God, and you'll feel like yourself again. Yourself in a new place, with your new husband. It's your chance.'

Millie felt her face frown, her forehead worrying into a crease. Was she thinking now? Was it her thoughts that stiffened her back, held her head erect and wormed around her stomach? Or was that gut and instinct, as Annie put it? Because Annie didn't know; Annie could only read her face, her body. Annie couldn't read her thoughts.

Could she? Did Annie know? Did Annie know what Johnny had done?

Millie covered her face with her hands, screwed up her eyes, counted slowly.

The key in her waistband.

Surrender. To surrender herself.

She thrust her hands into the potatoes. They felt warm, soft and warm.

'My, Millie, those potatoes are gone, aren't they? I can smell them from here.'

'We have no more, only these. I'll cut out the worst of them.'

Millie felt Annie's eyes on her cheeks, her forehead. She felt them trying to catch hers, like magnets. She refused, narrowed them, concealed them behind her eyelids. She focused on the potatoes, watched as the black crumbled away with a pinch.

The sound of Adam's whistling drew Annie's attention away from Millie and her potatoes. Millie watched as Annie's hands automatically fluttered to her plait, tightened it and smoothed back the strands that had slipped out.

'Any luck?' Annie called.

Adam strode in, his smile puckering into a whistle again.

'Well, you're looking mighty happy with yourself,' Annie asked, reaching her arms about his neck.

Millie looked away, saw Johnny's boots appear at the threshold. He watched their embrace. He didn't smile, nor acknowledge Millie.

'Yep,' Adam nodded, pleased with himself. 'First place we

tried. We're in; start tomorrow. I think he would've said tonight if his overlooker'd let him. But he was busy marching round, giving his orders. Couldn't understand a bleeding word he said. Scottish, apparently, but I'd heard naught like it.'

'And what is it, the work? Timber?'

'Of course,' Adam said, smartly, 'as Johnny predicted.' He rocked back and forth on his thin soles. 'They can't cut down those trees fast enough. Houses, boats, town halls, more houses, more boats. Me and Johnny'll have coinage out of ears; we'll have work for life.'

'Aye, and we'll have less of that,' Annie said, swatting him with her apron. 'You can never be too sure of work. But I'm glad, and not surprised. Are you, Millie? You'd see these two lads and know they were genuine.'

Millie nodded. 'But you won't be strong on these potatoes,' she said, holding a fistful of potato innards above the bowl. She opened her fingers one by one. The mush leaked out, landed in the bowl with a slap.

'Boil 'em up, Millie,' Adam said, generously, 'we won't notice if we have salt. Have we salt? And tobacco. If me and John-boy here have a pipe or two, we won't feel a bit o'rot. It's not like we h'aint had it afore, have we, Annie?'

Annie shook her head and set down her broom, joining Millie at the fire. Annie liked nothing better than cooking for Adam. She loved to be busy, to be made busy for Adam. It didn't matter if she ached to her bones, if her eyelids were closing.

And Millie wanted that. Millie wanted that feeling for herself and Johnny.

'What did you make of the place, Johnny? Is it what you imagined?' Annie threw the words over her shoulder. Millie heard Johnny clear his throat, inhale. He considered his words, exhaled.

'Aye, pretty much. There's one or two young 'uns that won't last five minutes, haven't the brawn.'

'And what'll happen to them?' Annie asked, tearing at the cabbage leaves.

Millie pictured his shrug.

'They'll be out. If you can't keep up, they won't let you back in.'

'And we'll keep up, won't we, Johnny lad? No worse than our rotten mills.'

'Far better, I'd say,' Johnny said slowly, tasting his words. 'There's more guaranteed work, for a start. The pay's better. And there's no one nagging you about church.'

Adam laughed a short, sharp bark. 'That's 'cos they pray to all sorts of gods in that sawmill.'

'What do you mean?' Annie asked, frowning.

'Men from all over; all colours of the rainbow, they are. Speaking in tongues I couldn't even begin to put a name to-'

'French?'

'Oh yes, Annie, love, plenty of French, I don't doubt that. But *other* people, folks of all sorts of hue, such like you've never seen afore.'

'They say there were a native people here, you know.'

'Ah, we won't find them in the sawmills, I don't think, Annie, love. But, me and Johnny, we were told there are Chinamen, Indians, all sorts.'

'Well, how will you speak with them? They won't have our English now, will they? How will you tell them what to do?'

'That's a thought,' Adam said, his voice dropping. 'How will we?'

'Same way we speak to you Lancashire lot in our mills: loudly and slowly,' Johnny answered. Millie could hear the smile in his words.

'Oh, you sod!' Annie said. Both she and Adam laughed throatily, their heads tipped back. Millie watched the brush end of Annie's plait dance across her buttocks. Johnny and Adam lit up, toed the crates into a circle.

'Remember this, Johnny lad,' she heard Adam say. 'We have neither a table nor a chair to call our own. But we'll laugh at this soon enough; we'll have our own set, and spares. We'll even ask you and Millie over to sit in them!'

'Aye,' Johnny said, inhaling deeply. 'In time, in time. And let's hope our wives will learn to cook better than this by then, too!'

Adam snickered quietly but focused his eyes on his plate.

Johnny took his plate from Millie with a grin, his eyes at her jawline. She sat down next to him. Even over the cabbage, she could smell the scent she knew to be only his. She hadn't noticed whether Adam had a similar musk, perhaps she hadn't got close enough, but Johnny's was unmistakeable: earth, sweat, the grease of wool, the traces of tobacco, salt. It was a smell she could taste, that appeared on the end of her tongue, unbidden.

'What do you think they're doing at home?' Annie said, her mouth softened by potato.

Adam put down his fork as though he was amazed, that the question had never occurred to him.

'Well, that I don't know,' he replied, thinking. 'What time will it be there?'

'Close to midnight, I should have thought,' Millie said. 'Mam will be fast asleep, Jane and Tudor, too. Mam will be up at one for the privy, then probably again at three.'

She felt their eyes upon her.

'She'll rise at four to light the fire, Jane will join her at half past. They'll both have to rouse Tudor at five when they hear the knocker-upper.'

'You remember well,' Annie said.

'I think of little else.'

'And a six o'clock start is good going, my petal,' Annie quickly said, to prevent Millie's words from settling. 'We was always on the dot at five, weren't we?'

'In winter. In summer, it'd be five, though it was not as though we'd get to finish any earlier; they knew what they were doing,' Millie said. She stabbed the cabbage, twirled its fronds about the tines of her fork.

'And did your lot ever put back the clock? We had that happen often enough; when five minutes miraculously becomes thirty. What about your family, Johnny?' Annie fished out a black lump of potato, the size of a molar, and set it on the edge of her plate.

He had cleared his and placed it on the floor. He took out his tobacco and pipe.

'Asleep, too, I don't doubt.'

'I must write to them,' Millie said. 'Send them this address.'

'We'll be gone before you get a reply,' Johnny answered.

'Then I'll send them the next address.'

'Why? So you can hear all about the mill and Mr Dunne's shop and the latest Temperance picnic?' he asked, his eyes flashing upwards.

'Yes, why not?' she asked. 'I think about it constantly, wonder what they're doing, what's changed.'

'Nothing's changed, Amelia. That's the point. You think that because you've left, it's all change, it's all different. But it'll still be as we left it: mouldy bread, people hoping for ten-hour shifts.' Johnny kicked his plate, and the fork clattered.

'Perhaps I don't want it to change.'

Annie placed her hand on Millie's.

'He's right, Millie, love. You've got to stop looking behind and instead look forward. And what a forward! These two boys will do us proud, won't they?'

'I'm certain they will,' she nodded, 'but there's no harm in writing to my kin, is there? They are still my kin, even if they are on the other side of the world. And I'll have to tell them what it's like here so they'll be prepared, when they come.'

She lowered her plate to the floor, looked at Johnny. His eyes narrowed.

'And I can write for you, Johnny. You'll want to write to your mam, won't you?'

Johnny stood up and moved to the front door. She heard him reach for his flint.

'You're not leaving that, are you, Millie?' Adam asked, shovelling her potato into his mouth before she could answer.

She swallowed hard. 'I will write,' Millie said again as Annie patted her hand.

She scanned the rough furniture on which they had prepared the meal: a board raised on bricks, a copper that would have to serve for food and laundry, a collection of chipped glasses and mugs where the enamel had worn away. It was a poor excuse for a kitchen; she would bet there were better equipped sculleries in the Saddleworth boarding houses, better in the inns in Manchester. And here they were, sailed ten weeks and confronted with the odds and ends left by other passers-through.

'If you two fellas have found work already, we'd better not hang about,' Annie said, folding her hands primly over her stomach. 'What'll it be, Millie, eh? Childer or laundry? Growing veg or kneading bread?'

Millie's heart sank. Couldn't there be a place in the sawmill for them, too? Surely, they needed women for something, packing or preserving, or whatever it was they did with finished wood? She could picture it: the men on one side, the air light with freshly sawn timber, women on the other, hair hidden beneath kerchiefs and gloves to stave off the splinters. They might sing as the girls did in Greenfield.

'There's enough kids down here to make you two rich,' Johnny said, thumping the clapboard with his knuckles. The whole house shook.

'But won't their mammas be here with them? Looking for work like we are?' Millie asked.

Johnny shrugged, the smoke from his pipe jerking upwards with the movement. 'You won't know until you ask.'

She was accustomed enough to children: the mill couldn't operate without their small hands and quick reflexes; she'd assisted the tiny ones at Sunday School when she was a child herself; she'd supervised Tudor from the moment it was obvious he'd survive. But here? They were likely to speak all different kinds of tongues, accustomed to all manner of different things. Annie had seen a baby wrapped in a sealskin, like it had been fished fresh from the sea.

'We can see in the morn, can't we? A walk up and down here and we can introduce ourselves to all the mistresses and ma'ams and see what we've got.'

'A right load of rum 'uns and wrong 'uns, I'd expect,' Adam answered, cocking his head towards the doorway. Voices belonging to a man and a woman erupted from beyond their door. They spoke quickly and furiously, the beginnings of one sentence overlapping the endings of the other, their tongues pummelling their teeth. The woman shushed the man, and he lowered his voice momentarily before resuming the same volume as before.

'Sounds like she's mithering,' Johnny said.

'What tongue is that?' Millie asked. It flowed so quickly, evenly, laced together, one bound to the next, predetermined.

'Ah, I couldn't tell you, lass, could be Yorkshire for all I know!' Annie winked and set about collecting up the plates. 'Where did you leave the other pail, husband?'

Adam jumped to his feet and opened the door behind which the couple were speaking. Their conversation broke off. Millie saw him raise his hand, dip his head. They began to speak again, more calmly, quietly, this time.

'It's gone!' Adam wheeled round, his eyebrows knotted. 'I left the second pail there, right there!'

'Well, that was a bit stupid, now, wasn't it?' Annie said, plucking her apron strings from around her middle. 'You should've brought it in with the other.'

'I didn't think these cheeky sods would steal it!' When Adam waved his hands above his head, Millie was reminded of Tudor's monkey at the Whit Fair.

Annie bade him to keep his voice down and chastised him for his language. 'Especially when it's your fault,' she said, and took down her shawl from the nail that hung on the back of the door. 'I expect I'll have to go and collect more water now, shan't I? And just when I thought I was finished for the night.'

'My fault? I should be able to leave a pail of water on the step without it a-wandering off, shouldn't I? Robbing arseholes!'

'Adam! Language! It's not even our bloody pail, anyway!'

'Isn't it?'

Millie laughed, a full laugh that made her shoulders drop and her spine soften. She looked back at Johnny. He smiled too.

'I haven't seen you smile in ten weeks, Amelia; longer,' he said. His fingers almost touched the bowl of his pipe. She wondered how he could bear it. 'It suits you. A sullen face doesn't.'

'I'm not sure sullen faces are meant to *suit* anyone, Johnny Barkwell.' She felt the holes in her shawl. They had widened. The threads, in differing weights and coarseness, sank away from each other, depleted. 'I'll go with her.'

Johnny gave the slightest of nods and both their smiles faded, as though they, too, had been packed away for the evening.

20

It felt warmer, clammier outside than it did in. The air's moisture teased their hair into curls. Beads of it waddled across their top lips and eyebrows. Millie and Annie dabbed at their faces.

'And in October! I shan't understand it! I thought this was the land of ice and snow?' Annie said, puffing. She threw her plait over her other shoulder.

The moon was bright overhead, illuminating the dirt path that picked its way through the clapboard houses that creaked and moaned as their inhabitants moved within. Through windows free of panes came sounds that Millie could place: babies wailing, a chorus of them, each with their own timbre and tone; the clanging of pots; the crackling and popping of fires. Noises also came from the windows that were stoppered with rags or sacking or even, in the case of one, the hide of an unidentifiable animal: voices, muted as the day dwindled and their owners were readying for their beds of hessian and straw.

Millie yawned, yearned for her own bed.

'Hark! What's that?' Annie grabbed Millie's hand, and they stood stock still.

'What?' Millie asked, 'what is it? It's only a baby, isn't it?' Another baby sobbed itself to sleep in the house next to them. It sounded so close by, as if Millie could reach out to it. She knew how it felt; if only she could sleep.

'There!' Annie's clammy fingers pinched at her arm. 'Not a baby! Animal!'

Annie pointed to the house on her left, a miserable house, leaning like an old man on a stick. It was thin and wizened, one room stacked on top of another on top of another, with a front door that didn't fit its jamb. 'There!' Annie said again, pointing to the patch of earth to the left of the front door. A knotty bush grew there, and beneath had been left a basin and scrubbing brushes. And this was their new neighbourhood, of which they should be proud? 'There's an animal there, where they wash the clothes!'

Millie looked closer. Annie was right. A small creature, no bigger than a cat but stockier, furrier, was nosing through the contents of the basin. It sat on its haunches and with little black hands removed the rags one by one. Sharply, it turned its head to the women, its hands holding a piece of sacking. It had a foxy snout but wide whiskers, and a black mask around its eyes.

'Why, it's like a little villain,' Annie inhaled. 'Perhaps it's he who took our pail!'

'Do you think it might bite?'

'I don't say we stand here long enough to find out. Come on, let's find this pump.' The creature continued to rummage in the basin.

Two boys, barefoot and bare-chested, took it in turns to open their mouth beneath the spout, the other operating the handle. They gulped greedily, their toes sinking into the slime.

'Come on, now!' Annie shooed. 'That's no way to treat the water! What about the rest of us?' The boys froze as the creature had done, watched the two women approach in silence, the water running down their chins and the shins of their tattered trousers. 'Well, honestly!' she huffed. They showed no response. 'Have you no pail or pot?' She lowered her voice. 'Certainly, no pot to piss in, it seems.'

The two boys stood back, silent. Annie offered up her pail to the tap while Millie moved the handle. The thin stream of water didn't increase in volume despite Millie's pumping.

'We'll have to get another,' Millie said. 'This won't last us the morning.'

'That'll be Adam's job. I'll see to that,' Annie said. 'It's his fault we're here at all. Honestly, what was he thinking?'

'I suppose he didn't think. I'd have left a pail outside at home and thought nothing of it.'

She saw the two boys watch their conversation, their eyes following Annie's moving mouth, then her own reply. They didn't know English, though she wouldn't have thought them any different from the boys of Saddleworth Moor. How strange this world was, that there could be people that looked alike, but unable to share a dialogue. What was the point of moving to a place where they couldn't even converse with their neighbours?

As they left, Millie glanced over her shoulder to see the two boys under the pump again, their red mouths gawping at the water.

'Where are their mammas? They should be a-bed,' she said, taking hold of the handle with Annie so that the pail hung between them.

'Perhaps they need us to look after them, you see, Millie; we need to think business now, be money-minded. Perhaps their mammas will pay us to put them in our care. Though,' Annie said quickly, 'I doubt they'd have the coin for it. Those boys will be at their mammas' sides in the factory, or gutting the fish, or whatever it is us women do round here. We'll have to find the better neighbourhoods. Go a-door knocking there.'

Millie felt sick. Door knocking? Mam would be appalled. She may as well go begging. And who would employ her to look after children without any references? It would be a mother that cared little about her progeny to take on two women that knocked on doors.

'Can't we just go with the men? To the sawmill?' Millie asked.

The path was darker now, fewer lights showed at the windows. Millie held up her skirts and tried to feel for a smoother path amid the stones and rubbish people had cast out of their houses.

'What, and our mouths grow dry with sawdust? I think not.' Annie set down the pail, arched her neck and lay a flat hand to the small of her back. 'I swear those spots have weakened me. I'm like a little old lady. A shuffle to the pump and I'm out of kilter, my breath clean snatched away from me.'

Millie stopped, too, and waited. She squinted into the darkness. Shadows moved and played, people perhaps, or animals, more of those masked creatures. She prickled. If she didn't go back with Annie now, if she were to stay in those shadows all night, then what would happen? Would Johnny come looking for her? Would Annie send Adam, as Mam had done with Tudor to fetch Jane from the fair? Would they call her name into the night?

She could watch them coming and use the darkness to hide, crouching beneath the windowsills and old wooden verandas to remain hidden. Nobody would know she was there as long as she kept to the darkest shadows, the ones where it was impossible to decipher your own hand from the black. Where your own existence became the silent breath in your nostrils, the twitch of your own eyelids. Bill O'Jack's had been like that, of course, if the windows were shuttered and there was no light in the grate.

Perhaps she could stay there, crouched and watching like an

animal, until dawn. And then what?

Annie picked up the handle of the pail again.

'Lordy! Hark and hail, the water pail,' Millie heard her mutter under her breath, and Millie, too, took the handle. 'Trot on, Millie-May, for I'm ready for my bed. Though I know the signs and tonight, he will keep me from it,' she sighed.

'What? Adam?'

'Oh yes, my wifely duties have only just begun. When he's whistling and smoking, I knows what's a-coming.'

'And you don't like it?'

'Oh, I like that he likes it; there's nothing that beats that silly grin on his face afterwards. It makes it worthwhile, even though my womb don't bring forth the goods.'

The words in Millie's throat refused to line up and match those in her head.

'We've got to keep trying, so he says, which is fine by him, as he likes that rumping and pumping. He always thanks me and wipes me down, which is terrible nice of him. For some of the things I've heard about husbands in my time!'

Millie shuddered. She pictured Annie's plait pushed into the straw, Adam's thin white limbs above her, his wet mouth wide with joy. She would see it soon enough, she supposed. They were sharing a single room, after all.

They heard a soft voice singing in the eaves, a man's voice. She strained to catch the words, but if they were English, the material in the windows caught them.

'That creature's gone,' Millie nodded in the direction of the upended basin in front of the gaunt house. Cloth and sacking were strewn about as though the wind had enjoyed washing day. Perhaps she should tidy it; she and Annie could do it, shock the householders into cleaning up after themselves.

In fact, they could both stay out, sweeping the lanes, talking under the moonlight; it was warm enough to. They could keep watch for the masked animal and learn the lanes of their new neighbourhood. What was there to go in for? They could tell more stories of home. Millie hadn't told her much of Granda, about the time he showed her how to make pheasant noises by squashing large blades of grass between her thumbs and blowing. Mam had complained of a headache the night she had returned and showed her the new trick and had sent her to bed without her supper. She hadn't recited the stories of his second wife, Father's mother, who had died before Millie was born but still reduced him to tears whenever her name was mentioned, despite the harsh tongue she was meant to have had. And Thomas, how he had been known to fix a drystone wall without so much of an instruction from the men that plied the trade. A wencher? She didn't believe it, she couldn't.

She could tell Annie about the Johnny she knew then, the one that gathered people about him and enlivened rooms with his presence. The way women lowered their eyes when he addressed them or spoke behind their hands at each other when he was nearby; blushing, when they thought Millie couldn't see them. And though she was no one really, no one of great importance – no great beauty, no remarkable intellect or wit, known only for working hard, and being sister to Jane Bradbury – that she had known she would marry him, knew she would be the one that would be carried by that thing he had, that thing that made men want to flank him and women want to touch him.

In the dusk, their hut appeared, the broken porch and the flimsy door and in front of it, the missing pail, emptied of water and on its side.

'Oh, the brutes!' Annie said, as she bent over to retrieve it. Millie saw her wince as her hand instinctively flew to her lower back.

'At least they returned it,' Millie said, the door flying open at her hand.

It had been easy enough to find the wealthy neighbourhood. Its white houses, large and robust like a sailor's salute, were raised high above sea level. It took them a full twenty minutes to walk there, and Millie feared she wouldn't remember the way back to the hut. Though why would she return to Johnny at the end of the day. For what good reason?

At the first house, Annie swore blindly they heard movement at the door. She bent her head to it. A maid on the other side drawing back the bolt before being called away.

'These housekeepers and their spies,' Annie said.

At the second, a harried manservant saw them down the steps with hand gestures befitting the shooting of hens, not women offering their skills. He followed them into the street, eyebrows heavy.

'Alright, alright!' Annie said over her shoulder. 'Let's leave the next couple then, lest Jimmy here has a fit.'

A knife grinder shook his head sadly at the foot of the next one they thought to try, one with a dirty porch window and steps in need of whitening, and they decided to heed his silent advice and instead try next door. To their surprise, a young maid beckoned them in and called the housekeeper.

They waited in the cool darkness of the hallway where a grandfather clock ticked irregularly and visiting cards lay on a heap on a small table. Annie leant over them.

'I couldn't tell you if that was our own language, or another's,' she said. Her breath disturbed them.

The housekeeper could be heard before she emerged into the

hallway, her keys jangling at her hip and her skirts sweeping the parquet. The maid that had let them in stood behind her, eyes downcast and waiting.

'Yes?' the housekeeper said. 'What is it?' She was Irish and had a small gold crucifix at her throat.

'We are two women, recently arrived-'

'I gather,' she replied curtly, scanning Millie from her unwashed hair to her boots and back up again.

'-and we are seeking respectful employment. We can wash, cook and clean; we can mind children. We could be sent on errands, we could-'

The housekeeper raised a dry hand.

'An array of talents, many of which I've heard the likes afore. Still, you're fortunate you called today as our washerwoman has married in the night and left us wanting. We're in the middle of the wash and there's more than we can manage. I presume you can make a start right away?' She looked at the clock beside the staircase. 'O'Dowd here will show you the copper.'

Millie copied Annie's enthusiastically bobbing head, dipping at the knees.

'You got a bit o'blue to bring 'em up?' Annie asked.

The housekeeper's lip curled in distaste.

'O'Dowd will show you; I don't know the details.' She flicked at the air as the manservant at the other house had done. 'I shall pay you what I would the other washerwoman. Don't think that because there's two of you, you'll be going home with the same.'

Millie nodded and shook her head at the words that required it. Obedient, dutiful, that's what Annie had said. *You're good at that.* But she hadn't been inside the house of a rich family before, never handled their things.

The housekeeper instructed O'Dowd to take them to the scullery.

'Well done,' Millie whispered as they clattered down the stairs. 'I'm sure I wouldn't have got my words out, if it was me.'

'It's made me think we're only just beginning. We're going to be lucky, Millie, I just feel it. What's your name, Miss?'

The maid looked behind her. The scullery opened out. It was cold and damp, but the large windows afforded plenty of light. A copper sat to one side, scrubbing boards leant against it. A mangle stood a foot away, primly keeping its distance.

'Mary,' the maid said. 'It's full,' she nodded towards the copper, 'and warm. I didn't know how I was going to do all this; it's taken me all morning just to get the water. You've saved my skin.'

'Don't you worry yourself, Mary, we'll take care a'this. Is it a month's worth?'

Millie watched Annie calculating the bundles. Every piece of linen from the house, every sheet, every tablecloth, saved up for washing week.

'Washing's every five weeks in this house; it was six in my last place. One week makes all the difference. I'd rather do it more regularly than take days and days like it did afore.'

'Don't blame you,' Annie said, rifling through the sacks. 'Come on, Mills, sheets first. Find all the big stuff, will you?'

'We normally start at four when the washerwoman's here. We're hours behind.' The maid's lower lip trembled. Her eyes were grey and shone wet like pebbles from the Tame.

'You go upstairs, Mary,' Millie said brightly, 'don't you worry about us. I'm sure you've got other work to do?'

The maid nodded. 'This will take a few days, though.'

'Don't you worry,' Annie said, bundling the sheets under her arms. Each time she disturbed them, Millie could smell warm bodies, breath, the sourness of sweat.

Mary dipped her head and lowered her little knees into a curtsey, before disappearing up the stairs.

'Did she just curtsey to you?' Millie laughed. 'My, you've already got authority and you've only been here five minutes!'

Annie held out her fingers, pretended to buffer a shining sovereign. 'What can I say, Millie-May? I must have the knack!'

'You've something all right.'

They loaded the bigger items into the copper and began to stir. It was an almighty soup to shift. Her arms would double in size.

'Thank god they've made the lye already,' Annie said, poking at a basin at the foot of the copper. 'Probably the old washerwoman was doing that with one hand and packing for her midnight flit with the other.'

'Haven't they got any lant?' Millie sniffed at the urns beneath the windows. She could feel the breeze licking at the misshapen panes. It was not a house that cared for its servants' comfort.

'Too posh for pish,' Annie said. 'You won't find any cow shit here, neither. Nor horse, too valuable. It'll be homemade lye and blue, a bit o'soap come Christmas.'

'How do you know all this, Annie? How do you know *everything*? At home, we'd wash every day, every couple of days, with mending on Sundays. Lant from the street. Shit when the stains were bad…'

'I know, I know, you don't need to tell me, petal, we's the same. But these richies, they have to do it all different. It don't matter when it's not you having to do it, is it?'

Mary joined them once her duties at the top of the house were complete.

'I don't suppose there's a break for dinner, is there?' Annie said, rubbing her belly. Mary's pebbly eyes grew wide, and she wiped the backs of her hands across them, then down her apron. She'd be blind by the time she was forty.

'Dinner? There's bread for supper, a bit of cheese if they've got it, or turkey. And beer. But anything else you best bring yourself.'

Annie didn't seem to mind and began a story about a field of turkeys near her father's house, which was stalked by a fox that knew their routine as well as a knocker-upper. And no sooner had she finished that tale, then she was reminded of another. Mary O'Dowd laughed as though she hadn't laughed for years, alternating the wiping of her eyes with her sleeves and her apron in between dunking and drying, scrubbing and soaping. Annie's knowledge of the doings of the village, of the comings and goings and the consummation of marriages, was exhaustive and Greenfield quite mundane in comparison, bereft of inimitable residents and peculiar goings-on. Sometimes Millie caught herself wondering if Annie dreamt some of her tales, or brazenly made them up to pass the time and amuse herself. Still, Millie didn't care if she did. She enjoyed Annie's company and the effect she had on others.

Between them, they pulled the last load of heavy sheets on to the maiden and hoisted it high in the air, fixing the pulleys so that the linen would dry over their heads.

'Shirts tomorrow,' Mary said, appearing with a jug of beer from the housekeeper.

'Oh goody,' Annie said, rubbing her red hands together.

As the water on her hands and apron cooled under the breeze from the windowpanes, she pulled on her shawl. It wasn't the mill with Alice, but it didn't seem a bad way to earn a penny.

It was gone nine when they arrived back at the hut. The men were smoking, their backs against the clapboard. She looked at the pot. It was suspended over the lit fire, but there was no water in it.

Annie pegged up her shawl and reached for the pail to fill it. She didn't chastise them as Mam might have done, but began immediately to divulge information about their day.

'You are brave,' Adam said, lacing her arms about Annie's waist. She handed potatoes to Millie, and they began to chip at their leathery skins.

Millie could hear Johnny attending to his pipe. He hadn't moved an inch.

'Was my lady knocking doors?' Adam asked. Millie rolled her eyes to herself as Annie wriggled in his grip, laughing. Still Johnny didn't look up.

'What do you think, Johnny?' Millie said. 'Are you impressed at our enterprising?'

'Very,' he said from beneath his whiskers, 'and more so when the coin rolls in.'

She wanted to throw the potatoes to the wall, watch them leave their earthy orbs on the clapboard. She would throw their plates next, dashing them against the wood, not caring if they broke into shards. She felt the blood in her forearms, her wrists. She could do it, if she wanted to. If she wanted to spend the rest of her evening picking up splinters of crockery in the dim light. If she wanted to feel his grip tighten about her wrist, his wet whisper in their ear. She wanted to feel something.

'We could probably open a washhouse by next week, the rate we're going,' Annie said, proudly.

'You probably could, you probably could,' Johnny said idly, pressing down the tobacco in the bowel of his pipe.

She would buy parchment soon and ink. Johnny needn't know.

'Come, Millie, let me show you the neighbourhood.' Johnny

stood. She felt his height behind her.

'I'm cooking.'

'Oh, you go on,' Annie intervened. 'I can cook up some potatoes. You come back when you're ready.'

'But I've only just got back.'

Johnny held open his hand. His skin was white where it had hardened. He needed some of the salves Teresa passed round the weaving shed. Camphor, was it?

'You heard the lady.' His hand snatched at hers and gripped it. He closed the door behind them.

'I've seen the neighbourhood; I've been collecting water. I've walked up and down here, looking for work, in case you'd forgotten,' she said, crossly. His grip about her hand grew tighter.

'And I want a moment with my wife. Is that such a crime?'

She cast out her free hand to help her balance. The lane was rocky, uneven.

They were silent. Two newlyweds, hand in hand. Johnny reciprocated nods with men blackened by dirt and work, and occasionally handed over his pouch of tobacco to those that gestured they needed it. The women, for the most part, kept their heads down, their bonnets or shawls pulled close, their eyes fastened on their tasks: the clothes they soaped in buckets, the children they scrubbed raw.

'Did you want to show me something in particular?' Millie asked.

'I thought I'd show you the sawmill.'

Why he had chosen this moment, when she had a meal to cook and a bed to get to, she didn't know. Adam would've eaten the lot by the time they returned.

And the sawmill looked much as a sawmill should: a huge,

hastily built warehouse with a bare square yard, in which the night shift was already toiling. The buzz and the scream of the tools pierced the air. Millie could taste the bitter tang of the sap at the back of her throat.

'Very nice,' she said simply, and Johnny's face clouded.

He drew her to a corner, bordered by two heavy gates behind which Saddleworth folk would've kept a bull.

He spoke softly, as to a child. 'I'm puzzled by your behaviour, Millie, quite in't dark, if I'm honest. We've sailed ten weeks to our destination, and now we're here. We've our lives to make. Why are you so set on making it difficult for yourself? For me?'

And Millie blinked, slowly, assuredly. The lines at his eyes were absent, his lips tethered to his pipe. She realised that she truly believed that she should let the shock at the death – the murder – of her relatives recede with the tide; that she should leave it to sink to the bottom of the sea where he had released it. That now it was said, and he was unburdened, it was done and forgotten. That she should move on and pretend it was nothing more than a declaration of a past dalliance with a woman, or a gambling debt now paid up.

He would not see it differently. When people stood in his way, he beat them: it was how he undercut his competitors at market, how he rose to salaried work, how he dealt with Granda and Thomas. Johnny Barkwell did not aim to appease, to make connections and friendships, though he might make it look that way: he strove to perform, progress, outshine. She considered her explanation. If she didn't voice it, he would never know.

'Though I don't intend to make anything difficult for myself, and certainly not for you, I do have to remind you,' she said, drawing in her breath and lowering her voice. A man had come to the gate with three sacks of wood shavings, their fragrance sweet. 'I do have to remind you that you are the cause of the death of my Granda-'

'This again!'

'Yes, this again! Johnny,' and she clasped his hands, squeezed them together, 'Johnny, you are the reason my grandfather and uncle lie in their graves.'

'I don't deny it, Millie, and I could've done. Many a man would've chosen not to tell their wives-'

'And because you have, I should be grateful?'

'Yes. And because it's done, it's happened. And you're here, with me.'

He tried to pull her towards him, but she turned her face so that his kiss landed at her collarbone.

'Millie, for the last time, you are blind to what your relatives really were. Your love and loyalty have been foolish, misdirected. Hell, I should be glad to have but a fraction of the admiration you have for them!'

'Well, you shan't,' she said, and moved away, her stomach twitching.

'You'll love me,' he said, catching her wrist. 'You'll love me as Annie does Adam. It'll take some time, but you'll do it.'

She turned to face the hut, the lane dark in front of them.

'I've ignored the fact you've shamed me, shown me up for not being able to write.'

She looked back at him.

'What?'

'Before. Showing off that you know how to write and I don't.'

'And now you're speaking nonsense.'

'The thing is, Millie, you *are clever*; there is something up here.' Out of the corner of her eye, she saw his finger jab at his temple. 'And you could use it to make a better life for yourself, for us.'

'Annie and Adam can't write either, you know; you're nothing special. And I'm nothing special that I can.'

He squeezed her wrist.

'You'll love me,' he said again. Inside, she laughed and shook her head, set her jaw. But externally, to Johnny, she assembled her face into a mask and turned back to the lodgings they shared.

21

The shirts, yellowed at the armpits, took more soaking and rubbing than the sheets had on the first day, but being fewer in number, Millie didn't mind. She hoped not to meet the man or men who wore them, though, such were the breadth of their shoulders and the girth of their stomachs.

'Fond of the food, the master of the house?' Annie had asked and Mary had coloured silently, her head bent over the stains.

They had broken earlier for supper, this time with slices of mutton.

'I've got you this,' Mary said, holding a limp scrap of paper towards Annie. 'I know you said you're looking for nannying, or something with the chillun, and there's a big house just five minutes from here with two young 'uns, so my friend says, and she's in service next door. They're French, but they'll take you.'

Annie showed Millie the paper.

'364 Seafarers' Way?'

'Yes, that's it,' Mary said. 'She had her housekeeper write it down for her. She's got a nice one, nicer than...' and she tailed off, her pebbles glinting glumly.

'This,' Annie said, holding the scrap aloft, 'this is our new venture. We'll be a-minding entitled young 'uns, doing laundry – we'll be rich!'

Millie pictured a solemn young child in britches. His hair

parted stiffly on one side, commanding her to pick up his spinning top, furnish his plate with meals. She imagined a younger sister weeping at every forbidden luxury.

'I'd rather not,' Millie said.

'Rather not be rich?'

'Yes, if it means—' and she thought of the masters' large shirts, 'if it means looking after spoilt children.'

'You've been influenced by that husband of yourn. This is where the real money is to be made, Millie-May. You've looked after Tudor; you'll be fine.'

'Tudor is my brother; I can tell him "no" until I'm blue in the face. But young rich things? I wouldn't know where to begin.'

'They're only littlies,' Annie said.

The water was the colour of dust.

'We'll pick them up when they fall, tuck them up. Two of them, did you say, Mary?'

'Two boys. Their mama is a teacher at the orphanage, so they're a decent family; well, so their housekeeper said, anyhow.'

'You know what you're doing. Why don't you go?' Millie said. She'd take large shirts over small children.

'Or why don't I show you, and we can both do it? Not that there's owt to show you; it's just common sense.'

'Oh, Annie, why do I always feel that you're right?'

She laughed and tapped her nose. 'You'll thank me. We'll be coining it in before you know it. We'll be keeping our men!'

Millie shook her head, imagined it. She could buy Johnny his tobacco and beer, portion it out on Fridays as he did for bread.

'When does the housekeeper pay us?' Millie asked.

Mary wiped her eyes. 'You'll get it when she's inspected it, when it's all dry, been through the mangle, folded.'

'Inspected it? Lorks-a-lummy!'

Tomorrow, Millie would buy parchment and ink with her first payment.

Millie guessed the two boys were no more than three and a year apiece. Their mother was gone at dawn, the cook told them in scant English, and she had far too much to do to be responsible for them, too. The cook had chosen that moment to let the meat cleaver thump to the chopping board, the carcass before them yawning into two.

'Upstairs.' The cook gestured with her eyebrows, and Annie and Millie took their leave.

'Blimey,' Annie whispered as they climbed the staircase. 'Talk about washing your hands of 'em, poor little critters. Didn't that Mary say this was supposed to be a nicer house?'

The two boys were incarcerated in facing cots. The older was standing, pointing at the window. His sing-song language – whether French or nonsense, Millie couldn't tell – ceased as the two women crouched to them.

Annie made her greetings and Millie curtsied low as though they were little country squires.

'Now, we be hearing your mama has gone off,' Annie said pointedly, 'but she'll be back,' she added quickly. 'And in the meantime, we'll take good care of you. What shall it be first?' She lifted the littlest from his blankets, his hands jammed firmly in his mouth. 'A rhyme or a game?'

The two boys, wide-eyed and silent, watched Annie as though she was a madwoman. The littler one, in her arms, looked away over his shoulder.

'Hello,' Millie said to the elder, feeling foolish. 'My name's Millie. What's yours?'

But his brow wrinkled, and he looked past Millie to his

brother in Annie's arms, who had begun to wriggle.

'Well, this is going to be a long day, isn't it?' Annie hissed. 'Let's see if there's a garden, at least. We can let them roam about there.'

They could hear the cook banging about in the kitchen. The boys were silent in their arms so they nodded towards the door they presumed led to the garden. Annie turned the key, and they slipped out. An herb bed gave way to a neat square of lawn, mown short. An apple tree shaded one end, while a heavy set of table and chairs presided over the other. A large box hedge screened what Millie predicted to be a kitchen garden and perhaps a cow or pig sty. It wasn't a big garden, but it would provide.

'Come on,' Annie said, settling the elder boy down. He looked about him in wonderment. Annie dragged the table to one edge of the lawn. The littlest clung to her momentarily as she swung him down to the grass. He began to sob, a shrill whine whistling through his wet mouth as tears leaked down his face. Millie stood before them, unsure what to do. She reached out her hands to him, but he turned away.

'There, there,' Annie hushed at him. 'I'll just be a moment.' Millie knew it wasn't her he was pining for, though, but the shelter of indoors, the comfort of warmth and silence. In the garden, the damp grass and the breeze that picked at his skin would be a new altogether unpleasant sensation.

'Hark at him!' Annie said. 'You'd have thought he'd never been outside, the poor wee molly. Aye, he prolly hasn't, has he? Or not in anything less than full jerkin or sheepskin or swaddled in blankets. I thought they'd like this.'

Annie sat down on one of the garden chairs and gestured for Millie to join her.

'Let's set our peepers on 'em, see what happens.'

The elder turned to look back at the two women. He peered at his brother and toddled towards him. As he stood over him, the younger's sobbing ceased. The elder rubbed at the tears on his brother's face and scuffed his wet hands along his britches to dry them. He looked back at Millie and Annie.

'He expects us to scold him, look,' Millie whispered.

'They're not allowed to do owt, are they? Perfect little gentlemen from the day they're born.'

The elder began to address his brother in the same manner Millie and Annie had previously interrupted. This time, he pointed and gesticulated, and the younger watched him like a member of his congregation.

'I shall have to ask their names again. I didn't catch them, did you?' Annie asked. 'But perhaps we should make our own names for them until they're old enough to tell us otherwise. I know naught about French, petal. I couldn't name a French name if it bit me on the-'

'Pierre,' Millie said, quickly. 'And I wouldn't say "arse" in front of them, neither. They might say it in front of their mother.'

'Well, *you* just said it!' Annie said. They laughed into their hands.

Millie felt the pain in her stomach ease then. She shouldn't be frightened; women looked after children every day; women had been doing laundry since laundry needed doing. And if she was busy, she didn't have to think. Maybe Annie had been right; what use was thought, when there was so much work to be done?

But then she thought of Johnny. If she ever became truly happy and comfortable in the Canadas – and she couldn't imagine it, but she did have that kind of disposition that made the best of things – if Mam and Jane and Tudor joined them and all was well, then would he be happy, too? Would they be happy together, like Annie and Adam? Somehow, she doubted it. She had the slightest niggling concern that he enjoyed her sullen with worry, clinging to his tailcoat with sadness. Why, he'd asked her to marry him at her lowest ebb, and he the direct cause of it? He'd announced their departure the moment they married. Perhaps it was his power he enjoyed better; yes, the fact that he could make a plan, change the course of their lives together, and there was naught she could do but acquiesce.

'I thought I had you then, flower. I thought I had a true laugh from you,' Annie said, tapping Millie's knee. 'But it was like you realised you were enjoying yesself and you were jolted from it, like a cart going over a bump in the road.'

Out of the corner of her eye, Millie could see Annie shake her head sadly.

'Or it's like when someone's gone to heaven and the person left behind reckons they can never feel happiness again,' Annie continued. 'Trouble is, that person's then got to live on for years, decades. What then?'

'I don't know,' Millie said.

'You've got to throw yourself into this, Millie. I know I keep harking on about it, but mend your relationship with Johnny, submit yourself to him.'

'It's he that brought me here, that made me! I wanted none of this!' Millie stood, eyes flashing.

'Fine. But what wife can truly choose their path? You've got to make the best of it. Make some babbies, like these two, here. That'll sort you right.'

'Babbies!' Millie threw up her hands. 'We have barely enough rotten potato to feed ourselves and you think bringing babes into the world will make me forget my mam, my brother and sister?'

'You don't think others have brothers and sisters? You don't think I don't miss anyone?'

'No, it's not that, it's-'

'You think you're speshal, Millie-May. The way you hold your head, the way you eye my hair and my waist. I've seen the way you judge my sewing.'

'Sewing? What? I-'

'I'll look after these two. You made it quite plain this was beneath you, anyway. You go back to Mary O'Dowd's, finish off there.'

'Annie,' Millie pleaded, 'you've got this wrong. I didn't think it was beneath me. I didn't know what to do! And you seemed so calm and confident, I-'

Annie held up a hand and fixed her gaze on the boys.

Millie cleared her throat, tasted at the words in her throat, but didn't sound them. There was no use. Annie's eyes had narrowed, her lips were clamped firmly together. She would not be speaking with Millie again.

Millie crossed the lawn and tiptoed up the steps, her heart beating in her chest. It was unfair. She did not want to be here; she did not want to be anywhere. She had love and had lost him, she had family and had lost it, and now even friendship evaded her. She clasped her hands to prevent them from shaking. She hoped Mary O'Dowd would still have something to wash, something to occupy her hands.

A woman in a stiff grey dress was handing an envelope to a messenger boy on the doorstep. Millie presumed it was the housekeeper. At her footsteps, the woman turned to Millie in surprise and addressed her, but Millie could not understand. It was like being in a dream, an animated face and a mouth opening and closing, but the panic of not being able to hear, or to know, what was expected of her. Like Granda's face, Granda's face with his glistening ear, wet with blood.

'I'm sorry, Ma'am,' she said, dropping a curtsey and dizzying as she rose. She had to go. She needed to. The hall was warm. The messenger boy stared at her. What was there to stare at? Why were there always eyes peering from every door, every window in this place? 'I'm sorry, but I cannot understand you.'

'Onglay,' the messenger boy said triumphantly and tipped his hat. He left at a jog.

The woman spoke again, but a fraction slower. Still, Millie shook her head.

'I am sorry,' Millie enunciated, her lips and teeth sanctioning every syllable. 'I can't speak any other language. But I have left my – the other woman in the garden with the children.' She nodded her head towards the lawn.

She felt a hand on her wrist. Millie looked up. The housekeeper's eyes had narrowed. She spoke faster, gestured back at the kitchen, the garden.

'I don't know what you're saying,' Millie said again. 'But go and see the other woman.' She shook off the housekeeper's hand and left. The messenger boy hadn't fastened the lock, and she kicked it open with her boot. She hoped she could remember the route back to O'Dowd's house without Annie. She would not cry, she told herself. She needed her vision clear, unmisted by silliness. Annie was not worth crying for, anyhow; she had no idea, no clue. If she did, she wouldn't have begun her lecture.

Babbies. As if children were the answer.

She imagined a boy, seal-coloured eyes like Johnny's, looking for rabbits, a loaded rifle wedged into his armpit. She pictured a daughter with a temper as short as Jane's. What traits could she, Millie, give a child? A willingness to be duped? Naivety and obliviousness?

Suddenly, a singer piped up outside the tavern on the

opposite side of the lane. He leant against the clapboard, the tavern's lantern swinging in the breeze above him, closed his eyes and sang. It was the ballad of Maria Marten, though the tune differed from the one Millie knew. She crossed the lane to listen to him.

He opened his eyes and signalled to the open trunk at his feet as he sang. It contained small sheets of paper, some illustrated with crude ink sketches. The letters were hunched and uneven, the paper creased or blotched with water. What had been the name of the ballad Jane had found? *The Greatest Crime of the Century*? She sifted through the sheets and looked for the phrase, but couldn't see it.

Perhaps her story hadn't yet made it across the sea. She felt a great surge of relief.

The singer broke off. 'What'cha looking for, lassie?'

'Do you have any parchment? And ink?'

'All thems beauty-ballads and you want clean paper to write your own!'

She pulled her mouth into a smile. She had her own money; O'Dowd's housekeeper had paid up when she had seen the sheets neatened in rows.

Men would toast first earnings with ale; she would have her own parchment. He fetched into the knapsack and drew out what she needed.

'You sure you don't want the tale of poor old Maria and the Red Barn? A real story, you know?'

'I know it well,' she replied, folding the parchment into her waistband.

'Then you coulda joined in!'

She thanked him. Once she was finished at Mary O'Dowd's, she would write home, her first true letter home. And no one should see it, but Mam, Jane and Tudor.

There was no sign of the Irish housekeeper. Mary instead appeared at the threshold, as if she had been keeping watch.

'I'm pretty much finished, Millie,' she said, shrugging. 'Having the two of you meant we got through it far quicker. I've only got little things left to boil.'

'Oh dear,' Millie said, 'oh dear.'

Mary looked about her. 'What's the matter? She didn't guarantee you the work, did she? Are you in trouble?'

'Oh no, no, nothing like that,' Millie said quickly. 'I just need something else to do. Those boys-'

'What? They were bad?'

'No, not at all,' she said again, her face flushing. She was alarming Mary, she could see. And there was no need; she shouldn't burden the poor girl with her quarrel with Annie. 'It's just I haven't anything to do for the rest of the day, and I really ought-'

'Look, I only have the silver to shine and I can't really invite you in here to do that. You are the washerwoman, after all. I'm sure you can come back in five weeks, though. I'm sure she'll have you back.'

'Yes, yes, of course,' Millie said. 'Thank you, you've been so good to us.' She squeezed the maid's rough hands and left the house.

Annie could knock on doors. Annie could bow her head to each housekeeper in the street in turn, keep her eyes downcast and her mouth sweet until each door in turn was shut in their face. But Millie couldn't, not by herself. She thought of Mam, pictured her small hands raised up to those huge, heavy doors. It wasn't right; it was begging. Work came through recommendations, skills sought after and reputations honourable.

She made her way back home. She could fetch some water so she wouldn't have to go later; she could write her letter to Greenfield. She was still using her time wisely. She would look through his pack, see if his Sunday shirt needed mending.

As the gulls and fishermen jostled for fish on the dock, she walked past quickly, the inns open and blaring with voices. But then the row of ticketing booths caught her eye. She had seen them on arrival, sandwiched between huts selling fish and pails full of shells, whether for food or decoration, she hadn't neared close enough to tell. The booths reminded her of the stalls at the Whit Fair, and had signs outside obstructing the pathway.

She could also buy a ticket.

She could buy a ticket with her own money, leave on account of her own steam.

She hadn't thought of that. Why hadn't she? Had she been awaiting Johnny's about-turn? For that would never happen. This emigration had been his plan. He would rather die in the sawmill than return to the mills of Saddleworth. But now Millie could have her own plan. It was surely costly, but now she was earning – well, she could be thirty-five by the time she was due to set sail, for all she cared, but it would still be preferable to staying. *It's a long road without a turn.*

She hastened a look over her shoulder. She was no remarkable sight; just another thin girl with hands rougher than the paper put in with caged birds and clothing that threatened to fall apart at the seams. She smoothed down her dress, running a hand over the key, and flattened her hair with a slick of saliva. She strode to the booths.

In the first, a short, thin man was sleeping on his chair beneath a newspaper. In the second, the sign had been streaked unreadable with rain.

But two men in a third booth saw her, beckoned her over with large hands and smiles.

One spoke first, his face tanned and his hair white. He nodded his head and smiled as he spoke. Quick interjections and pauses left open for her response.

'I'm sorry,' she said. 'I don't understand.' She looked over her shoulder. She had to be quick.

The man nudged his companion, who ostensibly tried another tack.

The two men spoke louder, shortened their sentences. They smiled encouragingly.

'I'm sorry, I still don't understand. But I want to go to England. Do you have a ticket for England?'

The first man nudged the second again, pointed to the ledger on the desk. The second man nodded. He seemed to think so. Millie leant over. Portsmouth.

'Ah, no, not Portsmouth. But England, yes. Do you have a ticket to Liverpool?'

'Liverpool?' She nodded. The two men scoured the ledger, flicking between pages.

'Husband?' the second man asked, looking her up and down. She felt her cheeks pinken.

'He is dead,' she said quickly. Her heart pounded. To use that word when Granda and Thomas-

'Alone?' he asked.

Millie folded her arms into her armpits. 'Yes,' she replied, and her knees shook.

The first man thumped the table and pushed the ledger towards her. A ship left for Liverpool every fortnight, first light on the Tuesday. If the weather was poor, it did not sail. The cheapest ticket: space in steerage.

'Do you accept instalments?' she asked, but the men looked blank.

She chopped at the desk with the side of her hand. 'One, two, three, four,' she said, moving her hand across the table. Her hand continued to chop. That amount would take time.

The first man watched, eyed her, then nodded. 'Yes,' he said. He understood.

'Thank you. I shall return,' she said, sounding each syllable and dipping her head.

She felt lighter. Her heart leapt in her ribcage. She would go home, and nobody could stop her. She wouldn't tell a soul. Her silence would be her power.

22

She was staring at the crease along the middle of the parchment, made where she had crammed it into her waistband, when she opened the door.

'And what do we have here?'

She stopped, looked up, startled. Johnny was lying across the bed, smoking, his boots dirty and crossed.

Her arms fell to her sides. It would be futile to lie at this juncture.

'I've got some parchment; I'm going to write home.'

She turned her back to him, set the parchment on the crate, her heart pounding. She needed something to do to distract herself.

'Ah, very good.'

She could hear him blow his plumes of smoke.

'Paid for how, might I ask? My dear wife is not spending my hard-earned coin on frivolities now, is she?' A cough crackled in his throat.

'One of the maids gave it to me, one of the maids in our new house. She was writing home and thought I might want to do the same. Which was very kind of her.' She blushed deeply at the falsehood, but Johnny wouldn't see it. She began to lay the fire. The mattress wheezed as he got to his feet, his boots deafening on the floorboards. She turned around as he picked up the parchment.

'And what have you got to tell them?'

'Everything, Johnny,' she said irritably, gesturing about the room, turf in her hands. 'Your work, my work, meeting Adam and Annie, the ship over. I don't know how I'll put it into words, but I'll have a go.'

'Very good, very good. And what will you say about me?'

'What are you doing here, anyway? Shouldn't you be at the sawmill?'

He crouched then, whispered into her ear. 'I asked you a question. What will you say about me?'

Without turning her head, she answered quickly. 'That you're well, that you have work, you are making friends.'

'Making friends! How jolly!' He sneered, rocking to his feet. He'd been drinking then.

Slowly, painstakingly, enjoying the sound of fibres being wrenched apart, he ripped the parchment clean in two and set the fragments back onto the crate top.

She turned to face him. 'What have you done that for? There's no harm in writing home, is there? Why would you prevent me?'

He took a deep draught from his pipe and spoke through the smoke. 'It's for your own good, Amelia. You need to think about your situation, about me; not your wayward sister and your busy-body mother, rubbing that key every five minutes when you think I'm not looking.'

'How dare you talk about my family in that way! Get back to work before you lose your place!' She turned back to the fire and angrily began to stack it, hands shaking. She would still write that letter; she would see to that.

'Yes, now there you speak sense. I suppose I ought. I shall see you later, wife.'

He bent down to kiss her, smeared his lips on her cheek and

slammed the door so that it bounced wide open. She closed it again and refused to look after his receding figure.

What had she done to deserve such hostility? First Annie, then Johnny.

She would write the letter. She dropped the turf and went back to the parchment. Its two halves were thin; she would only have room for two or three words per line. But she could explain that away. It would be short, this first letter. Something written in haste, eagerness to give news of her wellbeing, her new address. The detail could come later, when she was in a sharper mood. She wrote quickly, the nib scratching. It was not good quality, and she regularly had to retrace her strokes for the letters to appear.

Dearest Mam, Jane and Tudor

Forgive this paper; it's the first I could find, and cheaper for being split in two. But I am here, we have made it. There were times when I thought I wouldn't, when sickness struck the boat and food was scarce. But we've arrived and found lodgings that are not entirely unpleasant. It is cramped, as we share with another couple we met on the boat, an Annie and Adam Henderson, from Lancashire, but the company is welcome in such surroundings.

This is only a note so I could give you the whereabouts of our lodgings, so you can write me of your news. What of Granda and Thomas? I hope there are some developments.

She read back her words. It couldn't be further from what she wanted to say. She should mention him; it should appear strange if she didn't.

Johnny has secured work in the sawmill as planned, while I have become a washerwoman. There seems to be much work for many people, which is fortunate, as I understand there to be boatloads arriving by the day. It is quite overwhelming.

We haven't yet found a chapel, so we shall have to widen our search. I have taken to reading passages of our Bible to Annie, something we did to while away the hours at sea.

We hope to meet our neighbours soon and get to learn a little more of the people that inhabit our clustered street. A smile can go a long way, it seems.

But before you begin to laugh at my earnestness, I shall bring this to a close. Please write soon and bring me news of home. I miss it truly.

All my love,

Millie

She folded the two halves together and wrote out the address she knew so well. She'd need her next job before she could send it.

All this hiding and secrecy, when she could have been read like a book for the first nineteen years of her life.

The door fell open and Annie appeared, red-faced.

'I am so sorry, Millie, so truly sorry,' she panted. 'I should never have spoken to you in that way. It was entirely uncalled for. I gave myself a right telling off. I said, "Annie Henderson, you know naught of this girl and what she's endured and you've lectured and hectored and now you've gone and lost her."'

Millie stopped shaking and smiled, beckoned her over.

'Don't be daft, Annie Henderson. You haven't lectured and hectored. I'd annoy myself the way I'm dripping around. And you just want to get on and do well, and who'd blame you?' She felt suddenly weary, her body heavy.

'Are you alright, petal?' She said, peering into her eyes. 'Have

I given you quite a shock?'

'Oh no, it's just Johnny,' Millie sighed. 'He was here when I returned and we had a blazing row, that's all.'

'Dear, dear,' she said, cooing, 'what about?'

'That's just it; absolutely nothing. Again. I'm not conducting myself properly, I know it, for I'm attracting all manner of ill-'

'Ignore it, Millie. I'm truly sorry. Johnny will come crawling back, and I shall never speak to you in that way again – I quite forgot myself.'

A gloss of sweat shone across Annie's face. Her small eyes glittered.

'Your talking-to did me the world of good; I needed it,' Millie replied.

It was true. Annie had shown her that she needed to take matters into her own hands. It wouldn't be deceit and deception, exactly; more an absence of honesty. And she could live with that. 'Now tell me about those boys. When did their mother return?'

Annie seemed relieved at the ease with which their disagreement had blown over, and spoke animatedly about the children, how they seemed to enjoy their afternoon in the garden, and how she had been invited to return tomorrow, through a series of points and nods.

'And you have a letter written?' Annie said, looking at the ink on Millie's hands. 'I hope you didn't tell your mam about a horrid girl from Lancashire?'

Millie shook her head. 'I told her of a nice girl I've befriended. She might speak funny, but I've told Mam we've become like kin.'

Annie swatted her shoulder. 'I'm mighty proud you can write letters; I can't write a word. Perhaps, sometime, you could write one to my family, let them know I'm alive and well? Only short, like.'

'Of course,' Millie said, 'of course I would. You should've said earlier.'

'When you have the parchment and ink, and I'll pay you for it.'

Though Millie knew she couldn't accept Annie's money, it did make her wonder: who else couldn't write letters, but would pay for the service? She would need enterprise if she were to save more and quickly, and she'd have to do it without Johnny finding out.

The two women permitted themselves each a slice of bread, thickly spread with butter. The cabbage and bacon they had would only feed the men, so Annie readied that next while Millie went back to laying the fire.

'You know,' Millie said. 'I think we should divvy the work according to skill. You're better with the French boys; why don't you stick to the childer and I to the laundry? I'll come and help you if I finish my rounds first; or you can help me with the drying, should the night nurses arrive.'

Annie shrugged. 'Fine by me, lassie,' she said, 'though I think I win there. Looking after thems childer is play.'

Millie's limbs pulled at her. It was clear: her sudden lethargy was the result of exhaustion of having agreed to her own plan. It had taken every fibre, every sinew, of her body, of her mind, to yield and consent to the burgeoning idea. That to leave Johnny, and this cluttered, cacophonous country, was not only possible, but it would happen, by her own hand and her own actions. But she would have to be quick and discreet.

23

It had become routine. Millie could pass for any working woman, any new arrival she shouldered past on the street that worked hard, whose life was dedicated to earning. She rose before Johnny, Annie joining her, as they sliced bread and cheese for their husbands, wrapping an egg in a handkerchief if they had one.

Where Annie and Adam sang their goodbyes, snatching kisses and pushing hats down on opposite heads, Millie and Johnny were staid, formal, their hard fingers brushing as she passed him his food before she busied herself with some other task to avoid his eyes, his mouth already turned down around his pipe.

It would be Annie's turn to flee next, her hair already slipping from its knots. Annie's clientele was a stiff set of women, married to men whose fortunes fluctuated with the sea – merchants, brokers, excisemen – and so were forced to perform arithmetic in their heads whenever their butcher or their seamstress required payment. Annie's part in their lives was simple, she had said: to chivvy their children from one room to the next, ensuring they reached their lessons and meals on time, and to make their parents appear as socially successful as possible.

The most important part of the day, Annie soon learnt, was the moment when the mistress of the house could shine:

paying Annie for her services by counting the coins aloud into Annie's opened hand as she stood, head bowed, on the bottom step of the town house. It was a ritual amplified so that the neighbours could hear the sum she would be paid, whether or not she would be welcome the next day (she always was), and what her likely tasks would be.

Annie knew that this custom would be privy to payment and invitation to return, so she endured these women's pointing fingers and irritated manner as though she were someone else in her worn shoes: an aristocratic philanthropist in disguise, perhaps, reporting back to some earnest church committee on the working conditions of the impoverished.

'I'd rather be me, that's for sure,' Annie had said after recounting an episode where one of her mistresses' housekeepers had raged at her in a tongue she couldn't comprehend. 'It seems that if you've got more coin, you soon find more to spend it on. You end up worse off, mark my words.' Annie had seemed unperturbed by the experience of the woman's spittle flecking her face as she roared. 'She could've been insulting everything from the tip of my pate to the very frump of my shoes and I wouldn't-a known, so what's there to cry at?'

Millie alternated between a number of the townhouses, accustomed to their washing cycles. In most, she was the main washerwoman, left to collect the water, boil up the copper and make the lye herself, but her long hours meant that she was often joined by the other domestics who looked in on her, brought her tea or beer, occupied her with gossip about people whose names had slowly become familiar.

The lanes were always busy, regardless of the time she left their hut. There would always be children playing, leaping over empty oil barrels, challenging each other to knock-a-door-run, to hopscotch the loudest, the fastest, the furthest. There seemed not to be the half-timer system here as there was at home, and the children from ordinary families seemed not to go to school at all, and instead played in the street when they weren't put to task by their mothers. It was a shame, she thought, for they would never learn to read or write.

Rarely did their mothers seem to call them in, for they were usually lost in their own work, washing or preparing vegetables in their own lodgings, or, more likely, cleaning and filleting fish at the dockside, or working at the large tannery that could be smelt from the old town. It was the tannery women that Millie found most curious, swinging their lant jars as they walked and chattered, quite forgetting their contents. Their clothing smelt terrible, their skirts and aprons streaked with browns and greys that Millie tried to overlook, but the ways in which they shook their heads and laughed, their shoulders free from burden, pertained to a closeness, a social liveliness, that Millie missed.

The men in the lanes rose early and returned late, though there was one old man, older than her Grandfather, that sat on an upturned bucket, closed his sunken eyes and raised the peak of his cap to her each day as she passed him. She had taken to nodding by way of reply, but what he did all day, she couldn't be sure. He didn't seem to beg, yet he had no work to hand, no daughter or granddaughter visible to care for him. She wondered whether she ought to offer. She knew that Granda would never have asked for help; he'd rather have perished than ask Millie to bring him bread. But he, of course, had been more than capable of making his own: the hard, round loaves cooling on the sill, that he tore at with his fingers, his teeth. She could picture his hands, his fingers, but his face… the shape of his cheekbones, the colour of his eyes? She couldn't remember.

If Millie's rounds finished earlier than anticipated, Millie helped Annie, and when Annie's charges had been packed off to bed or their lessons or to church, she would join Millie at the tub or fireside, peggying the sheets until they resembled clean. They had an unspoken rule that whoever helped did it from the goodness of their heart to get the job done; the woman whose job it was would keep the fee.

There were the times, though, when Johnny would be waiting at the steps of the townhouse for Millie to finish. How he discovered which house she was working at, she didn't know; she presumed his fame had already spread amongst the men at the mill, and their wives, working as domestics, could tell him. When she smelt his pipesmoke, saw how he languished against a wall or a lamppost, she stiffened and tried to ignore the flutter of her heart, like a butterfly butting a window.

He'd dress it up as a kindness, a kind of gallantry. 'I've come to escort my wife home,' he'd say, or 'My wife mustn't walk these dangerous streets alone,' even though she did so each day. Their silence would be broken the moment they turned into the smaller lanes closer to home, when he commanded her to hand over her coinage. If she hadn't been paid that day, he would pat down her stays, call her a liar, accuse her of stealing from their own household, tell her that she was ungrateful for the caring, hardworking husband she had, and he had every right to throw her out into the street.

And sometimes, she believed him. Sometimes she allowed her head to drop and she would curse her churlish soul for thinking about her family, about Greenfield, about buying a ticket home, when other women around her – the maids she encountered, the other washerwomen, Annie – were full of new discoveries, of new friendships.

But then there were the times – fewer, admittedly – when, emboldened by good sleep or a compliment from an arch housekeeper, she hardened and looked back at his gunmetal eyes and lied through her teeth.

'Do you think I'd deceive you, Johnny? Do you think I'd keep money – our money – for myself?' And he'd look away, nod to a passing man, inhale deeply from his pipe, laugh.

It meant, though, that she had become like one of the rabbits Johnny had stalked at Bill O'Jack's. She could never fully engage in a conversation with Annie or the other maids, for she was listening for Johnny's approach; she could never pass through the harbour, with the men stacking their catches and the women hawking their fleshy wares, without snapping her head from left to right, watching for him to emerge from a knot of jeering men.

She kept it all to herself. When Annie enquired after her relationship with Johnny, she would pass it off with a vague comment – 'Oh, you know, the same' or 'Well, he still likes a drink' – and change the subject as nonchalantly as possible. Annie was shrewd, she knew, but even Annie couldn't detect her plan. For it *was* a plan, and the plan gave her hope.

Late November brought with it the cold that Millie had feared. She had barely slept when she rose to break the ice in the pail, her fingernails raincloud grey. She put on both of her pairs of stockings and her spare petticoat, stamped her feet.

'I'll have to put on my other dress, too,' she whispered to Annie. The cold had seemed to still the words in Annie's head and she simply nodded, indicating she had already done the same.

Johnny, pulling his collar high about his ears, coughed and thumped his chest. 'Have hot water ready for when we're home; the fire must be piled high.'

And when wasn't it? Millie thought, crossly.

'Course,' Annie said, letting his words thaw as she scooped her shawl over her head. 'I look like a medieval peasant,' she muttered, bidding Millie goodbye and hissing through her teeth as she opened the door to the lane. There was ice in the wind, tiny crystals glinting as they darted past the clapboard. In these temperatures, the ice would no doubt cleave to the dirt, freezing the puddles and tormenting the tread of her boots as she picked her way to the townhouses.

After the day's earnings, she would have her first deposit, carefully calculated to leave enough to Johnny without suspicion. If she didn't do it now, she might never do it. It would take just one instalment to set the full journey in motion. She wondered if it was wise, lengthening her route back to the fire by lingering in that fierce air. She wondered if the ticket sellers would be there at all. But they had jobs to do, just as she. And ships still sailed; the sea never stilled.

She pulled on the sheepskin mittens that had belonged to her father's mother. Granda had given them to her when she died, and Millie had buried them in her case, feeling guilty that Jane hadn't received such a thoughtful, useful gift. She doubted they had ever experienced such cruel temperatures. She fashioned her shawl into a hood, as Annie had done, and braced herself.

Despite the horizontal wind and pregnant sky, the lane was as populated as most mornings. This morning, however, the people were silent, tottering. They waddled, skirted around ice, slipped, regained composure. Millie joined their sorry dance, her lips pressed together, silvery.

The Smethwicks had a young English maid, Mattie, who had left behind her family to serve them in Quebec. She and Millie had become accustomed to swapping friendly words in the dark scullery that the Master of the house refused to light.

'Oh my, Millie!' Mattie said, opening the servant's door. 'You've surely got five minutes to warm yourself before you start? Here.' She ushered Millie's shaking hands towards the grate in the servant's kitchen. Millie drew a stool as close as she dared.

'Thank you,' Millie said finally, her teeth ceasing to chatter. She nodded at the other servants that came close to the fire, warming their hands between their tasks.

Thankfully, one of the footmen had collected the water for the copper the day before, and Mattie having lit the fire, the scullery felt warmer than Millie had anticipated. It was too dark for washing, Millie thought, examining the linen in front of the firelight, but it was pleasant. She yawned and listened for Mattie's footsteps, tried to push Johnny out of her mind and instead thought of the times she helped Granda with his washing. Silently, companionably, they'd sit side by side, listening to the wind torment the chimney. He was unusual in that he did his own washing, she now realised, rather than leaving it to her or Mam or Jane. But nobody would have called Granda a Mary Ann.

The fishermen worked quicker in the cold, forming neat lines to pass crates and creels to land. By now, Millie was accustomed to their dockside catcalling, their attempts to catch her eye as they leant against their patched boats, but the weather made them silent, their faces furrowed. The sea slapped at the stone angrily, froth teasing her toes as she stepped past.

The older man with the tanned face was buried beneath a stack of blankets, his hands around a mug of coffee. It smelt good. He tried to straighten himself, but the cold had stiffened his back. She scanned about her, but nobody ventured close, preferring to skirt closer to the dock to make their routes as short as possible.

'Not good weather,' he said, his mouth cracking into a smile. 'I go soon.'

'Very wise,' she said, wondering how much of her tongue he should understand. She spoke quickly, fearing any moment that Johnny would appear at her elbow, his breath on her lobe. 'I pay the first amount? To Liverpool?'

'Liverpool, Liverpool,' he croaked, pointing a gloved finger down the ledger. When it stopped, he took off his glove and scratched an X into the page with a pen.

She shook out her coins and handed them over. He made more scratches, pocketing the coins.

'You have recorded the amount I have given you?' She peered to see what he had written, but couldn't decipher the characters he left there, whether they were letters or numbers.

He looked up at her, creased his forehead and set the pen down.

'Yes, yes, yes,' he muttered, and she wondered whether he was answering her or saying the word to which he knew English people responded.

She shivered. She couldn't linger any longer. She gave her thanks, stated she would be back again as soon as she could. He pulled the top blanket around his ears and closed his eyes.

She hurried home, head down, imagining each time she heard the sound of a slipped boot on a frozen puddle or a cough in the lane that it was Johnny, ready to set his heavy hand on her shoulder, demand she tell him why she had been seen with the dockside ticket sellers.

But it didn't come, and she allowed her breath to slow as her numb fingers struggled to prise open the new latch Adam had installed. Though she fastened the door immediately behind her, fine ice dusted the floor. *Were wooden homes really the answer?* Though the thick, grey stone of Greenfield cottages took time and effort to heat, once they were comfortable, they remained so. And if the sun shone a little more fiercely than usual, their homes provided respite. Tudor had been known to lie flat out on the flags to cool, like a pig in his sty. But this clapboard seemed so thin, so temporary. It afforded no shield from the sunshine, provided no blanket to this cold. *I will die here*, she thought, simply, *I will die here if I don't leave.*

'Ah, Mistress Barkwell!' Johnny reclined on their mattress, a curl of pipesmoke lingering as if frozen. He had his boots on, his coat and a scarf or shawl she didn't recognise about his hair. His hands shook gently.

She frowned at him. 'And you can work the hours you choose these days?'

'Of course; it's the Barkwell charm.'

'What about Adam?'

'What about him? He's as under my spell as any of them! And besides, I shan't take the piss; I've only come back for another layer that I'd perish without.'

Even in this cold, Millie could feel her cheeks summon up their customary crimson. Had he seen her with the ticket seller? The sawmill was in the opposite direction to the harbour, but he wouldn't necessarily be telling the truth. What would she say if he had? That she was running an errand for Mattie, that her housekeeper sought another maid from England and she was to enquire... quite why Mattie hadn't done it and the washerwoman volunteered-

'And why does my wife look so perturbed to see me?' He patted the mattress beside him. The straw needed replacing; she could see it sagging beneath him.

'Because I don't want you to lose your place and I'm certain not about to lose my own.'

She removed her shawl and set about heating the water for her own washing, lugging over the deep tin bath. None of them had used it for bathing their bodies since they had arrived, making do instead with running cloths over body parts when the others' backs were turned. She heard him pat the mattress again, but she ignored it, and instead, stepped out of her stays and into her other dress. He whistled. She turned.

'Where are your shirt and britches?'

He laughed. 'My, I never knew my woman to be so forward! She wants the very clothes from my back, wants my flesh against hers!'

'I'm washing, Johnny, I'm doing our washing. Now do you want clean britches, or not?'

He stood then, and began to peel off his clothing, letting each layer fall to his feet. He made sure not to shiver, though she could see the hairs on his forearms standing on end.

'Your other britches, Johnny. Where are they?' She ran her hands through the tangle of sheets and blankets at the foot of the mattress so she wouldn't have to look at him. She found a shirt, his stockings and bundled them in with her cloth. Instantly, the water turned the colour of buttermilk. Though the room began to warm, she could hear the wind picking at the cracks at the windows, fingering the roof.

'Aren't you going to look at your husband, Amelia?'

'Not when I've work to do, no,' she said, jabbing at the bath with the dull end of the peggy. It sounded like a frenzied bird at a roof. 'Aren't you going back to work?'

He was behind her; she could feel his height and his breadth like her own shadow. He leant forward, draped himself across her, and dropped the clothes he had been wearing into the water.

'Oh, Johnny, you know this will take time to dry! What will you wear this afternoon?'

He laughed into her ear, a sound that began like a curdled cough and grew into the whine of a cat. She swiped at him, ducked under his naked weight.

There was a thump at the door, like a mud clot. Millie stood straight, looked at Johnny, but he hadn't heard it.

She left the clothes in the water and opened the door a crack. A small parcel, wrapped several times in string, sat at her feet. She bent down and squinted. Mrs A Barkwell, the ink blotched, the postmark clearly English but half missing. She snatched at it, rose quickly, her heart pounding, and shut the door behind her.

'What is it?' Johnny said. He leant on the peggy, still submerged in the water. She pulled at the string. It resisted, snapped back. She turned it over. Two letters, the string taut over the envelopes. She dried her hands against her skirts, nipped at the knots with a nail.

'Oh, damn and bugger!' she said, half-laughing. 'Make me work for it, why don't you!' It was Jane's hand, Jane's on the first one, at least. She knew those dramatic looping capital letters that Mam so deeply disdained: *one's handwriting should be as neat and modest as one's personage.*

'Give it here; I'll do it,' she heard Johnny say, but she ignored him.

'Oh, damn you!' she said again, louder this time, as the knots tightened. She took the parcel to the drawer, pulled out the carving knife and set it to the string, like a hussar to a mouse. It yielded immediately. She flipped open the first envelope, tore at its seal with her trembling fingers. The first sheet of paper was dated 2nd September. She opened the other envelope then, hacking at the paper with her fingers as though she were plucking chickens. She gathered the papers together and scanned their corners. Mam's hand, Jane's.

Unless you've already forgotten, you know damn well the address of this house.

2nd September

I suppose I should address you as 'Dearest Sister', but I don't much feel like it. Not when, since you've left, I've twice the number of visiting trips to conduct with our dear Mother, calling on all neighbours, Father's daft Aunt, and everyone in-between. I've coddled more babes and nursed more dying elders in these last two months than in the years prior, and I'm putting it down to your absence – we must have shared the pleasures when you were here – and Mam's incessant need to remain busy so she can't succumb to wondering what you're getting up to. Don't worry, don't feel guilty: there's naught to be done about it. She tells me that's what mothers do. Worry and busy themselves.

I suppose you haven't yet a permanent address, which is why we haven't yet received a letter from you, but I have decided to write now anyway, so that as soon as we know where to send it, it'll be on its way.

What have I to tell you? Well, you shall probably be unsurprised to learn that I have no great developments to divulge. Tudor is promised a small piecer role at Jennet's Mill through a friend of our dear Isiah Dunne. I shouldn't be ungrateful; Mr Dunne has been very kind in that respect and Tudor is quite overjoyed at the prospect – feels quite the man about the house – but I do wish it was through a connection other than Mr Dunne. There is just something about the man. He makes it so plain that he cares for Mam, which is just horrible, I feel, though Mam gets quite cross when I raise it. There is talk of a restriction on hours for people of Tudor's age, a twelve-hour day, though many are clamouring for ten, but I doubt it will come to anything.

Alice seems to hang about me now at work, as if I'm your replacement, so I shall be kind to her until the novelty wears off. But don't get any ideas about Gertie Barkwell – we may be joined by matrimonial lines, but I shan't be going to any Temperance Picnics with her. Don't mention a word to Johnny, of course, but I swear she gets worse by the day. Why, she used rags on her hair before work, the other day! As if she shall meet a gentleman suitor in the all-women weaving sheds!

What else is there to say? Well, Theresa's mother finally died, so Theresa will be quiet on that front for a little while. And don't dare you chastise me for any unkindnesses – you know how loathsome Theresa becomes whenever ailments come up!

I've been asked whether I'd help at Sunday School in the new year as Miss Williams is going to live with her niece in the Colne Valley. Mrs Brownstone will be taking over, but is concerned about running things alone – and who can blame her! – so she has apparently requested my calming, teacherly presence. I quite fancy myself as governess, so I may surprise you all and go along with it. I have to give my word by next Sunday if I'm to do it. I'd be a good teacher, wouldn't I? I was quite the disciplinarian with you and Tudor when you were small.

There have been no further movements on the inquest. I expected there to be another held, or for something to happen at least, but I think it must be a hopeless case, for there has been nothing. You won't quite believe me, I'm sure, but I'm secretly relieved. I'd now like nothing more than to forget this and carry on with our lives. I don't think it is disrespectful to wish that; I'd rather remember them *alive, than be constantly reminded of their death.*

Mr Dunne is carrying on with his tours of the inn, and tells Mam that people come from all over to see Bill O'Jack's and he may as well make sure they go away with the right information. He tells us it may nudge us towards justice, as someone may come forward, but I don't concur.

And that is all I know. Perhaps Mam will say more in her letter, but that's all, as far as I am concerned. I haven't heard anyone sing that ballad. Perhaps it didn't sell many.

As you may realise, from the changing colour of ink, this has taken me a couple of days to write, so it is no longer the second of the month, as it was when I started. But I think you'll agree that I write quite the pretty letter! A governess, an esteemed letter writer – I might have a chance at a life of letters, rather than wool and cotton, after all!

Write soon, if you can fit it between your many wifely duties and tell me more of your exciting new life.

Your sister,

Jane

Millie reread it and crumpled to her feet. She clutched the letter to her breast. She allowed the tears to fall, her nose dripping mucus onto her lips, her chin. She laughed though, let the laughs gargle out between her cries, and scrunched up her eyes.

She squeezed out the remaining tears and blinked. Mam's letter was short, perfunctory. It was an update, a note to convey the latest news – of which there was little, as Jane attested – and to wish her daughter well. Millie scanned it for the affection her mother gave in person so freely, but if the words were read as they were presented, it was absent. She signed off abruptly.

Obey your husband, your God. Work hard and you shall be

280

rewarded.
   Your Mother.

No postscript produced humour. Millie turned over the paper in the hope her Mam had written more, an addendum of love and warmth. But there was nothing.

'You know, I knew you were close to your family – what good girls aren't? But this, this–'

Millie looked up, quite forgetting Johnny stood there, watching her. His skin was beginning to purple. He trembled, and the peggy trembled with him, chattering against the bath.

'Get under a blanket, near the fire,' she said, looking back to her letters. She folded them carefully and slotted them in the back of her Bible.

'I never thought a family could be held in such high regard, more so than a husband. I mean, what have they got between them?'

'Kindness,' Millie snapped, 'humility, goodness.'

'Ah yes, *goodness*, of course. And I could've picked anyone you know, Amelia, anyone. I would've just said the words and they would've come running: Theresa; certainly, that Alice, she'd have given me a go the moment your back was turned; Dora. Who else?' She watched him scanning to remember the names of the women she had grown with, shared bread with. At least they had been saved from him, from this.

'But the thing that I don't quite fathom is that you seemed hungriest of them all; for me, I mean. I was honestly worried for your reputation, that time behind the mill…' He tailed off. 'And now, when I present it–' he gestured at his purpling body, '–you can't bring yourself. I thought you'd be quite the goer, that I'd be entertained, indulged, from cocksrike 'til night.'

'I suggest you think about getting back to work. Adam might

have some odds and ends lying about you can wear.'

She threw a blanket over him and took the peggy and tin bath from his grip so she could continue dunking the bloated cloth. She would read the letters over again when he slept, when he was preoccupied with Adam or picking at his pipe. She wouldn't allow herself to think until then. She wouldn't allow thoughts to form in her head. She took up a hymn, forcing her faltering voice to find the intonation, cracking over the syllables. It was a row and Alice would have been horrified to hear it, but it stopped her from thinking. Perhaps Annie had been right about thinking; thinking only brought about misery.

Annie appeared at the door, stamped the ice from her boots.

'Was that you I could hear singing?' she asked, rubbing her gloved hands together, and spied Johnny sitting at the grate beneath the blanket. 'What have we here?' Her eyebrows wriggled. 'Blimey, this is not the weather to be without your clothes, Barkwell.'

She gravitated to the fire as though magnetised and began to show body parts in quick succession: one hand, then the other, one boot, then the other; crouching down, her elbows, her face, her skirts. Johnny groaned, disgusted, and took himself to the mattress, the blanket enshrouding his body.

Ignore him, Millie mouthed. Annie blinked slowly.

'Give me five minutes and I'll help you. I just need to get life in these toes, find out if they're still attached to my feet.'

Annie winced as she peeled her boots off her feet and flexed her stockinged feet in front of the fire.

'I'm not sure I've known cold like it.'

'There's worse to come, Adam says. The men at the mill say that in winters past, that some of their number have been found frozen stiff in their beds!'

'Aye,' Johnny added from the bed.

'What a delightful thought,' Millie answered, heaping the soaped linen into the second tub. She would fill it with clean water once Annie had added hers.

Could Annie be of comfort to Johnny once she left? It was unlikely. Johnny was too critical of Annie's looks, of her width and stature, to take her seriously, and though Millie was no beauty, she had slenderness. 'I like to feel a woman's ribcage,' Johnny had told her once, running his fingers along her bones as though he were a musician and she his plaything to strike.

Millie had seen the way women looked at Johnny. Some blushed if he spoke to them; some, the braver, the brazen, invited him to speak, asked him for his thoughts on the matter in hand so they could hear the way he formed his words. All would nod quickly at whatever left his lips. He could have the pick of any in a heartbeat. But it was Millie's submission he wanted, her good sense trampled, shot down; her willingness and loyalty channelled to serve him alone.

He wouldn't have it for much longer.

Annie handed Johnny a shirt and a pair of britches belonging to Adam, before adding an assortment of her own washing to the tub. She told Millie of the English maid she had befriended that worked two doors down from the French boys. She was young, really young, and terribly homesick, Annie reported, and desperate to let her family back home in Essex know of her new life. Would Millie write her a letter, if she were to come to the house tomorrow afternoon, once laundry was collected and childer packed off?

Slowly, Millie agreed, though it was a shame that it was a service she could only really provide for the poor; if the rich were illiterate, then her instalments would grow in no time.

'We agreed the fee of a penny. I hope you don't mind, Millie, but she really couldn't afford more than that; not really that, if I'm honest, but she's fraught with it. Her housekeeper keeps chiding her for crying in front of the master.'

'I couldn't charge her, Annie! Not a child! The poor thing. Why on earth did she come here if she couldn't bear to leave?' she asked. *Why, indeed.*

'A penny will be fine,' Johnny said gruffly, pushing his stockinged feet into his boots, throwing on his greatcoat, and bidding the women goodbye. The door banged shut with the icy wind.

'Did I catch you mid-?' Annie winked, nodding at Millie's shift.

'No!' Millie said crossly. 'Absolutely not. He was just being… petulant, when I was trying to wash the clothes.'

'Are you sure? We need some kind of word we can exchange or some kind of gesture to signal when…' she sought the words, 'when *relations* are on the cards.'

How little Annie knew.

'I can think of some gestures, but I don't dare to show you, Millie,' she laughed. 'I best go and fetch more water, hadn't I? Things are looking low, my petal.' Annie wrapped the shawl back around her head and set off to the pump, pails clanging in the wind.

Millie sighed. Annie was more naïve than she thought, but perhaps it was better that way. If she detected what Millie planned, she may find it difficult to keep quiet.

The following day, Annie brought home the young maid. She was younger than Tudor, Millie could see, and her teeth clacked in her head, even when they drew her closer to the grate, their laundry shielding her from the hottest flames. She had circles under her eyes like the gills of fish, blue and translucent, and tiny hands that shook. She didn't have a pair of gloves.

'Thank you,' she said, her lips hitching at each word.

'She's done nowt yet, me love,' Annie said, fetching her a glass of ale. If only they had coffee, Millie thought.

Millie drew out a sheet of parchment from the drawer and smoothed it across her knee.

'Before we start,' she said, 'tell me something of your mam and dad. I'd like to know who it is I'm writing to.'

The maid relaxed a little, her shoulders softening as the fire's warmth made its way across her back. Her lips staggered into a smile.

'Well, they work on the farm, Mr Morris' farm. That's where we rent our cottage, see; he's the landlord. They work for him and pay their rent back to him. That's what I thought was so sad: to see my poor old pa in the fields, day in, day out; my ma up to her elbows in muck and then they give their coin back to him at the end of the week anyhoo, just for the fun of living there.

'I thought I'd get out of that, do something different. There's enough of us girls that work as domestics, so I thought I'd get myself a position. Little did I know they'd grow so fond of me that they'd take me away.'

The speed at which she spoke indicated a story long often thought, never told. Even Annie could only nod and purse her lips when she paused.

'But I've never written a letter, I wouldn't know 'ow to start!' she said.

'All you need to do is write from the heart,' Millie said, setting the nib to the parchment. 'You address them as ma and pa?'

The girl nodded. 'They can't read though, so someone will have to read it for them. You can't put in anything not for others' eyes,' she said, quickly.

'Of course. I'll read it back to you before we finish so you know what I've written down,' Millie assured her, though the girl looked as though she were about to repent for her sins before the preacher.

'I don't want to alarm them, neither,' she said, 'so best to tell them I'm having a whale of a time.' She looked miserable at that, wringing her hands in front of the flames.

'Well, we don't have to lie to them. How about "Dear Ma and Pa, I am writing to let you know of my safety, that I have arrived in the Canadas safe and well, and I am being looked after by" – what are the name of your employers? Is that a good start?'

Once prompted, the girl was able to spin out a letter that was convivial and contained one or two happy anecdotes Millie imagined spreading throughout the village, cottager to cottager. Millie read it back to her and the girl nodded, tears forming.

'I wish I were there to hear them read it,' she said, and Millie wanted to embrace her, tell her she felt exactly the same. But she didn't. Instead, she offered her the parchment and ink and asked her to sign her name.

The girl shook her head and rose to her feet. 'I can't, I never learnt my letters.' She fumbled in her pockets and held out a penny. 'I said I wouldn't be long. I'll have snow to clear from the pathways; it's come down thicker and faster than I was expecting.'

Millie didn't take the penny. She drew out her case from under her bed and took out a pair of woollen gloves she had knitted. The seams were crooked, and the yarn had been scraps from the factory floor, but they would be better than nothing. She felt guilty that she couldn't offer her sheepskin gloves, but she would be foolish to do that. She couldn't ever afford to buy the like again.

The girl took the gloves and drew them across her puckered hands. She thanked Millie, thanked Annie, and asked whether she would be willing to write another time, and read any that she might receive in return. Millie said that she would and waved her off through the snow, her boots sinking into the slush.

'That poor girl,' Millie said glumly.

Annie peered at the butter in the churn. 'Oh, she'll be alright when she grows up a bit, gets used to the idea. And you'll help her do that. I do think you could make a pretty penny at this, though, once word gets around. I can tell all the maids I come across!'

'But making money from maids? That's not what I had in mind. The poor souls can barely feed themselves.'

'The wolf's hardly far from our door,' Annie warned.

Millie sighed and began to slice the bread for tea.

24

She woke to the sound of kisses, before she felt them, short, sharp little bursts against her neck. His beard scratched her skin.

'My twenty-year-old wife,' he murmured between each one.

Millie hushed him, told him to think of Annie and Adam, just feet away, on their own straw.

'They are gone for the morn, sweet wife,' he replied, and she sat up.

'Gone? Already? Then shouldn't you be gone?'

Johnny placed his hand flat against her chest.

'No, they're gone early. Why do you worry, so? It's all arranged; an hour with my wife, alone, on her birthday morning.' He pulled her shift up over her head and she shivered with the cold. He stretched her out then, kissing each limb in turn, pinning each to the sheet. It was alright for him, she thought. He was clothed and hot with it. She clenched her teeth to forbid the trembles and clamped her eyes shut as he kissed her legs apart, kissed her there.

'Softly, softly,' he said, and the words made tiny vibrations that spread and warmed her body. Her ears grew hot, her face.

Was this part of it? Was this what everyone else did? she wondered, or was this what the preacher warned against? That once lips and tongues and breath were involved, would it mean that it evolved into an act of desire and vanity, rather than love? She could ask Annie, perhaps, but their union was a different one besides it continued despite the promise of children. And Millie wasn't sure how she felt about that.

'You'll love me,' he said then, his words muted by her flesh.

She wondered at his words. She had loved him once. And now?

She furrowed her brow and felt something rise in her.

It was how she had felt outside the mill, when she had first kissed him, that she could grow tall and wise, that she enjoyed, even desired, his attention. It felt as though the sun shone on her skin, bathed it.

She opened her eyes. It was the first time for weeks she had looked into his so closely. His chin grazed hers. 'You'll love me,' he said again, and she peeled his hands away from her. She shivered and pulled herself out from under him.

'It's cold,' she said. 'I shall put on some water to heat.'

She put on her stays, her stuff dress, her stockings, tucked the key into its usual place. She rolled her shawl across her shoulders. She could see ice between the floorboards.

Johnny lay back against the sheet, looked at the ceiling. She heard him strike the flint against his pocketknife.

'Where did Annie say she was going?'

Johnny didn't answer, exhaled.

'Well, I'll go and find her. You should go to the mill before they ask questions.'

'You should be grateful, you know,' he said. The water began to bubble. She watched the bubbles rise and break.

'I am grateful, Johnny. I thank the Lord every day for my health, my family's health, for there being potatoes and bread...'

'Potatoes and bread,' he shook his head and laughed. 'Anyone I could've chosen, anyone, and she is grateful for potatoes and bread.'

'I haven't time for this, and neither have you.'

She heard his boots clomp on the floorboards, heard the rasp of his laces.

Then she felt him behind her. She was slammed against the wall. He had his hand about her throat.

'I could do whatever I like with you, Millie. You do realise that? Most men wouldn't put up with this: this answering back, this telling me what to do, the sullenness. I decide to treat my wife on her birthday morning and you look at me with disgust. Many men wouldn't do as I do.'

Her heart hammered. Saliva pooled in her mouth.

Spittle coated his lips.

'Instead, you go around with that silly bitch, taking my money and spending it on whatever you choose.'

She tried to deny it, but her voice wouldn't be summoned. She couldn't swallow. She watched the muscles in his jaw.

His grip tightened around her throat and then released it as quickly as though she imagined it. Her hands flew up to her throat, and her eyes watered.

He took a hunk of bread from the board and let the door ring behind him.

She held out her shaking hands in front of her. They were redder, rougher than ever. They were the hands of an older woman, a miserable woman. Her shawl caught on the driest parts of her skin when she wrapped it around her shoulders, which gave her a shudder she felt in her molars. Her hands were sore when she lowered them into the water; they throbbed when she held the pen over the parchment. Her throat was sorer still.

She breathed, her chest rising and falling. She held her throat, slowed her breath. A tear ran down her cheek, but she wiped it away.

She took off the water and pulled on her boots. In Greenfield, her Mam, Jane and Tudor would wish her a happy birthday at the breakfast table, insisting she was free from any household duties that day. Her Granda had once made her a birthday loaf, attempting to fashion a letter A on top with some additional stickier dough. Granda had never learnt to read or write and his A had been more like an H, but Millie hadn't told him, instead prising off the H and eating it while it was still warm.

She would not cry.

This year, she would make a present to herself. After her washing, before she was due back for Mrs O'Mara, desperate for a letter for her elderly mother in Ireland, she would visit the ticket sellers and lay down her second instalment.

It would be as simple as purchasing fish heads at the dock or tobacco from the deaf-dumb man that wore a sign around his neck. She would walk to the dock, as any working woman might, hold out her coins, see that her name would be written there; return. She had done it once; she would do it again. And Johnny, she wouldn't think of Johnny.

Though she was sure she could feel her heart in her wrists, in her neck, her ears.

The older man's white hair was hidden beneath a broad-brimmed hat. He didn't seem surprised at her arrival, at the bag of linen she dropped to her feet. He flipped open the ledger and began to scan the pages. 'Liverpool,' she heard him mutter. The lines in his faces had grown deeper, as though a sculptor had taken to him with a chisel.

'Yes, that's right,' she said brightly, taking the opportunity to clap her numb hands together, but he didn't look up. His brown finger stopped at the spot on the page and he held open his other hand. She fumbled the coins into it, immediately wishing she had counted them out like Annie's mistresses did, but he withdrew his hand quickly and slipped the coins into his pocket. He took up his pen and scratched more markings into the page.

'You've got it?' she asked, and he raised his head and nodded. His hat needed beating. Hair, either human or animal, curled haphazardly across the felt while dust obscured its intended colour.

'Goodbye then, and thank you,' she said, though the man had closed his eyes and pulled his blankets up to his chin. *Happy birthday to me*, she thought to herself, flatly.

When Johnny arrived home, he waited on the threshold for her to look up from her sewing. When she did, he thumbed to the freezing air behind him. Avoiding Annie's gaze, she followed him out and behind the house.

'And what were you doing on the dock today? Whenever do you need to go to the dock?'

Her face grew hot. Had he seen her? He couldn't have seen her.

'When?' she managed to say, buying herself time. 'I pass through the dock to the old town. Maybe a couple of times today, there and-'

'Adam saw you, said he saw you talking to a man.'

'Oh yes, well, the house wanted fish heads and sent me out,' she said. 'There's a man that sells them on the dock. Have you not seen him?'

'But that's not your job, Millie. Tell them no. I won't have no wife of mine, speaking to men in a marketplace like a harlot.'

He lowered his voice and looked about him, as though he was being gracious. She a child who hadn't understood and should be corrected, set on the right path. She wondered what it would take for his hand to be about her throat again.

'I can't say no to a command, Johnny!' she said. 'They won't pay me otherwise; surely you know that?'

'I can't say I do,' he said, folding his arms in front of his chest.

'When the housekeeper tells me that her master has gout and wants fish heads for his stargazy pie, that the little maid is nowhere to be seen, and to hurry, I'm hardly to say no, am I?'

'So, you're a maid-of-all-work now?'

She had told him lies – quite inconceivable lies – and it had worked. All she needed to do was keep her voice calm.

'Yes, Johnny,' she sighs, 'yes, it seems I am, if it brings in the money. Now can we go inside? It is not much warmer there, but it is better than this.'

Johnny nodded, and she hurried into the hut, head bowed. Why did Adam feel the need to report on her whereabouts to Johnny? If he had seen her, and was intrigued, couldn't he have just stopped her and asked her himself? Now, she thought, she would have to look out for him, too. And what if Adam's suspicions were aroused enough to draw Annie in, ask her about Millie's doings?

25

Whereas spring in Greenfield heralded fresh rainfall and weak lambs, spring in the Canadas took longer to come, the deep snowfall reluctant to recede and glittering shockles refusing to melt.

But with the sun came chatter, the lane breaking out into an animated talk between neighbours, the like and volume of which Millie hadn't witnessed since Christmas Day. She caught neighbours lingering at thresholds to exchange news.

Johnny and Adam had got to know a party of local men, most of whom they worked alongside, and had taken to spending Saturday afternoons with them. They watched the cocks fight in the old town, and Adam had described the seasoned warriors with hooked beaks and tattered, featherless skin. Sometimes, there was a bear in chains, he had said, that stood on its back legs like a human and jittered to a tambourine when its marionette master shook its chains. Millie wondered what Johnny did there, how he carried himself among the men. Did he lead them, cajoling them into the next ale, the next hastily placed bet on the cock with the biggest claws, as he might've done at home? Or had he a new persona in the Canadas, something darker, more ruthless? She hardly recognised herself, after all.

And what did these men think of him? She knew that Adam admired him, and Johnny enjoyed Adam's company, careful to make sure he never exposed Adam's naivety, his inferior wit.

And surely there were women in the old town, women that clustered around the men: for romance, perhaps, but more likely for money, for ale, for sport. Did Johnny look up at them, catch the lined eye of a woman and smile? Did he speak with them, language permitting? Did he lay his hands upon their wrists, whisper into their ears? Or did he ignore them altogether, preferring to smoke and drink and observe the fight he had ostensibly come to witness?

Millie didn't know. But she knew that women would be drawn to him, that they would brush up against him like moths to flames. She had been that moth, lowering her eyes when he spoke and raising them quickly to catch his eye when she thought nobody else would notice. She had lagged behind Alice so that he might catch them in the lane, so that he would say her name and hear how his tongue lapped at the second syllable.

But where had that left her? Those stolen kisses and quickened stomachs and smiles stretched from ear to ear – what did they mean when they had resulted in this, a broken marriage and instalments paid to a ticket seller on the quiet?

Annie had encouraged Adam and Johnny on their Saturday afternoon 'happenings', as she called them. 'Why, they spend all hours at that mill, and all hours with us, they need some time to be men,' she explained, and didn't seem perturbed at the thought of rouged women trying to catch her husband's attention – didn't think of rouged women at all, it seemed.

Instead, she had asked Millie to see whether Mattie had any spare time on a Saturday afternoon, and rounded up other maids and laundry women and domestics, many for whom Millie had written letters or Annie had met on her childcare rounds, and gathered them together in the servants' quarters of a willing volunteer. Some women only had an hour to spare, dropping in before their employers, their husbands or their children called them, sometimes they had a whole afternoon to share, but the women adored those gatherings, garnering notoriety in the district as the place to share problems and news, find friendship.

And Annie loved it most, presiding over the shabby table around which they congregated, pouring tea from teapots or breaking rock cakes into bite-sized pieces, willing them enough to go round. Her forte was the shy women, and the recently arrived, slotting her arm through their shaking elbows, as she had done with Millie, and ushering them into conversations. She matchmade problems with solutions, linking women that could help each other through shared money, time, deftness with a crochet hook or the getting up of a tincture. And Millie enjoyed her status as right-hand woman to Annie's beguiling, effective leadership, spotting the black eye on a new arrival and bringing it to Annie's attention; arranging for the confinement of a maid recently discovered pregnant.

Millie's knowledge could be especially effective for anyone seeking a ticket back to England, of course, but no other women seemed to be in need of that. Despite their difficulty in finding work, their concerns for their husbands' drinking, the unwanted advances of their employers, they didn't seem to lament for home; in fact, they seemed steadfastly resolute that Quebec would bring them exactly what they sought: food, work, prospects. All it would take? A little time, patience and advice from new friends.

Millie instead kept the information to herself, shrugging off the comparisons between late spring in the new country and the old, the conditions in the mills and factories and farms, and continued to visit her ticket sellers, drawing up her shawl when she approached. She had to keep her movements a secret; after Adam's disclosure to Johnny, she couldn't risk anyone she knew seeing her at the dock: not Annie, nor Mattie, not Mary O'Dowd, not any of the other women that gathered quickly, furtively, in whichever woman's kitchen they could chance it most. She wondered if she would miss them when she was gone, these women that she passed the time with, but the only ache she truly felt was when she turned her mind to Mam, to Jane and Tudor, to home.

Johnny stood in the doorway, leaning against the wood. He held an envelope by its corner, pinched it as though it were a mouse found in the ale.

'I s'pose you'll be wanting this?'

Millie looked up from his shirt. Her shoulders ached; her fingers numb from repetition. She set down her needle and thread, squinting. 'What is it?'

'Oh, just some ramblings from home, I should've thought,' he said, swinging it in the air. Millie rose, moved towards him.

'For me? When did it arrive?'

Johnny shrugged and swung it in front of her face. As she reached up to grab it, he jerked it upwards, held it away from her. She stretched up on her tiptoes. 'Johnny!'

But still he teased her, lowering the envelope enough for her to reach for it and hoisting it away the moment her fingers brushed the paper.

'Johnny! It's my letter! Give it to me!'

'And where are your manners?' he asked, his lips thin.

'Please!'

He tossed the envelope to the ground, let it skid across the floorboards. Millie chased it, scooped it up like a hen after corn.

It was Jane's hand, a thin letter this time, no interjections from Tudor, then, and still nothing from Alice. She tore into it, held it up to the candle. She heard Johnny go back to his smoking on the doorstep, heard his deep inhales.

Millie drew out the single sheet. The lines were short.

27 May 1833

This is only a quick note, Millie, as it's late and I'm eking the last light out of this candle. But I wanted to let you know Mam is not well. She has caught a cold, which we thought nothing of, but then she developed a hacking cough. We put her to bed, but then she became feverish. She's still there, in bed, and some days she seems better and gets up to make tea, but then it's almost like a punishment for exertion because there are some days when she is set back, and shivering and sweating and calling for Father, which is rather disconcerting. I thought you should know, and I thought you would probably like to pray or light a candle or whatever it is we're meant to do. I'm sure all will be well – you know Mam is like an ox.

Your sister, Jane.

For Jane to write of the matter, Millie understood the gravity of her mother's condition. But her sister's positivity, her certainty that all would be well, and Mam's strong constitution, comforted her somewhat. She sat down on the chair, let the note rest against Johnny's shirt. She read it again.

'So, what do the old Bradburys have to say of such great import, eh?' Johnny said at her side. She flinched.

'Mam's not well, Jane says. She's coughing and feverish.'

He blew his pipe smoke down towards her.

'She'll be alright,' he said. 'She's getting on a bit, that's all.'

Millie wanted to grab him by the collar, wanted to pinch his cheeks with her thumb and forefinger. She wanted to draw him near, close, and growl into his face. What did he know about love and care? Why didn't he share in the aching hollowness of life without his family?

But she didn't. Instead, she picked up his shirt and began again to sew.

'You know, I really ought to discipline my wife, to show her that she is rude to ignore me, especially when I am showing concern for her family.'

She focused on making a neat hole so close to the previous stitch that it could never be detected. She pushed in the needle so that it shot cleanly through. The original hole was invisible.

'Many husbands would beat their wives, or shout at them until they shake.'

She pulled the thread through quickly.

'But I don't believe in violence.'

Millie's breath caught in her throat. It snapped out loud, like a cough or a laugh.

'Oh, you find that amusing, do you?' he whispered into her ear. 'Would you care to explain?'

She felt his presence crowd the back of her head. A sharp pain in her scalp, then another, then another. Johnny pressed each of her pins in turn, leaning on them, so their ends bit into her scalp, her skull. She bit her lower lip, refused to cry out, but swiped her hand behind her, tried to swat him away. He moved his feet back, shifting his weight so he could lean harder on the pins.

'It would have been a damn sight easier to have married someone like Annie. Of course, I'd have to turn her over, couldn't have a face like that looking at me, but you don't hear her going on about her family – she's barely mentioned them once. She just gets on with things, works hard, lets her husband bang away at her even though they're as barren as mules-'

Millie ducked her head, rose quickly.

'When did you become so cruel? Were you always so unkind?' she hissed, her arms pulsing with fresh blood. 'Have I been so blind, such an ill judge of character? What have I done to encourage such loathing?'

'Look at yourself, Millie! You mope around this place, sighing and leaping at the first sight of a letter. You're growing thinner by the day. You rarely speak with the husband that gave you the chance to leave a damp hovel in a backwards little island-'

'-that murdered her kin.'

'Oh, so that's what this is about! Her poor slain grandfather and uncle, such honourable bastards that made their honest livings by beer and cheating the innocent. They'd have sooner sold you, Millie, their own relation, than part with their booty, trust me. We're all better off without them.'

Millie's hands shook. She lost the needle in the creases of the shirt.

'So, you're playing God? You decide who is to live and who is to die?'

'I didn't touch them; besides, you know that.'

'But it was at your command!'

'They were lying, Millie, thieving from under my nose! What was rightfully mine! Anyone would've done what I did!'

Millie pulled apart the shirt. It roared as it ripped. Once her arms could move no further, she threw it to the floorboards and ran to the front door, pushed it open.

She ran between the throngs of women in the street. She picked over the rags and pots and pans and faeces, rolled her ankles on the compacted dirt. Conversations were snatched silent as they observed her, and though she itched to turn her head to see if Johnny followed, she didn't dare. She kept her arms bent, her hands clasped together, so he couldn't grasp at her fingers and pull her back.

The lanes opened out gently as the smell of the sea grew stronger. Gulls hawked at the dockside, shouting loudly at the fishermen who, deaf to their pleas, hauled in their own catch in silence, their movements deft and rehearsed. In the sun, the smell was stronger, the fish sweating in their crates, shiny topless men sweating into the waistbands of their trousers. Barefooted children ran perilously close to the edge, skipping over ropes, while the blind beggarwoman groped her way around the perimeter wall, addressing each cluster of people she happened across.

Millie avoided the people and ran behind the fishermen's boats. The bigger ships drew in there, further round the bay, announcing their arrival with their horns. She turned a corner, and leant against a wall, panted. Though the harbour was deserted, Millie had seen each new ship heralded here by crowds of people waving and cheering, airing their hats. It seemed a kind welcome, really – local people suspending their activities and making their way to harbour as each and every ship arrived – but Millie was not compelled to do it. What if these new arrivals had been given no choice, like she?

But she had a choice now, and she had chosen to return to Greenfield. She would board her ship here, keeping as low a profile as she could muster, holding her breath until the waving and cheering had subsided. She stood in the shadows and caught her breath.

She saw Annie's plait first, like the rope the fishermen used. It hung in a straight line down the centre of her back. Annie inched up on her tiptoes, scanning the fishermen, the women that wandered between them offering flowers or flesh. Millie wasn't sure whether to run to her or hide. She waited for her to turn. Annie pasted her small hand to her forehead to shade her eyes. Her armpits had yellowed. She moved closer.

Millie stepped out from the wall and waved a limp hand.

'Millie! Where in God's name have you been?'

Millie took Annie's hand. They were too close to the ticket sellers here. She pulled her into a ginnel beside one of the boarding houses. An old woman, her creased cheeks rouged red, tutted at them. They watched as she crossed the lane into the alley that faced them and leant against the clapboard, fanning herself. She arranged her skirts so that the tiniest sliver of ankle could be seen above her boot.

'I have to leave, Annie, you have to help me.'

'What are you chattering on about now, Millie-May? My, your Johnny's been-'

Millie raised her hand upright.

'Listen to me. I am leaving. I'm taking the ship home. My mam is not well, and I need to go home. I'm not to be imprisoned here any longer.' Millie clenched her jaw to stop her teeth from clashing together.

'Have you lost your mind?' Annie said, her eyebrows jumping.

'I have never felt clearer of mind, to be honest, Annie,' she replied. 'But I'm going to need your help to do this.'

'Oh no, no, no,' she muttered, plucking at her plait and tickling her chin with its brushy end. 'Don't whats-it me in this, *implicate*. Your Johnny will kill me.'

'No, he won't kill you, but he might kill me if he found out. So, I'll need to leave in the dead of night. You'll have to help me. We'll get him drunk, and you can let me slip out, wave me off.' Millie's voice lowered to a whisper. 'It won't be for a month, perhaps longer, there's more money I need to save.'

'Oh Millie, it's not safe. You can't do that alone. I'll be afeard you'll come to awful harm. What's so bad here? We're just beginning, you and I, things will work out. We've got our Saturday afternoons-'

'I told you,' Millie said. She placed her hands on her hips. 'I'm leaving. So, will you help me, or won't you?'

Annie nodded then chewed the end of her hair. 'I shall miss you.'

'You shan't,' Millie said. 'You have your lovely husband to look after.'

Annie brightened at that and breathed deeply. 'I see that you won't be dissuaded.'

Millie shook her head.

'He said you tore his shirt.' Annie placed her hand on Millie's. 'He said you lost your rag and shrieked and pulled it in two in front of him.'

'Did he say what he did to me to provoke me?'

Annie's eyes filled then and sniffed. 'He said you received a letter.'

'Well, then,' Millie answered, and she led her out of the ginnel towards the direction of their lodgings.

At the hut, Millie made to enter, following Annie. But the door was slammed once Annie had passed through, narrowly missing Millie's fingers. She looked up in surprise.

'Johnny?' Millie said, pushing her words through the cracks in the door. 'Let me in, Johnny.'

She pressed her ear against the door, heard Annie's squeak.

'She chose to leave this household, so she shan't re-enter.' Johnny's reply, on the immediate other side of the door, was plain enough. Annie responded again, a pleading tone.

'Johnny, just let me in,' Millie said, thumping the flat of her hand against the door. She could already feel the faces peering out of the neighbouring hovels, the beckons to other family members to gather and watch.

'No, Annie,' Johnny said, enunciating each syllable carefully to ensure Millie heard. 'I have every right to teach my wife that she can't come and go as she pleases. That this house, spartan as it might be, was secured for her to live in by her husband. That it is a privilege to reside in such a house when there are others cast out in the streets for much smaller crimes.'

Smaller crimes. He had no right to talk of crimes.

She would not give him the pleasure of causing a scene. She turned on her heel and glared at the small face that appeared in the place of a windowpane in a facing hut. The small face immediately disappeared.

She would walk the lanes all night if she had to. She was unafraid.

She began, holding her head aloft. She would saunter, swing her hands, as though she was taking the night air, a stroll between duties. She rolled her shoulders, breathed deeply the stench of emptied chamber pots, pretended not to see the disapproving glances of women finishing their evening's work.

But as her skin began to prickle for want of her shawl and the catcalls increased in number, emerging from unseen mouths, she decided she would go back – and plead if she had to. It was her home, too; she cooked there for him; she washed there for him. She would endure it; temporary as it would be.

Annie was sweeping the boards in front of the door; futile, Millie thought, but it had meant their neighbours had gone back to their own obligations. Annie brightened when she saw her.

'He's gone,' she hissed, beckoning to Millie. 'He and Adam

have gone for ale. So, get in here, quick-as-like.'

'And now you see why I want to leave?' Millie sighed, closing the door behind them.

Annie nodded once. 'I can, my lass, I can, though it takes guts to do what you're bent on doing. I'm not sure I could do it.'

Millie took off her boots and sobbed, allowing Annie to stroke her back and hush her as though she were a baby.

26

It was the younger man this time, his ankles crossed on the desk in front of him. At her approach, he raised his eyes, his eyebrows, and brushed away curls of tobacco from the ledger.

He greeted her. It was a word she had heard on the lanes, batted between the women, the men, the children. But it wouldn't sound right on her lips, too tentative and alien, like when they'd asked Mattie to say 'ginnel' and they'd all died laughing at her southern pronunciation. Instead, Millie bowed her head, held open her palm. Her final instalment.

'The last time,' she said. The man looked at the coins there, glanced up at her. 'No more.'

She watched as the man picked up his pen and made another mark against her name. The page had become worn with indentations from his pen.

'No, this is the last time. I have paid,' she said. 'Paid up.' She set down the coins on the desk and sliced at the air. 'No more.'

The man shrugged, raised his ankles to the desk again, and slouched back in his chair.

'I shall be leaving on the ship next week,' Millie said, pointing to the departure in the ledger. 'Me, there.' She pointed at her heart, then back at the ledger. The man looked up at her through thick eyebrows and smirked. She could see his tongue as he spoke. Then he shook his head and settled further down in his seat.

Millie's breath quickened; she felt a tremor in her stomach. He was mistaken. She had paid up, she had paid every last instalment, the figures had been imprinted in her mind. She could recite them; she could see the numbers when she closed her eyes. She would be going home; this was what they had agreed.

'No!' she said, louder this time. She rapped at the ledger with her knuckles. 'I have paid. Can't you see?' She couldn't make a scene, but he had to see.

Millie plucked the pen from his fingertips and wrote down he total amount, circled it. She looked at him to see if he understood. He shrugged again, his mouth creasing into a dry smile. His lips were cracked, split. She drew an arrow from the encircled number to her name, added a tick.

'Done,' she said, 'completed. All paid up.'

His hands rose to his ears, parted, empty. He didn't know, he was indicating, he didn't care. *But he should care*, Millie thought. *He had to care.*

'What? What do you want?' she asked him, leant over his desk. She looked quickly behind her, brought her head level with his. He leered then pulled his lips back to bare his teeth. She thought of the dray's cob, how she, too, showed her teeth when she wanted something, when she was hungry for something.

She couldn't call a constable or ask Annie for help. But there was something she could do. She wondered if it would have the desired effect, that he would hand over her ticket as soon as she was done. She had seen Johnny softened by it, his irks fading with each convulsion provoked by her touch.

It would be quick, she thought, watching him as he sat back in his chair, his arms resting behind his head. He hadn't a wife; she could tell by the stains about his collar and the sprawl of his whiskers. It would be quick and then she would be free. She would not have to think on it again.

'You will give me my ticket,' she said, pointing at the desk.

He opened his eyes again. 'Go away,' he said in English, 'finish.' He drew one finger across his throat and closed his eyes again.

'No,' she said, firmly and pulled him up from his chair. She drew back the tarpaulin. Behind the stall was a chamber pot full of dark piss. Its smell soured the air. But it wouldn't take long. She pushed him against the wall, her fingers fumbling at his trousers. He helped her then, brushing her fingers away as if he had expected this, as if this is what happened, the final instalment. As she touched him, she heard his gasp, and she grew bitter. This was all it took. A few short, sharp tugs and her trip home would be secured? She wanted to laugh at the idiocy of it. She let her eyes glaze over, let the wall's sooty blackness sink her in to night.

She felt his hand on her wrist then, slowing her movements. She slackened her hand a little. She heard him pant, the air whistling through his nose hairs and over his cracked lips. He moaned a little then, too, a feeble kitten whine. He shook her wrist then, so she looked up. He pointed at her mouth, his eyes pleading.

'No,' she said, shaking her head, and she gripped him harder then, shaking him, driving him on. She ignored his whines, the pants that grew louder. It would be over. This would be over.

And it was. His whole body shook, bouncing violently against the wall. She drew away, wiped her hand along her apron, and slid back in front of the tarpaulin. She would not remember this, she told herself. This would be a mundane necessity, as simple as emptying the night soils.

He appeared from behind the tarpaulin, his grin wet. His eyes twinkled. He spoke then, smiling between words, made kissing sounds with his lips, rolled his tongue. She held open her hand. She wished it were gloved.

'Give it to me.'

He opened a drawer in the desk and drew out a small book of tickets. He flipped open the page and slowly copied her name from the ledger, in wobbly, uncertain capitals. He tore it then and placed it in her hand. His hand felt damp, clammy.

'Don't be late,' he said, the words unnatural in his mouth.

She snatched the ticket and turned on her heel.

Annie had been right: to pull herself out from beneath Johnny's dead weight, to peel back his arm, and slip into the cool of the room without detection, would have been impossible. Though he slept heavily, bodily, he certainly would have wakened.

She had suggested a late shift, some sheets that had to be completed before midnight, returning only when he knew that sleep would be on his mind. Then she should feign a task that had to be completed before daybreak, something for her most prized customer. Annie would help her, of course.

It hadn't been hard to find a night shift. Mattie's cold had turned to influenza and Millie had covered for her in the days leading up to the ship's departure, Mattie too weak to argue. It was gone two when Millie left the big house, though Millie felt as awake and as alert as the middle of the day. She thought of her case at the foot of her bed, tucked out of Johnny's sight. She didn't need to touch the ticket and key in her waistband to know that they were there; she felt their presence each time she pressed her feet onto the lane and drew on their hope and power.

But she was less certain about Johnny. She hoped he had already fallen into a deep sleep; that her absence hadn't caused him to smoke or drink between snatches of sleep, as he had been known to do. She hoped Annie and Adam's routine had influenced him. He had a full day's work ahead; he'd be up in less than three hours.

The latch lifted.

Breath from noses, from open mouths, reminded her to breathe.

It was dark, but Annie had lit the fire. She was seated next to it.

'Hello,' she whispered. 'I've managed to stay awake. And they're both asleep.'

Millie nodded, afraid to respond. She kneeled next to her and took the sheets that she had left out. The water was warm. Lowering her hand in, breaking the surface of the water, sounded like the crash of a wave against the dock. Millie couldn't remember who they had agreed to say these sheets were for; who they actually belonged to. But it didn't matter. Nothing mattered. Just silence. And time.

They soaped the sheets slowly, their heads bent to it, their hands illuminated beneath the translucent sheets like a child's shadow play.

'Annie?' Adam groaned from their mattress. The two women lurched, looked at each other.

'Yes, love?' she whispered.

'It's late; come to bed now,' he said, his words smothered by sheet and shirt and hair and darkness.

'Won't be long, petal, we're very nearly there.'

They awaited his reply, but it didn't come.

Millie opened the door to empty the soapy water as Annie walked the smaller tub of fresh water to her hands. These would be the cleanest, most thoroughly washed sheets anyone could wish for.

'This is a joke.'

It was Johnny. His words were too straight and clear to be sleep-shrouded.

'I'm sorry, Johnny, but it's got to be done. I promised it. We won't be much longer.' Millie's voice lurched between whisper, and speech.

'I'm up in two to three hours. Nothing is worth this.'

'We're rinsing now, Johnny.' Millie sat back on her heels, looked at Annie.

Quickly, then you go, Annie mouthed, dipping her forehead to the door, and Millie nodded, her stomach heavy.

They waited for Johnny to settle. Millie held her breath. Counted to sixty. Then again.

Annie opened the door as Millie grabbed her case.

'Go, go!' Annie mouthed, draining the water from the sheets onto the dirt. The moon showed Annie's cheeks to be wet. When she pressed them to Millie's, they felt cool and slick against hers. Annie's small hands rubbed the back of Millie's head, her shoulders.

'What will you tell him if he wakes up?' Millie asked.

'I'll think of something. You go. Hurry.'

She heard Annie press the door silently back into its jamb but didn't wait to hear her fasten the latch. She ran, keeping to the shadows the huts threw across the lanes. The ticket sat in her palm between her damp flesh and the handle of her case.

Millie ran on her tiptoes, ignoring the scorch in her throat, the prickling of her eyes. She trained her ears on the lane ahead, her eyes adjusting to the murk. She looked to the hovel where she and Annie had first watched the racoon pick its way through the washing-up bowl, but both had been replaced by a stack of cartwheels.

Too late, she saw a man sitting on the steps in front of his hut. Their eyes met, but she looked away. He would tell of a running woman, her skirts and a case in her hands. It would do the rounds at daybreak; there'd be a hunt for her. Johnny would be furious; not just at her deception, but his name being the topic on everyone's lips.

Her plan would only work if Johnny were to stay asleep long enough for the ship to set sail.

There was movement at the dock. Men were still coiling up ropes or mending nets, their movements slow, trancelike. She kept her head down and skirted round them, imagining Johnny's voice to bolt out of the darkness.

The ship was not taking passengers yet, though many had begun to gather. She would be easy prey out here, in the open. She scanned the dock, holding her hand to her head to keep her shawl in place. There was a wall in shadow, where men had stacked creels and crates and ropes. She ran and lodged herself next to one of the sturdier stacks. She would be seen only if she was looked for. She would stay here until the first opportunity to board. *Please, Johnny, stay asleep. Do not stir.*

The boat had been in for days, and though she'd seen its hulk on the horizon, she hadn't dared to look at it closely, in case it should be spirited away. But now, even in the half-light, she could see its majesty: its bright whiteness, its complex set of lines and pulleys and ropes that seemed impossible to master, but somebody did, many bodies, up there on the masts, exposed and swaying. At first, she could only see one man, a small, tanned man with his shirt about his waist, taking a cloth to the railings, but as the light grew bolder, he was joined by other men, checking ropes, sweeping the decks, whistling. Another man strode about in their midst, jotting things down and blowing his whistle to get their attention. She couldn't recall if it looked like the ship she had arrived on, The Great Countess; she supposed it must do. When she thought back to that day in September, all she could remember was sickness, a feeling of dread and gloom, her silence beside Johnny. Men waving caps and the cracks in people's boots. Her thoughts then, like now, had been of Greenfield.

She wondered what would have changed in the time she had been away. Nothing, she hoped; she hoped it would be exactly the same. The same hymns sung in chapel, the same songs sung in the mill, the same nonsense spoken by Mam and Jane at their wheels. She hoped the heather bloomed the same purple, the same filthy water whirled about the Tame, the same fullers stretched their fibres in the fields. She knew the creak of the door when the King Bill closed for the night; she knew the cry of the knocker-upper when he reached the houses of the men he liked least. She hoped she could slip in and start up where she left off, without anyone realising she had truly ever gone. She knew her grandfather and uncle were lost, but she could be found.

The skies grew brighter. The docks filled as though it were a play and a narrator had announced the players on stage. Men loaded tiny sailing boats with nets and set out impatiently to sea, while ticket sellers shouted for last-minute customers, the man to whom she had paid her final instalment not amongst them. Women hawked anything they could – seafood and fish, ribbons and parchment, lucky figurines of crude ships – while men shouldered them out of the way, carrying through crates and boxes which they heaved on to trolleys.

Queues began to form. She had to be near the front. A queue could protect her. Or would it only confirm her presence, show her up? There were fewer women, fewer families, amongst the men that stood nervously at the prow, checking their tickets, muttering to their companions, patting pockets, rifling through their knapsacks. 'Keep one hand on your pennies and t'other on your tuppence,' Annie had said, deadly serious, pushing some of her own pennies into Millie's hand.

And despite Annie's *Millie-Mays*, and *Petals*, and *Flowers*, and *Loveys*, she had seen Millie's anguish, her determination to leave, and she had helped her. She hadn't agreed with her, she hadn't approved, but she had helped. Millie knew it was a risk that Annie would be the first one he turned to. She pictured him with his hands at her collar, Adam pleading, but she dissolved the image with a blink. Annie was canny, and Millie owed her. She wasn't sure that she would be able to repay her.

She looked about her, wondered what to do, imagined Johnny waking, feeling for her. She pushed it out of her mind. He was gone; she would be gone. Still Millie's heart pounded. She would set sail almost to the moment Johnny would realise her gone.

Tell him I'd have probably gone to fetch water, Millie thought, *tell him I'd probably gone to empty the pot. Anything to delay him, make him take up his tobacco.*

'Quite the sight,' a voice started beside her. Millie jumped. It was the blind beggarwoman. 'Or so they tell me,' she added with a chuckle. It caught in her throat and she coughed one loud hack, which sent a pat of spittle to their feet. 'You will need to move quickly if you're going.'

'I know,' Millie said.

'What I lack in this-world sight, I make up for in foresight, a gift from my mother who could do the same, God rest her soul,' the beggar continued. 'Would you like to know what your future has in store?'

Millie bristled. She wanted to be left in peace. She needed to think. Could the woman detect that?

'No, thank you,' she said.

'Ah, a most unusual answer. Can I invite you to tell me why?'

'Because I shall only live it, anyway; I have no control, whether I know it or nay.'

'Wise,' the woman said, taking Millie's hand, and Millie shuddered. She yearned to yank it back, but thought of Mam and manners and endured it, a shiver starting at the top of her neck, creeping down. 'I am sure you shall be rewarded for such a wise outlook.'

The gentlemen were boarding now. Millie could only spy two women amongst them, one fanning herself despite the cool breeze. It would not be long before second class, then steerage. More passengers arrived; spectators gathered at the shore. Men in official caps spoke to passengers at the front of the ramp, gestured with their arms one way, then the next. The people responded, shuffling their feet in the direction of the pointed fingers. The spectators moved further down, at the insistence of a man with a whistle.

Come on, she thought, *hurry*.

The breeze changed.

'Down! Move further down!'

Millie saw a small man with a white apron move through the crowd, holding aloft a bird in a cage. It was brown, a flash of yellow beak.

The light nibbled at the shadows. She jammed her heels against the wall.

'Your turn soon,' the beggar woman said, tottering to her feet. 'And then you shall be far away from here, closer to your grandfather. Which, I think, is what your heart desires.'

The woman moved away, one hand feeling the roughness of the wall to guide her. Millie watched her go.

One of the cap wearers rang a handbell and the second-class ticket holders took to the ramp. They talked amongst themselves. The weather, Millie presumed, the likelihood of a smooth crossing. She saw them swap tobacco and newspapers. She urged them silently to hurry, to board them quickly and efficiently.

The man rang the bell again and steerage huddled forward, a brown-grey mass like field mushrooms. She watched, waited for the mass to swell. She couldn't see any women. She would need to make a run for it.

The sky seemed to lighten at every blink, wisps of clouds like the sky's own sailboats on an azure sea. She had hoofbeats in the hollow of her chest. As she pushed her body away from the wall, she feared her legs couldn't carry her the short distance to the prow. She tottered, her arms flailing away from her sides. *Pull yourself together*, she thought, *think of Granda*, but her knees trembled and her tongue stuck itself to the roof of her mouth. She tried to swallow, but no saliva came. Instead, her ears rang and her eyes twitched and she wondered what in God's name she was doing, but she pushed on and ignored the pairs of eyes, the men's eyes, boring into her, scorching her skin with their gaze: inquisitive, fearful, malignant.

She joined the crush of bodies, hers noticeably smaller and slighter. She kept her head bent, focused on counting the holes in the threadbare jacket of the man in front, linking them with invisible threads. He stood stock still, erect, listening, and she listened with him: the shuffling of boots, the shifting of coarse fibres, the clearing of throats, the striking of flint. The sea lapping at the dockside, the throb of boots along the ramp. Then further, the city waking: the clanging of pails, the squeak of boats being launched to sea, the ringing of bells and firing of whistles, the cries of seagulls and hawkers.

It was enough to charge her. This would be her moment. She wouldn't let them take it from her. She wouldn't be seen, stuck in a mass of men. She needed this.

She took the key from her waistband and held it in her palm, folding her fingers around it. She began to wind between them, threading her limbs through the gaps that appeared between bodies, between cotton and fustian.

'Hey!' she heard more than one man call.

She heard a commotion behind her. Further back, men were shouting, jostling. The noise was coming towards her like a wave.

'Millie!' She stopped, dared not to turn. It was her name. She hadn't imagined it. It was her name. 'Millie!'

'That you, Miss?' A man at her side elbowed her and it was the momentum she needed. She pushed to the official in the cap and threw her ticket to him.

'Please, sir, my ticket!'

'See-voo-play, grassius.'

His pinching away of the stub of her ticket seemed to take an age. She watched every fibre separate. Finally, he gave her back the remainder. It had been that tiny square of paper that separated her from home. She rushed towards the dark of the steerage, tiny bunks familiar, like cotton in mud.

'Millie!'

She ignored her name and ran into the corridor, the other passengers swelling about her.

'Women! Left! Les femmes! A gauche!' a voice shouted after her and she turned. There was a room for women, the door open. One bunk already had a shawl draped across it, so she took another, low and in the corner. She slammed the door and leant her weight against it.

'Excuse me! Excuse me!'

A thundering of feet past the door. She strained to listen.

'You don't have a ticket!'

'Sir, no ticket!'

A burst of bodies against the corridor, hands grappling. Was it

318

really him? She replayed the voice. It could've been; it could've been Adam. It could've been strangers, her name learnt from the alarm raised in the lane.

He would have to rip her from this ship if he was to find her. He would have to cause a scene.

There were more voices, shouting, but she couldn't distinguish the words. She stood, opened the door a crack. There were three officials holding tight the body of a man at the far end of the corridor. He had ceased to squirm and stood rigid, facing the way she had come. The hair, dark and mussed, was his. There was a tear in his fustian at his shoulder. One of the officials leant down to retrieve his cap and swept the dust off it. Once it was replaced on his head, he placed his hands around Johnny's wrists.

'She won't be here unless she has a ticket. And you don't have a ticket, so off you go.'

Together they marched Johnny towards the light of the passenger ramps and out of Millie's sight.

Shaking, Millie threw down her case at the end of her bed, shook off her boots, and climbed on. The provided blanket smelt of dust and mildew, but she drew it up to her chin. She tucked the key back into her waistband, felt its familiar nip, and listened to the jeers of the men outside as they bumped and butted into each other, finding their way onto the ship.

Her toes groped across the wooden footboard, beating the bounds of her new existence, and clamped her eyes shut. She would feign sleep even if it didn't come.

27

It was the shuffling that woke her, the sounds of feet distressing sheets or hands riffling through belongings. But she kept her eyes closed, mimicked the breath of someone deep in contented sleep. She did not want questions; she did not want to answer questions.

'Bonjour! Hello?' a voice asked.

Millie resisted the urge to reply, to introduce herself, as a polite woman would.

'Ah, suit yourself,' the woman responded. The rustling grew louder.

Finally, she heard the thrap of a leather buckle being fastened. A door opening, footsteps receding.

Millie opened one eye carefully, squinted through her eyelashes. She was alone. She sat up, shaking.

She had done it. What would she tell Mam? Could she lie to Mam?

Her stomach tilted, and she pressed her stockinged toes to the floor. The sea was calm so far, it was her own doing that churned it so. *Your own doing*, she chided herself, *all your own doing*. Her stomach bucked and though she retched, nothing came.

She raised her hands above her, scanned them from her littlest finger on her left hand, across to the littlest finger on her right. They were child-sized, weren't they? Despite the wedding ring, now dinked from work and looking older than its eleven months, her hands were small, slight. They could still fit between the warps, still piece together the slivers, the rovings, the yarns as they broke; she would still be of use. She could slot back in a widow; no questions asked once they saw her weeds.

She watched her hands shake, how they seemed detached from her body. She couldn't feel the trembles in her shoulders, her armpits, and they were attached, weren't they? There was just a lightness there, as though her arms could simply float away, that her hands would immediately if they weren't already bound, in bondage to her wrists.

And she had been in bondage, hadn't she, really? Bound to Johnny and feeling her way round what was needed, what he needed, what they both desired to keep peace and fairness and kinship. And Annie had served her apprenticeship; she had progressed to that next level, the stage to which all women aspired. Annie had peace and fairness and kinship, but she also made her husband happy, found contentment in doing so. And, presumably, she felt God smiling at her, felt His smile within her, warm, when she went to bed, when she awoke and prepared for the new day.

Millie hadn't felt that smile. She had felt heavy and leaden, a soft sickness that seeped from her sinews into her bones, so that every action felt laboured, every interaction – even with Annie, even with the women on a Saturday afternoon – had seemed inauthentic, a fake, a forgery. As though she were on stage and watching herself from the rafters, watching her body comply, watching her brow furrowed in concentration at getting it right, setting it right, making sure she didn't arouse suspicion.

So, who was she?

Now that she was here, alone, aboard a ship sailing for home, who was she?

She sat up in bed just as the ship's floor lurched, and really did lurch this time, for the other passenger's case – a tiny leather thing with a fustian handle – slid towards the door. And this time, the nausea couldn't take it any longer and a hot, sticky mess looped onto the floor at the foot of her bed. She coughed and was silenced by the gargle of more liquid that followed the same path and splattered, like the sound of the offal falling from a strung beast.

Granda.

She panted now, felt the sweat pool at her collarbones, the heave of her stomach as it threatened again. But this time it was dry, and she lay back for a moment, wiped the corners of her mouth with her sleeve and wondered how she would clean the floor and remove the stench she knew had clotted the air. She decided not to do anything about it, but to feign sleep until sleep came.

He speaks so closely to her ear. In fact, he draws her hair away from her ear, pushes it behind, so that his lips graze her lobe. She feels his beard, the coarse hair stubbling her skin. He made it onto the ship without a ticket.

I did it, he says, *I did it I did it I did it I did it.*

He doesn't pause for more breath, it just comes, heating her ear, the breath cooking her skin, blistering. It is like a child's game, a chant in the lane, but it isn't triumphant, it's insistent, as though it is the skein on a loom, pushing it further and further, around and around. The same skein, getting finer and finer, winding itself around the mechanism instead of being sent on its way to become something else. It stays the same, the same phrase, pronounced in the same way, the same diction, intonation.

I did it I did it I did it I did it.

Then he sinks in his teeth and she feels the blood rush and she shrieks. Kicks, her feet entrapped in the loom when all she wants to do is get away. But she cannot, so she shrieks harder still, her voice curdling in her throat, her hands slicing at the air. Hot air, that won't be chopped, but comes back at her harder, closer, enshrouding her.

A hand then, on her shoulder, and words that aren't his.

'Hush now, my pet, what a nightmare!'

Hands pressing her down. Just two hands, she thinks, just two, one on each side.

'Sleep now, come now.'

She opens her eyes, and it is as dark as night. There is nothing to do but obey. Sink down into the depths of night and feel the weight of those hands and submit.

There are voices, there are always voices, but these are hushed and further away.

A gentle heat on her closed eyelids and the sound of children playing overhead.

'But sir,' a woman's voice says with concern. Millie recognises the sound of concern. 'She howls all night and sleeps all day; shivers and shakes as though there are demons in her. And I've never seen her take a morsel of bread.'

'I'll fetch the doctor, but he'll want for coin.'

There is silence but for the squeak of a shoe.

'A chaplain then.'

And next time she wakes there are hands in her moist armpits, the fabric sticking to her skin and lodging there. She momentarily thinks of Annie, how she soaped the armpits of her dresses and still they yellowed and how she saw them once, full of curled brown hairs that so accurately matched the colour and consistency of the hair on her head that Millie could have laughed.

They pull her upwards and thumb open her eyelids. She sees them then: a man of the cloth, next to a man of poor cloth – most definitely not made in Lancashire or Yorkshire, too shoddy for English work – and a middle-aged woman with a shawl pulled up over her head. She looks like a mill worker's mam. But Millie's own mam has kinder eyes, a softer mouth.

'Sit, can't you,' the clergyman commands and Millie straightens her legs and her back, but they begin twitching again. He lets go of her head and she doesn't mean to, but it lolls away from his hands and thumps the thin wall behinds her bed. It smarts at first, a sharp pain that radiates out across her scalp, sending signals. It settles into a dull ache.

'Laudanum,' she hears him say, 'opium, or drink. I don't know where they get the money for it. And the cost of a ticket. She is a passenger, I take it, and not a stowaway?'

She supposes the man in the poor fabric nods or checks his notes because it is not mentioned again.

'You shall have to keep watch–'

'But I don't know her from Adam! And I've already cleaned up her vomit enough times!'

'You shall have to keep watch,' he says again to the woman, sterner this time, so she listens and will do as he says, 'and make sure she receives no more of the stuff. You will need to give her bread and water and see that she takes it. You will settle up with her when she has her wits.'

Millie hears the woman nod her acquiescence for her shawl sputters against her dress.

'We shall leave her in her disgrace. She shall feel God's wrath for it.'

And as Millie slumps back down into her bed, her eyelashes beating against her cheek, she realises it is her they are talking about. It is she that shall feel God's wrath, it is she who is in disgrace, and she fears he may be right, though she cannot quite pinpoint the reason why.

Instead, she settles back down into the nest of sheets that have become like her second skin, cocooning her, and falls back to sleep.

There are times when she remembers where she is – a ship on the sea – and she chuckles at the preposterousness of it. But when she laughs, there is a sigh or a tut, and then she becomes afraid. Because a ship on the sea is not a stable thing. One almighty gust and they could topple or turn and that would serve her right, serve her right for embarking on such things. Embarking! One embarks a ship, but one does not embarkwell, if not feeling theirself, does one? And she is a Barkwell now. So, she is once again failing, failing in her duty, to live up to her name. Her new name, her married name. And her Granda didn't chance for to see it! For she is a wife now, never forget. Oh, Jane remarked as much! Remarked-as-much, Mrs Remarked-as-much.

And there are times when she wonders if she is in heaven, sitting on the clouds, for the motion is such. Up and down and left and right. Her stomach quite leaves her at points, and she hears them groaning above. The woman next to her coughs into a bucket, like the sound of a thirsty fox in one of Johnny's snares. Johnny!

She is shaken this time. The two hands are curved about her shoulders as though they fit there. Millie's body is pushed and pulled, pushed and pulled, until she commands her eyes to open.

'Here,' the woman says, peering closely at her. When Millie's mouth opens in surprise, the woman shies away at the stench.

'Come now, they tell me your name is Amelia. And I know you've not eaten in days, p'raps longer. So please, eat this.'

She offers a heel of bread in her palm as though to a cat or a hedgehog. When Millie doesn't take it, but sits there, gaping, blinking, the woman sets it down next to her, on sweat-soaked sheets, next to a thigh or a knee, or some other body part horribly contorted.

'And when you've finished, there is water, clean water, in a sealskin pouch beneath my bed. Drink it all; I can refill it later. I am going to take the air on the deck and I suggest you do the same.'

The woman leaves then and Millie recognises the sound of her boots, the same sound that has been ever-present since she arrived and pulled the sheets up around her ears. This self-same woman has been moving in and out of the room, going up and down deck, finding and drinking water, probably conversing with other people, as if getting on such a boat and travelling such a distance is such a meagre, everyday occurrence that it doesn't warrant a comment.

She draws the bread towards her and sniffs. It is most certainly bread and probably hard. She crumbles the edges with black fingernails and trickles crumbs into her mouth. They stick to her teeth and her tongue and catch in her gullet so she tries to reach the woman's water pouch. Her bed is further away than it looks so Millie is forced to swing out her feet from the sheets and inch them across the floorboards which are rough and grooved w And as Millie slumps ith the indentations of many pairs of dirty feet crab-crawling across them and Millie's knees feel as though they are the strongest knots of bones ever to have lifted such a weight, they tremble so. But finally, her fingers brush the pouch and peel back the lid to find the water sweeter than she ever remembered water tasting. She gulps it down, breaks the bread into greedier pieces and follows that with the remainder of the water. It sinks slowly to her stomach and lodges there. It feels strange but comforting.

She lies back down and lifts back her dress. There is a warm smell that wafts with the action, a kind of earthy closeness, and she wriggles her stays so that she might view her stomach. She fancies she sees the bread and water protruding, as if testing the flexibility of her skin. A tiny pot belly, like the truly starving, were said to have in the slums in Ashton-under-Lyne, when the workers were striking and their tiny pot bellies sent them crawling back, willing to work for any sum. But she isn't truly starving, is she? She is satiated; that small nugget of bread could keep her going for weeks, months! She has the energy of a newly initiated mill worker, of the men that operate the mules. Wouldn't Tudor be operating a mule now, did Jane say?

She remembers the key and lifts it into the air, ogles it.

She leaps to her feet. She can feel the springiness in her toes, feel the keening of energy in her fingertips! She would go on deck! She wraps her shawl about her shoulders, places the key back into her waistband. She imagines it has made a mould for itself, a nest amongst her flesh.

'Where do you think you're going?'

She jumps at his voice, looks for him. He isn't leaning against the open doorway smoking, as she expects. He isn't in the corridor peering in. But he has found her.

'Looking like that? You're to be seen in public looking like that?'

Millie turns this way and that. She looks up, but he's not there. Why would he be there, on the ceiling? She chides herself. She gets down on her hands and knees and searches the dark letterbox of space beneath her bed, scoots a hand across the floor and feels nothing.

'Sharpen yourself up, Millie. Come on, you're not a child now.'

'Where are you?' she asks the tangy air. 'Show yourself!'

He is silent now, of course. He knows when silence has the most effect.

She sits back down on her bed, notices the damp of her sheets through her skirts.

She looks about again. Johnny Barkwell is not here. He is not here.

She feels the energy seep from her, evaporate. It takes all her breath to draw up her legs, drape her arms about her knees and cradle them. She lays her head on top.

He had heard about the ways in which women, left to their own devices, spoilt, could have their lives ravaged by the insufferable heat of their menses. He could see it in Jane already, he had said; it was why she had not yet been married. *God give the man strength that took her.* Millie had laughed at first, wondered where he got such information. Jane was just headstrong, she had replied, determined and well read. But he hadn't liked that; said that she was also over-familiar with giving her opinions.

And perhaps he had been right. Perhaps this is it, this he described, an unburdened, unbidden force she is unable to quell, rising up in her. Perhaps it will remain that way, and she shall become slave to it.

'Oh, you're up.'

The woman reappears and Millie lifts her head. The woman looks at her and wrinkles her nose. Her eyes narrow. She is the age her voice determines, around fifty.

'And you have eaten?'

Millie nods, straightens out her legs. Her shawl slips and lands in her lap. She suddenly feels the weight of her hair on her shoulders. She cannot remember the last time she washed it.

'Thank you,' Millie says, but it arrives like a whisper. The woman seems not to have heard.

'You need to air your bed, air yourself. Take yourself on to the deck. I can't be forced to sleep next to *this* any longer.'

Millie stands and looks back at her bed. There is a blanket at the foot, halfway to the floor.

She is aware, too, of a smell, not unlike the smell that announced Johnny and Adam's return from the sawmill. Of soft vegetables, sodden straw. Millie lifts her arms a fraction and notices how the smell intensifies.

'Have you another?' The woman asks and Millie frowns, looks at her. 'Have you another dress?' The woman says again, her tone much harder. She thinks Millie a simpleton.

'No,' Millie says. She stands there, her arms floating away from her body as though her dress is wet.

'Go, then,' the woman shoos her to do the door and Millie obeys, staggering out to the shadows which throw themselves across the corridor.

She shields her eyes and shuffles to a door that she can see at the far end, one that opens onto a set of squat, perfunctory steps upwards. Her knees tremble as she takes each step in turn, the worn wood smooth beneath her bare feet, and she hauls herself up by her arms, feels the stretch in them as she swings each foot forward. She hears them then, the other passengers, their talking, the throaty laughs of men hoping for the best. It is loud, and the wind adds to the volume by shouting in her ears, teasing her hair upwards. Two older men nearby turn to look at her as she surfaces, and she realises she looks like some drowned woman, a girl feared dead in the millpond but has woken, risen, with weeds still clawing at her hair, her dress clogged and lagging.

The men turn back to their conversation. She collapses onto a seat and looks out to sea. It is as before: a cold grey blanket stretching out for as far as she can see. No other vessels, no land. There are clouds above, though, woollen wisps teased out as though by a stiff brush. The seat is more like a bench, large and substantial, and she feels as though she has been smeared into it. She feels her breath lengthening, her heartbeat slowing.

She chose to be here.

Later, when Millie returned to the dormitory, she found the woman had changed her bed linen, paired up her shoes at the foot of her bed and lain out a dress she didn't recognise. The woman was sitting on her own bed, reading her Bible. Her spine stiffened. She lowered her Bible when Millie arrived. She saw her brace herself.

'You can wear my spare until we are nearing Liverpool. I'll want it washed and returned then.'

Millie nodded and fingered the fabric. It was shop-floor fustian, but it was clean, cared for.

'Thank you,' Millie said.

The woman looked at her Bible again.

'And thank you for the bread and water.'

She pursed her lips in reply.

'I'm not a drinker,' Millie said, her cheeks flushing hot with shame. Mam wouldn't hear this, would never hear of this. The woman flinched. 'Nor nothing else. I don't touch a drop.' Millie sat down on her bed and saw that the woman did not believe her. 'I'm a Methodist.'

The woman nodded this time, a quick flash of her greying head, as if to bring the conversation to a close.

'I didn't feel well,' Millie said. 'I still don't, if truth be told. I've never felt so cold and hot all at once, my head muddled and not sure whether I was asleep or a-'

'Right, good. Well, you shan't if you don't look after yourself. There's plenty of bread and water to go round. Where's your husband?'

The woman's gaze had settled on Millie's ring finger.

'Dead,' she replied quickly. 'He died in a sawmill accident. It's why I'm going home.' She remembered Granda's phrase he used instead of the word '*death*': going home. 'I couldn't live there alone. I'm returning to my family in Greenfield, in Saddleworth.'

The words came as quickly as the rabbits on the land surrounding Bill O'Jack's.

'Saddleworth,' the woman said, offering no condolences. 'And how will you get there?' The woman looked at her then, full in the face. Her jagged lips, her watery eyes. Millie could see she thought her of dubious repute.

'I-I suppose, I suppose I shall have to work to find the fare, unless I find anyone going that way in need of a companion.'

'A companion?' The woman's eyebrows soared high on her forehead.

'I mean,' Millie said, 'someone to keep them awake, someone to talk to. I imagined a mail coach already travelling that way; that's how Johnny and I got to Liverpool in the first place.'

The woman's eyebrows settled. 'Don't go advertising yourself as a companion-'

'I wouldn't-'

The woman held up a hand to silence her.

'Don't go advertising yourself as a companion, a woman by herself. You find yourself another woman as a companion and go yourselves together.'

Millie's face glowed with heat. What did this woman think

she was? Of course, if she'd thought about it sensibly, that's exactly what she'd do. And that's what she'd say she'd do. But she hadn't thought about Liverpool. Only Greenfield.

'Where are you going?' Millie asked.

'Carlisle,' the woman answered, as though irritated at the question. 'My employers' man is meeting me.'

'That's far, isn't it?'

'It'll take some time, yes.'

And Millie could see that the woman didn't know what lay in store for her and that she was afraid.

'Now, are you going to change into this dress or not? There's a washstand in the cupboard next door, which I asked the chaplain to install for you. Not many on board will have access to a washstand, so make the most of it and tell no others.'

Millie thanked her, thanked her again, and went to the tiny room next door to peel off her dress and wash.

The woman barely spoke to Millie again and kept her distance. Millie confined herself to the room. Mostly, she attempted to read her Bible, but the words swam before her. She could pass hours, she realised, with her eyes drawn to the same passages, but without making sense of the letters that lay there. Mostly, she thought of Granda and Tom, and how Mam, Jane and Tudor were weathering, whether people still stared at them in the streets or hushed their conversations when they came into view.

And there were times when she still thought she heard Johnny – his particular way of exhaling his pipesmoke, or the way he coughed into his fist – but that was when she concentrated hardest, searched for the real sounds about her ears and counted them: one, a male passenger on deck, being slapped on the back to ease his cough; two men huddled about their ales and laughing; three, a man calling his wife, a Polly, or a Molly, most certainly not a Millie.

And then it came, the great roar of men on deck, like the sound during Wakes Week when the men raced ponies on the moors. Millie looked up from her Bible and blinked. She scrambled to her feet and up the steps to the deck.

England had come into view. She would soon be home.

28

Though it was the hills she knew so well, could trace the line of them in the air with her finger, the rise and fall of the land looked different from the cart. The additional foot or so in height gave depths to the ravines she hadn't seen before, made the green of the sheep tracks more vibrant. The curvature of the North face of Noon Sun seemed flatter, more sheer; Alphin loomed away, solitary, priggish.

Sleep weighed heavily in her bones, sagging her low into the cart amongst the packages and parcels, but the sharp wind, fluting across her skin, kept her alert. That, and the beat of her heart, a gallows drum, which had maintained since she first took her steps back on English soil.

The driver sat hunched over his reins, his hat pulled down on his head. His horse's ears relaxed sideways. For all she knew, they could have both been asleep, rocked into slumber by their own motion, their own propensity to keep going, one hoof in front of the other. They were not excited to reach their destination; there was no exhilaration in returning here after their journey, shorter than hers by any account. And he wouldn't have assumed anything on her part, either. She watched him look her up and down. Take in her brown stuff dress, shawl, and small case. Only a domestic servant returning from service, or, if he were to take in the gold band on her ring finger, a recent widow returning home to consider her next chapter.

And this was the part she would play. She would need weeds, of course. She could borrow Mam's. But once she was wearing black, it would be easier to mourn, easier to face Esme and George and Gertie. And she could tend to Mam with a quickness, a brevity, that could be excused by her mourning dress. She could avoid the questions about the Canadas, about the sights she had seen and the people she had met, until time had lapsed, and Mam was well again. *A newlywed with all her life ahead of her*, they would think, *returning home a widow to tend her mother*. And they would leave well alone.

Nausea rose up inside her, bubbled in her throat. She inhaled deeply through her nose and held on to the side of the cart. It sank again, as quickly as it had come.

The tracks were quiet, the valley was as still as a Sunday afternoon, though the clouds hemmed and hawed together, plotting. It would be a few hours yet before the mills spilled out, and more hours still before the looms ceased for the evening. She could surprise Mam with warm milk, mop her brow and set back the curtains, ready the kitchen with tea before Jane and Tudor arrived home, speechless with astonishment. She imagined the making haste to embrace her, each vowing never to argue again now they had been granted this second chance; Tudor forgetting his impending manliness and kissing his sister's cheeks.

The clouds opened. The rain was heavy and thick and seeped into her clothing. Her shawl slopped to her scalp, the water rushing off it into her lap.

'You alright back there, lass?' the driver called through it. He sat lower in his seat.

'Yes!' she shouted, though their ears were filled with rain and the sound of it, and she didn't know if he asked her another question. She buried her case, with its reread letters, beneath a trunk and felt a particularly large, cold droplet lower itself onto her spine and travel its length.

The clouds were so low they looked as though she could part them with her hands, push them aside like tobacco smoke. She squinted, bobbed her head to see if she could see Bill O'Jack's beyond the Wellihole, but it was sheltered, obscured by the hills and the cloud. Greenfield was folded into the land, haphazard lines of dark, dank houses that appeared to be stuck steadfast, governed by the hasty topography of the land. If she blew hard enough, she thought, they could disappear.

But the cart would need to drop down lower first, work its way into the valley. The Brew in Mossley looked as it always had done, though the butcher had painted his sign blue. No other shops had changed hands; the door to the scrapper's stables at Woodend still lunged on its hinges.

At the Wellihole, the rain simpered into a drizzle, and the smell of long grasses and the turgid water of the Tame rose up to meet her. She hadn't smelt that smell in the Canadas; could it only be found here? Hunger gnawed at her stomach, gave way to a roiling nausea. She turned her head to face her favourite view, the one she had conjured so readily whilst she'd been away. The fields rolled out like a bedspread, flat and lush, as though she herself could canter through it to greet the hills that, from here, gave the lofty illusion they were far away, grand and destined for higher things. But she could reach them after only an afternoon's walk, the mist hiding their peaks and simple slopes. If only she could grab at them, kiss them and embrace them, tell the view how happy she was to see it.

And then the road, her road, the road on which she had lived for nineteen years. The sickness surfaced again, collected in the corners of her mouth and seared her tonsils. She bent her head deftly over the side of the cart; let it pour away without a sound. Her stomach sighed, and it came again, a tide this time that sloshed against her teeth and railed against her nose. Her ears rang with it.

'You alright lass?' she heard the driver call again, but even if she had the strength to answer, her mouth couldn't find it. He reined the mare to a halt, but Millie raised her arm, flapped her hand, eyes closed.

The cart rolled on. The street was silent, the cartwheels muffled by the dirt. How like the earth packed streets of Quebec it was, she noticed, how had she not made the comparison before?

'Just to the chapel,' she croaked, and she worried he would have to lift her from the cart like a scarecrow. Her limbs threatened to splay out from under her.

There would be bread in the larder, butter in the dish. Mam may have even been able to persuade Jane to buy honey from Mr Dunne's, though she didn't care for it and felt their money was best used elsewhere. 'I can walk from there.'

He held out a hand as she went to step down. She was glad to take it and felt the bend in her knees and the weakness in her ankles as her skirts grazed the Greenfield earth. He nodded his head at her and took only one of the coins she offered him, refusing her eye contact and climbing back aboard.

The chapel door was ajar and though she longed to push it open and breathe in the dark air, it would have to wait. There would be plenty of time for reacquaintance. She clasped her case to her chest with one hand and plucked at her skirts with the other.

She was home. She stood at the ginnel's end, breathing hard. None of the neighbours were at work in their yards, none cutting up newspaper for the privy or looking up from their tubs. And she was relieved. The rain had driven them indoors.

This would be her moment, her private moment. She passed the doors quickly, then reached her own back door. There were no boots there, so Tudor was still at the mill. She lifted the latch, heard it make the sound it always did: the sliding and clinking of metal against metal, worn smooth by everyday use. The door releasing, the air rushing out to greet her, that same smell of bread and wood polish and leather, of fabric drying, wetting, and drying again, of warmth and breath and safety.

And the sound of her boots on the flags.

'Tudor?'

It was Jane.

Millie set down her case, shook out her hat.

'Try again.'

Jane rose immediately, a man's boot and needle in her hands. She looked tall, Millie thought, tall and gaunt. Her face much paler than she remembered, her dark hair accentuating the milkiness of her skin, the blackness of her dress even more so. Millie hadn't remembered that dress. She smiled at her and Jane stared back, her eyes settling on Millie's stomach. Then Jane came tumbling towards her, their skirts mingling, entwining. And she sobbed. Jane sobbed into her neck, plastering again her dress to her collarbones, her shawl to her dress.

'My! I'd imagined a homecoming, but this!' Millie laughed, which made Jane howl then, her breath coming thick and fast through her nose, her mouth. They tightened their arms around each other, felt the beat of their hearts, the brittleness of their bones. Millie laughed again, enjoyed this sudden strength she had, for she held Jane upright. 'Jane! It turns out you did miss me after all! If this is from you, what shall I get from Mam? How is she? Where is she? A-bed?'

Jane pulled away from her.

'Did you not get my letters?'

Tears stuck to Jane's face like porridge oats, suspended part way through their tracks.

'What letters? What letters, Jane?'

Her sister looked fearful then, her forehead twisting up and away from her eyebrows.

'Oh Millie, you don't know.'

'Where's Mam? Is it Mam, Jane?'

And Jane nodded slowly, then quicker, her head bobbing lightly on her shoulders, her eyes filling again. 'Is that not why you're here? I wrote to you; I wrote to you several times. I knew it would take some time to reach you, but what could I do? I wrote right away.'

'Is she gone?'

Jane continued to nod. 'She didn't recover. Her suffering was slight. She was comfortable. Thank the Lord.'

The room swooned; the mantelpiece seemed to dance before her. Millie held the table; let the chair squeak across the flags so she could sit. She couldn't fathom how efficiently her body could fashion tears when she had so little strength. Still her stomach gargled, rolled.

'When?'

'A few weeks ago.'

'When exactly?'

'The second of August.'

She had been at sea then, flinching at the sound of every man's voice.

Jane took the seat next to her. She drew Millie's hand into her lap. Both hands were hot, wet, and sticky. She told her about Mam's final days that she became unaware of her surroundings, forgetful. She asked for windows to be opened and once they were beseeched that they were closed as quickly. That Tudor was as patient as Jane was angry, and the two clashed unceremoniously until Mr Dunne took them aside and asked them to hold their tongues for the sake of their mother.

And Mr Dunne made arrangements and held the service at St Chad's.

Jane looked glumly at the boot that needed repairing. 'He has been kind and generous, Mr Dunne,' she said, looking up at Millie.

'Mr Dunne?' Millie asked.

Millie felt the hardness of the chair beneath her, felt her buttocks grind into it. If she sank any further, she would disappear. The chair would consume her.

Jane hadn't pinned her hair. It sat wildly over her shoulders; locks tangled. She hadn't combed it for days. Millie watched the muscles in her jaw tense, release, tense again.

'He has been kind and generous,' Jane said again, though her gaze rose beyond Millie's face and settled somewhere behind. 'He offered to buy this place, to take it out of mine and Tudor's hands.'

'This place? Our house, you mean?'

Jane continued. 'We couldn't have afforded it. So, we were grateful.'

'You've been paying rent to Mr Dunne?' Millie's voice rose. The sickness with it.

'No, not quite. You see–' and Jane paused, her breath sucked in, 'Mr Dunne lives here now and we agreed that if I should keep for him, then all would be well.'

'Keep for him? Keep house for *him*?'

And then Jane nodded.

Millie sat back against the chair. Her head felt light, but her heart throbbed deeply in her ribcage. It was like a millstone.

'And Tudor? How does Tudor take all this?'

Jane's expression didn't change.

'Tudor is calm. He takes things easily since you left and Mam died. Like he doesn't much care, like things can't get much worse. And I suppose he has a point. He spends his waking hours in the mill. Did I tell you he has a mule now?' Jane's eyes lowered then landed on the doormat or the flagstones. 'I should imagine he's already thinking of taking a wife, just so he can be rid of me, of this.'

Millie grabbed Jane's hand again and dug in her nails. She needed a rush of feeling, but Jane just looked at her in surprise.

'And you – you who railed against marriage – don't mind keeping house for Isiah Dunne?'

Jane's lips looked as though they meant to smile, but thought better of it.

'We're not *married*, Millie, thank the Lord. It is a domestic arrangement; it satisfies all parties.'

'Satisfies all parties?'

Jane looked away. 'You weren't here; you weren't to know.'

'I can't believe Mr Dunne owns this house, our house.' Millie slunk back into her chair. 'And you're stitching his boot!'

'And Bill O'Jack's, Millie, he owns Bill O'Jack's. Mam was glad to be rid of it. And who should take it from her hands?'

Millie searched Jane's face. There were lines at her eyes, lines she didn't recall seeing before, and there was a blue tinge beneath her lower eyelashes as though the skin had been pulled so taut that it had bruised of its own accord. Her lip trembled.

'So that's it,' Millie said, slapping her hands against the table harder than she intended. Jane flinched. 'Anything of any worth, anything any of us ever built, is gone.'

'We haven't ever built anything, Millie. What have we built? Bill O'Jack's was bricks and mortar, the house is bricks and mortar, but we didn't *build* either of them. We're just people passing through this world: living, dying, passing through. We haven't made our mark on anything.'

Millie let the words wash over her, let the subsequent silence gather at her ears. Mam gone; Granda and Tom gone; her marriage. And Mr Dunne presiding over it all, the puppeteer gathering the strings.

She rose. She set the water to boil and took out two cups. Tasting the bile in her throat, she searched the drawers for mint leaves. She found two, curled and browning, and straightened them out before dropping them in to the cups. She turned. Jane had returned to the boot, tugging the heavy thread through the leather. It made a sound like a nib against parchment.

Jane didn't look up from the boot when Millie brought the cups to the table. 'Why are you here, Millie? Where's Johnny?'

Millie slopped a little of the water over the side, watched it pool on the grain of the table. Mam would have leapt up to wipe it away.

She told Jane about the sawmill accident, the man who had run to raise the alarm. How a team of them had carried him back to the lodgings they shared with Annie and Adam, set him down upon a clean bed of straw she and Annie had prepared the moment they heard the news, packing off the two little maids for whom she had been writing letters.

How, for a day, Johnny had seemed strong, making jokes from his sheets and asking Adam to prepare his pipe, but then he had slipped into a fever, which gathered first at his temples and his hairline, before breaking out across his body. He shook next, and his eyes creased as pain introduced itself. To wash his body and keep him cool, Millie used the rags Annie borrowed from neighbours, pointing urgently when they didn't understand.

But the blood continued to leak and with it his colour drained. He was buried, Millie said, in the clothes he wore for their wedding.

Jane leant over and squeezed Millie's hand, absently rubbed her knuckles.

'Oh Millie,' she whispered over and over, 'oh, Millie. I did wonder. People don't leave to return.'

Her recitation had gone well. Jane hadn't asked any questions. She would say the same to Esme, George, and Gertie; she would tell it exactly thus each time.

'A widow at twenty,' Millie concluded.

'But you're home now,' Jane said.

'Can we go to Bill O'Jack's?' Millie asked, sitting upwards.

Jane looked at the clock on the mantelpiece. Its tick seemed irregular, a strong, confident click-click-click, then a trip on the fourth or fifth before it righted itself.

'I promised Isiah that his meal would be on the table by five; he has business to attend to this evening.'

'So, we have an hour. Come on.'

The two women walked in silence and listened to the wind torment the tall grasses that grew up from the verges. It tormented their necks and ears, too, taking unexpected sideswipes at them. But Millie breathed deeper and calmer and fuller.

As always, the mist hung in low clouds over the hills, threatening to spill, keeping the valley's washerwomen on their toes. The sun was secreted behind them, wondering whether the effort to break through was worth his while. The plantation was patchy, as though previously felled trees hadn't been replenished. It broke just as Millie remembered it, a gap in the wall that dipped down onto the track to Bill O'Jack's. The track was as churned and as furrowed as it had been in the days before Millie had left. She remembered every last detail.

'What does Mr Dunne do with it?' she asked.

Jane looked out into the valley. 'Still people visit from all over. It remains as it was.'

'Does he plan to do anything with it?'

Jane shrugged and stood at the fence post at the top of the track. She lifted the lip of the letterbox, let it fall. It clattered, and somewhere they heard a pheasant shriek. Millie took the key from her waistband, the ribbon a dirtier grey than it had ever been, and placed it in the open letterbox.

'What's that?'

'It was a key to a box where Granda kept his coffee and sugar, yeast and things.'

'And you kept it with you all this time?'

Millie nodded. 'Silly, I know.' *Let the gore-seekers find it, hold onto it.*

'I shan't go down there, but you can, if you want.' Jane folded her arms.

The mud sucked at Millie's boots each time she lifted them. She moved to the coarse grass and walked more easily.

The yard needed sweeping. Dried mud knocked from boots and horseshoes lay across the stone. The top stone on the mounting block had crumbled away from frost and ice, most probably. The door was ajar, as she had expected.

She pushed it open, watched it swing on its hinges, knock gently into the wall behind.

The End

Historical Note

When I moved to the edge of the Peak District in 2015, the climate proved a surprise: how quickly clouds gathered and burst; how, on certain days, my house could be enveloped in a thick mist that refused to shift. I noticed that the unpredictable, merciless weather accentuated the harshness of the landscape, and I wondered how the people that lived here in its boom – in the early nineteenth century, when the wool and cotton trades exploded and the hamlets swelled into overcrowded towns – worked their fifteen-hour days and survived winters without modern amenities.

Then I discovered the Bill's O'Jack's murders. The isolated Moorcock Inn, or Bill's O'Jack's – which I have changed to *Bill O'Jack's* here, for ease on both the eye and ear – lay on the road between Greenfield and Holmfirth, the land flattened by heather and weather. In 1832, the publican and his son were murdered, their bodies found by a young female relative.

It was not the unsolved crime that caught my writerly attention as such; more the desire to understand how a close-knit community coped with such infamy, lacking in the judicial, therapeutic, and psychological resources we would draw on today.

As these questions ruminated, I focused on the (unwritten)

story of that female relative. As Livi Michael acknowledges, 'The historical novel is perhaps most frequently used as a vehicle for the suppressed voice'[1] , and I was drawn to Millie, a working-class woman who would know only too well the narrow proximity between life and starvation. History has left us little about the real Amelia Winterbottom, but I wanted to explore how she might cope with this incident, something that she and her peers would have believed to be meted out by God, with stoicism and duty prescribed as the medicine and sticking plaster. *Out of Human Sight* came from these questions.

In 1832, and the years thereafter, the Bill's O'Jack's murders were so notorious that gore-seekers from across the country visited the pub to see the scene from themselves, and commemorative ceramics were released on the fiftieth anniversary, which can still be seen in Saddleworth Museum. Today, the story doesn't seem quite as well known, but for those more familiar with the facts, you will recognise that I have made changes, omissions and embellishments, both minor and significant. These aren't to play havoc with history or mislead the curious, but to ensure a well-rounded, complete and human-centric story of fiction.

I hope this work of fiction will re-ignite interest in the real-life, still-unsolved Bill's O'Jack's murders of 1832. Bill and Tom's tombstone, complete with chilling epitaph that influenced this novel's title can still be seen in the corner of St Chad's churchyard in Uppermill, and the foundations of Bill's O'Jack's itself can still be seen from the Holmfirth Road, beneath those heavy skies.

1 Livi Michael, 'Approaches to the Historical Novel', in The Art of the Novel, ed. by Nicholas Royle (Norfolk: Salt, 2015), pp. 112–120 (p. 114).

Acknowledgements

Many generous people have offered their insight and expertise during my writing of this book.

Firstly, I am indebted to the Northodox team who, though a young company, have been eager and ambitious from the outset. It has been a pleasure to work with you.

A huge thank you to staff and students at The Manchester Writing School, Manchester Metropolitan University, who spent a good deal of time with excerpts of this book. It is subsequently all the better. Big thank yous in particular to Susan Barker, Oliver Harris, Livi Michael, and Nicholas Royle, and Han Clark, Harriet Clough, Gary Kaill, Christine Knight, James Lavender and Sara Sherwood.

Thank you to Mossley Writers and other writer friends – Laura Bui, Clare Fisher, Janelle Hardacre, Louise Hopewell, Tawseef Khan, Karen Powell – who provide constant inspiration and support.

I am also incredibly grateful for the colleagues, friends and family who read early drafts, and offered their thoughts and goodwill, especially Emma Blunt, Andy Charman, Graham Crisp, Helen Ewles, Rachael Kerr, Liz Knapp, Lynne McVernon,

Will Mackie and New Writing North, Giles Milburn, Tiffany Sabin and Nikesh Shukla.

Saddleworth Historical Society and Saddleworth Museum made available excellent resources about the case, the period and the area, as did Michael Buckley, Lily Hopkinson at St Chad's, John Lenton, and Gary Ridley at Greenfield Methodist Chapel, all of which proved invaluable for the researching of this novel. Thank you. It must be said: any anachronisms and historical errors are mine.

Finally, I would like to express my utmost, heartfelt thanks to my parents, Pat and Loz, to Matt, and to Chris and Imogen for your unwavering love and support.

NORTHODOX PRESS

HOME OF NORTHERN VOICES

 FACEBOOK.COM/NORTHODOXPRESS

 TWITER.COM/NORTHODOXPRESS

 INSTAGRAM.COM/NORTHODOXPRESS

 NORTHODOX.CO.UK

SUBMISSIONS ARE OPEN!

WRITER &
DEBUT AUTHOR   [ ]

NOVELS &
SHORT FICTION   [ ]

FROM OR LIVING
IN THE NORTH   [ ]

A NORTHERN STEAMPUNK ADVENTURE

CLOCKWORK MAGPIES

EMMA WHITEHALL

CATHERINE WIMPENEY

HER SISTER'S SHADOW

A PSYCHOLOGICAL THRILLER

'SEARING!' – Trevor Wood

THE SILENT BROTHER

BROTHER

SIMON VAN DER VELDE

'ORIGINAL AND COMPELLING, HAD ME READING
WELL INTO THE NIGHT' – Awais Khan

SUSAN WILLIS

THE
CURIOUS
CASEFILES

A COLLECTION OF SIX SHORT STORIES

Printed in Great Britain
by Amazon

17051386R00212